CI NG

RICHARD

A captivating historical romance of forbidden Tudor love

SANDRA HEATH WILSON

JOFFE BOOKS

Revised edition 2020
Joffe Books, London

First published in Great Britain 2014

ISBN 978-1-78931-305-5

For my best friend, Kelly Ferjutz

CHAPTER ONE

April 1483

FOURTEEN-YEAR-OLD LADY CICELY Plantagenet, second daughter of the late King Edward IV, was returning to Westminster Palace after walking in the garden by the Thames. In deep mourning for her father, her heavy skirts dragged the grass behind her. As she reached the palace, she trod on a sharp pebble and bent to attend to it, and was astonished to hear what was being said in a room overhead. The window was wide open, and the speakers did not lower their voices.

It was often the case that an overheard conversation could be dull, sometimes amusing or even sad, but this one was shockingly informative, and definitely not intended for any ears but those of the two persons engaged upon it.

Cicely stood again, listening. Her half-brother's voice was its usual drawl. Thomas Grey, Marquess of Dorset, was twenty-six years old, plump and incompetent, and to her he was Thomas the Tub, but he was her mother's favourite, the elder of her two sons by her first marriage. 'Your Grace, your Council awaits . . .' he declared, and it seemed that the words were accompanied by a comic bow.

Then Cicely realized her mother was present as well. 'Hush, Thomas, this is not a matter for jest, because we may not win the Council over.'

'We will, Mother. Your royal son will be brought from Ludlow without further ado, to be crowned Edward V, and Gloucester will be powerless.'

'Thomas, Thomas, victory will not be certain until the crown is on Edward's head. He is only twelve, and my husband ordered that his brother, Richard of Gloucester, is to be Lord Protector in his minority. We cannot hope to keep this from Gloucester for long. My brother-in-law is far from a fool, the Council has no reason to love us, and Hastings may yet see that Gloucester is informed. Perhaps he has already done so.'

'*Hastings?*' Thomas showed the utmost scorn.

'Do not underestimate him. Common Jane Shore — born the equally common Elizabeth Lambert — may have been my husband's favourite mistress, but her bed is already open to all. You fool yourself that you are the only one to dibble her, because Hastings, Lord Chamberlain of England, does as well.'

Cicely's lips parted. Thomas the Tub and Lord Hastings were Jane Shore's lovers? Already? With Father barely cold in his tomb? Mistress Shore clearly did not mourn for long, even for a king!

The queen continued. 'Be sensible, Thomas, she is a whore and will couple with power. She will satisfy you *both* until it is clear which one is the more important. The other will then be dropped like a stone into a river. Hastings is an unknown factor as far as I am concerned. Yes, he served my late husband, but he is no friend of mine.'

'Nor is he a friend of Gloucester's.'

'Gloucester. Oh, how I loathe that lopsided snake.'

Cicely gazed up at the window. Lopsided snake? Her uncle's body was not quite regular, and his one shoulder rested slightly higher than the other, but it was very hard to notice. Surely, there was no good reason why her mother should speak of him in quite such a derogatory way.

Thomas continued, 'Believe me, Hastings will not want Richard of Gloucester as Lord Protector. You are being over-cautious, Mother. Come, what you seek is within your grasp.'

'Is it, Thomas? Do you really think so?'

'The day is ours for the taking. Let us confront the Council with what we wish for.' He laughed.

'With what we *intend*,' his mother corrected.

'With what we will *achieve*,' he replied. 'Our family is going to push Richard of Gloucester into perdition and rule England through Edward V. It is as good as done.'

Cicely heard their steps as they left the room. Her mother was trying to reverse Father's last instructions, and appeared to be on the point of success! Richard, Duke of Gloucester, was not going to be Lord Protector after all. At least, not if her mother and her Woodville family had anything to do with it.

Elizabeth had been a Lancastrian widow, her family adherents of Henry VI, who had become slow-witted, when she turned the head of the Yorkist Edward IV, five years her junior and Henry's deposer. Even though Edward pleaded on his knees, she denied him her body, telling him that although she was not good enough to be his queen, she was too good to be his mistress. Edward was so ruled by lust that he offered marriage, and thus she had become Queen of England. All these years later she was still beautiful. On her, the same rich mourning robes worn to unflattering effect by her second daughter, appeared to glow.

The Woodville marriage had shaken the realm, but Elizabeth had done her duty by presenting her king with many children, of whom only two sons and five daughters remained. When Edward's initial obsession with her was at an end, she made no objection to his multitude of mistresses, thus maintaining her position and ensuring the advancement of her rapacious family.

Cicely was now old enough to form her own opinion of her mother, and was deeply ashamed. Suddenly, going into the palace was no longer to her liking, and so she turned to resume her walk. The weak spring sunshine glanced off the Thames and downstream London quivered in the haze. The steeple of St. Paul's seemed not content with the summit of Ludgate Hill, but tried to reach to Heaven itself. There were rain clouds in the west, but they were a long way off. The apple trees were in blossom, the daffodils had gone over, and the bells of London tolled continuously for her father. How could he be no more, that huge, handsome man with hair like polished copper, who had kept his kingdom at peace for so many years and was loved by his people? His life had come to an end earlier this month of April in the year 1483. He had been within two weeks of his forty-third birthday.

Pausing, Cicely studied her reflection in a puddle. She was pale with large grey-brown eyes, at present spoiled by crying. Her long, unruly hair, very dark chestnut in colour, was worn loose as became a maiden, but it was not shaven back from her forehead as was the fashion. Her older sister Bess was shaven, and so was their mother, but Cicely did not like it. It was a fashion her mother would probably soon oblige her to adopt, but until then she liked to be as she was. On top of her head there was a close-fitting silver chain caul that was held around her ears and it caught the sunlight when she moved. Her mourning clothes were hot and unbecoming, and she was glad of the playful breeze from the Thames.

She sighed, for she did not look at all as a Plantagenet princess should. Why could she not be more like her seventeen-year-old sister, Bess, who was a true member of the splendid royal family, tall, graceful, blue-eyed, with the straight red-gold hair that was so admired? *Straight* hair, not a tangled untidy mass that refused to obey brush, comb or pin. She, Cicely, looked forward to the day she married, whenever and to whoever it may be, because such unbecoming locks could then be concealed beneath a headdress. She was the only dark one in a bright coppery family — no, not quite the only one, for she was like her uncle of Gloucester, who in turn, she was told, was like her grandfather, the great Duke of York.

She thought of the uncle who was now the foremost lord in the land. Some said he had been that even before her father died, because Edward IV liked his pleasures and handed more and more responsibility to his loyal, steadfast brother. Not for nothing had Edward chosen Richard to be Lord Protector. And now her mother was trying to deny Richard his rightful place. He had not even been *told* the king was dead! Unless someone like Lord Hastings had sent word, of course. It was very dangerous indeed to plot against Richard. Dangerous or foolish. Both, probably, because if Edward IV had wished his brother to have charge of the new boy-king, then that was what *should* happen.

Cicely tried to recall Richard, but it was so long since she had seen him that she could not bring him properly to mind. He was of perhaps a little less than medium height, slender and with hair exactly the same as hers. Yes, that at least she could recall clearly. His face eluded her. But if her father trusted him and held him in more favour than any other man, then she, Cicely, half Woodville, half Plantagenet, would do the same.

She went to the garden wall and stood on tiptoe to look over at the crowded river. Boats of all sizes were coming and going at the palace's great stone landing, and the freshness of the apple blossom behind her was pleasing, but she knew that as summer drew on, less pleasing scents would intrude as London became hot and dusty. This time of the year, when everything was coming to life again, had always been the time she loved most, and since commencing her monthly bleedings two years ago, she had felt more stirred and excited by spring than ever.

It was a muted excitement that seemed to reach into every part of her, a quivering thrill that made her breasts tighten and aroused an unknown hunger deep inside her. And she had such dreams, rude dreams of lying naked with her future husband, letting him touch her, and touching him in return. Such things were not to be confided, not even to her confessor. Perhaps especially not her confessor!

She had no one in particular to give his face to this anonymous husband, because no marriage had been arranged for her, unless one counted her brief betrothal to the heir apparent to the Scottish throne. Princesses had no choice, except to obey. She had even been termed Princess of Scotland for a while, but was glad there was no longer such a contract, because the thought of leaving England was too dreadful.

As for gentlemen she already liked here in England, there was only her distant cousin Ralph Scrope, but she had only exchanged glances with him. He was two or three years older than her, and was usually in the north in the Duke of Gloucester's household, but had been here at court for some months. With his inviting smile, hazel eyes and light brown hair, he pleased Cicely, and was the first young man she had ever looked upon with interest. Or who had looked at her the same way. At least, she was not aware of anyone else. She felt colour entering her cheeks, because in her imagination she had done a lot more than *look* at Ralph.

She remembered speaking of it to Bess. Well, not of her carnal imaginings regarding Ralph in particular, but of her emotions in general. The conversation had been prompted when she unguardedly mentioned a dream of the previous night. It had been a dream that shocked her into awakening.

'Cissy!' Bess had been horrified by her younger sister's unexpected worldliness. 'You should not speak of things like that, it is not seemly.'

'I do not *feel* seemly, Bess, not when—' Cicely had broken off and gone a little pink.

'When what?'

'Nothing. I just feel . . . peculiar these days.'

Bess smiled. 'It is the spring, Cissy. When the sap rises.'

'Is it?'

'Well, partly. It is also a need to become a woman, a true woman, no longer a maid.'

'Do you feel it too?' Cicely remembered looking intently at her sister.

Bess fixed her eyes upon her embroidery. 'I have felt it for a long time now. It began a whole year before my first monthly bleeding, and it has been with me ever since, except that it is no longer simply in the spring, but *all* the time. Especially when I think of him.'

'Who?' Cicely had been curious. Had her sister been speaking of a real lover?

'Oh, just a man,' Bess replied lightly, and stitched busily again.

'Yes, but who is he?'

'No one you know, and no one I can do much about. Now then, Cissy, you feel as you do now because you are older. Sometimes it seems you are older than me! You certainly see and understand so many things more than I do.' Bess smiled a little wickedly. 'A good tumble with Ralph Scrope would be the answer.' She was rewarded by the deep flush that raced to her sister's cheeks.

Cicely had been cross. 'Do not make fun of me.'

'I am sorry, I did not mean it. After all, who on earth would want to roll with Ralph *Scrope*!'

'Bess! Anyway, I hardly know him.'

'Even so, I have seen you making sheep's eyes at him. And he at you. I will warrant he has no desire to return north to our uncle's household. Mother suspects him to be a spy.'

'He does not *seem* like a spy.'

Bess laughed. 'And how should a spy seem? If he is a good spy, he will simply become more or less invisible, amiable to everyone, noticed by no one.'

'Presumably he would be our uncle's spy, and if he *is* then he will surely have sent word to the north.'

Bess looked at her. 'Possibly. I had not thought of that.'

The remembered conversation vanished as Cicely's wandering thoughts were pulled abruptly back to the present by a sudden gust of wind sweeping from the Thames. It strengthened the sound of the bells downstream, and grief for her father engulfed her again. The smell of incense still seemed to cling to her, like wood smoke in autumn, and if she closed her eyes she could clearly see the priests in their flowing robes. She could also still hear their sombre chanting as her father had been brought to Westminster Abbey to lie in state. The people crowded the way, crying for their lost king. They forgave him his vices and faults, except his marriage to one of the now hated Woodvilles, but even that was set aside as he was conveyed to his last resting place at St George's Chapel in Windsor.

She had wept throughout, much to her mother's annoyance. Such a display of sorrow was not to be tolerated in one of Elizabeth Woodville's daughters.

At Ludlow in Shropshire less than a week later, Elizabeth Woodville's brother, Earl Rivers, who had charge of the little prince who was now Edward V, set off with him, and with Sir Richard Grey, younger of Cicely's two half-brothers, for London with a royal procession of two thousand men. He had been summoned urgently by his sister, but had also received a message from Richard of Gloucester, requesting him to meet him at Northampton, that they could ride into the capital together. Clearly Gloucester was now well aware of his duty as Lord Protector, and this awareness had yet to be communicated to Elizabeth Woodville. Rivers was in a quandary.

Sunlight glinted on the armour of the men-at-arms, and the royal banners waved as the fine horses clattered on the cobbles of the towns through which Rivers' great cavalcade would pass on the way to Northampton. With Rivers and Grey at his side, the boy-king rode at the head of the procession. The new monarch was tall for his age, but not handsome in the mould of his magnificent father. His reddish hair was dull and straight, his face spoiled by a weak jaw, and he was a disappointment to subjects accustomed to the spectacle that had always surrounded Edward IV. The late king's son was a tiny candle beside such brilliance, but thanks to Woodville influence, he was also puffed up with his own importance, and not very pleasant.

Rivers did not wish to cross a man as strong and competent as Gloucester, yet neither did he wish his Woodville family to give up the reins of government and power. He decided the latter was more important than the former, and laid a plan he hoped would deceive and delay Gloucester.

It did not work. Gloucester found out and took possession of his royal nephew. Rivers, Grey and his other noblemen were arrested, and the Ludlow entourage of two thousand dismissed. Rivers and Grey were fools to think they could outwit Gloucester at first hand. The duke was only thirty, but more astute, puissant and loved than any Woodville. He was also a clever, accomplished, battle-hardened military commander. That was why Edward IV had so heavily relied upon him, and rewarded him so handsomely for his unswerving support.

Gloucester now had important backing from his cousin, Harry Stafford, Duke of Buckingham, who was three years his junior. Stafford was a strutting peacock of a lord whose bloodline placed him close to the throne, and he had long festered over injustices at the hands of the Woodvilles, one of whom he had been forced to marry when they had both been children. He regarded the Woodvilles as lowborn, and he hastily allied himself with Richard in order to strike back at his hated wife's hated family.

That same day swift riders were sent to bring the news to London. They would reach the capital at around midnight. Gloucester held back at Northampton to await developments. He had the new king, and had no need to do anything precipitate.

It was almost midnight, and the news had yet to arrive, when Cicely again overheard her mother and Thomas the Tub. She and Bess were in a closet in the queen's apartments, hastily attending to embroidery threads that should have been tidied much earlier in the day. The sisters exchanged uneasy glances as they heard movements in the apartment itself.

'I wish the Council would come to a decision,' their mother said. 'The more they hesitate, the more likely it is that Gloucester will learn what we do.'

'Gloucester is done for,' Thomas replied confidently.

Bess gave a sharp intake of breath and whispered a single word, 'Richard', but Cicely was too afraid to take much notice. It was intolerable to eavesdrop again on her mother's scheming.

Elizabeth spoke. 'Done for? I will not believe it until I have him standing defeated before me. In the meantime, Thomas, you are forbidden to confide in that widowed harlot Jane Shore, do you hear? I do *not* want my private affairs whispered about between the coverlets. What she hears from you is certain to be whispered to Hastings.'

The sisters thought their presence was undetected, but suddenly the door was flung open and their mother confronted them. 'Why are *you* here?' she demanded.

They started to their feet, the colourful threads falling to the floor. Bess indicated the rainbow shades at her feet. 'Mother, we came to sort the embroidery . . .'

Elizabeth Woodville gazed coldly at her eldest daughter. 'Take it all and be gone.'

As they hurriedly retrieved the threads, the sisters became aware of a loud hammering at the outer door of the apartments, and then their half-brother's dismayed voice.

'Mother, the Council has received word from Gloucester. He knows all and has the king! He also has my uncle Rivers and my brother!'

Of one accord Bess and Cicely fled from the closet, and their mother's furious shriek of disbelief followed them.

Wringing her hands, Elizabeth turned frantically to Thomas. 'What shall we do? Gloucester is not likely to forgive or forget.' She paused as a new thought entered her head. 'Sweet Jesu, what if he still harbours a grudge because of Clarence. . . ?'

George, Duke of Clarence, had been the middle of the three Yorkist brothers, the one who plotted and schemed, and paid the ultimate price for treason against Edward IV.

The queen began to shake and sob, and Thomas lost his nerve, trying desperately to find a solution. The only one that presented itself was flight . . . or sanctuary. The moment the latter occurred to him he said it aloud, and the queen's sobbing ceased.

CHAPTER TWO

THAT NIGHT CICELY was rudely awakened by her sister shaking her.

'Cissy! Wake up!'

'Bess? What is it?' Cicely rubbed her eyes.

'Listen.'

They lay together in the bed, and heard turmoil throughout the palace. There was shouting, banging, people hurried to and fro, and from outside the racket of horses and wagons in the yard. Afraid, the sisters sat up, and then Cicely drew the bed hangings aside and slipped out to look for someone in the adjoining rooms, but found no one. She soon ran back to Bess.

'We are alone!'

Bess's eyes widened, and she got out of bed as well. As she snatched her robe, the draft set the flame of their night light dancing wildly in the darkness.

'Oh no, Bess! Do not leave here. We do not know what has happened. It may be something dreadful.' Cicely gasped. 'Perhaps the Duke of Gloucester is here!'

'That will not be something dreadful,' Bess responded swiftly. 'Quite the opposite. Anyway, if we do not look, we will never learn what is going on. Are you coming, or would you prefer to stay on your own?'

Cicely picked up her own robe reluctantly and followed her sister out of their apartment. They were greeted by a chaotic scene. There were crates and boxes, plate, jewellery and furnishings, and ladies and gentlemen were hurriedly stuffing more and more treasures into hastily brought chests and sacks, which were then dragged out by soldiers and pages. The air was alive with curses and frightened voices. Then out of the commotion bustled a familiar and reassuring shape, their childhood nurse, Biddy, her headdress wobbling, her grey gown crumpled and dusty. She pushed them firmly back into their apartments, followed them inside and closed the door on the shambolic scene in the outer rooms.

Bess gripped the nurse's arm. 'What is it, Biddy? What has happened? Has the Duke of Gloucester arrived?'

'The duke? No.'

Bess's disappointment was almost tangible, Cicely thought, noticing again how very anxious her sister was for their uncle to be here.

Biddy said they must be dressed, and as she helped, she told them what she knew. 'Now it is known the Duke of Gloucester has your brother the king, your mother is fleeing for sanctuary in Westminster Abbey, as is everyone else who threw in their lot with her party. The Marquess of Dorset has left; the queen does not know where he has gone. But you, your younger sisters and your other royal brother, the little Duke of York, are to join her at the abbey.'

Cicely was dismayed. 'But we have done nothing. Our uncle will not harm *us*!'

'That is as may be, but go you must or the queen will have my head. Come on now, it is not far along the underground passage.'

Bess crossed herself in horror. 'We do not have to go that way, do we? Oh, Biddy, there are all manner of infernal creatures abroad in that tunnel!'

'Be still! A royal lady should not be afraid of spiders and such like things. The rats will run in the opposite direction from your torches, of that you can be sure. The tunnel it is, for the queen does not wish to be seen going into the abbey, although I will admit that all the plunder she is sending there will be witnessed by the whole of London as it cannot be brought along the narrow passage.'

'Plunder?'

'Yes, the queen is stripping the palace of all she can before the duke arrives.'

They fell silent as she finished dressing them. When they were ready, Biddy led them to the tunnel entrance, where they were met by a small party of men-at-arms who escorted them down into the cold, damp subterranean way. They could distinctly hear the pattering of small rodent paws, but at last they emerged at the other end, where they immediately heard hammering and shouting ahead.

'What is that?' Cicely asked nervously.

Biddy glanced quickly at her. 'They are breaking a hole in the abbey wall, so that all the treasure may be brought inside.'

Now they were in the abbey itself. Carved gargoyles leered at them in the ghostly light of the torches as they mounted more steps, this time leading to a landing where a high, arched door faced them. The landing gave into passages on either side, where they could see more doorways, but it was on the one before them that a guard knocked loudly. It swung slowly open, letting light flood out, bringing with it a welcome sense of warmth.

Followed by Biddy, they entered a room filled with many familiar faces, including their three little sisters, Ann, Katherine and Bridget. The second of Edward IV's sons, Richard, Duke of York, always called Dickon, lay asleep on a pallet close by, although how he slept in such a noise Cicely could not imagine. His tousled coppery hair was ruffled and his arm outstretched to reveal at his elbow a crescent-shaped scar, the result of a fall from a horse. But it was their mother who held their attention. She sat on the rush-strewn floor, her black gown billowing around her, and she beckoned her two eldest daughters.

'Gloucester shall not take my other children too — they shall stay here with me, with me!' she cried, pulling them down to the floor beside her.

Bess frowned. 'Mother, the Duke of Gloucester will not harm us. You are his brother's widow and we his nieces and nephews. He is an honourable lord.'

'Honourable?' The queen laughed harshly. 'If he is, my child, it will be George of Clarence who has first call upon that honour, not Elizabeth Woodville and her children.'

Cicely was puzzled. 'What has our dead uncle, the Duke of Clarence, to do with it?'

'If only you knew. If only you knew.' Elizabeth closed her eyes.

Cicely was none the wiser. 'But you are the king's mother. Our uncle will respect your position, I am sure of it.'

'So am I,' Bess added firmly.

'Ah, the voices of youth and innocence. So you are sure of it? Well, you credit your uncle Gloucester with much more tolerance and understanding than I do.'

'You have *never* liked him, have you?' There was a cold note in Bess's voice, an edge that reminded Cicely of Elizabeth herself.

'Nor has he liked me. It is mutual, I promise you.' The queen's old caustic tones returned. 'Well, I still have Dickon, do I not? *He* is the healthy one, the true Plantagenet prince. Edward is so sickly that it may yet be that *I* have the next king after all.'

Cicely looked away. Her mother lacked all true maternal feeling, and possessed far too much cruel personal ambition.

'But Edward lives for the moment, Mother,' Bess responded, 'and our uncle has him. I am glad, because you will not win this. You are an evil woman, and I despise you.'

Shaken, Cicely got up. There were times when Bess and her mother seemed almost the same person. They were both cold and heartless when they chose to be.

Elizabeth gazed at her eldest daughter. 'My evil is in you too, Bess. Do not ever doubt it, for I see my own eyes in yours. A looking glass will have told you this long since.'

Bess flushed and got up, pretending not to have heard. 'Cissy, we may as well try to rest for I fear this will be a very long night.'

The two sisters found a secluded corner and sat down. Cicely glanced at Bess. 'I have never heard you speak to Mother like that before.'

'I should have.'

'She is right, you *are* a lot like her. I had not realized it fully until a few minutes ago.'

'Do not say that, for she is the last person I wish to resemble.'

Cicely was silent for a moment. 'How long will she keep us here?'

'I do not know, Cissy. She is terrified of our uncle, so it may be some time.'

Cicely wondered suddenly about the Duke of Gloucester. 'I suppose she is wrong about our uncle? I mean, well, we do not know him very well, do we? He is always in the north and was hardly ever at Father's court. The last time I saw him was when I was . . . actually, I do not know when. I know he was here this last Christmas, but I did not see him because I had the measles. For all we know he may do all the things she fears!'

'No!' Bess's voice was surprisingly emphatic. 'He will not harm us, I know he will not. *I* met him again last Christmas, and I can tell you that he is definitely *not* what Mother now claims.' She paused, aware of how vehemently she had spoken. 'I liked him, that is all, and we all know that Mother is only fearful for herself.'

Cicely hesitated, but her curiosity was too great. 'Bess, why are you so certain of him?'

Bess's eyes were luminous in the dancing light of the torches. 'I know him,' she said softly.

Cicely did not say anything more, but Bess's attitude puzzled her. No, it made her feel a little uncomfortable. Why should talking about their uncle bring about such a change in her sister? If it had been some young courtier of whom they had been speaking, she could have understood the look on Bess's face — but the Duke of Gloucester? Not only was he Bess's close kinsman, he was also married with a small son, another Edward Plantagenet, and was known to be devoted to his wife and child. There had never been any whispers of him having strayed from his wife's bed, which was unusual for such a highborn prince, but it seemed to be so. She *had* to have misread Bess's attitude. Richard of Gloucester was their father's brother, their blood uncle, and for Bess to even *think* of him in any other way was wrong.

The last time Cicely recalled seeing him he had been with her father. The brilliant Edward had his arm slung idly around his younger brother's shoulder, laughing loudly at some shared joke. The Duke of Gloucester was quieter in his mirth, his laughter drowned by the roar of the king. Edward had seen his daughter and held his hand out to her, drawing her towards them and saying to his brother, 'Well, Richard, with that hair she is more your daughter than mine, eh?'

Try as she would, Cicely could recall no more. Her uncle's reply was lost forever in the depths of her memory.

A day later, those in sanctuary heard the cheers as the Duke of Gloucester entered London with his nephew, Edward V. And the Duke of Buckingham. At first they only heard a dull roar in the distance, but then the sound became almost deafening as the procession passed the abbey itself and went on to the palace. It was not by accident that it took that route, Elizabeth Woodville declared, for she was sure the duke was making certain she heard his triumph. Loudly.

April gave way to May, and Elizabeth Woodville and her children still claimed sanctuary at the abbey. Cicely and Bess were miserable in such dreary confinement, but Dickon was utterly wretched. He was subjected to the suffocating attentions of his once-aloof mother and was so unhappy with his lot that he scowled at everyone and sat in stony silence at the table when everyone ate together. The queen feigned not to notice the little boy's resentment, and plied him with sweetmeats and wheedling talk.

The Lord Protector had not been idle since his arrival in London, sending many a member of the Council to entreat his brother's widow to come forth from sanctuary, her children with her, but Elizabeth refused to even see the messengers. After a while the duke tired of seeking to reason with her, and broke off his efforts.

One day, however, there came a visitor to the sanctuary who *was* seen by the queen, and that visitor was none other than Mistress Jane Shore, the woman who for more than seven years had been the paramour of Edward IV and was subsequently sharing her ample favours with Thomas the Tub and Lord Hastings. Jane had been born Elizabeth Lambert, daughter of an affluent London merchant, but preferred to be called Jane. Shore was her married name.

Cicely was reading to her mother, and let the precious book fall when the lady was announced by a flustered lady-in-waiting. Her mother was irritated, but too intrigued by Jane Shore's visit to do more than frown. Certainly the need to dismiss her daughter was overlooked.

Into the room Jane swept, gloriously beautiful in dark red damask, for she wore mourning for no man, not even a king. Her flaxen curls were unrestricted, even though her maidenly days had ceased when she was only eleven. She halted before the queen with an insolent smile upon her fair face. There was a glaring absence of a curtsey.

Elizabeth was icy. 'Mistress Shore, if you have come to seek your latest guardian, I am afraid you will have to look farther than the abbey of Westminster. I do not know the whereabouts of the Marquess of Dorset.'

'Dorset?' Jane laughed aloud, and Cicely put her hand to her mouth to conceal a smile. Her father had loved Jane Shore, who had seemed to love him in return, although maybe the haste with which she turned to Thomas the Tub

and Lord Hastings suggested a rather inferior emotion to love.

Jane was still laughing. 'Jesu, if I looked to your firstborn for guardianship then I would indeed be in a sorry plight, Your Grace. No, he is of no consequence to me now, for I have found myself a proper man, not a little barrel of small cock and even smaller ability in bed.'

Cicely's eyes widened. Jane dared to use such a word in front of the queen?

Jane continued, 'My lord of Hastings is a very ardent lover . . . almost as ardent as was the late king himself! Just not quite as big, if you know what I mean. I do like a well-endowed man — there is so much more pleasure, do you not agree? Or perhaps you were always too much of a stone to be appreciative.' Her green eyes danced, but Elizabeth feigned indifference, turning away as if bored.

'You clearly have nothing to say that is worth hearing, so please leave.'

Jane stood her ground, brazenly picking up a walnut from a dish on a table. She dropped it quite deliberately, Cicely thought, and then made much of bending to retrieve it, thus giving Elizabeth Woodville the full benefit of her plentiful bosom, which the late king had often said was his preferred pillow of a night.

The queen was reminded of his words, and her face darkened with annoyance. 'Mistress Shore, your continued presence displeases me.'

'Your Grace, I have not come merely to cross swords with you. My mission is of far greater importance. I will come to the point. Lord Hastings and others wish to remove the Lord Protector from office and bring you forth to resume your rightful place, as the mother of the new King Edward V.'

Cicely's lips parted with a mixture of shock and dismay.

Elizabeth was cynical. 'Really? And why, pray, should I believe anything *you* have to say to me. Surely you do not think me so naive as to credit *Hastings* with a sudden change of heart?

I had not thought Gloucester such a fool as to send you, of all people, with a tale like that. He must be desperate to have me out, and chooses a charge of treason with which to do it.'

'Your Grace, I do assure you that Gloucester, of *all* God's creatures, knows nothing of this. If he did, then Hastings would surely lose his head and I would forfeit a man who knows exactly how to use his splendid, er, cock.'

Elizabeth became even icier. 'You think ever of your lust!'

'Whereas you know only of power. Did you *ever* enjoy the king's bed? I know I did, every single moment of it. He could sometimes stand for me for hours on end. Yes, really. And I rode him as often and as passionately as I wished. Even you must know how satisfying it is to have a king's member between your legs? And such a member. Do you know, I have often wondered what it would be like to tumble Gloucester. He may be slender and slightly twisted of body, but his face . . . oh, such a face. That long, dark chestnut hair, those fine-drawn features, and those compelling grey eyes. Or are they dark blue? Somewhere between, maybe. Anyway, he is beautiful, do you not think? Yes, a true man, with great beauty of visage. I will warrant he knows an exquisite thing or two about matters of the flesh.'

'Have you *no* dignity?' Elizabeth demanded frostily.

'Not when it comes to men. Good God, woman, have you not *looked* at Gloucester and seen so much more than a crooked body? I would not decline a night with him, and would certainly roll him over more energetically than his wan little wife. Anne Neville will never do right by him. What does he see in her? She is not flesh and blood, just a piteous presence.'

'You disgust me. I have no wish to hear the lurid details of your carnal dealings with my husband or your apparent hunger for his deformed brother.'

'Well, at least it can be said that my lust is well placed — power would bring *me* precious little gratification. Beauty does not make a real woman, just an emotionless image.'

Cicely gazed at her, absorbing what she said. Jane Shore loved men for themselves and it was a trait with which Cicely Plantagenet felt affinity.

Elizabeth raised an arm to strike her husband's former mistress, but then thought better of it. She looked keenly into Jane's scornful face, and after a while she said, 'Very well, Mistress Shore, tell me your tale, for to listen will cost me nothing and may serve to amuse my afternoon.'

Jane's chin came up. 'Your Grace, I do not seek to merely amuse your dull life. My Lord Hastings is gravely distressed by the mistake he made in telling Gloucester of the late king's dying wish; in fact he is so distressed that last night he was quite limp and incapable. Not by this morning, of course, for he is a man with great needs, but it is a measure of his desolation that he now wishes with all his heart to remedy his error. I know not what he intends or how he expects to accomplish it. He has not told me; merely that he wishes you to know he is intent upon putting everything right. He assures you that Gloucester will soon be dealt with as he so richly deserves. Unfortunately, for that means I may never have the tantalising duke in the hay.'

To her surprise, the queen burst into laughter. 'Oh, come now, Mistress Shore, surely you do not imagine I am completely isolated here! I know what has happened to your beloved Hastings. He has not surged to power on the crest of a wave as he had expected because Buckingham is now at Gloucester's side. *Another* ambitious noble who believes he has a claim to my son's throne.' Her cold eyes glinted maliciously as she witnessed Jane's discomfort. 'Well, Mistress Shore, I am right, am I not? Hastings' nose has been pushed out of joint, and now he is the thwarted child, trying to get his own back.'

The beautiful Jane pursed her sweet lips with a twitch of anger. 'I would not have put it quite like that. Whatever my lord Hastings' personal reasons, the same cannot surely be said of the others involved with him.'

'And who, pray, would they be?'

Jane listed a number of prominent Lancastrians, spiritual and secular.

Elizabeth snorted. 'God's truth, a nest of adders, and all with the same reason for hating Gloucester, the loss of power and influence. Jesu, I almost begin to pity him.'

Now it was Jane who laughed. '*Pity* Gloucester? I may find him an interesting prospect as a lover, but I do not pity him!'

The queen leaned towards Jane, her voice contemptuous. 'How you harp upon him, mistress, for I fear he must be the only man in England to remain unmoved by your obvious attractions. You are not accustomed to such indifference, are you?'

Jane flushed angrily. 'You are wrong, Your Grace.'

'Indeed? Then I must have been mistaken last Christmas when you fairly threw yourself at him, to his intense discomfort. God's blood, the man is such a prude I thought he would vomit!'

'A *prude?* Oh, he is not *that*!' Jane laughed again. 'Believe me, he has a quietly devastating appeal that he rarely chooses to use. If he did, there would not be a woman at court who would not part her legs for him. Even you.'

'Rubbish, he's a prude. Whatever, it was most disappointing when you failed to hook him.'

'Disappointing?'

'Well, his faithfulness to his wife is the laugh of the court. Oh, he has bastards, which to his credit he acknowledges, but all were conceived before he married. At least, if he has had any since, it is an amazingly well-kept secret. The late king probably populated a small town, but not one such brat was acknowledged after his marriage to me. They were all known of, but adultery is frowned upon, is it not? An unmarried king may sow his oats as he will, but not once he has taken himself a queen.'

Jane's lips pressed together.

'I do not doubt that Richard of Gloucester is red-blooded enough to have several mistresses at once,' Elizabeth continued, 'but if he does, my husband the king certainly did not hear. He would have told me if he knew such an interesting morsel of scandal about his youngest brother. So I do not think Richard has anyone but his duchess to warm him at night, which must be a chilling experience, for she can barely warm herself, let alone him. I really hoped you would haul him to your bed, just to prove he was a natural man. "Loyalty Binds Me" is his motto, is it not? It clearly means "Only Anne's Bed For Me".' She chuckled.

'You are entirely wrong about my actions, Your Grace,' Jane said again.

'Oh, *you* may not have thought of it yourself, but I would not put it past my husband to put you up to it. He would have curled up with mirth to think of such a scene.'

Jane gave a half-smile. 'I had no idea you were so interested in what I did that night.'

'Tried to do,' Elizabeth corrected. 'However, you may carry a message to Hastings. I will welcome his attempts to remove Gloucester from God's earth, but mark me well, if aught should go wrong, I will deny everything.'

'He would not expect otherwise.'

Elizabeth's lips compressed at these words and she was stung into defending herself, although she immediately regretted the impulse. 'Mistress Shore, I *must* deny all knowledge. I have my children to consider.'

Jane's scornful disbelief was not concealed as she swept from the room as grandly as she had arrived. She had not feared the queen before and did not fear her now.

Elizabeth stood still for a moment or so after the door closed, and then gave a howl of rage and dashed her fist upon a table, Cicely's presence still forgotten. Only when she turned, uttering an oath that would not have been out of place in a fish market, did she see her second daughter. Clearly shocked, she seized Cicely's wrist and hauled her to her feet. 'What a little earwig you are. You may go now. Reading can wait until another time. But mark well that you hold your tongue about what you witnessed here today. One careless word and you will rue it. Am I clear?'

'Yes, Mother.' Cicely caught up her skirts and ran from the room, fearing her mother would change her mind and make her rue things *now*!

But the queen's threats ceased to matter the moment the sisters were together again, and after securing a sworn promise of secrecy from Bess, Cicely related everything. And that meant everything, including Jane Shore's thoughts of Richard of Gloucester.

Bess flushed angrily. 'How monstrous she is. She would bed a horse if it were all there was to hand.'

'Bess!'

'I take nothing back. How *dare* she speak of our uncle so crudely.'

'She speaks of every man crudely,' Cicely observed. 'But she likes men for themselves, not because they are powerful. I like that in her. It is honest.'

Bess said nothing.

'If only we could be free again, able to return to court and—'

'You would have the Duke of Gloucester *murdered* so that you can dance again and have a new gown?' Bess's words were acidic. 'They spoke of overthrowing him. Do you really believe that only means removing him from office and sending him back to the north on a promise of good behaviour? Of course it does not, it means putting him to death!'

'No, of course that is not what I want.' Cicely drew back. Murdered? Put to death? She had not meant any such thing!

'Then what *do* you want? Just because you have gazed wistfully at Ralph Scrope you think you know everything. Well, you do not. You do not know anything at all. I would rather stay here for the rest of my life than have my dear Richard's blood upon my conscience. Not a drop of it would I spill, do you hear? Not a drop! I will not be party to this plot! I would rather betray Mother to him than see him harmed.' Bess got up and hastened from the room.

Cicely stared after her. My *dear* Richard?

Hastings' scheming came to nothing. News soon reached the abbey that discovery of the plot had led to Hastings being beheaded immediately. Such had been the Duke of Gloucester's fury and disappointment that he did not hesitate. The other conspirators escaped with their lives. It might have been better for the Lord Protector had he rid himself of all of them, but he was lenient. Jane Shore received no harsher punishment than having to perform an act of penance. She appeared before St Paul's Cross, barefoot, wearing a kirtle with no concealing underskirt, carrying a taper.

Cicely could not help wondering if such leniency — and subtle humour — only made Richard of Gloucester even more attractive to Jane. Yes, she imagined it would.

CHAPTER THREE

ON A BRIGHT June morning, the Council arrived at the abbey, where they were received by the queen. Wishing to play the beleaguered widow, Elizabeth had all her children present for the meeting.

It was fully expected that Richard of Gloucester himself would lead the Council, and Cicely waited in anticipation. Any mention of him drew abuse from her mother and a strangeness from Bess, and between these two stood Cicely, more than a little confused and now half-frightened of him. But he did not come.

The Archbishop of Canterbury spoke first. 'Your Grace, we are here to implore you to —'

She interrupted. 'My lord archbishop, I understood I was to meet with the Lord Protector himself, not his minions!' The words brought an angry muttering from the rest of the Council.

'Your Grace,' the archbishop responded after a moment, 'the Lord Protector deemed it wiser not to come himself. He thinks only of sparing you any embarrassment.'

'His own embarrassment, more like.' She rapped her fingers on the table before her. 'Very well, if I must deal with you, what is it you wish me to know?'

'Your Grace, we again urgently entreat you to come forth from this place. It is not right for you and your family to remain here. It serves no purpose —'

'No purpose? No purpose?' Her voice rose angrily. 'Is it then *no purpose* to save my life and the lives of my children by seeking sanctuary?'

He spread his arms. 'But your lives have never been endangered, Your Grace. The Lord Protector *assures* you of this. He respects your position as queen and your children as brothers and sisters of the king, and as his own nephews and nieces.'

At these familiar words Cicely glanced at Bess, and saw her triumphant smile.

The archbishop continued: 'Please believe me, Your Grace, no harm will befall you.'

Elizabeth sighed, as if dealing with a dim-witted child. 'My lord archbishop, Richard Plantagenet has every reason for wishing to be rid of me and I therefore find it impossible to expect any good intention of him. I am a thorn in his side while I remain here and he wishes to have me out. Once that happened, I would conveniently vanish one day and a suitable story would spread of my sudden mortal illness.'

The archbishop was shocked. 'I must protest, Your Grace. The Lord Protector is a man of his word, and wishes to live at peace with you.'

Bess's eyes were now bright with excitement. *Surely* her mother must capitulate.

'Pah!' Elizabeth Woodville was at her rudest. 'Richard Plantagenet is your cousin, is he not, my lord archbishop? You are *so* full of praise for him.'

The acidity of her tone and the implications behind her words provoked the mild archbishop into righteous anger and he abandoned all attempts at sweet reason. 'Very well, Your Grace, as you remain so determined, I am instructed to receive into my custody the person of His Grace, the Duke of York.'

'You jest!' she cried, taken by surprise.

'No, madam, the king himself wishes the company of his brother and has urgently requested the Lord Protector to send for him.'

There was a hush in the room as the queen stared at the Council and the Council stared back. Without a word the archbishop placed a paper on the table, and by craning her neck Cicely recognized her brother Edward's inelegant scrawl. The queen read the letter and then folded it slowly between shaking fingers.

'I will *not* give my other son into the clutches of the Lord Protector.' Her eyes were lustrous and tear-filled as she employed her considerable wiles upon the men before her, but it was from another direction that an unexpected interruption came.

Dickon flung himself on the rushes at her feet. 'Mother, *please* let me go to Edward. Please, I do not want to stay here.'

'Silence!'

'But Mother, I—'

'Enough!' Her voice quelled him, but as he sat up his eyes were brimming.

The archbishop was victorious. 'Your Grace, you cannot keep him here against his own will and that of his brother the king. That is to violate the holiness of sanctuary as truly as if we were to seize you now and force you from here.'

This was defeat and Elizabeth knew it. There were too many witnesses for her to attempt denial of her son's wishes. She stepped back from the little boy, her chin held high. 'You may take him, but my daughters remain here with me.'

She saw the protest and anguish in the girls' eyes and dismissed them peremptorily to their rooms before they too could speak their minds. Then, turning once more to the Council, she said, 'You may tell the Lord Protector that nothing short of a public avowal of allegiance to my son, and of his good intentions towards my family and me, will induce me to leave here. And I *mean* public! The whole realm must know we are safe from his malice.'

The archbishop was so incredulous he could only gape.

'Those are my terms. Good day, my lords.' In an imperious swirl of black, Elizabeth left the room, and the door was closed upon on her delighted son and the angry Council.

For a while the monotony returned, the days passing at a snail's pace, with endless sitting, reading, embroidery and music. The summer months were fine, the sun flooding the old stone of the abbey with its golden warmth. Often Cicely sat at the window with Bess, although they were barely able to see more than a few yards in either direction because the walls of the gloomy building were so thick. The courtyard always seemed deserted, even the birds seemed absent. How Cicely longed for the open happiness of the palaces and gardens, and for the freedom of daylight and sunshine, but she said nothing to Bess for fear of further charges of intent to foully murder the Lord Protector.

One day in late June, their solitary existence was shattered when the Archbishop of Canterbury came once more to see the queen. He was very troubled and most insistent that he be received by the queen alone. Cicely and Bess hoped against hope that he brought news of their possible release. However, what he had to say concerned an entirely different matter.

Once again it was Biddy who came with all haste to tell the sisters. She was as white as a sheet and trembled from head to toe. They made her sit down and tell them what ailed her. It appeared that she had been about to knock on the door of the queen's apartment when she heard raised voices from within. The queen was distraught and the archbishop's voice was insistent.

'What were they saying?' Bess demanded impatiently. 'Surely nothing can be *that* bad?'

'It can, my lady. To begin with, your uncle Earl Rivers and your half-brother Sir Richard Grey have been executed at Pontefract for treason. And, far worse for you, it seems your father's marriage to your mother has been declared bigamous, your father having already been betrothed to one Lady Eleanor Boteler, Talbot as was, daughter of the old Earl of Shrewsbury.'

Bess was shaken by the first revelation, absolutely shattered by the second. 'And . . . and the Lord Protector has allowed this?'

'Yes.'

Cicely sat back weakly. 'How *could* he?' she breathed.

There was an urgent tapping at the door and one of their mother's ladies entered to beg Bess to come at once because the queen was as one demented now the archbishop had left. Bess gathered her skirts and ran along the passage to her mother's room, with Cicely following close behind. They found the queen so agitated that she hurled ink at her terrified ladies as they huddled in a corner. They squealed and ran out, almost knocking Cicely from her feet as they passed.

Bess was firm, making Elizabeth sit down, while Cicely brought a goblet of wine. It was accepted, because their presence was apparently soothing. But when Elizabeth spoke, it was not of her dead brother and son, nor even of Lady Eleanor Boteler, but again of the dead Duke of Clarence. 'George Plantagenet comes back from the grave to destroy me,' she whispered. Her face was ghastly and her eyes bright with fear.

Bess frowned. 'What is the matter, Mother? What do you mean?'

'Mean?' The queen sat upright, as if suddenly awakening from a nightmare. 'I mean nothing! I am merely feeling unwell. My head aches so.'

There was authority in Bess's voice. 'Mother! Your brother and son *were* guilty of treason, as you are too, for plotting against Father's dying command that the Duke of Gloucester was to be Lord Protector. We have a right to know everything because if you have been declared the mere mistress of our father, then *we* have been declared bastards!'

'Yes, and by your precious uncle — do you *still* defend his every action?'

'Mother, I would merely know his reasons.'

'He wants the throne for himself, is that not obvious?' Elizabeth gave a disparaging snort of a laugh.

'That is not good enough, Mother. You and I know that he could take it by force were that the case. But he would not do that. Think of him what you will, but he would never use arms against us. Whichever side of the blanket we are, we will always be his brother's children. There is more to all this and I intend to be told! What has our uncle Clarence to do with it?'

Cicely's legs began to tremble so much that she leaned against the wall and sank to the floor. She was surely asleep, and would soon awaken. . . .

'Very well, Bess, you wish for the truth and you shall have it. All of it.' Drinking the last of the wine, Elizabeth stood a little weakly, refusing to let Bess help her. She went to the fireplace, cold, black and dark, and with her back towards them, began her story.

'Your father married me knowing he was already betrothed to the widowed Lady Eleanor Boteler, daughter of John Talbot, the first Earl of Shrewsbury. Married to her, to all intents and purposes. Certainly they were married if he bedded her after promising marriage. Which he did. It was the only way he could get between *my* legs, so no doubt he did the same thing with her, except that in her case he really did make her his wife. Unwittingly, no doubt, for he was young and rash, but it was done all the same. Unless, of course, there was another before *her*. Who knows? He was capable of anything when it came to women. But as things went on, he found himself trapped with me. I knew nothing of it all, and believed myself truly wed to him. He rewarded Lady Eleanor well for her silence by showing favour to her family. She was very pious, kept the secret and died four years after the bigamous ceremony with me. I am told she died a very sad lady. I sympathise, for I now share her fate, because her death did not make any of you legitimate. Your father and I were never truly married.'

Cicely stared. 'Never?'

'No, child. I was never his wife, merely his mistress.'

Cicely blinked back tears. Her father fully intended his bastard son to ascend to the throne?

Elizabeth sighed. 'Others knew, of course, but your father purchased their silence. He paid enough for them to stand by him. Gloucester did not know, of course. He and your late uncle Clarence were the last two men your father wished to have in on such a secret. Clarence because his son was in fact the rightful heir, Gloucester because Edward valued his loyalty and support, which might not be so freely given if this great lie were to be discovered.'

She paused. Speaking of it at last was both purge and greater weight. 'All might have stayed well and hidden had your father not given offence to the Earl of Warwick, whom he taunted about me. You see, the earl — who was often called the 'Maker of Kings', because whoever he supported did indeed ascend to the throne — had been instructed to negotiate a French marriage for Edward. Warwick was justifiably incensed to find he'd been sent on such an empty and insulting errand. He left the court and took Clarence, by then his son-in-law, with him. Clarence was married to Warwick's daughter Isabel, and Anne, whom Gloucester had wished to marry, was the wife of the Lancastrian heir, Edward of Westminster, Prince of Wales. Whether York or Lancaster, a daughter of Warwick was destined to be Queen of England.'

Cicely's brows drew together. 'So Lady Anne has had two husbands? I thought she and the Duke of Gloucester had been a love match since childhood.'

'She certainly turned willingly from him to marry Prince Edward. She was in love with the prince, or so it was believed at the time. Edward was killed at the Battle of Tewkesbury in 1471. By then she was almost fifteen, and Richard seventeen, maybe eighteen, I do not know for certain. Anyway, Richard took her back and they have been married ever since. God help him for having such a cool marriage bed.'

Bess smothered a gasp. 'How can you say this? It is *known* that the duke and his wife love each other very much!'

'And maybe *he* does.' Elizabeth's eyes met her eldest daughter's. 'It is whether she has ever fully returned that love that is in question.'

Bess turned away, as if she had learned something momentous.

Elizabeth went to sit down again, and leaned her head back. 'We wander from the point, for I was speaking of Warwick. Your uncle Clarence had been certain the Maker of Kings would turn upon your father and put *him* on the throne instead, but Warwick went over to the mad Lancastrian King Henry VI, to whom I and my family once adhered, but by then poor Henry did not know what day of the week it was. So Clarence, realizing Warwick was now aiming to put the House of Lancaster back on the throne, crept back to the House of York and made his peace with your father. At least, so it seemed on the surface. Clarence somehow sniffed out the truth about Lady Eleanor Boteler and tried to use it to his advantage. George was unscrupulous, tactless, foolish, faithless and much given to drinking, and believed he had discovered something that would ensure the crown passed from Edward to him, and thence to George's own son. Not to Edward's *illegitimate* son by me. He even came to taunt me in person.' The queen smiled reflectively. 'He said I was no better than the king's other doxies, and he was right, as a confrontation with your father soon revealed.'

Cicely felt an odd need to offer comfort, something her mother would never have done in return. 'But you did not know, Mother. You were tricked.'

'Oh yes, but it was probably no better than I deserved. I thought I manipulated your father into marrying me, but in the end it was he who manipulated me. The king warned Clarence to hold his tongue or face the consequences. But Clarence either did not believe the threat or did not care, and continued to drip his poison. Your father eventually lost patience and arrested him on a charge of treason against the realm. Easy enough to do, given George's past waywardness. That was when Richard of Gloucester came with all haste from Yorkshire, unable to believe the sorry state of affairs between his brothers.'

Elizabeth remembered. 'By then Gloucester was twenty-five, and in many ways more capable than his brothers put together. But he always, *always* supported your father. I know how Edward relied on him, and I suppose he was right to do so. *I* did not value Gloucester, however, because he proceeded to plead with your father to spare Clarence. That was the very last thing I wished to happen. Fortunately it was also the very last thing your father wanted. Gloucester was never told the truth, of course, and was left believing my marriage was true and Clarence a traitor.' Elizabeth gave a short laugh. 'Gloucester spoke well for his brother's life. A most engaging man, your uncle, but your father stood his ground and Clarence was condemned.'

The queen glanced at her jewelled fingers, and on resuming the story, her voice sank to the merest whisper. 'That was really when Gloucester began to despise me. He had never liked me, nor I him, but now he realized that I was in some way responsible for George's plight.'

She got up and went to the window. 'Your father hesitated for many days to sentence his brother Clarence to death, for it was a terrible thing to do, but in the end Clarence was secretly executed in the Tower. When Gloucester learned of it, he was shocked and distressed. Lady Eleanor Boteler was long dead by then, and as far as I knew there was no one else to speak of it. Your father and I could continue to play at man and wife, and that would be the end of it.'

She turned for a moment. 'I was wrong, though, because there were those in Eleanor's family, the Talbots, who knew of it but had been persuaded or rewarded to remain silent. And Robert Stillington, a priest who all those years before had known of the pre-contract, perhaps even officiated, is still alive today. He is now the Bishop of Bath and Wells. I strongly suspect him of having informed Clarence, but that cannot be proved. If he did, it would explain something of Clarence's behaviour. Now Edward IV is dead before his time, and the good bishop has spoken up to prevent a bastard from ascending the throne of England. He has gone to Gloucester, who has chosen to believe him and is to take the throne for himself.'

Bess was immediately protective. 'Mother, there is no *chosen* about it! If all that you have just said is the truth, we *are* illegitimate, and the Duke of Gloucester *is* the rightful king. Our uncle Clarence was attainted and his children barred. That only leaves Richard. Why should he discard his own son's birthright for the sake of his brother's illegitimate children? And if other whispers I have heard are true, Father was not legitimate either, but born of a brief dalliance between our grandmother and a mere archer!'

'That is calumny! God's blood, girl, you would say *anything* to help Gloucester's cause! Cannot you at least *pretend* to think purely where he is concerned? Have you never heard the word consanguinity? That man has ruined us. He thinks *nothing* of maltreating his beloved brother's widow and children, yet *you* harbour unclean thoughts of him.'

Bess recoiled, pale-faced. '*He* has not ruined us, Mother, you and your hated Woodvilles have done that. If I were Richard, I would do all I could to see them overthrown. His is the royal blood, not theirs! And you are *not* Father's widow, are you? You are just another of his splay-legged bitches!'

Cicely scrambled to her feet. 'Bess!'

Elizabeth went for her eldest daughter, meaning to hit her with as much force as could be mustered, but Bess ran to the door and out of the room.

Cicely tried to follow, knowing her mother would interrogate her, but she was not quick enough. Elizabeth could still be nimble when she chose, and seized her second daughter's arm.

'What *is* this between Bess and Gloucester?'

'I know nothing, Mother. There *is* nothing. How can there be when it is so long since Bess last saw the duke?' Cicely faced her squarely.

'She saw him last Christmas, and that is not so very long ago.' Elizabeth searched her daughter's eyes. 'Has he returned her feelings? Has he . . . touched her?'

'Say what you will of him, I feel sure he would be proper with her.'

'How would you know? *You* have certainly not met him in a long time.'

'Then be honest, Mother. You have known him ever since you met Father. Do *you* think he would?'

Elizabeth smiled. 'No, I suppose I do not, but even a saint can fall by the wayside. Although not this saint, I fancy. But that does not make Bess's adoration any better. She *does* love him, does she not?'

Cicely lowered her eyes. 'I would only be guessing, as you do.'

Elizabeth smiled again. 'Jesu, I know you will not appreciate this, but you, too, are like me, Cicely. Bess has Woodville tendencies, but not the quick mind to accompany them. She is swayed by foolish Plantagenet passions, whereas you . . . Well, I do not know exactly what it is about you that makes you so different. I see the way you watch and learn. You may only be fourteen, but you behave more like nineteen, a nineteen with a great deal of insight. You can analyse what you see and hear, and I suspect your judgement to be superior. You will always know the right thing to do, the right advice to give, although whether you can apply it to yourself may be another matter. You can also, without trying at all, induce others to trust you. On reflection, in your case, perhaps I did lie with Richard of Gloucester after all, but it was so unexceptional that it entirely escapes my memory. You certainly make me think of him.'

'I am not accustomed to your praise, Mother.'

'That is praise?'

'I believe so, but whomever my father might be, please do not say I have your coldness.'

Elizabeth laughed. 'Oh, dear me, no. There is a spark in you, Cicely, a light that tells me you will fight to the last for what matters to you. Here you are, standing midway between Plantagenet and Woodville, and you have the best of both. Oh yes, there *are* some good things about the Woodvilles. Not many, I grant.' Elizabeth searched her daughter's face. 'If you put your mind to it, I dare say you could go far. You will certainly be able to influence men.'

'I want love, not machination.'

'You will soon learn to discard such romantic notions.' Elizabeth gave an ironic laugh. 'I really had not noticed how much you have matured. You are becoming a beauty. Maybe you will trump Bess.'

'I do not think so, Mother. My looks and colouring are *not* the fashion.'

'Changes of fashion have to commence somewhere. Why not with you? Which reminds me, you really must have your forehead shaved back.'

'No.'

'We will see about that.' Elizabeth moved away. 'Now, regarding, Bess, I wish I knew what it is about Richard of Gloucester that makes women want him so. Whatever it is, he has more than his fair share. You can tell your sister that if she *does* harbour a fleshly desire for him, and allows it to be known, I will carve her heart out with a blunt knife.'

CHAPTER FOUR

RICHARD'S REVENGE UPON those who had conspired against him at the time of Edward IV's death was astonishingly temperate. Only a few had really incurred his wrath. Cicely could not help thinking that if she had been her uncle, she would have dealt much more harshly with all his enemies. There would not be any left to cause trouble in the future!

The country willingly and gladly accepted Richard of Gloucester as King Richard III. There was still discord from Lancastrians, Woodvilles and dissatisfied Yorkist nobles, but the people knew Richard would rule justly, as he always had on his lands in the north. His fame went before him.

The day of the coronation, 22 June 1483, was one to remember, even for those seeking sanctuary. As the sun stood at its highest, an expectant hush fell over the capital, and then the first fanfare sounded in the distance followed by the cheers of the crowds. The choir music began in the great church and the cheering grew more rapturous, rising to a deafening roar as the royal procession entered the abbey itself. The singing and chanting seemed to go on forever, but after the passing of more than an hour, there was a pause in the music.

Cicely closed her eyes, imagining it all, and then the joyful carols rang out once more. Outside the crowds sensed that the moment had come and renewed their wild cheering, this time with even more enthusiasm. At length those in the abbey knew the procession was returning to the great banquet at Westminster Hall, because the cheering became more distant until it blended with the air of excitement that had enveloped London for the past week.

Bess wished to be alone, and so Cicely made her way to her mother's apartment, there being no one else with whom to sit. It was not often she sought her mother's company, but it seemed appropriate today. Elizabeth Woodville, now to be known as Dame Grey, as she had been on the death of her first husband, was alone, seated at her table, a quill hovering over a letter yet to be commenced.

She looked up. 'What brings you here, Cicely?'

'Nothing really. Bess wants to be on her own, and—'

'And I am better than nothing?' There was a faint smile.

'Yes,' Cicely replied deliberately.

Her mother chuckled. 'Oh, what have we come to, Cicely? Not so very long ago we were the most important ladies in the land, along with Bess, of course, but now look at us. Your father has much to answer for.'

Cicely sat on the window seat and poked idly at a cobweb that hung against the lattice.

'Is Bess still eulogizing her confounded uncle?' Dame Grey asked.

Cicely did not answer.

'We have spoken of it before, Cicely, but I have to ask you if you know any more now than you did then. Just how far *does* this go with her? I may not have been a warm mother, but I do not like to think of her in such pain.'

Cicely could not hide her astonishment. Had her mother *really* just said something kind and thoughtful? She stood, wishing she had never come here. 'Even though she was Father's favourite, Bess does think more highly of Richard.'

Elizabeth leaned back in the chair and picked up the quill again, to stroke the tip. 'Why, of *all* men, did she have to pick him? If the wiles of Jane Shore leave him cold I cannot imagine that the inexperience of his own niece will have any effect. I fear Bess will discover him to be far less than she imagines, for he is completely and utterly devoted to Anne Neville. Although I suppose I should now call her *Queen* Anne.'

'I have heard that he has a son and a daughter by other women.'

'Ah, yes. The girl is named Katherine, but I know no more. The boy is John of Gloucester, and he was born shortly before you, Cicely. *And* before Richard of Gloucester married his Anne, should you wonder otherwise. I believe John of Gloucester is to be knighted in September, and our new king's only legitimate son, Edward of Middleham, will become Prince of Wales at the same time.' Elizabeth drew a long breath. 'But this takes us away from the matter of Bess's feelings for her uncle, and indeed, if they are reciprocated.'

A voice from the door startled them. 'Rest assured they are not, Mother. *I* am the evildoer, not him.' Bess stood there, her face scarlet with humiliation and anger, and they knew that she had been listening to them. Then she left again, the heavy door swinging to behind her.

Cicely ran after her, but once in the refuge of their own room, Bess turned on her like a tigress, and slapped her with all her might. The force made Cicely stumble back, her cheek marked red by Bess's ring. She lost her balance and fell to the rushes. Bess stood over her, her hands clenching and unclenching with the violence of her emotion.

'You little bitch! You little maggot!'

'Bess . . .' Cicely whispered through a haze of pain and misery.

'Do not make excuses, for Jesu's sake do not make excuses — I *heard* what you said!'

Cicely felt a hard knot of anger in her stomach, and struggled defiantly to her feet. 'Very well, if you are so eager to believe the worst of me.'

'Of course I believe the worst, I heard you!'

'What did you hear, Bess? Tell me. If I said so much, perhaps you will enlighten me, for to be sure *I* do not remember.' Cicely's voice was very like their mother then, the same ice-cold crispness belying the inner fury.

Bess faltered and the first doubt crept into her face. This was a side of Cicely she had not seen. 'Well, you and Mother spoke of . . .' She bit her lip and her voice sank to a barely audible whisper. 'You were discussing the way I feel about our uncle.' Having said it aloud at last, she sank to the bed, trembling. 'Oh, Cissy, I have never known such misery and shame.' She put her hand out blindly to her sister, and with a rush of feeling Cicely took it and sat to put a comforting arm around her.

'Bess, dearest Bess, you know that I was not tittle-tattling to Mother. And believe it or not, she is sad to see you so unhappy. And she would have known nothing at all had you not betrayed yourself by shielding him so often and so violently. Your feelings are written so large that even I can recognize them for what they are.'

'I am so ashamed of myself, so disgusted, and yet I cannot conquer it. The very sound of his name sends my pulses racing. He is my *uncle* and yet I crave him.' Bess began to shake, her eyes pleading with her sister to forgive such iniquity.

'My poor Bess.'

'Cissy, I tell you if he were to beckon his finger to me I would willingly give myself to him.' Bess hung her head once more. 'Have you any notion of how I felt today? He was so near, in the same abbey, but I could not even *look* upon him. He is enshrined in my heart, every detail, every flaw. I love him so much,' she breathed.

Cicely sat silently with her, holding her close and just listening.

When Bess spoke again, her voice was very soft. 'The last time I saw him he was about to depart for Middleham. He had taken his leave of Father, saw me outside and came over to say farewell. He kissed my cheek and hugged me, telling me that the man who married me would have the most beautiful princess in the world. If you could have seen him then, Cissy. He was so handsome and gentle, so slender and yet so strong, wearing a thick travelling cloak over the wine velvet doublet and grey hose he had worn in the great hall as we broke our fast. And he wore thigh boots, I remember. I do so like thigh boots. It was impossible to know that his back sometimes causes him pain, for he would not let that be known to anyone. I adored him so much in that moment that I could hardly stand. I desperately wanted to tell him how I felt, but to him I was only his niece, and he did not see beyond that into my heart. The desolation I felt at his leaving left me in no doubt; no doubt at all that I love and desire my own uncle.'

'Bess, if the Pope can — rarely, I know — give dispensation for uncles to marry their nieces, then in God's eyes it cannot be a truly evil crime to love Richard. Can it? I wish I could say something more to help you, but I cannot.'

'Dispensation or not, nothing can change the fact that Richard is married already, and adores his wife. I cannot bear to think of her. She has him and I do not. She may not even love him, but I would, Cissy. Oh, how I would. He would be deeply shocked if he knew anything of this, and I would lose him forever then. At least I have something of him now, a smile, an arm around my shoulder, or a kiss on the cheek. I imagine so much, you know. I lie in bed at night, thinking of how it would be if I went to him as he slept.'

Cissy was startled. 'I do not think you should tell me anything more, Bess.'

'But I need to, Cissy. I have to let you know what it is to be me. I *do* imagine making love with him. I *do* imagine going to him. It would be summer, the night would be warm and he would be naked and asleep. His hair spreads against the whiteness of his pillow as he dreams — of what, I do not need to know. I reach out to touch him . . .'

'Oh, Bess.' Cicely really did not want to hear more, but knew she had to let her sister confess everything.

Bess smiled, gazing through her tears at nothing in particular as she spoke of her fantasy. 'I cast off my clothes and stand at his bedside, looking down at him. I see his dear body, so slim and pale, so perfect to me, in spite of fate's unkindness to him. I adore him with my eyes. Can you imagine such a moment? To gaze upon the man you hunger for, to see him so accessible and unknowing? To hear his gentle breathing, and want his physical love so much that it is agony? I bend down and slip on to the bed with him. I move close, and stroke his chest, with its dark hairs, and my hand moves down to his loins . . .'

Cicely was shaken by such frankness. Her breath caught, and her eyes widened.

Bess hardly noticed. 'Oh, Cicely, I find him so very alluring, unbearably so, and now I am caressing that part of him that can join me to him in the act of love. He is aroused by me, Cissy, and he pulls me close. Those fine lips that I look at so often when I am with him, find mine in a kiss, and I am in such ecstasy that I fear I may faint of it. His kisses are so tender, yet at the same time needful. It does not matter to either of us that we are uncle and niece. I feel his body come to life for me. Just for me, Cissy. He makes such sweet love to me, kissing my lips, my throat, my breasts, and that which is concealed between my legs. I feel him inside me, and my maidenhead offers no resistance. He is my lover, my beloved, my life, and for these secret minutes he belongs to me.'

Cicely gazed at her. 'I — I do not know what to say, Bess,' she whispered, her heart contorting with compassion.

Bess exhaled slowly and then looked at her with a sad smile. 'I pray that if ever you fall in love like this, it will be with a man you can actually have. Certainly not Ralph Scrope, for he is not the right one for you.'

Cicely pulled herself together. 'I hardly ever see Ralph. How can I when he is at court and I am in here?'

'And the times you did see him?'

'I liked him well enough. I blushed most dreadfully.'

Bess smiled. 'Did your heart quicken, did your skin feel hot, did you feel weightless, breathless, that you were with the only reason you are alive?'

Cicely shook her head. 'No. Definitely not.'

'Then, believe me, you are not in love. When you are, it will strike you like a flash of lightning. When I see Richard again it will be as fresh and poignant to me as the very first time.' Bess pressed her lips together ruefully. 'Making love with him can only ever happen in my imagination, but to me it is almost real. Sometimes I feel I *have* lain with him.'

The conversation was broken by the bells of London once again beginning their joyous clamour rising jubilantly on the summer air. Bess went to the window. 'Richard, by Grace of God, King of England and France, Lord of Ireland. May God bless and keep you safe,' she said quietly.

CHAPTER FIVE

A MERE TWO weeks after the coronation, Richard and his queen set off on a royal progress around the realm, to be greeted everywhere with joy by the ordinary people who loved him. The Duke of Buckingham, still riding high in Richard's favour, lingered in London a while and then returned to his estates in Wales, specifically his castle at Brecon.

There, as Richard continued north through England, the duplicitous duke plotted, with the connivance of his Lancastrian prisoner, the sly Bishop Morton of Ely. Buckingham planned to rise against the king and either take the throne for himself, or assist the claim of the so-called Lancastrian heir, one Henry Tudor, exiled in Brittany, who called himself the Earl of Richmond, although that title was now in Richard's possession. Tudor's claim was tenuous, and descended through his mother's illegitimate Beaufort line, which had been specifically barred from the throne. But he and his supporters could not have cared less about flying in the face of such weighty legal considerations. It was never to be proved which aim was in Buckingham's mind. The only certain thing was that he wanted to remove his cousin Richard from the throne, even though the new king had treated him well and rewarded him lavishly.

Unrest began the moment Richard set out on his ill-fated progress, and included an unsuccessful attempt to 'free' Cicely's brothers from the royal apartments in the Tower. Hurt and embittered, Richard struck back immediately and crushed the revolt. Buckingham was captured and executed at Salisbury. He begged to see Richard, to explain, but Richard refused.

Henry Tudor's formidable mother, Margaret Beaufort, had boundless ambition for her precious son. She was descended from John of Gaunt, and was now married to her fourth husband, the influential Lord Stanley, whose allegiance could change with the wind. Margaret was a pious schemer, a plotter, a woman prepared to commit high treason to get what she wanted . . . and what she wanted was to see her unworthy Tudor son upon Richard's throne.

Before Buckingham showed his true colours and rebellion raised its ugly head, Margaret paid a visit to Dame Grey in the abbey. She glided silently into Elizabeth's presence, her small eyes bright and sharp, her mouth tight and cold. She wore a white wimple, and her sombre black garb made hardly a sound on the rushes. 'Your Grace,' she murmured, making low obeisance to the startled Elizabeth.

'Lady Stanley, you forget I am no longer queen, merely the widow Dame Grey.'

'I forget nothing, Your Grace, I merely address you as you should be addressed. In the eyes of the realm you are still the queen of Edward IV and the mother of Edward V.'

Elizabeth's eyes narrowed suspiciously. Margaret had aspirations for her own son, not for Edward V.

Margaret continued, 'My visit, alas, has an unhappy purpose, for I bring you grievous news indeed. Richard has had your sons murdered.'

Elizabeth clutched the table, her heart beating wildly. Her mouth ran dry and her body turned icy with fear. She, so often shrewd and quick, was suddenly foolish and gullible. For these few seconds it escaped her that Margaret almost certainly had an ulterior motive. 'How . . . how do you know this?'

'I know because their bodies have been seen. By, amongst others, my half-brother, who conspired to enter the Tower in order to free them.'

'Your half-brother? Oh, yes. John Welles. From your mother's second marriage, I believe. No, her third.' In her anguish, Elizabeth did not think of asking the clever Margaret who the other witnesses were; she thought only of her children. Her dead sons.

Lady Stanley continued: 'The foul deed was done before Richard left on his progress.'

'But why? I know they might one day have attracted the disaffected, but they were only boys, and illegitimate.'

Margaret was consolatory. 'Their murderer sits upon the throne but he is not secure — there are many who would rejoice to see him dead, as no doubt you would yourself.' She looked sideways at the stricken woman.

Elizabeth's head was reeling and she sat down, clasping her shaking hands in her lap. The news had shaken her so much that she hardly knew what she was saying. 'But if Richard dies . . . who takes the throne? Buckingham?'

'That strutting boaster?' Margaret almost spat.

Elizabeth's eyes flickered. 'He was your stepson, I believe, Lady Stanley? By your . . . second husband? You have had so many I have quite lost count.'

'He may *think* the throne to be his ultimate destiny, and since he too is descended from Edward III, his lineage is indeed grand. But he is gravely mistaken if he imagines Richard's enemies will flock to *his* banners.'

Elizabeth was startled. 'Banners? Buckingham really does intend to *rebel* against Richard? I do not believe it.'

'Nevertheless, it is true, and he is bound to fail. He is no match for the crick-bodied Plantagenet when it comes to military matters. But he *will* keep the usurper occupied long enough for *us* to strike.'

'Us? My lady, I fail to see why on earth you have come here. To tell me my sons are dead, yes, but not to what you now refer. You are only interested in your son, Henry Tudor, whose claim to the throne is *much* smaller than Buckingham's, and *infinitely* smaller than Richard's. None of this is of any consequence to me. My sons are dead, and I certainly have no stomach to see Henry Tudor on the throne.'

Margaret's thin lips curled, for what she had to say next galled her to the very bone. Forcing aside her distaste for Elizabeth, the loathed Woodvilles and the House of York, she seemed all sincerity. 'But surely you have the stomach to see the true blood of Edward IV — *your* blood — upon the throne? Your Grace, I have a proposition of the utmost gravity and import.'

Elizabeth waited with deep suspicion.

The sweet, flat voice continued: 'My son, Henry, will invade to overthrow the usurper and avenge your husband's great memory. He will reverse the declaration of illegitimacy placed upon your children, and restore Edward IV's blood to the throne by marrying your eldest daughter.'

Elizabeth was more herself now, and not fooled by any supposed desire to restore Edward IV's blood to the throne. Henry Tudor needed Yorkist support to gain the throne, and a promise of marriage to Bess would bring him just that. His own claim was questionable, but with Bess by his side. . . . She stood and was face to face with the Tudor's mother. 'Lady Stanley, you have given me no *evidence* of anything, and it is a fantasy to believe that your son will attract such huge support that he will overcome Richard.'

The dark Margaret was inwardly enraged, but smiled. She sought written proof of Elizabeth's consent to the proposal. 'I cannot give you proof, you must know this.'

'It is hard to believe Richard has acquired so many enemies in so short a time.'

Margaret gave a short laugh. 'Oh, behind his attractive face there is an evil soul, as is evidenced by his contorted body. He has *always* had many of these detractors, my lady, for his is not an easy nature, and now he has acquired many more who hate him by virtue of his usurpation of your son's throne. The names of *my* son's supporters have amongst them the highest in the land, but I may not divulge them to you without first having your agreement to the marriage.'

Elizabeth was cold and regal. 'You do not trust me, Lady Stanley? Surely you do not believe that I would support my sons' murderer? If that is indeed what Richard III is.'

The reply came hastily. 'You must understand that many lives are at stake and even to such a great personage as yourself I must safeguard them to my utmost. However, there is one whom I shall name. Your eldest son, the Marquess of Dorset, is now back in England, awaiting word to act.'

'Thomas?' Elizabeth felt her heaviness lift. Her resolve was strengthened, and suddenly, illogically, she accepted all that Margaret said. 'And what form must my consent take? Written, I presume, since you must have evidence of agreement, must you not?' She uttered these last words to force the Tudor's mother to admit that her son's claim rested almost entirely on Bess.

The thin lips parted as Lady Stanley gave the ghost of a smile. 'Naturally, Your Grace, there must be a signed document that you will agree to support my son's claim, provided he swears to make your daughter his queen, thus restoring your husband's blood to the crown. York and Lancaster will be reconciled, and England will look forward to peaceful prosperity.'

By now Elizabeth began to see the advantage of such a marriage, for she would again be the mother of a monarch with all the wealth and power she craved. On such a surge of renewed ambition, it was only too easy to be convinced that the country as a whole would, after all, rise against Richard. As she penned her letter of consent she wept for her lost sons, feeling special remorse about the little Duke of York, for if she had not wanted to create an impression in front of the Council, he would still be here with her.

Lady Stanley hastily sanded the letter, and the moment Elizabeth had appended her seal, departed with almost indecent haste, lest Elizabeth demand the names of the other conspirators and so-called witnesses.

When October came, Buckingham's revolt was quashed, not only by Richard but by the weather, which put the rivers Severn and Wye in flood and prevented the duke and his army from crossing into England. Buckingham was captured and beheaded. The speed with which Richard disposed of this second attack upon his authority unnerved those others who plotted against him. But he was again too lenient. John Welles, Margaret's half-brother, was arrested, deprived of his lands, and then freed. Henry Tudor himself did not even disembark from his ship. He came within shouting distance of the shore, where Richard's soldiers shouted they were friends come to conduct him to London in triumph. But the wary Henry, suitor to Bess's hand and seeker of Richard's throne, sensed the trap as surely as does a wild animal, and remained safely aboard his ship. He sailed back to Brittany to wait once again.

Richard returned in triumph to his capital, supreme and safe upon his throne. It was to be February 1484, just before Cicely's fifteenth birthday, that he at last came to the abbey in person.

CHAPTER SIX

CICELY'S NIGHTMARE OF being trampled by a horse awakened her with a start. She sat up and pushed her hair back from her forehead. Jesu, what a horrible dream. She was hot, her skin was damp, and she felt as if something momentous was about to happen. Something that would change her life forever. It was an astonishing feeling, almost shattering, and it made her heart pound.

Bess sighed in her sleep and turned over, but Cicely's attention was suddenly drawn to the window because she heard the sound of flesh-and-blood horses in the courtyard. Curious, she slipped from the bed, pulled on her warm robe and carried a small table to the window. Standing on it, she was able to ease herself on to the ledge and then open the glass to lean out to the cold air of the February night. Men were talking and stamping their feet and now she could hear the horses more clearly. She could smell them too, that warm, sweet animal scent she had always loved — even though horses did not love her, and she was a barely adequate rider.

It was snowing, and there was already a blanket of white on the ground. Edging forward a little more, to see into the courtyard, she saw the horses and men. Two lanterns swayed and guttered, and apart from the dozen or so men on foot, she saw two more huddled figures on mounts, well wrapped against the cold. As the men slapped their arms around themselves and cursed the season, she noticed a large dappled stallion by a small door into the abbey. Then the banners caught her attention — the white boar cognizance of the king himself!

Gasping, she wriggled back into the room. Fearful thoughts chased through her panic-stricken mind. He had come to take them, to force them out under the cover of darkness and snow, to imprison them in the depths of the Tower as he had imprisoned and then killed her brothers! Forgetting Bess, she fled across the room in her bare feet and out into the torch-lit passage. Her flying feet were taking her to her mother's apartment when she saw her uncle.

He was coming up the stone staircase that led to their refuge. His tread was light and swift, and he was alone. His fur-lined cloak was wet with snow, some of which still clung to his thigh boots. At the top of the steps he removed his gauntlets and his hat, which was pinned with a costly emerald and pearl brooch. There was no table, so he dropped both gauntlets and hat on the floor. She saw how thickly his wavy, very dark chestnut hair fell to his shoulders. It would tangle, she thought, for its texture was like her own.

He was about to take off the heavy cloak, his precious rings shining in the smoking light of the torches, when he realized she was there. She sank down on the floor, against the wall, unable to move or speak. His face grew serious, and he let his cloak fall carelessly with his other things, before coming towards her.

He was clad in a green velvet doublet and black hose; the doublet's arms were slashed to reveal heavy gold embroidery, and he had a presence that was far removed from the monster her mother accused him of being. Around his lean waist was an emerald-studded belt from which hung a sheathed dagger, and across his shoulders rested the magnificent livery collar of York that her father had worn so often, although the pendant that swung from it now was not the lion or sun in splendour, but the white boar.

She flinched and closed her eyes tightly as he put out his hand. There seemed a desperately long pause before he spoke. 'My poor Cicely, what *have* they been telling you about me?'

His voice was gentle, not fierce or angry, and she opened her eyes to look at him. At last he was before her, clearly, and she gazed up at his handsome, aristocratic face. Jane Shore was right, he was beautiful, but in a very masculine way, and he reached out to something deep inside his second niece. She had been a child when last she saw him, but she was older now and could see more surely because of it, and in that single moment she knew exactly why her sister was in love with him. And why Jane Shore would not have hesitated to lie with him.

He was not a muscular man by any means, but of slender build and slightly less than middle height, and would have been taller but for the affliction to his back. She knew he had been straight enough as a boy, for so her father had told her. The sideways curve of his spine had come when he was only ten or so. But it did not matter that his body was not perfect, for his rich clothes hid the fact anyway. All she saw was him. He was spellbinding, and everything about him passed into her soul.

'Why do you fear me, Cicely? I would not harm you. I am your uncle, not your enemy.'

At last she found her tongue. 'My brothers . . .'

'Ah, yes. You believe it all, do you?' As he bent to take her hands and pull her to her feet, she could smell the costmary on his clothes. With unexpected attention, he pushed her untidy hair away from her face, and then stepped back to look at her from head to toe. 'You have grown somewhat since I last saw you, and I am glad to see you do not shave your forehead.'

'You are?'

He nodded. 'You look very well as you are.' Then he smiled. 'So, you are growing up, but believe me, your troubles are only just beginning.'

'Troubles?'

'It does not matter, I meant nothing.'

'Yes, you did.'

His grey eyes swung back to her in surprise. 'You would argue with me?'

'Would you mind if I did?'

He hesitated, but then shook his head. 'I do not believe so.'

'What did you mean that my troubles are only just beginning?'

'That the course of life does not always go as we hope.'

She gazed at him. 'Has yours?'

'Jesu, lady, you ask a lot of questions. No, my life has not gone as I hoped, but there is little I can do about it.'

'Maybe it would have done if you had chopped off the heads of all your enemies. Every last one.'

He was amused. 'Possibly, and I have reaped the consequences of the oversight.'

'Do not be so merciful again, Your Grace.'

He gazed at her for a long moment. 'You have changed more than I imagined. Perhaps I should have you sit on my Council?'

She smiled, drawn to him more and more. Not even her father had allowed her to speak with such latitude. 'I will do so if you wish it, Your Grace.'

He laughed suddenly. 'I do believe you would.' He studied her again. 'What do you think, Cicely? Was I right to ascend to the throne? After all, it did you no favour.'

'I know my father's pre-contract was real, Your Grace, so yes, you were right.'

'You bear me no grudge?'

She shook her head. 'No grudge, Your Grace. Because you were right,' she said again. She could hardly believe she was so forthright with him, but he invited it and she admired him for it.

'Well, since you are evidently now a lady, I must tell you I have been given to understand that your father consented to your marriage to Ralph Scrope.'

'Oh.' She felt her cheeks go crimson. Was there anyone who did *not* know of her passing interest in Ralph?

'Is it true? Because if it is, I will see that it comes about.'

She gazed at him in dismay, unable to speak.

He gave a slight laugh. 'You are not speechless with delight. You do like Scrope, do you not?'

'Well . . .'

He searched her eyes in the torchlight. 'But not enough for marriage?'

'No. Something Bess said made me realize—' She broke off, her face suffusing even more as she remembered what the conversation with Bess had entailed.

He looked curiously at her. 'I hardly dare enquire exactly what Bess said.'

'Please do not.' She noticed he played with the fine ruby ring on his right thumb. He wore other rings, but the ruby was truly magnificent.

He smiled. 'Then the matter is over and done with. I had gone so far as to have a contract drawn up, for believe me, Scrope is eager for the alliance. He is the son of one of my northern supporters, a man I like and respect, and . . . well, Ralph is waiting down in the courtyard, hoping to speak with you.'

She drew back. 'He is? But . . . I have barely spoken to him, Your Grace, and certainly have not intimated any wish to marry him.'

'So he presumes?'

'Unless my father really gave him permission, yes, he does.'

'Do not worry, Cicely, for you have heard the last of such a match. I will not coerce you into Scrope's bed.'

'I want to marry for love,' she found herself saying.

'An ambition I can only respect. We all wish to marry for love, I think.' He touched her hair again. 'If you change your mind, or if there is ever a man to whom you give your heart, you have only to tell me. I may be many things, but I will *never* stand in the way of true love. Unless, of course, you tell me you want a hound like Henry Tudor.'

'Never.'

'Good.'

He was an odd, rather exciting mixture of composure and unease. 'You . . . are not at all what I expected,' she said.

'Expected? Did you not remember me?'

'Not really. Oh, I did in a way, but not as clearly as Bess does.' She lowered her eyes, wishing her sister's name had not slipped from her lips again.

'It has not pleased me to see you frightened of me. It was the same with your brother when I met him at Stony Stratford. It did not please me either that he is such an officious little prig, but we have the Woodvilles to thank for that as well.' He pursed his lips. 'I should not have said that about your brother.'

'Why not? It is the truth. Dickon is far better.'

'Oh, he is.'

She had spoken of her brothers in the present tense, and so had he.

'So, do I take it that you are no longer afraid of me? Or do you still imagine that because my body is not straight, my soul must be crooked? That I eat small children when I break my fast? That the only reason I would come here would be to seize you all and imprison you in a deep dungeon?' He waved an arm to mock the shadows.

'Why *have* you come?'

He leaned back against the wall in a less than regal slouch. His grey glance moved over her again, sweeping from her bare feet to her hair and then to her earnest face. 'To attempt sweet reason with your lady mother — if such be indeed possible.'

The sarcasm was not lost upon Cicely. 'She hates and fears you, so perhaps you waste your time.'

He gave a dry laugh. 'Your mother has good reason to fear me, given her most recent treachery. But Cicely, if I wanted to do away with you all, and if I am a godforsaken monster, do you honestly believe I would not have flouted sanctuary before now and had it all over and done with?

Your father did that after Tewkesbury, so there is a precedent. Then I could be at ease to enjoy my next platter of spitted child.'

'Do not say things like that.'

'Forgive me, I only meant to tease.' He put his fingertips to her cheek.

He was tactile, approachable. Disarming. She gazed at him as he lounged against the wall, his jewels flashing in the moving light.

His voice became more serious and authoritative. 'I wish to speak with your mother. Please tell her I am here and will speak to her now, not at *her* convenience.'

Cicely was aghast. 'Tell my mother *that*?'

He straightened. 'Yes, now. I trust there is a warmer place than this landing?'

She indicated the arched doorway near where they stood. Inside was the large room where they all sat together during the day, and the fire was struggling to survive. She left the King of England bending to put another log on the feeble embers and then press it down with his heel.

But as she hurried to arouse her mother's ladies, she found Bess next to the clothes he had left on the floor. 'He is here, Cissy?' Bess's voice shook with the force of emotion that coursed through her just because he was only a few yards away.

'Hush, Bess, for he may hear! You cannot go . . . well, you know.'

'No, I do not. What do you mean, Cissy? Do you think I am about to rush to him and rape him with my eyes and words? Maybe I will even fling myself carnally upon him in front of you?'

Cicely drew back. 'Do not say that, Bess. I do understand your feelings, truly I do. Perhaps now more than ever before.'

Bess's eyes softened. 'He is everything I say, is he not?'

Cicely nodded, for it was true.

'I *must* see him, Cissy.'

'If you do, you had better know that he has sent me to bring Mother to him. Given the way she feels about him now, do you honestly believe she will hold her tongue out of respect for you? Bess, she will accuse him of all manner of vice, all manner of disgusting intentions towards you, and in so doing she will ensure that he looks upon you with aversion. Is that what you want?'

Bess hesitated, torn, and then gave a reluctant sigh. 'I hate you when you are so logical, Cicely Plantagenet. Now *you* have been alone with him, whereas I, who love him so very much, must stay away.'

Leaving Bess where she was, Cicely hurried on to her mother's apartments. There was soon a great deal of panic and commotion as Elizabeth's ladies rushed from their beds to prepare their mistress. Bess had gone when Cicely returned to the king. He was forcing a second log on the fire, and was unaware of her presence until she closed the door. He whipped around warily, but then saw who it was. 'Cicely! Dear God above, I thought — well, it does not matter what I thought. Never be a monarch with enemies, for it is a truly unhappy state.'

'Is there ever a monarch *without* enemies, Your Grace?' she asked, going to his side.

'Uncle. I am your *uncle*, Cicely, not some unreachable figure upon a throne. And you are right, there will probably never be a king free of enemies.'

'I — I have awakened my mother's ladies.'

He nodded. 'I know. I appear to be a true fox among the hens.' As she laughed, he smiled too. 'I am glad you are now at ease with me.'

'You remind me of happier days, when my father . . .' Her voice died away, for her father seemed a very awkward subject.

'Do not shrink from speaking of him to me, Cicely. I loved him dearly, and if he were still here, I would still serve him.'

'Even if you discovered the truth about Lady Eleanor Boteler?'

'How abominably direct you are.' His grey eyes were riveting in the firelight. 'Whatever my opinion of your father's marital maze, he was still the rightful king, so, yes, I would have served him. But I could not stand by after his death and allow his illegitimate offspring ascend to the throne. The pre-contract proved *my* right to the throne, your uncle Clarence's son having been barred by his father's attainder. Not only was I the king, but I had my own son's rights to consider. He is my heir. There is also the matter of England. The land cannot sustain a minority rule at this time. It requires a man of some experience. That, I am afraid, happens to be me.' He smiled.

'I think you are right on every point, Uncle,' she answered.

'You do?'

She nodded. 'Yes.'

'You are astonishingly mature, Cicely.'

'I have had time to think since being in here.'

He laughed. 'No doubt, but you can blame your mother for *that*.' He became serious again. 'Cicely, I have not relished what has happened to you, your brothers and sisters, who are all my close blood kin, even if outside marriage vows. Your father wished me to be Lord Protector, but instead of his instruction being carried out, your mother and her family caused rebellion, my exclusion and would probably have done away with me. I had to execute Rivers and Grey, for they had committed treason, but it was another act that hurt you. And since then there has been another rebellion. I have asserted my authority and behaved as I think is right. Nevertheless, you have not deserved what has happened to you, and for that I ask for your forgiveness.'

'There is no need, for I have already said I think you had no choice but to act as you did. You were honourable. If you had not become king, England would be still torn by many ambitious nobles squabbling for influence. You are the only man who can control them all. You are also the one with the greatest claim to the throne and the greatest ability.'

'*How* old are you?' he asked on an amused note.

'I am in my fifteenth year.'

'So you are fourteen?'

She blushed. 'I am in my fifteenth year,' she said again, 'and next month, on 20 March, I will commence my sixteenth year.'

'The Feast of St Cuthbert. My chosen saint. So, being in your fifteenth year is that important?'

'Yes.'

He smiled. 'As you wish.'

'I *do* wish, for it is not pleasant to be half-child, half-woman.'

'Oh, I think we can safely say you are a woman, Cicely Plantagenet, for you certainly keep me on my kingly toes.'

It was so easy to speak to him. He did not look down on her as tiresome, nor did he show impatience or any of the other attitudes adults so often adopted when faced with awkward, if not to say insolent, questions from one as young as she. The impulse to touch him was too great to resist. She put her hand on his forearm, where the slashing of his sleeve revealed the rich embroidery.

His hand moved over hers. 'Cicely, your father played me for a fool. A loyal fool, but a fool nevertheless. He kept the pre-contract a secret from me and by so doing intended to deny me *my* right by letting his illegitimate son ascend the throne. And he permitted me to plead for my brother Clarence's life, when all the time he meant to have him despatched. It is hard to forgive such things.'

'You are true to yourself, I think.'

He gazed at her. 'I have never spoken of these things before. God alone knows why I am telling you. Can I rely upon your discretion?'

'Of course. You were loyal to my father, I am loyal to you.'

'It is that simple?'

'Partly.'

'Ah, there is a reservation.' He waited for her to explain.

'I will also be loyal to you because you are honest.'

He raised an eyebrow. 'There are many who would not agree with *that*!'

'They do not know.'

'Know what?'

'You.'

He paused. 'That is a great compliment, I think.'

'No one could speak with me, tolerate me, as you do and be bad.'

'And that is carved in stone?' He smiled.

She smiled too. 'Yes.'

He suddenly put an arm around her shoulders, and the gesture seemed intimate because of the way his back curved, but it was merely warm and appreciative. 'You are an exceptional lady, Cicely. I look forward to when you come to court. You would of a certainty be wasted on the likes of Ralph Scrope.' He kissed her cheek, and there was mint on his breath, sweet and fresh.

Then he took his arm away. 'I think I should ask if your sisters are well?'

'The little ones are in excellent spirits. Being in sanctuary does not mean anything to them.'

'And Bess?'

Her heart lurched. 'Bess?'

He tilted his head. 'You *do* have a sister named Bess?'

'I — Yes, of course. She is well too.'

'And still beautiful?'

'Yes.'

He smiled. 'She is very much my brother's child, whereas you, Cicely, look very like me. But I can assure you that your mother and I have never been that close. Oh, what a dire thought.'

Oh, how she longed to ask him about Jane Shore! His view of the incident would be so enlightening. This thought led Cicely to another. Was he really faithful to his queen? It was now even harder to imagine he had no mistresses, for he was so desirable, both for himself as well as his power, but if he did have mistresses, there were still no whispers, no names mentioned. Nothing. She gazed at him, for it was also hard to think that Anne Neville had ever preferred another to him.

The expressions on her face interested him. 'I think I should definitely not ask what you are thinking.'

'Definitely not.'

'Then I will refrain.' He pushed his hair back, and she noticed that he had lost part of the small finger of his right hand.

'What happened?' she asked, pointing to it.

'Too much childish enthusiasm at swordplay. You see? I am malformed *and* missing parts of myself. At this rate there will be little left of me to eventually bury.'

'But what there is will still be honourable and honoured.'

He gazed at her. 'You quite rob me of words, Cicely.'

'You give me words. I have never met anyone like you before. Well, not since I have grown up.'

He smiled.

'I will always honour you.'

He continued to gaze at her. 'And I you, I believe.' He touched her cheek again, lingering a little, and then drew his hand away again. 'I wish you to stay when your mother arrives. What I have to say to her I desire you to hear as well.'

'She will not like that.'

'Possibly, but I think my rank exceeds her, do you not agree?'

'Yes.' How he fascinated her with his lightning changes from uncle to king, his easy manner closely followed by tension. He was as taut as a bowstring, and yet throughout remained so accessible.

Elizabeth threw open the door and strode into the room, wrapped only in a loose robe over her nightgown. She halted in disbelief when she saw him. 'So, you *are* here. I thought it must be a jest.'

Cicely hung her head in shame that her mother could show so little respect to the King of England.

'Some may call me a jest, madam,' he replied, 'but you had better be sure I am not.'

Seeing Cicely, Dame Grey signalled imperiously for her to leave, but Richard raised his hand. 'Cicely will remain. If you wonder why I have not requested Bess's presence as well, it is because I wish to spare her the personal pain of your actions, of which I imagine she knows nothing. You or Cicely will tell her afterwards, but she will not learn it direct from me.'

Elizabeth looked squarely at him for a moment, and Cicely almost expected her to tell him how her eldest daughter felt about him, but then, without requesting his permission, she went to sit by the fire. As Cicely positioned herself behind her mother, she was sure there was suppressed amusement on his lips. He glanced at her for a moment, and yes, he found Dame Elizabeth Grey entertaining, although that fact would not have been perceived by many.

Then his attention was fully upon her mother. 'You have pledged your eldest daughter to Tudor, madam, and I will know your reasons.'

Cicely's lips parted in shock. Bess was pledged to Henry Tudor?

All Elizabeth's hatred flooded back. 'There are four dead reasons, Your Grace.'

'Explain that remark, madam, for I do not wish there to be any room for misunderstanding between us.'

'Very well. You executed my dear brother Rivers, and my younger Grey son. And, even more heinously, you have done my royal sons to death most cruelly.'

He stroked his chin thoughtfully. 'Rivers and Grey were guilty of treason. As you also were, of course. As to your sons by my brother . . . How came you by this wondrous information?'

Her lips compressed stubbornly and she turned her head away to stare at the leaping fire.

'What promises did the reptilian Lady Stanley make to you?'

'If you know so much perhaps you will tell me!' Her face was ugly with malice as she looked at him again.

'Your insolence is unbecoming, Dame Grey. Must I remind you that *I* am the monarch here?'

It was said levelly, but there was sufficient warning in it for Elizabeth to shift awkwardly in her place.

'Now then,' he went on, 'have you or have you not promised Bess to the Tudor upstart?' She did not meet his penetrating grey gaze, so he continued, 'You promised Bess because Henry Tudor's mother told you I had foully murdered your sons — my own nephews! She is not unbiased, I think, or did you not think of that? You accepted what she said without question, and signed your name to a letter of consent. I marvel at your crass stupidity. Did you not recognize that scheming woman's purpose? God's blood, I knew what you *said* of me, but I did not think you actually *believed* it!'

Elizabeth's face had drained of colour. He knew everything when she believed her actions were undetected.

Richard turned away, leaning a hand on the chimney breast as he kicked at the burning logs. 'Lady Stanley tricked you, madam. Your sons are not dead.'

CHAPTER SEVEN

ELIZABETH STARED AT the king. 'Not dead?' she whispered.

Richard drew a heavy breath. 'Lady Stanley told you they were in order to dupe you into signing your name to what she wanted. Her purpose is to sway uncertain nobles against me, in the hope of ending my reign and seeing Henry Tudor in my place. Disgruntled Yorkists would be influenced by the promise that Bess would be his queen. Well, Tudor's mother has not succeeded, and I have seen that her Stanley husband confines her to one of his estates. I will not have her miserable, arrantly hypocritical visage near me. Stanley himself only holds on by a thread. And so do others, so take care. I *am* capable of harsh action, as Hastings, Rivers, Grey and Buckingham discovered to their cost, and as some of your other kinsmen and allies may yet discover.'

He looked at Cicely. 'Cicely, Lady Stanley carried my queen's train at the coronation. Did you know that? You are right, lenience seldom works with an implacable foe. Always remember it, even if I have not as often as I should.'

She felt his bitterness.

Deciding he lied about her sons, Elizabeth's lips had curled back derisively. 'Well, you crooked, uneven tyrant,

I wish Lady Stanley and her son *had* succeeded. Oh, how I wish it.'

'Mother!'

Elizabeth twisted around to look up at Cicely's shocked face. 'What is this? I now have *two* daughters who leap to this monster's defence?'

Cicely's eyes became bright with caution, and she wondered if her mother would have adopted such an attitude with any other king. But then, had not she, Cicely, taken liberties with his tolerance?

For a moment Elizabeth remained angry enough to say what she pleased, but then thought better of it and fell silent.

Richard looked from mother to daughter. 'What is it you do not wish me to know, Cicely?'

Elizabeth responded haughtily. 'It is not your business, king or not.'

He ignored her. 'Cicely?'

'There is nothing,' she replied, meeting his eyes unhappily. She found it very difficult indeed to lie to him.

Richard raised an eyebrow, but did not press her. He had time for her, as she did for him. His attention returned to Elizabeth. 'Do not rely upon my chivalry or forbearance, madam, because at this moment the thought of seeing your mischief-making head upon a block holds much appeal.'

'You would not do that! You are many things, Richard of Gloucester, but you have never raised your hand against a woman.'

He found that laughable. 'So I do have one redeeming feature? That is solace indeed. However, it is clear that I really should mend my ways, because women are certainly raising their hands against me.'

'Oh, how glib you are. Even *I* am influenced, almost wanting to like you, although I know you have killed my boys. Maybe not with your own hand, but certainly you gave the order. I know it in my heart.'

'Your *heart*?' He grinned.

Elizabeth's fingers tightened on the arm of her chair, and Cicely knew her mother was battling with herself, wanting to fly at him and claw the mockery from his face, yet knowing it would be a grave mistake.

'And if I prove to you that your sons live?' Richard asked her.

'What will you do? Show me from a distance two boys of comparable height and colouring and tell me that they are my children?'

'You really begin to tire me, madam, and I find you as displeasing as I ever did. I am not concerned with *your* welfare or how long you choose to remain here, but I *am* concerned with your daughters. It is for their sakes that I am come here this night. Your sons live and are well, and if I prove this to you, I want your word — written, of course, since that appears to be your chosen way — that you will allow your daughters to leave without delay. You as well, if you so wish, but please believe me, I would be happy for you to moulder here. Oh, but I *do* want the treasure back. It belongs to the crown, not the Woodvilles, even though they may believe otherwise.'

Elizabeth flushed, but remained arrogant. 'And if I refuse all this?'

'Then you do not see your sons, and you remain here indefinitely. I will not weary myself or my Council with tedious talking and pleading. You are here of your own volition, madam, but if your daughters require me to take them under my protection, I will heed their wish.'

Cicely put a timid but appealing hand on her mother's arm. 'Please, Mother.'

Elizabeth took a long moment, but at last she submitted. 'Very well, Your Grace, I give my word that if my sons are alive, I will come out of sanctuary, my children with me. You will have my letter of consent, although I cannot take back that which I gave to Lady Stanley. But what will you do with us after that? I cannot imagine you want us near you, reminding everyone of your late brother.'

'I have no qualms about reminding anyone of Edward IV, madam. I loved and served him as a loyal brother should.' Richard glanced at Cicely, his eyes alight as he again remembered their conversation.

Elizabeth gazed at him. 'I wish I understood you, Richard Plantagenet.'

'I am relieved you do not. Now, you will need something warm to put about your shoulders. The night is cold.'

Elizabeth stiffened with suspicion. 'I am to go to them? Why do you not bring them to me?'

'You surely do not think I would be idiot enough to bring them *into* sanctuary? No, you must come outside to them. Not to the streets of London, merely the abbey courtyard. I will not abduct you, you have my word. However, you may remain here if you wish and I will depart, taking your sons with me. They will not be in London for much longer anyway. I cannot have the likes of John Welles, Lady Stanley's overenthusiastic half-brother, planning to get in either to dispose of or rescue them. It would certainly suit Henry Tudor to have them dead.'

'Would it not suit you as well to have my boys dead?' Elizabeth ventured.

'No, madam, it would not. I have no intention of murdering my nephews.'

'You can *say* it, Your Grace, but—'

'You have my solemn vow,' Richard broke in coldly. 'Have you ever known me to break my word? So, if you wish to see your sons, now is probably the best opportunity.'

Elizabeth put out her hand involuntarily. 'I will come!'

He took a rug that had been draped over a chair and put it around her shoulders. 'Once again a king dresses you, my lady,' he murmured.

'I am given to understand there are many ladies who would wish *you* to dress them, Richard Plantagenet, having undressed them first, of course.'

'Oh, my conquests are legendary.'

'They should be, but you do not appear to have the wit to do anything about it. Or do you?'

He met her eyes. 'That, madam, is for you to speculate upon.'

She looked at him for a long moment, and then swept from the room, leaving the door open. She would wait at the bottom of the stairs.

'Do you wish to see your brothers, Cicely?' Richard asked.

'Yes. Please.' He went out to collect his hat and gauntlets, and then gathered his cloak from the floor and brought it back to rest it gently around her shoulders. Again there was that odd intimacy about him, that hint of an embrace. But it was innocent. She doubted he even knew he did it. 'I am glad to have made your acquaintance again, Cicely Plantagenet.'

She returned the smile. 'And I to have made yours, Uncle.' She was his slave. Had he asked her to stand on her head and bounce, she would have endeavoured to do it.

But then something drew his sharp attention outside the door. Bess stood there, wearing only her night robe. Cicely's heart sank, for she could almost *feel* her sister's hunger.

'Bess?' Richard smiled.

'Your Grace.' Somehow Bess managed to curtsey to him. Cicely knew what emotions were rioting through her sister, just to be face to face with him again.

'Uncle. Call me Uncle.'

Cicely could only guess how much Bess hated that word.

Bess looked at the cloak around Cicely's shoulders. 'You are going somewhere?'

Richard nodded. 'To the courtyard. Your brothers are there.'

'My brothers? They *do* live?'

'Yes, although I had hoped that at least *someone* here would have credited me with clean hands.' There was a hint of bitterness in his voice.

'I always believed in you, Uncle,' Bess replied, not entirely truthfully, for she had confessed to Cicely of entertaining fleeting doubts.

He looked at her, and said nothing.

She came closer. 'May I come too? To see them?'

'Of course.' He cast around for something to keep her warm. There was only the curtain beside the doorway, so he tugged it down, clearly with more strength than it seemed, for it gave way immediately.

Cicely felt the brink come close again, for now Bess would confront their mother in his presence. And Bess knew it. She watched as he put the curtain around her sister, and saw how Bess's eyes closed with the intense joy of it. His lips were close as well. It meant little to him, but more to his eldest niece than he could ever imagine.

Suddenly Bess's hand moved over his, making him stay. 'Uncle . . . ?'

Cicely gazed at a nearby torch.

'Yes, Bess?'

'I . . .'

He waited.

'I . . . do so want to leave this place.'

'And so you shall, for your mother will have to honour her word.' He moved away from her, and Bess closed her eyes again, trying to hold on to the exquisite pleasure of his touch.

Cicely remembered Ralph Scrope and was anxious. 'Uncle, I do not wish to speak to Ralph Scrope.'

'He will not approach you, Cicely, I will see to it.'

'Thank you.'

They descended to the door to the courtyard, where Elizabeth waited. Bess faced her mother, her face set with determination, and after a moment Elizabeth gave ground. There was nothing to be gained by forcing unwelcome knowledge upon Richard. Not now. Unless, of course, her sons did not live after all.

Richard conducted them outside, and Cicely saw Ralph standing with the king's dappled horse. He smiled at her, the same carefree, engaging smile of before, and his light brown hair lifted as a breeze sucked down into the courtyard. He was tall and well made, attractive in almost every way, but she did *not* wish to marry him. He took an eager pace forward, but then saw the brief shake of Richard's head. His face changed and he quickly stepped back again, his eyes downcast. He remained thus as Richard led Elizabeth and her daughters across the now-thick carpet of snow. Cicely was dismayed that because she was shorter than the king, his costly, fur-trimmed cloak dragged the ground behind. Snowflakes fluttered, catching on her face and in her hair, and her bare feet were already so cold. As Bess's must be too, although Cicely doubted her sister was capable of feeling the cold when Richard was near.

The men who had been stamping and cursing were instantly silent and respectful at the king's approach, and obeyed immediately when he signalled to them to help the two small, muffled figures still mounted to descend. They were led to the king and their identities revealed.

Edward, so briefly the new king, and Dickon, the little Duke of York, were immediately recognizable in the torch-lit courtyard, and Elizabeth sobbed joyfully as she ran through the snow to snatch them to her breast and weep loudly. She did not seem to notice the sudden chill as the rug fell from her shoulders into the snow.

Cicely stooped to retrieve it, full of relief and gladness that her brothers were alive, as Richard had said, and she bent forward to kiss them both as they huddled against their mother. She heard Dickon say her name and she smiled at him. Edward barely acknowledged her, but then he was always disagreeable. Being of poor health did not improve him, although he was no worse now than he had been the last time she saw him. They both looked well cared for.

Bess went to them then, and as Cicely straightened to stand back, she became aware of the king's eyes upon her. This time she could not read his expression, but guilt scythed through her for having ever been unsure of him. She found herself going to kneel before him, to draw his gauntleted hand to her forehead.

'I had doubts, Uncle. Please do not think less of me for it.'

He raised her swiftly. 'I could never think the less of you for your honesty, Cicely.'

'I did not know you until tonight, but now I think I do. Please know that I will always support and love you.'

He smiled. 'Our spirits are as kindred as our blood, Cicely Plantagenet. Do you not agree?'

'Yes.' Then he turned his attention to Elizabeth, to whom Cicely had now returned the rug. 'Well, madam, you see before you your sons, alive and well. I trust you will abide by the word you gave me?'

He beckoned Ralph to bring the stallion, and the hooves clip-clopped slowly, not quite muffled by the snow. Cicely felt Ralph watching her, and at last looked up to meet his eyes, still hazel in the light of a torch. She felt his anger and resentment, and knew it was not *her* he had wanted, but the rank and influence he would gain through her. Thanks to Bess, she had made the right decision.

Richard mounted, and did so as lithely and easily as any other man. It was only when he hesitated in the saddle that she remembered his uneven back. Then he was himself again, as if nothing had happened. He was Bess's perfect Richard again, the rich green velvet of his doublet dotted with clinging snow, as was his hair. A snowflake brushed his lips, and Cicely saw how Bess watched it, wishing *she* were that snowflake.

His men took the boys away from their mother's desperate arms, and as Ralph returned to his own mount, without looking at Cicely again, Elizabeth hurried to grasp the bridle of the king's horse. 'Why? Why do it this way, at night, with my sons hidden beneath cloaks? Why do you not show them to the realm?'

He soothed the excited horse as he looked down at her. Cicely was sure he meant to deny her mother an answer, but then he changed his mind. 'I have already been forced to deal with two assaults upon my throne, assaults in which *your* name has been somewhat prominent, madam. I will not flaunt your sons before the people as if they are my trophies. The spoils of war. I am not such a man to do that. If they are not seen they will eventually not spring to the instant mind of anyone with a grudge against me. That is why — not to harm them or kill them, just to keep them from scheming minds. I will not always keep them like this, only until I am established and the land is settled. I weary of rebellion and will avoid all provocation if it is in my power to do so. Does that suffice?'

She clung to the bridle, her voice urgent. 'Does this mean that I will not see my sons when we come from here?'

He did not answer her and at last she had to release the dancing, impatient horse. Without a further word he urged his mount forward, raising his hand in salute to Cicely and Bess, and then he was gone into the twisting snow. His horsemen followed.

Elizabeth stared after him. 'Richard Plantagenet, I hate and despise you still, and yet . . . before God, I must admire you,' she whispered.

Bess, standing next to Cicely, whispered as well. 'And I must always love you, Richard.' Then she hurried into the abbey.

As Cicely and her mother went inside after her, Cicely suddenly remembered she wore his cloak. When she reached the room she shared with her sister, Bess was waiting, the cloak very much on her mind as well.

'It is his.' The words were a statement, not a question.

'Yes.'

Bess seized it and wrapped herself in it before inhaling its scent. Costmary. Him. 'Tell me everything, Cissy, for I must know exactly what he said. Did he mention me?'

'Oh, Bess, this has to stop,' Cicely began. She would never tell Bess *everything* he had said, because she had promised him she would honour his confidence. And somehow, she did not want to tell her sister anything at all, no matter how innocent. It would still be betrayal.

'Stop? It will never stop, Cissy. Never. I have seen him again, touched him again, and his spell has enchanted me ten more times over than before. I want him so much, *need* him so much, and yet he loves only Anne Neville.'

'He will never love you like that, Bess.' Cicely said it gently, for it was true. She had seen tonight that Bess was not anything to him that she should not be. Nor would she ever be.

Annoyed, Bess did not reply, but went to curl on the bed, still wrapped in his cloak, her back to Cicely.

CHAPTER EIGHT

IT WAS NOT only the cold wind of 1 March 1484 that caused Cicely's teeth to chatter, but also the intense excitement of imminent freedom. She and Bess stood behind their mother at the top of the abbey steps, awaiting the arrival of the king. Their younger sisters were there as well, in the care of their nurses.

Over to their right was a colourful assembly of lords and clergy, many of whom Cicely recognized and who smiled at her and her sisters. Others remained stony. The scarlet, fur-trimmed robes of the mayor and aldermen of the city of London glowed in the thin sunlight, and a crowd of curious Londoners had gathered before the steps, for the news had travelled quickly that not only were Dame Elizabeth Grey and her daughters leaving sanctuary, but that the king himself would be making an oath of friendship towards them. The crowd was for the most part quiet, although there were some jeers from a more unruly element, eager for the humiliation of the hated Woodville who had wrongly been Queen of England. There was an air of tension over the whole gathering, for Richard would soon appear.

Cicely stole a glance at Bess, whose eyes were bright with anticipation. Her cheeks were flushed as she gazed along the road from Westminster Palace for the first sight of the man she loved. The fluttering of royal banners could be seen, indicating that he would soon set out for the abbey, and Cicely felt a knot of apprehension for her sister, who stood on tiptoe to look past her mother's flowing black veil. Having met Richard again as her older self, Cicely now knew not only his spell, but his fleshly indifference to his eldest niece.

Then the first cheers were heard in the distance as the king's cavalcade rode out from the confines of the palace. Down the road it came, standards streaming in the breeze. Above the noise of the crowd Cicely could hear the hooves on the cobbles and then at last saw the white boar on the clothing of the riders. At the head of the procession, riding the same dappled stallion, Richard had the royal circlet on his dark head, because today he was to make an oath as King of England. He acknowledged the cheers with a gauntleted hand and a smile, and made a brave sight in his gorgeous crimson and gold clothing. Few noticed his back, even fewer cared. He was a handsome Plantagenet, still young, already known for his justice and care of the people. Richard III was no weakling, and would reign England well because he was not solely concerned with his nobles. The people appreciated that, but some of those nobles were resentful. There would always be discontented nobles.

Immediately behind him rode two gentlemen in rich clothes; one was Francis, Viscount Lovell, and the other was Sir Robert Percy. They were Richard's friends from his early days at Middleham in Yorkshire, in the household of the king-making Earl of Warwick. Like many of Richard's faithful followers, they had been appointed to positions of honour and trust in his new administration. Among the riders behind him, Cicely saw Ralph Scrope, looking handsome enough in Richard's livery. Beside Ralph was a young man she did not know. He wore pale blue, was tall with long silver-fair hair, and she could not help but notice his good looks and smile when Ralph said something to him. Whoever he was, she found him attractive . . . and a little familiar, although she knew she had never met him.

At the base of the steps Richard halted, raising his hand high to quieten the cheering, and a hush fell upon the gathering, broken only by the stamping of the horses and the occasional mewing of seagulls over the river. He turned his horse towards the noblemen and burgesses of London and began to speak, his voice carrying through the silence with clarity. He promised that if the daughters of Edward IV and their mother came out of sanctuary into his custody they would be treated as befitted their station and would come to no harm or insult at his hands, that he would arrange suitable marriages for them and that, with God as his witness, he would uphold his word.

Only when he finished speaking did he glance up at the abbey steps, and his face was expressionless as he looked at Elizabeth. 'Madam?' He could so easily have addressed her as Dame Grey.

She straightened proudly, and with her head held arrogantly began to descend the steps towards him, her daughters following. Cicely did not dare look at her sister, for she dreaded that Bess's feelings would be impossible to mistake. Their mother halted before Richard and knelt. He dismounted and Elizabeth took his hand to kiss it. A great cheer rose from the crowd to see the hated Woodville on her knees before the man she had sought to destroy. Elizabeth closed her eyes with humiliation, but he did not gloat over his triumph and made her rise almost immediately — he had no use for mean satisfaction.

He spoke quietly for none to hear but Elizabeth and her daughters. 'You will have no reason to regret your actions this day, and I truly hope that there will be no regrets on my part either.'

The former Queen of England looked up into those serious grey eyes and was surprised by the sincerity she saw there. Her reply was the only one she could give. 'Sire, you will never regret it, this I promise.'

Her words seemed to satisfy, for he remounted and to the continuing cheers of the crowd and royal party prepared to return to the palace. Not once had he looked at Cicely or her sister. Bess lowered her eyes disappointedly and Cicely squeezed her hand.

A voice spoke beside them and they turned, startled as a man addressed Elizabeth. 'Dame Grey, Viscount Lovell, your servant.' The newcomer sketched a bow to them; he was of an age with Richard, stockily built, with dark curly hair and a swarthy skin, and his voice denoted that he had spent a lot of time in the north of the land. He said he was to conduct them to their new quarters at the palace of Westminster, where Richard's court was at present gathered.

Cicely wondered why Richard did not speak in the same way; after all, they had spent the same time at Middleham. Richard's voice was . . . she did not quite know, because if there was an accent, she did not detect it. It was simply his voice and unlike any other.

The royal procession set off, with much of the vast crowd running beside it, eager not to miss a single moment. And so the fugitives left the abbey; not for them this time the ignominy of underground passages in the dead of night, instead they rode palfreys in a great cavalcade led by the king himself. Cicely rode beside Bess and delighted in the freedom and sights of London — even the smells, some of which were more than a little noxious. Anything and everything was preferable to her young heart than the hated abbey. She wanted to laugh out loud and urge her mount into a headlong gallop, to scatter the bustling Londoners to the four corners of the earth, but she resisted the impulse, and turned to Bess. 'Is it not wonderful to be out of the abbey?'

But Bess was staring miserably at her mount's ears.

'Please do not be sad today; not today when we are free at last.'

Bess gave her a watery smile. 'I am sorry, it is just . . . he did not even look at me.'

'Nor at me,' Cicely pointed out. 'He simply spoke to Mother, that is all. You must try to be more cheerful, for you do yourself no good by moping like this.'

These tactless words drew Bess's anger. 'Do not preach about something of which you know nothing, Cissy! One day you will come to realize exactly how foolish and heartless you sound right now! '

Cicely was hurt. She understood how Bess felt, but was determined not to let anything ruin this day. Unthinkingly, she urged her palfrey forward, but having not ridden for quite a time was too generous with the command. She was not a good rider anyway, so instead of moving just a little away from Bess, the palfrey took her swiftly to the head of the procession, passing a frowning Dame Grey who did not approve of such unladylike behaviour. To Cicely's relief she was able to rein her mount in before she overtook Richard as well. As it was, she found herself beside Francis Lovell, whose horse did not take kindly to her sudden arrival.

Hearing the slight commotion, Richard looked around and laughed on seeing the reason. Cicely was mortified, stammering her apologies to the viscount as he struggled to quieten his startled mount. At length he too laughed. 'I fear, my lady, that you have been too long out of the saddle.'

'Yes. I am so sorry, my lord. I will never amount to much of a horsewoman.'

'No harm was done, and I believe the king would forgive his favourite niece.'

'Favourite?'

'Oh, I do not think there is any doubt of it.'

As they approached the palace, Cicely thought of Richard's queen. How would Anne Neville be? She had so seldom come south to London that she had left no lasting impression. Through her the great Earl of Warwick's ambition had been realized — one of his daughters had become Queen of England. But not even Warwick could have dreamed of the circumstances that would bring this about.

'Is the queen in London?' she asked Francis.

'Indeed, yes, but only until the morrow, when she and the king leave for the north. The land is peaceful at the present time and they wish to conclude the progress that Buckingham's rebellion interrupted. And also to visit Prince Edward at Middleham.'

'The king's son is not here with them?'

Francis shook his head sadly and lowered his voice to be sure Richard would not hear. 'The prince's health does not improve and is a great source of worry to the king, as it should be to the realm. It is bitterly regretted that the prince does not have the strength of John of Gloucester, whose health and vigour outshines the prince tenfold, even though he be only the son of a lady in the Countess of Warwick's household. The king was but fifteen when he sired John, and now John himself is older, at sixteen. He is tall, fair, handsome and dashing. I fancy you will like him.'

The journey was almost at an end, for the outer buildings of the palace were almost upon them. They rode through the great gate, past the bell tower and into the courtyard, halting at last in the shadow of the old palace, and as Richard hastened on inside, Francis jumped lightly down from his horse to assist Cicely to dismount. She smiled and reached down to his arms. Her mother and sister were helped down as well, and as Cicely straightened her gown she was aware of the rest of the cavalcade filling the area. There was some laughter, and when she looked towards the sound, she saw the young man who had caught her attention earlier.

As he dismounted she thought again that he seemed familiar. Whether he felt her scrutiny she did not know, but suddenly he turned to look directly at her. He smiled and bowed. When he straightened, his long silvery hair fluttering in the breeze, she saw him say something to her. She could not hear, but thought by his lips that he said, 'Greetings, Cousin.' Who was he to address her thus?

Francis observed, 'A-ha, I see that my prediction is correct.'

'Prediction?'

'I said you would find John of Gloucester to your liking.'

Her lips parted, and she turned to watch Richard's son and his companions going into the palace. At last she realized why he seemed familiar; he had his father's eyes and manner.

CHAPTER NINE

THAT NIGHT CICELY fidgeted impatiently by the window of the rooms she and Bess had shared before, now theirs once more, and refurnished richly, in keeping with that of the king's eldest nieces. Outside it was almost dark and across the river the lights of part of the city glimmered faintly, shining on the moving water. In the glass she could see a broken reflection of herself, dressed in a fine lavender silk gown that was trimmed with bands of delicate white fur. On her head there was a small cap of white lace, from beneath which her dark hair hung loose. The queen had kindly provided her husband's nieces with a fine wardrobe each, and Cicely was overcome with delight to wear such rich and fashionable clothes.

Bess was in the room as well, and Cicely turned with an envious sigh, thinking her elder sister, now eighteen, was without doubt the loveliest creature in England. But Bess was changing her gown for the third time, having waved away both peach and rose, and she was *still* dissatisfied with her appearance, even when wearing gold. To Cicely she had looked exquisite in all of them. The harassed ladies-in-waiting fussed around her, plucking at the embroidered brocade and arranging the golden folds to perfection. Bess tapped her slippered foot anxiously. 'What do you think?' she demanded of her sister.

'Oh, Bess, you know you look well, as you always do. Do not try any more. Now *do* come on or we will be late and that would not be proper on our first night at court.'

There came a timid knock at the door and a page entered bearing a message that their mother awaited their presence in order to go down to the hall. They looked nervously at each other, for tonight they were virtually on trial before the entire court. With quaking hearts they followed the diminutive page to where Elizabeth waited, clad from head to toe in the deepest mourning. She would have covered her face as well, had not Bess advised her that it would be going a little far, because if Elizabeth were in that deep a grief for Edward IV, she would not have attended court at all, but would retire to some secluded manor or even a nunnery. Elizabeth also made use of a walking stick, having twisted her knee when alighting from her palfrey earlier. The aid was genuinely needed, but looked an extra affectation on top of all the unrelieved black. Like Bess, Cicely believed her mother made them look nothing more than foolish.

The noise of the merry-making in the great hall reached their ears long before they came to the head of the staircase leading down to the huge gathering below. Minstrels were playing, lords and ladies danced an elegant measure, and a man was singing falsetto. As the names of Edward IV's former queen and her two elder daughters were announced, an immediate hush fell upon the court and everyone turned to look. They descended slowly, aware of whispers behind raised hands, the occasional mocking smile and aware most of all of Richard and his queen on the dais at the far end of the room.

Cicely walked a little behind her mother and Bess, for it seemed the natural thing to do. Bess's beauty and regal Plantagenet bearing was drawing the same appreciation that Elizabeth Woodville herself had once enjoyed, although where Elizabeth was concerned the admiration had been very grudging. Now the interest on the men's faces was blatant, and the jealousy of the women equally obvious.

Cicely's nervous glance moved to Francis, who stood with Sir Robert Percy. Francis winked and smiled encouragingly as she passed, for which she was grateful. Sir Robert inclined his head as well. He was perhaps a few years older than Francis, a well-built man with straight tawny hair, an open face and a hint of congeniality in his easy manner.

She also saw Ralph Scrope, splendid in sage green. His disgruntled gaze followed her across the floor, and when their eyes met, he turned away. She glanced around for John of Gloucester, but could not see him.

The walk towards the dais seemed interminable, with the tap-tap of Elizabeth's stick sounding like a clock ticking away time itself. Cicely's faint courage was fast disintegrating. She knew that her cheeks were aflame and was dismayed that her inexperience was there for all to see. She had so wanted to conduct herself as a young lady, to look as graceful and collected as Bess. But perhaps Bess's composure would soon waver when she came close to Richard. Already a little tension was entering her; Cicely could almost *feel* it.

At last they came to the foot of the dais and went to their knees before their king, Elizabeth with some difficulty. Richard, who wore gold-embroidered velvet of the same grey as his eyes, came down to raise her. 'I welcome you to my court but understand your discomfort, Dame Grey. Are you able to be presented to the queen?' His golden circlet gleamed as he indicated the steps of the dais.

'Richard Plantagenet, if you imagine I intend to *not* be presented to your queen, as is fitting, you are very much mistaken. You may have declared me mere Dame Grey, but I am *still* the consort of Edward IV,' she responded emphatically. She knew it was wrong to address him thus, but was too proud to entirely forget that *she* had once been Queen of England.

'Then please allow me to conduct you.' He could have put her in her place, reminded her that although she may have consorted with his brother, she had never, in law, been Edward's consort, but he allowed her the dignity she sought.

Elizabeth held her head high as she mounted the steps, but her teeth were gritted not only to quell the pain in her knee, but to also quell her anger. She was not accustomed to being less than a queen. It was one thing to be hidden away in the abbey, quite another to face the highest in the land again at court.

Cicely studied Anne Neville, who did not look at all strong. Her dainty, very pretty face was the colour of parchment and her blue eyes had dark rings around them. She was gracious and friendly towards Elizabeth, who was finding the night very difficult indeed.

When Elizabeth had been escorted to one of three chairs set out to one side of the dais, but not actually on it, Richard turned to Bess who, like Cicely, remained on her knees before him. He raised her, and Cicely saw how her fingers moved momentarily around his. He thought it was her nervousness, but her observant sister knew better. Bess managed to mask her feelings, and showed no other outward emotion as she too was conducted up to Anne, who received her with the same courtesy and favour as she had Elizabeth. As Bess was complimented upon her appearance, Cicely felt so sorry for Anne, whose primrose gown drained away what colour she had. Even her long, pale, almost strawberry-coloured hair, swept up beneath a rich, heavy headdress, was lacklustre. It was also shaven back from her forehead, a mode that Cicely knew Richard did not like. The gem-studded belt at the queen's tiny waist showed how painfully thin she was. She looked as if he could snap her in two with one hand.

As Bess went to sit with her mother, Richard turned to Cicely. 'Come, sweet Cicely,' he said with a smile, bending forward to take her hand. She managed to rise with what she prayed was sufficient elegance, but her hand shook and he felt it. 'I fear this is all necessary, Cicely,' he said quietly, that he would not be heard by everyone.

'I am trying not to fall over myself.'

He smiled. 'You will not do that, for I am here to prevent it. Cicely, you will soon cease to be subject to such intense curiosity.'

'I hope so,' she answered honestly.

He glanced around the silent, almost echoing hall, and with a sharp gesture signalled the minstrels to resume playing. The dancing recommenced, as did much of the merriment, but many eyes were still turned towards the king and his younger niece at the foot of the dais.

Richard looked her from toe to head, and smiled. 'You are becoming more beautiful by the day, Cicely.'

'You tease me.'

'No, I do not. Your loveliness is a match for your sister's. It is . . . warmer.'

'Now I *know* you are trying to make me feel better.'

He smiled. 'That is more like the Cicely I recall from the abbey. I was beginning to fear you had lost your spirit. You must think better of yourself, because in so many ways you put your sister in the shade. And before you suspect me of bolstering your courage again, let me add that I am not the only one to admire you.'

'Oh?'

He put a conspiratorial finger to his lips, but did not satisfy her curiosity. 'Come, for my queen wishes to meet you.'

He led her up to Anne, and to her relief, she managed to kneel with some semblance of elegance. Anne inclined her head and smiled. 'Lady Cicely, you are truly welcome. You and your sister have become beautiful young ladies now, yet it seems not long since you were mere children.'

Even her voice is pale and thin, thought Cicely as she kissed the skeletal hand. She was drawn to Richard's kindly, hollow-eyed queen. 'Your Grace, it is kind indeed of you to receive us so well and to have given us such magnificent wardrobes. We are very fortunate.'

'Fortunate *and* fair.' Anne smiled and raised her with a gentle hand. 'You are my husband's dear nieces, the children of his beloved brother. How else should we receive you but in kindness?' Then she drew a long breath, clearly feeling unwell, and her eyes moved meaningfully to Richard, who took Cicely's hand quickly.

'Come, you were the first of my brother's children with whom I spoke and so you shall be the first with whom I dance.'

She was nervous as he led her to join the dancers. She and Bess had maintained their dancing lessons in the abbey, but was she good enough to tread a measure with a king? She was aware of Bess's jealous gaze as she moved in time with Richard, twisting and turning, her hand ready when he had to take it. He moved with a light grace that belied the distortion of his back. He may not have been a giant as her father had been but, slender or not, his was a commanding figure, and in Cicely's eyes he was by far the most handsome man in the room. But her eyes were that of a loving niece, not of a niece who would be his lover.

As they performed the intricate steps, she saw how his eyes wandered continually towards the queen, who had begun to cough. One of her ladies was pouring her a goblet of wine, but still Anne coughed. Richard forgot the music and stood motionless as the dancing continued all around him. Cicely moved to his side. 'Please go to her, Uncle.'

His grey eyes swung to her. 'Forgive me, for I mean you no discourtesy.'

'I know that.'

He caught her hand and squeezed appreciatively as he led her from the floor and up to the dais, where he left her in order to go to Anne, whose coughing had abated a little, although she looked like a wraith. Someone else was standing next to her now, John of Gloucester, leaning familiarly over to distract her by whispering something amusing in her ear. He was dressed in a mustard doublet and hose and a sleeveless, fur-trimmed jacket of russet velvet, and was already as tall as Richard. His silver-fair hair curled loosely to his shoulders, and as he looked kindly down at his father's queen, Anne smiled up at him and patted his arm fondly.

Then Richard was there, leaning down anxiously. 'My lady? Anne?'

'Please forgive me, my dearest lord, but I am feeling a little tired and would return to my rooms. It is nothing that cannot be soothed by a good rest. I will be well enough to travel in the morning.' He took her thin hand and pressed it softly and lingeringly to his lips. It was not a mere gesture but an affirmation of love. But what sort of love? Cicely wondered, thinking of Anne's first husband. The queen's thin fingers closed momentarily around his and then he assisted her to stand. She bade Cicely and John a good night and then was gone with her ladies.

Cicely felt sad as she watched the wraithlike figure move slowly towards the staircase. She knew — as did Richard — that the queen was not long for this world. But there had been something tepid in the way his wife had responded to him. Had it been because she was so unwell? Or was there some truth in the story that she had loved her first husband more?

To Cicely it seemed there might have been unshed tears in Richard's eyes as he turned quickly to his son. 'John, she is more fragile with each day. I fear greatly for her.'

'Perhaps now, with summer almost upon us, she will improve, Father.' John's hand moved out to him but then withdrew again.

'I can only pray so.' Richard mastered himself again, and spoke more briskly. 'But now, I will present you to your sweet cousin.' He drew her forward. 'Cicely, this is my son, John of Gloucester.'

All she saw were John's grey eyes as he stepped forward and bowed low over her hand. 'Cousin Cicely, I am your servant.'

'Sir.'

Richard clearly wished them both gone, for Anne was still on his mind. 'John, I have just put up a lamentable performance in the dance — you must make it up to my niece, lest she believes all men of the north to be clumsy oafs.'

As John conducted her down to join the dancing, she noticed how Ralph watched. His expression was set, and there was something on his face that conveyed he was now her implacable enemy.

Of that dance she would remember but little, for she seemed to float on air. Her flesh quivered every time John's hand touched hers. Never before had she experienced such emotion, and she needed all her strength and purpose to control the excitement that ruled each faltering step. But what of him? Did he even see her as a young woman, or was she merely a tiresome cousin with whom he must dance? His face betrayed nothing, and they spoke not a word.

The stately dance came to its end and as the dancers bowed low to each other, Cicely's attention was snatched away as Richard, still clearly worried about Anne, remembered his duty and approached Bess for the next dance. Bess came to life and light, claiming everyone's attention as she bent and turned to the music. She might have been formed of golden gossamer, and her shining gaze was turned so often to her king that Cicely was afraid she went too far. *Please do not, Bess. Please.*

John spoke softly. 'Cousin Cicely, shall we dance again? Or am I forgotten?'

She turned with a start. He was leaning carelessly against the carved stonework of a pillar, an attitude so reminiscent of his father that she almost gasped. He was in the shadows, his fair hair dulled by the dim light, and he was curious. 'What is it, Coz, do you see a ghost?' Even his low laugh was Richard's. He straightened and came closer, his hair restored to its silver-fair colour in the light from wall torches and the great wheel-rim candle holders suspended overhead.

'I — I must apologize, sir,' she managed to say, feeling gauche. 'It is merely that you were so like your father just then that it quite startled me.'

'It is no king you see before you, Cicely, only poor John of Gloucester, your devoted cousin and servant!' He bowed extravagantly, and then hesitated. 'Have I presumed by addressing you by name?'

She looked into his eyes again. 'No, sir, you do not.' She felt hot, because she knew that was not the answer she should have given.

'Will it be even more of a liberty if I beg you to call me John?'

'I . . .' These moments were far too forward. She should be aloof and pretend to be offended. But why be artful? She liked him very much, and was sure by his attitude that he liked her. 'As I believe I was saying . . . John . . . your resemblance to the king is noteworthy.'

'Why so? He is responsible for my existence on this earth and so I would expect to resemble him in some manner! *Your* resemblance to him is more remarkable. You seem more like father and daughter than uncle and niece — it has been commented upon.'

His words touched a chord in her heart and she was back in time, her father's arm slung carelessly around her. '*Well, Richard, with that hair she is more your daughter than mine, eh?*'

'Cicely?' John was awaiting a response.

'My father once used those words, and so has yours since.'

'He likes it that you resemble him. My father, that is. It amuses him that it has been wondered if he once coupled with your mother behind your father's back.'

'I know. He told me.'

John was startled. 'He did? That surprises me.'

'I find it easy to talk to him, and he to me. I do not pretend anything to him, nor, I think, does he pretend to me.'

'I am jealous that he is so deep in your confidence.'

'Jealous?' She smiled. 'He is my uncle.'

'True.'

Their attention was drawn away because there was a stir as Richard conducted Bess back to her chair and then took his leave of the gathering. He was unable to stay away from Anne a moment more. 'I do so feel for him, John,' she whispered, tears pricking her eyes.

John nodded. 'He has much to bear. His son, my half-brother, is not at all well. It is the same with the queen.'

'He and the queen love each other very much, do they not?'

'Yes. Why?' John looked at her.

'Oh, nothing, it was just an observation.'

He glanced at her a moment longer, and then lightened the moment. 'I am truly glad you *are* King Edward's daughter, because you otherwise would be my half-sister and I would blush to feel as I do.'

She blushed. 'Now you do presume, sir.'

'And will presume even more. I find you most to my liking, sweet Cicely.' He smiled, his eyes laughing.

'You tease me.' That was the second time she had been called sweet Cicely tonight, once by Richard, and once by his son. Other people had called her by that name as well, for the herb sweet cicely was common enough, but tonight it meant more.

'No, upon my heart I do not.' He placed his hand on his breast. Then he looked towards Ralph, who continued to watch from his place further along the hall. 'Poor Ralph, he had great hopes of you.'

'Does the whole of creation know about it?' she demanded crossly. 'He had no right to presume. I gave him no reason at all to think I would marry him.'

John put his hand on her sleeve. 'I do not for a moment imagine you did.' He smiled. 'After tonight I will no longer be in his confidence, I think.'

'Did he *really* think I wished to marry him?'

'Well, he gave my father cause to think it was a virtually settled matter, until you left no doubt it was not *your* wish. I am glad Ralph means nothing, because I mean to pursue you.'

She laughed. 'And what makes you think I will regard you with more favour than I did him?'

'I know you do already,' he answered quietly.

'We have known each other for barely half an hour, and so you cannot possibly—'

'But I do know, Cicely. And so do you.' His eyes were serious, his voice soft.

'That . . . is *very* forward,' she whispered. Her heart was racing.

'Is it not part of my irresistible charm?' He spoke lightly, but drew her hand tenderly to his lips, dwelling over the moment.

It could so easily have been art on his part, a knowing way that he had employed many times before with great success, but somehow she did not think so. 'John, I—' Something snatched her attention away to Bess, who was accepting Francis Lovell's invitation to dance.

John released her hand. 'Your sister is very beautiful,' he observed. 'She has turned the heads of many men here tonight, and yet she notices no one. Is her heart given elsewhere?'

She avoided his grey gaze. 'I think she is a little shy, that is all.'

'Shy?' He snorted. 'Cicely, please, she is most certainly *not* shy. She flirted outrageously with my father, testing her wiles, no doubt.'

It was perilously close to the truth, and Cicely could not help drawing back. 'Forgive me, I — I must go to my mother.'

'Have I offended you?' he asked anxiously.

'No, of course not.'

'Then do not go.'

'I must, John.' She wished she had held her silly tongue, because she really wanted to stay. But it had been said, and she would look foolish if she changed her mind. She was angry with herself. If she could not remain calm when something, no matter how innocent, was said about Bess's manner towards Richard, then she would do far more harm than good.

For a moment his hand stayed her, but then he accepted. 'Promise me we will speak again?'

She smiled gladly. 'Of course.'

'I live until then,' he said quietly. Again, it could so easily have been light flirtation, but she knew it was not. They looked at each other, silent exchanges between them, and then she hurried away. She still felt as if she lacked substance, and her heart pounded as it had never pounded before. She remembered what Bess had said, and knew that tonight she had met someone who would always mean a very great deal to her.

She reached her mother, who was seated where she had been throughout. 'Mother? I thought I would come to speak to you.'

'Really? How very thoughtful,' was Elizabeth's dry response. 'So, you flutter your doe eyes at Richard's bastard?'

Cicely did not reply. Could not her mother set sarcasm aside, just for once?

Elizabeth's critical glance moved over Cicely's gown, and her lips pursed. 'Hmm, you look well enough, I suppose. I would not have thought lavender was your colour.' Then she gathered herself. 'Well, as the king has departed, we will also. I have no wish to appear over-eager to enjoy the delights of court life once more.' She stood, allowing no dissent from her dismayed daughter, who so regretted leaving John of Gloucester that she could have wept with the frustration.

Bess was summoned from the floor, and Elizabeth led her daughters towards the steps up which Richard had gone only minutes before. Immeasurable pride carried Elizabeth, and she gave no intimation of the effort she had to make to disguise her hobble. She glared at her daughters when they moved to assist her.

If Richard had still been present, Bess would not have left so willingly, but without him she had no interest in staying. As they reached the top of the staircase, Cicely turned, seeking but one face in that crowded hall. At last she saw John, still standing where she had left him, but accompanied now by Sir Robert Percy and Ralph Scrope, whose face was a study. He appeared to have just said something to John, and not received the response he required.

For a fleeting moment she and John of Gloucester looked at each other again. He smiled, and she knew that she was already more than a little in love with Richard's son.

CHAPTER TEN

CICELY AWOKE THE next day to the sound of the royal cavalcade beginning to gather before the palace. She remembered that this was to be her first complete day free of the abbey, and with a flush of uncommon warmth she also recalled the moment Richard had presented his son to her, and then how they had danced together. Not that she could remember much about the dance, for she had been so excited, so swept away with happiness that she feared she would not even remember the steps. But after that, she remembered every word, every touch and every smile.

Afterwards she had sent Biddy to ask discreet questions about him, and now knew that he had been born in 1468 in the great Yorkshire castle of Pontefract. That was his other name, John of Pontefract, but he was generally known as John of Gloucester. It was also known that he was very high in Richard's favour. Of greater interest to Cicely was that Biddy had been unable to find any rumours of him having a sweetheart. There was one cloud upon her new horizon, however, because she did not know if he would accompany the king and queen when they set out for the north that morning.

Later, after hearing Mass in the royal chapel, Cicely and Bess joined the great gathering in the hall for their breakfast, where Cicely was further disappointed by John's continued absence. Indeed, none of the younger men in Richard's household were there, because theirs was the task of preparing the uncompleted progress for the long journey.

Elizabeth had remained in her rooms, saying it was because her knee was now much more painful, although whether this was true her daughters could not decide. Certainly their mother had not enjoyed her lesser position in the great hall the previous night.

Cicely was daunted by the enormous variety of food and the smell of rich spices that hung heavily in the air, and she ate only bread. She had eaten well at her father's court, of course, but after so long at the abbey, with the plain fare that was provided there, this was all a little much.

Bess smiled, taking a huge piece of meat from a platter, and cutting it deftly with a knife. 'Come on, Cissy, why do you not eat a little more? You cannot starve simply because your John is not here.'

'You seem in a very good mood, considering our uncle is leaving today,' Cicely observed, but before Bess could reply, the queen entered the hall and they all had to stand.

Accompanied by her ladies, Anne came directly to the sisters. She had donned a bright blue travelling cloak but her sweet face was ashen against the vivid colour. She motioned to everyone to be seated again, and then drew closer to Cicely and Bess. 'It saddens me that I must leave London so soon after your return to us, but I hope to deepen our friendship when I return.'

Cicely smiled at the queen, whose gentleness touched her. 'We are honoured, Your Grace.'

Bess smiled as well, but Cicely sensed her lack of spontaneity. Anne shared Richard's bed, and that was something Bess, so suffused with unutterable jealousy, could not forget.

Anne did not seem to notice, however, for she was speaking of Middleham and Yorkshire and her only son, Edward, whom she so longed to see again. She pulled on her gloves at last. 'I must leave you now, and bid you farewell until our return.'

Cicely stood in haste. 'Your Grace, may I accompany you to the yard? I would very much like to.' She was hoping to see John there, but Anne was delighted and they walked from the great hall together. Bess remained behind, because it was believed Richard would also come that way, and she hoped for a chance to speak to him. Be with him. Only for a moment, maybe, but it would be all she could have for weeks.

As they came out into the morning sunshine and paused at the top of the palace steps, Cicely gazed down at the bustle of waiting horses and baggage, and also a curtained litter bearing the queen's arms. Anne looked sideways at her. 'I suppose *you* cannot imagine having to forgo riding in favour of a cumbersome litter.'

Cicely laughed. 'You did not see me yesterday, Your Grace. It was not edifying. I could scarce remember what it was like to be on a horse.'

Anne smiled. 'A very diplomatic answer.'

At that moment someone emerged from the palace behind them, and they turned, thinking it might be Richard, but it was John. Cicely's eyes began to shine, and her lips parted slightly with the happiness that suddenly leapt through her.

Anne noticed and leaned closer. 'He is comely, is he not?' she whispered.

John bowed low to his father's queen and then to Cicely, but there was no way to read his face. Cicely's spirits fell, not only because of this, but because by his clothes he was clearly to accompany his father on the journey.

Anne broke the awkward silence. 'I . . . er, will proceed now, for I think the king approaches.' She beckoned to her ladies, acknowledging the farewells of Cicely and John.

Alone with John for a moment, Cicely looked at him miserably. 'Please forgive my foolishness last night.' She had to bite her lip and stare hard at the stone steps, for she was afraid to see no welcome response in his eyes, but he took her cold hand and kissed it.

'Sweet cousin Cicely, there is nothing to forgive, but if it gives you pleasure then I will say I forgive you.'

'You jeer at me?'

'No, never that, Cicely. Never.' He kissed her hand again. 'Please, I think too much of you to hurt you.'

She smiled, her fingers tightening against his. 'You are going to the north as well?'

'Yes. But I will return, of that you may be sure. Can I trust you not to find another in my absence?'

She gazed at him. 'You know I will not.'

'And you know that I will not play you false either. You *do* know that, do you not?'

She nodded. 'Of course,' she whispered, closing her eyes as he leaned forward to kiss her upon the cheek. His lips were cold from the March air, but so wonderful to her. 'God be with you, John of Gloucester.'

'And with you, Cicely Plantagenet.'

'You are a Plantagenet as well,' she reminded him.

He smiled and would have said more had not a herald announced the king. Richard emerged with his northern lords and gentlemen, who all wore his white boar badge. He was richly attired in mulberry velvet. Mulberry — murrey — was the colour of the House of York. There was a heavy cloak over his shoulders and the circlet of gold rested around his forehead, but before he could approach his son and younger niece, Bess emerged from the shadows nearby. They were just beyond Cicely's hearing, but she could see the love on her sister's face as she spoke to him. His followers continued politely down the steps, but Cicely was dismayed to notice their exchanged glances.

Richard put his hand to Bess's cheek and smiled, and then left her to come quickly towards John and Cicely. His hair fluttered in the breeze from the river as he smiled at her. 'It seems my brother's daughters wish to bid me farewell in person this morning.' He raised an eyebrow as he saw her hand, still tightly clasped in John's, and he put a gauntleted finger to her chin, tilted her face up and kissed her cheek. The freshness of mint touched her. 'I fear the time has come to part, Cicely,' he said, 'but know I will do all I can to ensure my son's swift return.'

She blushed and felt foolish, but he smiled again and then was gone, descending the steps to the great dappled stallion as it was led forward. As he mounted, Cicely saw John's dun horse being brought as well, and with great reluctance she released his hand. He paused, and then bent his head to kiss her fully upon the lips. It was a kiss that fluttered hesitantly upon her mouth, uncertain of its reception, but for a final second it grew strong as it was returned.

He gazed into her eyes for a moment and then hurried down to his horse. Some of his companions cheered and made comments, until Richard silenced them with a raised hand. Then he, John and various nobles who had been in the palace with him accompanied the queen's litter out of the yard. They would soon join a much greater procession of lords waiting on the outskirts of the capital. With much noise and clatter, the slow baggage procession began to trundle out as well, but was soon left behind.

Cicely watched until the last packhorse had passed beneath the gateway and then walked slowly back into the palace, wondering how long it would be before she saw John again. His kiss still tingled on her lips, and she did not know if she was deliriously happy or wretched because it would not be repeated for weeks, maybe even months.

Bess barred her way. 'My, how swiftly things progress, little sister.'

'Not more teasing, please.'

'Come on, it is a fine morning, so let us walk in the garden.'

Soon they were treading the grass in the walled garden, beneath the apple trees which were stirring with blossom at the approach of spring. Daffodils nodded against the stone wall, although they were yet to open in the chill March air.

The sisters leaned against the parapet, where Cicely had leaned the day she overheard her mother and Thomas the Tub, and looked down into the eddying waters of the incoming Thames tide.

Their reflections swayed as Bess glanced at her sister. 'Well, I most certainly did not imagine you would so soon face the futility of suppressing an emotion as fierce as love, but you feel a great deal for your John, do you not?'

'Yes.'

Bess sighed. 'Perhaps you begin to understand why I love Richard. Everything about him strikes an answering chord in me. When he failed to come to the hall after you had gone, I could no more have stopped myself from waiting by the steps than I could have flown. I know my conduct is reprehensible, especially when Anne is so kind and friendly towards us. It is my shame to admit how much I resent her.' She looked at Cicely. 'Do you believe he lies only with her?'

'I cannot answer that! Bess, you may be in love with him, but his private life remains none of your business. Perhaps the queen is too ill to be a wife in all the senses of the word, and perhaps he is forced to seek solace elsewhere. I could not blame him if he does. He deserves to be happy. I love him too, you know.'

'And you have more of him than I,' Bess replied sadly. 'What can I do to stop this feeling? I do not care that he is so close in blood, that to lie with him would be wicked before God, because I would do so if I could.'

'Oh, Bess . . .'

'You have no notion of how fortunate you are to love John of Gloucester, because *he* is not beyond your reach. Nor would he wish to be.'

'Bess, please . . . *please* do not ever be tempted to reveal your true feelings to Richard.'

Bess gave her a rueful glance. 'Do not worry, Cissy, I will not be so foolish.'

'And can you imagine how *he* would feel?' Cicely asked softly, thinking of his kindness. 'He would not only be dismayed because you are his niece, but also because he is not a man to heap blame solely upon you. He is so tactile and warm by nature that he would wonder if he had seemed to encourage you. Richard should not be burdened like that, Bess.'

'His wife and heir are in poor health, Cicely. *I* could give him a healthy boy,' Bess replied in a detached tone.

Cicely recoiled. 'Sometimes I do not know you at all, Bess.'

'Sometimes I do not know myself.'

The quiet of the garden was interrupted by the laughter and chatter of children as their three little sisters came out of the palace with their nurses. Bess hurried to dance around with them, and did not see Margaret, Lady Stanley, emerge as well, seeming almost to float across the grass, carrying her open prayer book in her hands. Her black skirts slithered silently as she approached Cicely. Her pinched face was sour and her thin lips pursed. Maybe she could no longer *un*purse them, Cicely thought.

'Good day to you, Lady Cicely.'

'Good day, Lady Stanley.' Cicely was careful to execute a respectful curtsey, but as she did so she wondered why on earth Richard had allowed such a bloodsucker back to his court. He should keep Henry Tudor's scheming mother as far away as possible until she drew her final breath. And she would draw it very soon indeed if Cicely Plantagenet were Richard.

'Lady Cicely, it has been noted that you are becoming acquainted with the king's bastard, John of Gloucester,' Margaret observed.

'He is my cousin, my lady, why should I not become acquainted with him?'

'Do not let your hopes run too high.'

Cicely met her gaze. 'What do you mean?'

Margaret dissembled. 'Oh, simply that the course of love is always difficult. I know, for I have had four husbands.'

God help them one and all, Cicely thought.

Margaret's cold glance moved to Bess, who chased little Bridget around a nearby apple tree, making her squeal. 'How very undignified,' Henry Tudor's mother murmured, watching.

A sudden cold hand touch Cicely's heart, for she could see Margaret's hatred for the young woman who in her eyes had committed a heinous crime by making it known she did not want Henry Tudor as her husband, by showing her preference for Richard's protection. Margaret resented it greatly that her son needed Bess — or Cicely herself — if he ever overcame Richard and mounted the throne. To keep the peace, he needed to unite York and Lancaster, or constantly risk his own overthrow.

Gradually Bess became aware of her scrutiny, and came quietly to join them, her chin lifted with pride and defiance.

Margaret was all honey. 'I bid you good morning, my lady.'

Bess inclined her head. 'My lady,' she replied.

'It gladdens me to see you so happy, but no doubt you will miss the king during his absence.'

Cicely wondered if there was a double meaning in the query. Had Margaret too perceived the truth about Bess?

Bess smiled. 'Of course, my lady. How could I not? He is my dearest uncle and I love him.'

'Even though he has had you declared a bastard?'

'Yes, even though,' Bess responded immediately. 'He can do no wrong in my eyes.'

'So I am given to understand.'

Cicely was dismayed. Bess was definitely being whispered about at court.

Margaret's eyes were hooded as she acknowledged them both and then moved away over the grass like a black shadow. The sisters shivered, and then Bess pulled a face. 'Oh, Cissy, can you just *imagine* what her precious Henry must be like?'

'And can you imagine four husbands having to bed such a spiteful bag of bones? What valour and determination they must have had. I gather Lord Stanley no longer does, because she has taken a vow of celibacy, or some such thing. How thankful he must be.'

They giggled together, but meeting Margaret again had been an unpleasant reminder of the threats Richard still faced if he was to keep the throne.

As Henry Tudor's mother disappeared into the palace, a man who was just leaving had to stand aside for her. It was Francis Lovell, and he bowed to Margaret, although not with particular respect, but then he saw Richard's two eldest nieces watching, and gave them a broad grin as he strolled across to them, past the younger girls still at their play. His stocky figure was very reassuring after the spectral Margaret.

He swept them a respectful bow. 'I trust you are enjoying your freedom, my ladies?'

'Oh yes,' Cicely responded.

He gave her an arch look. 'Yes, so I have noticed, Lady Cicely.'

She flushed and lowered her eyes. It was sometimes really horrible to be young, because everyone older seemed to think it was their right to tease.

'You have not gone north as well, sir?' Bess enquired.

'Within days I will. The king gave me various tasks to complete here first.'

Cicely looked at him. 'Why has our uncle allowed Lady Stanley to return?'

He spread his hands in disbelief. 'I wish I knew. She is a rotten apple well able to spoil more in the barrel. I do not always know what is in the king's mind.'

Bess curled her lip angrily. 'After what she did, at the very least she should have been thrown into the Tower and left there to contemplate upon her actions. *I* would have had her evil head!'

'So would I,' Cicely added.

'Such savage words from such dainty lips?' Francis feigned horror, but then became serious. 'You must realize that had Richard executed or even imprisoned Lady Stanley, then the same fate would necessarily have fallen upon your lady mother, for she was every bit as guilty in that conspiracy.'

Bess stiffened. 'Sir, my mother has given her word that the king will have no cause to regret giving her his protection, and she will be true to that. There you see the difference between Dame Grey and Lady Stanley.'

He nodded. 'I sincerely hope you are right, my lady.'

'I am. My mother will *not* fail Richard, for *I* will see to it.'

Cicely could tell that he was not entirely convinced in Bess's ability to control her mother, but where Richard was concerned, Bess had no equal as defender.

CHAPTER ELEVEN

Only weeks later, the bells of London tolled sorrowfully, their solemn booms resounding across the dark April skies and finding an answering echo in the ominous rumbling of thunder. The great stone tower by the river landing of the palace vibrated with the noise of its three giant bells, and across the courtyard at Westminster Hall still another bell shuddered through the still air. The heavy clouds crowded the heavens and the breathless air lay oppressively upon the land. The river was silent, not a boatman plied his trade, and craft wallowed idly on the dark waters lapping undisturbed against the wharfs. The myriad white swans glided without a whisper on the moving waters, unconcerned that tragedy had befallen the king and queen.

Once again wearing black, Cicely stood by an open window that overlooked the courtyard, watching a slow procession approaching. It was a very different spectacle from the one that had left in March, because Richard and his queen returned to their capital in deep mourning for their ten-year-old son, Edward of Middleham. He rode alone at the head of the procession, his horse caparisoned in funereal black, his clothes of a like colour. His bowed head was bare, without hat or even circlet, and his dark chestnut hair fell forward to shadow his sorrowing face. His slight figure seemed remote, almost distant, yet he was there, bereft and grieving, not looking once at the silent crowds lining the way. The crisp clatter of the horses was overwhelmed by the resonance of the bells and growls of thunder.

Of poor Anne there was no sight, for she travelled in the litter, the curtains tightly drawn. Her anguish was so intense that Cicely was to learn she found it difficult to even walk without support. The loss of her only child was a mortal blow to this delicate, frail queen, who could not bear Richard another. He was now a king without an heir, and Anne knew there were many who would deem it her fault for being so feeble. Perhaps he did too. No one knew his thoughts.

Behind the clustering roofs and steeples of the city, a blaze of lightning illuminated the skies, glancing brightly off the river. The answering thunder broke overhead almost immediately, and the heaviness of the air seemed to press Cicely with its humid fingers. In an effort to bring some coolness to the room, she placed her hands on the embrasure and leaned out a little. A faint breath of wind arose and the first large drops of storm rain began to fall, their force whipping up the dust on the ground below.

The dust soon became mud in the ever-increasing downpour, and the bruised leaves of the herb garden filled the air with their newly released scent. Straining her eyes through the rain, she sought John among the riders behind the king, but it was Richard himself who claimed her attention as he at last looked up at the palace. He did not seem to notice the torrential rain, or indeed notice anything at all. He appeared to be looking directly at her, but she knew she was invisible to him. He was a father in the purgatory of his child's death, and the queen had retreated from him, unable to offer him any consolation at all. His expression was stern and his lips hard, and he made no attempt to cover his head as the rain soaked his hair so that it clung to his face and neck. Cicely found it harrowing to see him thus, and wanted to go down to meet him, but knew she could not.

She watched him dismount at the palace steps. The yard was filled with horses; his men in clothes as black as his, but with his white boar emblazoned on their breasts. He looked at no one as he hurried up the steps into the palace, and only one figure went after him. John, also clad in black. She stretched out a little more, to see him for longer as he followed his father. He glanced up, his taut face a measure of the sorrow he shared with Richard and Anne, but he knew Cicely was there, for he smiled briefly before disappearing into the palace.

Anne's litter moved on towards a side door, from where she could be helped out of it and carried up to the royal apartments. Her head lolled and she seemed almost grey, as if what little spark there was in her had been snuffed. She saw nothing, said nothing, and knew nothing as she was borne into the palace.

Cicely watched the rest of the procession stream into the rain-drenched yard, the horses hanging their proud heads as reluctant servants hastened out to their tasks, and then she went to find her sister.

She found Bess seated at her embroidery, her eyes bright, her lips tight. The needle flew in and out, and she did not look up as Cicely entered. They sat in silence for a long time, until at last Bess lowered the needle. 'He *will* be mine, Cissy. Only Anne stands in my way.'

Appalled, Cicely leapt to her feet again and ran out. Her sister's lust for Richard had begun to extinguish all the good that was in her. He would *loathe* her for what she felt and said.

For most of that terrible day the thunder rolled around the skies, vying with the persistent bells. In the humid palace the sounds were at war with one another and Cicely's head rang with weariness. She longed to see John, but he had not come to see her, nor even sent a message. Sitting by the open window in her rooms, breathing in the lingering scent of the herbs as it lay strong upon the air, she wished the rain would stop so she could walk in the garden. At least it fell less heavily now and in the distance there was a break in the clouds, through which beams of sun reached down to the sodden earth. Soon she would be able to go out.

At last the storm became little more than a faint drizzle and, not even taking a cloak, she hurried down through the palace and out into the afternoon, where dampness floated like cobwebs in the brightening air. The grass was soft beneath her slippers and the hem of her gown soon became wet, but she did not care. The scent of blossom was sweet, and as she inhaled she heard the guttural grumbling of the storm in the distance.

She went to the part of the wall where she had been before, and leaned over to watch the boatmen as they plied their trade after acknowledging the king's sorrow by staying ashore throughout the morning. Their voices were subdued, and when one of them laughed, the others scolded him. She noticed a large white swan bobbing on the water directly below her, and almost immediately it hissed and stretched up, wings flapping. She bent to pick up some tiny stones, and tossed them at it.

'Do not threaten me like that, sir, or I will have your feathers to stuff my mattress!'

Almost as if it understood, the swan moved away, its black legs pumping through the water. Her reflection was broken, swaying wildly on the wavelets, and as it became gentle again, she saw she was no longer alone, for John was standing beside her.

She whirled to face him, her breath catching with pleasure. 'John!'

He gazed at her. 'Cicely. . . ?'

She saw the change in him. Richard and Anne may have lost a son, but he had lost his half-brother. 'Oh, my poor John,' she whispered, stretching out her hand.

He linked his fingers with her, and then suddenly pulled her close. 'I have missed you so, Cicely,' he breathed, his lips moving in her damp hair. 'When it happened, I could hardly bear my father's misery. I have never seen him like that before, not even when your father died.'

She held him tightly, pressing her face into the rich stuff of his doublet, savouring every second of their first embrace, even though the circumstances were so sad.

He drew back to cup her cheeks in his hands. 'I feel as if we have been together all our lives. You feel the same, do you not?'

She nodded. 'Of course I do, for I missed you every moment you were away.'

He bent forward to put his lips to hers. It was a far different kiss from the one they had shared in March, for now he made no attempt to hide his love. The kiss was long, sweet, and more exhilarating than Cicely could have ever imagined. It was her first true kiss, unhurried and not restrained by watching eyes, and she wished it would never end . . . wished it could lead to so very much more. Her body was awakened by desire, and the passion that swept through her now was new and so ravishing that she felt she might almost die of it. She breathed his name as restraint began to slip away from her. If anyone looked from a palace window they would see, but she did not care. Nothing else mattered, only him.

He was no less aroused, and so held her gently away. 'Sweet God, I love and want you so much, Cicely.'

'And I you.' She could have wept for the ending of those blissful moments.

'It would be better if we talked of something else, I think.' He smiled self-consciously. 'You rule my heart, my lady.'

She took his hand and kissed it tenderly. 'I cannot believe this is happening, John.'

He closed his eyes as her lips caressed his skin, and then had to pull his hand away. 'Jesu, I feel as if I will explode.' For the first time he glanced at the palace windows, but there was no one watching. His father would put up with much from him, but not the public deflowering of a favoured niece!

Drawing a very long breath to steady himself, he looked at her again, and on impulse searched in his purse, bringing out a little golden ring set with a single sapphire. 'Will you wear this for me?' he asked, holding it out, and then smiling. 'Oh, I do not mean on your fourth finger, for we would rightly be chastised for such speed and presumption. Maybe you could wear it on a chain around your neck? Oh, I do not know, nor do I care *how* you wear it, just that you do. It was my mother's, and I want you to have it.'

'But if it was your mother's, surely you want to keep it?'

'My father gave it to her when he was almost the same age as me, and now I want to give it to you. He will understand.'

'Will he? I do not know anything about her, John, but it could be that he loved her and would not wish his ring to be on any other lady's finger but hers.'

'She was a lady in the Countess of Warwick's household. They knew each other when he was in the earl's household. Not long after I was born, she gave me to my father because she was to marry a brutal man who believed her to be a virgin. My father tried to prevent it, but she married anyway. Six months later her husband killed her; my father believes it was because he discovered she had a child. I know no more. My father saw that I was raised as his son. I have not lacked for love or luxury.'

Richard had been about John's age when he became a father, and the thought raised uncertainty in her. 'Have you . . . lain with many?' Her cheeks were hot as she asked the question.

He smiled. 'What would you have me say, Cicely? That I am as pure as you?'

'No, for that would be foolish. You are a man; it is expected that you bed as you choose.'

'Cicely, I *have* lain with others, but never with the feelings I have for you. You are so important to me that I cannot bear to think of ever losing you.'

'You will not lose me, John of Gloucester.' She slipped the ring on her little finger, which she then closed tightly to be sure it stayed there until she could put it on her favourite golden chain.

He put his arm around her shoulder, and they leaned together to look over the wall. She gave a little laugh. 'I cannot believe how much I have changed since my father died.'

'My father thinks you very wise.'

'How very dull I must be.'

He shook his head. 'No, for you to have won his favour so completely is a measure of how he respects you. You make your sister Bess seem most immature.'

'Do not say that. It is hard for her to know that she is no more than a useful bride to someone like Henry Tudor.'

'And so are you,' he pointed out. 'The Tudor must promise to marry one or other of you, because only you two are old enough to consummate such a marriage. He needs the deed done as quickly as possible.'

'He will *never* take the throne, John, *never*! And I would rather burn in Hell than lie with him! So would Bess.'

He leaned to brush her cheek with another kiss. 'How fierce you are, my lady.' Then he drew away. 'I feel so guilty for being happy when my father is so sad. Do you know how he sees this bereavement? The loss of his son is God's reprisal for taking the throne. Nothing anyone says will convince him otherwise; he can no longer seem to see that the throne is his by right of your father's bigamy. He is so burdened with conscience that I begin to fear he will break beneath the strain. There is no one more loyal to him than me, and yet even I am concerned about his ability to rule now — as unsure as I think he himself is. He governs with his heart and not his head, and in these dangerous times that is a crime!'

'But it is a fine heart, is it not?'

'Aye, sweetheart, it is a fine heart, but will one day lead him into a folly from which no one and nothing will be able to rescue him. The queen looks nigh unto death and he sees her drifting away from him. Jesu, the night the news of Edward's death arrived at Nottingham, he was so stricken, so overcome with grief, that when someone was heard to suggest he should put the queen aside and marry a healthy bride, Jesu, I thought he would kill the fellow with his bare hands. No, he will never put Anne aside, and so he will have to name an heir, probably his sister's eldest son, the Earl of Lincoln, who, incidentally, is expected here imminently. He has been in the north in connection with my father's affairs there. I will like to see him again. I like Jack of Lincoln.'

Cicely thought of her dashing twenty-two-year-old first cousin, whom she had always liked very much. She also coveted the amethyst ring he always wore. It was *such* an amethyst. 'Jack will be a worthy heir, but it seems so wrong that Richard has you, so strong and healthy a son, yet cannot name you to succeed him.'

'Ah, such is the fate of royal bastards.' He smiled. 'I speak as one to another, of course.'

'Of course.'

His humour was brief. 'Sadly, I think Anne herself will solve the problem. She thought herself unnoticed but one day just before news arrived at Nottingham of the prince's death, I saw her cough into her handkerchief and it was specked with blood.'

Consumption! Cicely crossed herself. 'Oh no. Is that not how her sister Isabel, Duchess of Clarence, died?'

John straightened suddenly. 'Listen! Is someone calling you?'

They looked towards the palace, and there came the sound of a woman's voice. 'It is my mother! Whatever possesses her to call for me herself? I had best present myself immediately.'

Seizing his hand, she hurried towards the palace, where they encountered Dame Grey just inside the doorway, still with her walking stick, although her knee had mostly recovered.

Elizabeth's eyes moved over her daughter, whose fluster was plain to see. Her glance flickered to John, who met it squarely. Her arched eyebrow was raised, but she turned to Cicely. 'The queen wishes to speak with you, madam. Urgently it seems. I despatched a page but he could not find you! God's blood, girl, you look like some serving wench, more at home in a tavern than a palace. You shall not present yourself thus but will change at once. Come!' Without a further glance at John, she seized her daughter's elbow, but Cicely stood firm, refusing to allow her arrogant mother to so slight him.

'Mother, I will present to you John of Gloucester.'

Elizabeth looked sourly at her daughter but was forced to acknowledge the son of Richard Plantagenet by coldly inclining her head. He was partly in shadow, and his resemblance to his father was once more apparent in the faint smile upon his lips as he bowed over her hand.

Minutes later, in the rooms Cicely shared with Bess, Elizabeth studied her second daughter closely as she presented herself for approval.

'I am ready now. Do I look well enough?' Cicely asked.

'As much as you ever do in black,' was the discouraging reply. Then the hawk-eyed Elizabeth noticed the chain that was newly around her neck. It was long, and disappeared between her breasts. 'It is some time since I have seen that. Why do you suddenly wear it again?'

'Impulse.'

Elizabeth gazed at her. 'What do you wear upon it?'

Cicely drew away. 'Nothing, Mother, it is just a chain.'

Elizabeth stood suddenly and caught the chain, pulling it into view before Cicely could prevent her. Seeing the ring, Elizabeth exhaled. 'So . . . you have a love token. John of Gloucester, one imagines.'

'Yes.' Cicely took the chain from her mother and dropped the ring between her breasts again. 'Is my appearance now suitable for me to present myself before the queen?'

'Well, it is a vast improvement on previously, when you looked like a common whore after rolling in the grass with Richard Plantagenet's by-blow.'

'I had merely been out walking, Mother, not anything else. Why must you always be so unpleasant? I marvel Father ever desired you to the extent he clearly did.'

'Be unattainable, my dear, and you will achieve anything you want from men. They are ruled by their lusts. Believe me, this is good advice.' Elizabeth gave a very small smile. 'I had thought better of you than to pant after a king's bastard!'

'Why so, Mother? Like clings to like, after all a bastard is what you and my father have made of me.' With a stony face, Cicely curtseyed and swept from the room.

Richard's queen lay upon the huge royal bed, supported by many rich cushions; her face was ghastly, her huge eyes silhouetted by dark, bruised shadows, and her hair hung limply against her breast. She held out her hand to her husband's niece, and dismissed her ladies. When they were alone she leaned wearily back against the cushions and closed her eyes.

'Cicely, I wish to have you near me. In my inner household, where only those I truly depend upon can come. You are only young, I know, but I also know, by the respect the king has for you, that I will be able to place my faith in you. Forgive me for wanting to lean on you so much, but I need someone to talk with, to share my sorrows with, and my ladies, even those most close until now, simply will not do. There has to be one special person to whom I can turn for everything of an intimate nature. There is no one else here with whom I feel so completely at ease. I can no longer be truly myself even with my dearest lord, with whom I once shared everything, because I need to hide so much from him.'

Cicely's heart was filled with compassion, but part of it rejoiced to hear Anne call Richard her dearest lord, because it meant she *did* love him truly after all.

Anne paused as a fit of coughing overtook her, and when she took her handkerchief away from her mouth, Cicely saw the spots of blood that John had mentioned. The queen nodded. 'Yes, the mark of death is truly upon me. Richard does not know, nor must he. To let him see daily proof of how much my health now fails would be to weigh him even more than he already is. I try to shield him from it. I have not been at his side as much as I wished, since—' Renewed tears welled from her eyes. 'Since we lost our dearest son,' she whispered.

Cicely took her hand and held it gently. 'I am so very sorry, Your Grace. And of *course* I will help you however I can, but surely the king *has* to be told?' She found herself taking the soiled handkerchief and searching for another.

The queen pointed towards a cabinet. 'They are in there. Cicely, he does not have to be told until it is unavoidable.' She took a deep, shuddering breath, both to drive away the new tears and to regain the strength to continue speaking. 'I should not confide this to anyone, but I have kept him from my bed by saying I am too frail. I will not even let him sleep at my side because I am so afraid that I will be the cause of his death too. I know he needs me, just to hold me and share everything as we used to, and I *do* want him to be with me, so very much. There is no man more sensitive and understanding, more precious to me, but I could give this vile curse to him as well. Do you understand?'

Cicely's eyes also filled with tears. 'Oh, my poor aunt . . .'

Anne smiled a little. 'I am ashamed to share the secrets of my marriage bed with you, a maiden, but if you are to help me, and understand me, you need to know how I truly feel. It is so comforting to be able to speak to you. Maybe it is the honesty in your eyes, and the staunchness of your spirit. I know Richard feels it, and even though I hardly know you, I feel it too.'

The queen tried to sit up a little, but found it too weakening, even with Cicely's help. She paused to regain her breath and smiled as Cicely managed to put some more cushions where they would help the most. 'It is because of the telltale blood that I wish to speak with you, for I *must* conceal my condition from Richard for as long as possible, and to do so I will need a helper, someone to take away my handkerchiefs and replace them with fresh ones without drawing attention. Someone to make me comfortable when I need it, without my having to instruct it. You have helped me twice since coming here now, and on neither occasion did I have to ask you. So my heart tells me to turn to you, even though you are of such tender years.'

'I will do all I can,' Cicely promised, reaching out to put her strong young fingers around Anne's skeletal ones. 'When do you wish me to join your inner household?'

'Immediately. Richard will soon return to Nottingham, from where he can easily march to any part of England Tudor may choose to invade. I will wait here until I have regained a little strength, and then I will go to join him. That means the entire court will accompany me.'

'Should you not stay here? Travelling is so very arduous, especially in a litter.'

'I will not leave him alone, Cicely. He needs me to be near. I may no longer be the wife he once had, but I still love him.'

'And he loves you, Your Grace.'

Anne managed a smile. 'Just think, Cicely, being so close to me will mean seeing more of John of Gloucester, which I am sure will please you.' She closed her eyes. 'If only he were legitimate, for it would resolve so very much.'

CHAPTER TWELVE

Bess was not at all pleased to hear of her sister's new position so near the queen. Cicely had not said anything of what Anne had told her. As far as Bess was concerned, Cicely had simply been summoned to a place that ought to have been granted to Richard's eldest niece.

'By right it should be me,' she declared.

Cicely looked at her. '*You?* Bess, you can barely bring yourself to be civil to the poor queen, so why on earth would she wish to have you at her side?'

Bess tossed her head, but said no more on the matter.

It was then that Cicely received another royal summons, this time from Richard himself. As she prepared to go to his apartments, she saw the stricken look in Bess's eyes, the unshed tears and deep hurt. 'He never thinks of me, Cissy, it is always you. What do *you* have that I do not?'

'I do not know.' But Cicely wondered if Richard sensed something in Bess that made him feel uneasy. She took her sister's hand for a moment and squeezed it reassuringly, but it was not easy to offer comfort when she so disapproved of Bess's behaviour.

She hastened to Richard's apartments, wondering why he wished to see her . . . and wondering too how he would be. He had not been seen since his return. A page admitted her, and she was conducted to one of the private chambers overlooking the river. Richard was not there; no one was there. She glanced around. It was clearly one of her uncle's personal rooms, for there was evidence of him all around, from his books to his circlet, lying on a table where someone had put it, for he had not worn it on his return. One of his rings was there too, the one with the huge ruby.

She drew the chain from her bodice, and looked at the ring John had given her. It was warm from her body, and because it was John's, she raised it to her lips.

'A tender moment, Cicely?'

Richard's voice startled her, and she turned swiftly to see him in the doorway. He had changed his clothes, no longer black, but grey, simple and unadorned, and his doublet was only partially fastened. It was not like him to be so remiss, and yet it went with his ruffled hair and his hollow eyes. It was as if something crucial had been driven from him. The shadow of grief was there to such a degree that he almost seemed like his own ghost.

He came towards her, looking at the ring she still held. 'John wastes little time, it seems,' he murmured, not with anger or disapproval.

'Do you mind very much, Uncle?'

He met her eyes. 'No, for it is his to give as he wishes.' He glanced at her black gown. 'No mourning, Cicely. I intend to let it be known. I do not want to be reminded of my child's death, rather of his life. Do you disapprove?'

'No.'

The faintest of smiles crossed his lips. 'I knew you would understand.'

'Uncle . . . ?' She longed to embrace him, to hold him close and somehow alleviate his sorrow.

'Please do not say anything,' he said quickly, raising a hand that was clearly defensive.

'But I must, Uncle, for I love you dearly and it breaks my heart to see you in such agony. I did not know the little boy you have lost, even though he was my cousin, but I do know you, and the poor, dear queen. I comfort her, but need to comfort you as well. Do you not see that?'

'Please, Cicely . . .' He turned away, his voice tight as he struggled with his emotions.

But she would not let him spurn her help. 'It is *I* who must say please to you. *Please*, let me show I care.'

'I already know you care, Cicely.'

'Do you?'

He met her eyes again and smiled a little. 'Oh yes.'

His sadness wrung her heart. She felt so many things towards him, but to see him tortured with despair was almost too poignant. His pain was hers too. 'Please let me be closer to you, or I will die of your grief,' she whispered.

'If I let you hold me, for that is what you will do, the little composure I still have will be forfeit. I do not think either of us wishes that.' He turned away. 'It was not to leech upon your strength and kindness that I have sent for you.'

'Leech? I give both gladly.'

The hint of a smile played around his mouth again. 'I stand corrected.'

She put out a hand to touch him, but he moved away. 'I believe you are to enter the queen's inner household?'

'Yes, with your permission.' Please do not let him ask her why.

'My permission? Yes, yes, you have it. If it pleases the queen to keep you close to her, then it pleases me.' He paused. 'Cicely . . . take care of her for me.'

'I will do all in my power, Uncle.'

He nodded. 'I know, but I needed to say it.'

She gazed at his face, so very handsome, so enticing. He was affecting in every way, and no one could ever be indifferent to him. Bess's description returned. Yes, he was beautiful, and more physically and mentally magnetic than he seemed to know. He would always move and inspire others, and make them his eager servants forever. And yet he behaved as if unaware of this inherent power. There was nothing vain about him, or any arrogance in his character. And there was nothing she, Cicely, would not have done for him. Just as she was about to break the silence, he spoke of Bess.

'I have the feeling that your sister may not have been so eager to come to my court as I first thought. Does she regret Henry Tudor's failure to depose me?'

Cicely stared at him. 'Regret? Oh, *no*! Why do you think such a thing?'

'Because she makes little effort to hide her dislike of the queen. Perhaps Bess feels that she herself should be wearing the crown as Tudor's wife? It both angers and hurts me.'

Somehow Cicely managed to meet his steady gaze. 'Bess loves you, Uncle.' Oh, how true. 'And she loves the queen. You mistake her manner.'

He twisted his lips. 'Really? I need more persuasion, I fear. You forget that I understand you as much as you understand me. You are not being entirely forthcoming about your sister.'

Cicely lowered her eyes guiltily. 'But you *are* wrong to think she wants Henry Tudor to take your throne. Nothing could be further from the truth.'

He did not respond, and as the seconds passed she felt she had to say something. 'Uncle, forget Bess, for it is not important now. Is there anything *I* can do to help you with . . .' She did not finish, for what words could she use to describe the awful vacuum that was now at the centre of his soul?

'Help me?'

'Do anything to make a little difference?'

He smiled. 'You help me by being close to my queen.' He went to the table and picked up the circlet. 'Well, I must play the king again, eh?'

Something broke inside her and she ran to him, flinging her arms around him and holding him so tightly she feared she would stop his breath. She knew he did not want it, but he was in her embrace now, and she willed all her strength to transfer to him. 'You do not *play* the king, Uncle, you *are* the king! A very good king. England is your realm, and you rule and defend it as truly and dedicatedly as could be wished. Do not doubt yourself or feel less of a ruler because you are afflicted by such cruel grief. We look to you for your strong and unswerving leadership. My father loved and admired you, and would have been lost without you. I will not let you sink beneath this, I will *not*!'

'Cicely, you disobey my wish and take advantage of my patience.' He tried to pull away, but it was half-hearted.

She tightened her hold. 'I do? Then, king or not, I am *glad* to defy you! *Someone* must be here for you. The poor queen is ill, she no longer has strength, but *I* do, and I will be here. For her. But mostly for you! You enslaved me that night at the abbey. You took my breath and my heart away with your kindness, humour and forbearance. When you smile, I am made so happy, and I would fight Satan to help you.' Tears brimmed in her eyes. 'I cannot do much, but if I can help you to smile again, I will. And if that is defiance, then so be it.'

He struggled against his emotions, and her embrace did not waver. Instead she held him more, and at last his arms moved gently around her, and she felt his lips upon her forehead. 'Jesu, Cicely, you will make me the most conceited monarch on earth.'

She heard the faint echo of his former self, a trace of the humour that so bound her to him. 'Perhaps I am the most conceited niece, believing I can help to heal you all by myself.'

'I do not deserve you, my sweet Cicely.' He caught her wrists and unlinked her arms, drawing first one hand to his lips, and then the other. His eyes were very dark and unhappy, but somehow he managed the smile she sought. 'John is very fortunate.'

'I am fortunate that he likes me.'

He touched the ring on the chain. 'If he gave you this, he more than just *likes* you, Cicely. I am glad, for I could wish for nothing better.'

She searched his eyes, for there was a note in his words that made her think his thoughts had returned to Anne. 'I *will* look after the queen, Uncle.'

He nodded again. 'For however long it takes, mm?'

She gazed at him. 'Please, Uncle . . .'

'Do not look so anxious, for I am not about to inveigle you into betraying her confidence. The moment she told me she had requested your close presence, I knew why. You are everyone's confessor, are you not? Tell me, Cicely, who is *yours*?'

'From now on it will be your son, Uncle.'

He smiled. 'Well, know that I am also at your disposal.'

'Confess my innermost thoughts to the King of England?'

He put his hand briefly to her cheek. 'No, to your fond uncle.' He smiled. 'You may go now, Cicely, for if I am indeed to be the king you say I am, there are duties to which I must attend.'

She dropped a deep curtsey, from which he was swift to raise her. 'No, not this time. Your love and good sense have helped me more than I could have imagined. I thank you with all my heart.'

Her tears had their way as she left him, and her steps took her straight to Bess, whom she confronted in a way she had never thought herself capable. 'Listen to me, you miserable, self-centred bitch! Do you know what Richard thinks of you? He believes you regret Henry Tudor's failure to invade and claim you. He thinks you hoped to be a Tudor queen instead of just a Yorkist princess.'

'Yorkist bastard,' Bess corrected, gazing up at her in astonishment. 'Please do not be so reticent, Cissy; say what you really think.'

Cicely did not care about the sarcasm. 'You have hurt him, Bess, you have hurt the man you adore to the exclusion of prudence. Is that what you want? He has noticed how you are towards the queen, and if *he* has, then you may count upon it that everyone else has too. There are whispers and sniggers about you, or had you not realized? I am ashamed of you, ashamed that you are my sister. You do not deserve his kindness and consideration, and so help me, if you continue to hurt him, I will scratch your evil eyes from their sockets!'

Bess stared at her. 'Cissy?'

'I have made myself clear, I fancy.'

'I . . . I have hurt him?' Bess seemed dazed.

'Yes. And angered him,' Cicely added for good measure. This was long overdue, and she only wished she had been driven to it sooner.

Bess's lips trembled. 'He said so?'

'Yes. He loves Anne, Bess, and nothing you do will ever change that, but you have changed what he thinks of you. Face up to the truth, about him and about yourself. Be our father's daughter from now on. Can you imagine what *he* would think to know all this of you? You were his favourite, his beautiful Bess, but he would never forgive you for what you do now.'

Tears shimmered in Bess's lovely eyes. 'I have hurt Richard?' she whispered, so stricken that it was all she could manage.

'Confront the demon that has possessed you, Bess. Drive it out and seek forgiveness. Seek an audience with Richard, reassure him of your loyalty to his queen and his cause, for as God is my witness, he deserves far better than you have seen fit to offer. But *I* will accompany you,' Cicely warned, 'and if I see *anything* perverse in your conduct, I will drag you from the room. Do what is right for *him,* Bess, not for yourself.'

Bess sat like a crushed mouse. 'He will not see me,' she said in a small voice.

'He will if I request it.'

'Ah, yes, for you have him around your little finger.' Bess was expressing a fact.

'Because my love for him is what it should be,' was Cicely's short reply.

It was soon done, and Richard had been reconciled by Bess's abject apologies and distress, but there was still a reserve in him that Cicely knew would be a long time mending. If it ever would.

Anne changed her mind about staying on in London for a while, having decided to accompany Richard to his chosen headquarters in the centre of his kingdom. The journey would take them away from the heat and smell of summertime London, and out into the wider countryside and the beauties of Sherwood Forest. And so Richard's entire court moved north as well.

Nottingham, the Castle of Care, where Richard had heard of the death of his son, had very sad, very raw memories, but it was the best situated fortress for Richard's purpose. There he waited, like a patient spider for a cautious fly. The whole realm waited for the uprising and invasion, but the months drew on and it did not come.

Cicely was kept very close to Anne, and occasionally heard comments — private asides among the other ladies — that it was surprising the late king's *second* daughter had such a place of honour, not the first. Bess conducted herself with restraint, trying hard not to do anything that would cause unwelcome comment, but Cicely knew how very difficult it was for her sister. Bess's love for Richard Plantagenet only increased. Sometimes he stopped to speak to her, but he was not at ease with her as he always was with Cicely.

John was at Nottingham as well, of course, and he and Cicely spent every moment they could together. Their love grew, as did their passion, but they did not consummate it, for that could have embarrassing consequences, both for themselves and for the king. Everyone knew of their love, including Ralph Scrope, whose gloomy presence was the only shadow over their happiness. He took to watching them whenever possible, and was like a footpad creeping behind them. John and he were no longer friendly, and there had been a scuffle that ended when John shoved Ralph's head into a pile of horse dung. It did not deter Ralph for long, for he soon began following them again.

Cicely went discreetly about her duty to the queen. She could not be with Anne every moment of every day, but she was there as much as possible, always being to hand to change the telltale handkerchiefs, always aware that Richard knew about it anyway. Anne grew daily more weak, pale and ailing, and finally the day came when he could no longer pretend he did not know how desperately ill she was.

That particular day had dawned bright and fine, and Anne had been feeling unusually well. Richard was not occupied with matters of state, and when Anne expressed a wish to go riding in the forest, he elected to accompany her. Out into the warm sun rode a colourful cavalcade, down from the great rock upon which the castle perched, and north from the town into the cool glades of Sherwood Forest, towards the hill upon which Richard's favourite hunting lodge stood. But they did not go to Bestwood Lodge today, for they wished to stay out in the open air.

The sun dappled the earth, filtering through the bright leaves of the oak trees and playing on the thick bracken. Cicely rode with John, her heart singing and her eyes shining, for never had she known such happiness as on that hot summer's day. The horses' hooves thudded dully on the rich cushion of green, and all thoughts of invasion and danger were easily forgotten.

Deep among the trees, the royal party paused for a while by the cool shaded waters of a small brook that trickled among ferns and moss. They sat on the grass, talking and laughing as servants set out a virtual feast of food and drink. Anne chose to sit beneath the heavy spreading branches of an ancient oak tree, and Cicely sat with her. The queen's eyes were unusually bright and her cheeks flushed with colour — her former loveliness apparent once more, but unnaturally so. Cicely was anxious, and wished to remain close, but when Richard and his two old friends from the north came to join them, Anne kindly dismissed her to spend a little time with John.

Bess was with a group of ladies, and to Cicely's chagrin her eyes once again devoured Richard. Bess's determination to conduct herself properly was already on the wane, and no one present misinterpreted it. Except Richard, across whose mind such a thing still did not pass. There were other whispers now as well, and many a wondering eye glanced at him, curious and inquisitive. How could he possibly remain unaware of his lovely niece's adoration? Perhaps he returned her incestuous desire, but was better able to hide it?

Cicely left John, went to her and leaned down. 'Be *honourable,* Bess!' she hissed warningly, and then returned to John. Bess kept her eyes lowered, but by the set of her mouth it was plain she resented Cicely's renewed interference.

CHAPTER THIRTEEN

NOT LONG AFTERWARDS, Cicely and John were able to slip away together. As the sounds of laughter and talk died away, they put an arm around each other's waist and strolled, close and intimate. The brook chattered softly beside them, unseeing and indifferent, intent only upon its busy journey, and the cool waters looked inviting to Cicely, who was warm in her stuffy, formal gown.

She stopped, looking back through the trees, but they were completely alone now. Pulling off her slippers, she hitched her rose-coloured skirts up and tied them, then stepped into the brook's narrow channel. John laughed aloud as she shivered at the iciness of the flowing water. 'This is no way for a king's daughter to behave. You are shameless!' he said, lying on the grassy bank and putting his hands behind his head to watch her.

'Fie on you, sir! It is no way for a king's son to behave, ogling shameless women in the heart of Sherwood.'

His eyes moved lazily over her, openly inviting. 'If you will step this way, my lady, I will do more than merely ogle.'

'And will you not come to me to prove your point?'

'Ah, no, sweet lady, I think a king's son outranks a king's daughter. *You* shall come to me!'

Her eyes became more serious, and after a moment's hesitation she stepped out of the water and went to look down at him. 'You seek to tempt me, sir?'

'I do hope so.'

She knelt beside him. 'What will be my reward?'

'I offer a kiss.'

'Only one?'

'Well, if you are sufficiently tempting, you may have two.'

She bent down to put her lips lovingly to his, and then drew back. 'That is one, sir.'

'I need another, to help me decide,' he breathed.

She lay down to kiss him again, more yearningly this time, for it was so very good to be intimate with him like this. They did not often have the chance to be really alone, and she wanted to go as far as they dared. She wanted to sample the pleasures of physical desire, because she had now learned how very much she liked such things.

Lovemaking enticed her, John enticed her, and she so wanted to know what it would be like to have him inside her. The muscles in the apex of her legs undulated at the mere thought of it. She was a virgin, but her thoughts were not pure, and she knew that she would always love to make love. It was what she was made for, and self-knowledge told her she would never cease to feel this way. She slid her arms around him and pressed closer, her breasts crushed within her bodice.

He pushed her gently on to her back and leaned over her. 'Are you tempted now, Cicely?' he whispered, smiling down into her eyes. His silvery hair brushed her face, and she could feel his breath. There was no mint, just his sweet breath.

'I am,' she admitted, for her body was fiery with need. She wanted to give herself and receive him in return. The temptation was ravishing, and her willpower so very frail.

Her skirts were still hauled up and tied from those moments in the brook, and he was easily able to put his hand on her thigh. 'Do you wish me to tempt you even more?'

She gazed up at him. 'I . . . I want everything, John.'

He caressed her skin, his fingers moving further up between her legs, and she made no move to stop him. The feelings that ran riot through her now were well nigh unstoppable, nor did she wish to struggle against them. She was excited as never before, and when his hand moved gently where she had never been touched before, she could have wept for the pleasure of it.

He leaned further over her, and pulled her hand to his loins, where he was now fully aroused and ready to make love. She closed her eyes as she touched him, for it made her feel so close to him in more than just the physical way. And her excitement intensified. New sensations quivered between her legs as his knowing fingers pushed and stroked. He had made love to others, she already knew that, but now his experience was revealed. Yet, with her, he was tentative, unsure . . . His hesitancy endeared him still more, and bound her to him.

Bound. The word checked her passion, for it made her think of . . . She did not know what it made her think of, just that suddenly the spell was broken.

He felt the change in her. 'Cicely? What is it?'

'I . . . do not know.'

He rolled aside and sat up. 'If I have been too forward, too—'

'No. No, for I invited it. Forgive me, John, I really do not understand myself. I really do want you to make love to me.'

He smiled, and put his arm around her. 'Sweetheart, it is probably as well that we stopped. It really would not do for the king's son to get the king's favourite niece with child.'

She smiled bravely, for in truth she was close to tears. 'I do love you, John of Gloucester.'

Sounds carried on the light breeze, and he glanced towards them. 'I think they are about to leave. Come, we must rejoin them.' He scrambled to his feet and held his hand out again.

She accepted, and when she was standing, she untied her skirts quickly and allowed them to fall. They were crumpled now, but there was nothing she could do about that.

A stealthy rustle among the bushes made them both turn. Someone was there! Cicely's heart stopped, but then John caught a glimpse of Ralph Scrope slipping away.

'Scrope!' he breathed. 'I vow I will impale him on a pike!'

'Oh, he must have seen everything.'

'Then he will have to do what's necessary to relieve himself,' John snapped.

She flushed, recalling her exposed legs. 'I do not care what he has to do, John, I am more concerned that he has seen far more of me than he should.'

John caught her close. 'No, he cannot have seen much. I was between him and you.' He smiled. 'He will not dare to say anything, for I will go after him if he does, and he knows it. He is not a brave fellow, Cicely. Strutting, yes, but brave, no.' He hesitated. 'But there is something about him I really do not trust.'

She recalled being told by Bess what their mother had said of Ralph. 'Mother suspects him of being a spy.'

'Really?' John's eyes moved swiftly to hers. 'It was said in seriousness?'

'I believe so. She thought he was your father's spy, but he could be anyone's.'

'I think I should speak to my father about him. He should be told everything, no matter how seemingly trivial. Come, we will have to run.' John took her hand, and they hurried back through the trees.

As they came to the clearing, where the servants were preparing to pack everything away and the horses were being made ready again, Cicely saw Anne rise. Her handkerchief fell. John's hand tightened, informing Cicely that he had also seen. And then Anne herself realized, but she was already walking away with her ladies. She glanced anxiously back at Cicely.

Richard was leaning easily against the tree beneath which they been seated. He was alone and relaxed — perhaps because Anne seemed better — and he did not at first notice as his niece endeavoured to secretly gather the blood-spotted square. But then he saw her from the corner of his eye and straightened. 'Cicely?'

She concealed the handkerchief and said nothing.

He held out his hand, and reluctantly she surrendered the evidence. There was much blood, too much for him to pretend Anne was getting better. The precious rings on his slim fingers gleamed in the afternoon sunshine as he crushed the handkerchief and pushed it into the purse at his waist. He met his niece's anxious gaze. His sad smile was so faint it might almost have not been glimpsed at all, and then he walked lightly away towards the horse, trying to appear unconcerned to the rest of the party.

During the long ride back to Nottingham Castle he gave no hint of his discovery as he laughed and smiled with Anne. He turned only once to glance at Cicely, who felt she had failed the queen. John leaned across to put his hand on hers. He knew how she felt.

Later that day Cicely made her way alone to the top of one of the towers, where Richard's lookouts drew discreetly aside to let her be as private as possible. The light was fading but the setting sun still slanted dazzlingly in the west. She was able to see for many miles, over the town of Nottingham to the forest beyond, and away to the misty purple of the horizon. She had been unable to bring herself to tell Anne of the afternoon's happening. If Richard said nothing, how could she? She picked unhappily at the old stonework of the battlements, crumbling small flakes away and flicking them over to fall into the courtyard below.

She turned as she heard someone coming up the steep steps of the tower, and to her dismay Richard appeared in the narrow doorway. He dismissed the lookouts and as he approached, she knew he had followed her.

Should she curtsey? The moment seemed to call for it, but he prevented her. 'I have no time for ceremony, least of all from you.' The breeze played with his hair, and he stood beside her, twisting the ruby ring as he too looked into the distance. 'Cicely, I cannot pretend to her any more. She is closer to death than I had prayed, and she needs me.'

'And England needs you as well,' she found herself saying, even though she had not realized the words were on her lips.

'You think I do not know that?'

'If you should become ill . . .'

'I have not yet, so do not imagine I will at this late date.' The words were dryly uttered.

'But if you do?' she persisted.

'I want to fly in the face of reason, Cicely, and here you are, the very personification of reason.'

'Not reason. I know what *she* wants.'

'She has said it to you?'

'That she fears giving you the contagion? Yes. It worries her greatly. She loves you and wants to protect you.'

'I am not a babe in need of such protection!'

'No, you are the king.'

He looked at her. 'Ah, you lead me full circle, and by the nose at that.'

'Full circle, yes. By the nose? I think not.'

'Be damned, madam,' he murmured.

'Better me than you.'

He smiled. 'Be damned again.'

'I will be if anything should happen to you because *I* was not vehement enough now.'

'The Almighty excelled Himself when he produced you, I think.'

She smiled. 'He excelled Himself more with you. Uncle, you know how I prize you, so if you imagine I will just stand by and let you always do as you wish, you are very wrong.'

'Just who is the king here?' he enquired lightly.

'Why, you, of course.'

'Yet *you* decide what I can or cannot do?'

'No, I can only tell you what I think. Is that not what you wish of me?'

He gazed at her. 'Sweet Cicely, I no longer know *what* I wish of you. Suffice it that I do not think I can do *without* you. You are my conscience. I receive more common sense from you than from the entire Council.'

'Then know that I am right about the queen. If nothing else, please observe her wish in this. For it *is* her wish, even though it breaks her heart.'

'She follows her sister Isabel, and there is nothing I can do to prevent it. I am the king, but am helpless to keep my wife in this world. How could the virtually unstoppable Earl of Warwick have produced two such beautiful but delicate daughters? My love for Anne is no longer one of passion and fire, such as you and John now share, but has become steady and enduring.' He paused. 'It cannot be anything else.'

She felt there was some double meaning to those last words. But what? The sun had all but slipped behind the horizon and she shivered as the chill crept into the darkening night, but he seemed not to notice and was deep in his thoughts and memories. When he spoke again his voice was quiet, the breeze almost stealing the sound from his lips before she could hear. 'They all leave me — my brothers, my son and now my wife.' He looked at her, the sunset alight in his eyes. 'What shall I do, Cicely?'

His guard was down and his isolation exposed to her, and she was so moved that for a moment she could not say anything. Or do anything. Then she could only whisper, 'Do? You have to be king. There is nothing else.'

'And when everything I touch turns to dust?'

She went to him then, not hesitating to hold him close and put her cheek to his. 'You touch *me,* but I have not turned to dust.'

He returned the embrace, but only briefly. 'I should not have weakened enough to say what I just did. It was hardly a display of strength and leadership.'

'Even a king needs someone to speak to as himself and not his high office. You know that, and so do I. That is why I will always come to you if you require me.'

He drew back to look at her. 'You never fail me, Cicely. I do not speak like this with anyone else.'

'Whatever you say to me will never go further.'

'I know. I trust you, Cicely.'

'It is trust well placed. I became your eager servant that night at the abbey, and nothing I have seen of you since then has changed my mind.'

'Perhaps if you could see into *my* mind, you would not think the same.'

She was puzzled. 'What do you mean?'

He moved away. 'Nothing that I intend to confess. Yes, I have to be king, but what sort of king am I? It is being said that I usurped my nephew's crown for my own advancement and glory. There is no suggestion that I had no choice but to accept the throne. I *am* the legitimate king, and England needs a man, not a child. But now all those close to me are being taken away. Is that my punishment?'

'No! Please do not say that, do not even think it!' She went to take his face in her hands. 'You are going to be a great king, a truly great one. If everything seems to be slipping from you now, there will come a time when all is well again. You are the only man to rule England. There is no one who can come even close to you, in blood or ability. You are incomparable. What more can I say to you? How can I help you? Please tell me, for it matters more to me than you can know.'

She almost kissed him. On the lips. All over his face. It was *such* a moment for her, such an essential moment that she could not help the way she felt. He always affected her. There was something about him that grazed her very soul — perhaps it was *everything* about him — and she could not bear to see him brought as low again as he had been immediately after the death of his son. It distressed her so much she was shocked by the violence of her reaction. 'Please,' she whispered. '*Please* do not despair.'

He put his hands over hers. 'Oh, Cicely . . .' he said softly, and released himself from the contact.

'You mean so much to me. I have never felt as I do about you. Not even my father.'

He smiled at that. 'Indeed. Well, I am sure you feel much more towards my son.'

She paused. 'John? But that is different.' Was it not? In truth she did not know how she felt right now, because it was Richard who engrossed her.

'It is rather to be *hoped* your feelings for John are different.'

'Different, yes, but not less.'

'Oh, Cicely, you will run rings around him. As you do around me.'

'I do not run rings around you,' she answered. 'You just allow me to do it, which is rather different.'

His glance swept over her. 'Little escapes you.'

'Because we are alike.'

'Yes.' He met her eyes.

'You do know that I love you?'

'Yes, Cicely.' Then he added, 'As I love you.'

She embraced him again, her cheek once more pressed to his. 'Do not give up, for I will *never* forgive you if you do.'

'Oh, a fate to be avoided at all costs.'

'Indeed so.'

'Then I will not give up.'

She looked into his eyes again. 'Promise me.'

'I promise.'

'If *ever* you need me . . .'

He smiled. 'I might rather dominate your company, and I do not think John would appreciate that.' The sunset shone in his eyes again, and upon his hair, finding its dark copper glints. Then he glanced towards the fading sun as if noticing it for the first time. 'Come, it grows cold up here.'

She took the hand he extended, but did not immediately move. He turned to look quizzically at her.

'Never be sad on your own again,' she said. 'Always send for me. While I live I will *never* let you down.'

'Perhaps that is one reason I followed you up here, or had you not thought of that?'

She gazed at him. 'I am honoured.'

'I am not a paragon, Cicely.'

'Yes, you are.'

He pulled her hand. 'Come.'

CHAPTER FOURTEEN

WITH THE PASSING of the long summer it became apparent that Henry Tudor would make no attempt to invade that year, and there came the prospect of trouble-free winter months ahead. Richard's tension lessened, for he knew that his realm was safe for the time being from the awful bloodshed that must follow any determined invasion.

But nothing could hold back the relentless progress of his queen's illness. Anne's brief rally was over and once again she began to sink. Her dry, feeble cough was often heard in the Castle of Care, but at least she now knew that Richard was fully aware of what was happening to her. Cicely's advice to him had now been bolstered by his advisers, who strongly urged him not to go to his wife. He could not bring himself to obey completely, and still went to see Anne every day, but he was never alone with her and certainly no longer shared her bed.

One good thing for Cicely was that Ralph Scrope had been sent away to Yorkshire, for which she was entirely thankful. He had been a spectre at a feast, and his constant stealthy stalking had begun to frighten her. How had she ever looked upon him with favour? On learning of it all from John, including that there were suspicions about Ralph's loyalty, Richard decided it would be a wise precaution to send him away from all chance of discovering anything that might be considered helpful to Henry Tudor. Richard had been loath to do it, because of Ralph's father, but it had become ever harder to know who supported the crown and who did not.

Cicely had not escaped a rebuke from Richard, who thought she should have gone to him immediately, not only about her mother's passing suspicion regarding Ralph, but because Cicely herself might have been in danger. 'I could have helped you in this long since, had you but trusted me enough to confide what was going on.'

'It was not that I did not trust you, Uncle. Please do not think such a thing. I simply did not think.'

He raised an eyebrow. '*You?* Not think? Well, I suppose there has to be a first time for everything.'

She met his gaze and then looked away again.

'Cicely, you are not to let anything like this happen again. Is that clear? I will not tolerate your being intimidated in any way while at my court. Or anywhere else, for that matter. Do I have your word?'

'Yes, Uncle.'

'Sweet Cicely, your wellbeing is of the utmost importance to me. Always remember that.' He smiled. 'I know you can read me like a book, which is not a comfortable feeling, believe me, although I do manage to keep some important pages to myself, as no doubt you do from me. But between us there must always be trust, complete and inviolate. I cannot settle for anything less.'

'There *is* that trust, Uncle.'

He seemed about to say something else, but then dismissed her.

The court remained at Nottingham until the final days of the autumn, when Richard at last decided to return to London. All through the summer Bess had hovered near him, like a moth to a flame, but he did not even seem aware of her presence. He was alone in this, because it had become plain enough to everyone in the queen's household. She was not liked as a consequence.

On a frosty autumn day before the court finally departed for the south, the ladies were gathered in Anne's apartments to look at a newly arrived consignment of rich cloths. They stood in small groups, as near as possible to the flickering log fire, chattering and laughing as they examined the fine fabrics intended for the queen herself. It was one of Anne's better days, and she was able to sit in a chair by the flames, inspecting the beautiful silks, velvets and brocades as they were displayed before her.

Cicely was among the ladies and discovered a soft blush-rose satin that she held against herself, imagining the gown it would make for the Christmas season. Anne saw and sent a page to bring her. The queen was so frail she could barely speak above a whisper. 'Do you like that pretty satin, Cicely?'

'Oh, yes, Your Grace, I do.'

'Then it is yours.'

Cicely's eyes shone. 'Thank you!'

'No doubt you imagine yourself wearing a wondrous gown as you dance with your John?'

'Yes, and I hope it will be *every* dance, for I do not want him to partner anyone else.'

Anne smiled. 'Oh, how well I understand. I felt the very same when I first fell in love with . . . Richard. If I could, I would *still* dance every dance with him. I will never dance again now, but must be present at Christmas.'

Cicely could not help but notice that moment of hesitation before Anne said Richard's name, nor could she help wondering if, after all, the name the queen wished to say was that of Edward of Lancaster, her first husband, the then Prince of Wales. It was a dismaying thought.

'So, Cicely, which of these do you think will suit me best?' Anne indicated two bales of brocade that had been placed before her. 'Yes, I know they are both very alike, and that cherry is perhaps not my best colour, but I believe I will stand out. Do you think so?'

'Yes, Your Grace, I do.' Cicely looked at the cherry bales. The only real difference between them was that one was embroidered with gold, the other with silver. There was no doubt in her mind that the gold would better suit the queen. 'This one, Your Grace,' she said, running her fingertips over the rich surface.

'Then it is settled.' Anne nodded at some waiting pages, who took the unwanted bale back to the table with all the others. Then she smiled at the ladies, who had fallen silent expectantly. 'You shall *all* have a gown for Christmas, ladies. Please make your choice.'

With cries of delight they fell upon the cluttered table, but no one went near the cherry bale, for to choose that would be to draw a comparison with the queen, and there was not one among them who would wish to risk that. Anne began to cough a little, and Cicely brought her a draft of the herbal brew the physician had made for her. It was soothing, but made no difference to the advance of her illness.

Just then the king was announced, and everyone curtseyed low as Richard entered. He wore a doublet the colour of walnuts, and wine-red hose, with a sleeveless dark-brown coat trimmed with black fur. The coat swung as he paused to look around. 'Ladies, your cackle is audible throughout the castle,' he said, inclining his head to include them all.

Anne smiled. 'You exaggerate, my lord,' she said, trying to speak above a whisper but failing.

He came to her. 'How are you today?' His eyes were warm with feeling.

'See?' Anne replied, taking the hand he held out to her. 'We are all choosing our gowns for Christmas. I have this excellent brocade and Cicely has that blush satin.'

'And very desirable you will both look.' His glance moved to Bess's solitary figure. 'What of you, Bess? Do you not wish to choose a gown?'

The question was so sudden and unexpected that many of ladies gasped. Bess started as well. 'I — I was going to wait until everyone else had chosen, Uncle,' she managed to say, but the look in her eyes almost stripped him naked.

There was an immediate stir, and his gaze moved curiously around everyone, before returning to Anne's suddenly set face. The queen was angry that Bess made so little effort to conceal such inappropriate desire, and today could not conceal her own resentment.

Richard's glance turned to Cicely, who avoided meeting it, a fact that to him spoke volumes. He knew something was wrong, and that it concerned Bess, but felt obliged to continue. 'Come, Bess, choose now, before the gannets have taken everything.' He went to the table and beckoned.

Bess rose slowly, aware of the hostility in the room as she went towards him. The ladies drew back from the table as she passed.

Richard was clearly bemused as he gestured at the bales. 'Which do you like, Bess?'

'I . . . do not know,' she said haltingly.

'What of this?' Of all the bales, he indicated the cherry and silver brocade.

Bess hesitated, but then nodded miserably. 'Yes, Your Grace, I like it well enough.'

'It is settled then.' The continuing silence made him clear his throat. 'Ladies, I know I have committed some crime, but for the very life of me I do not know what it is. I may be king, but I am not fey.'

Anne could not leave him floundering. 'Come, my dear lord, let us talk a while,' she said in her pathetic whisper.

He went to his wife with some relief, and Cicely felt so sorry for him. He had no idea that he had unwittingly chosen the very cloth that was bound to foment more whispers. Anne and Bess would be alike, but opposites as well, and it would be Bess who shone. Nor would Anne tell him, because Cicely heard him ask, and the queen replied that he had imagined it. As always, he did not press further.

The other ladies began to talk together again, resuming their choosing of the cloths but a little more decorously this time. They turned their backs on Bess, who tried to gather her bale. She fumbled and it spilled, unrolling its way across the rush-matted floor. No one went to her aid, except Cicely. Whatever else lay between them, she and Bess were still sisters.

Bess was grateful. 'Why did he choose this cloth, Cissy?' she whispered. 'There were so many there, but he chose this one.'

'And you should have had the wit to decide on something else.'

'I know now, but did not think in that sudden moment.'

Cicely paused, the collected brocade spilling over her arms. She kept her voice as soft as possible, so that no one could overhear. 'Bess, you will *have* to be more alert to it all. You still persist in making plain your feelings for him, and the ladies will not forgive you. Nor will the queen. Perhaps especially the queen.'

Bess stole a glance towards him as he leaned over Anne's shoulder to whisper in her ear. 'I am enchanted, Cissy, in his thrall so completely that I will never escape.'

'Do you wish to?'

'No, for to say that would be to deny what is in my heart. Even though his great love for Anne is so very obvious to all, and I am destroyed by this white-hot desire, I look at him, and my body exults. And when I lie in bed at night, he becomes mine.'

Cicely gazed at her. 'You *have* to control it. You almost *raped* him with your eyes.' She handed the bale to the pages, and as they bore it away to the rooms she shared with Bess, she continued, 'If Anne should complain to him, you will be removed from court and sent somewhere that not only keeps you from him, but places you beyond Henry Tudor's reach as well. You do know that? It might be a doorless turret in the middle of an Irish lake, for all I know.'

Bess smiled wanly. 'If you ever wish to know what it is like to be cursed, just ask me, for I can describe every torment.'

After a few minutes, Richard took his leave of his wife, acknowledging the ladies again, and when he had gone, Anne looked at them all. 'The king fears that I am tired, and with the long journey to London tomorrow he insists that I rest. You may all leave now. I will send for you if I require anything. Cicely, I wish you to assist me to the bed.'

Cicely curtseyed, and waited until she and the queen were alone. 'Will you wish to disrobe, Your Grace?'

'No, for I am determined to be with Richard when he dines, but I *will* be free of this unwieldy headdress.'

Cicely hastened to remove it, slipping it from its pins and then easing it from Anne's head. Then she brought a hairbrush and smoothed the lank rosy hair. Anne closed her eyes. 'That is very soothing. Can you imagine that I was once as beautiful as your sister?'

'Oh, yes, Your Grace, I know it well. I think perhaps you were much *more* beautiful than my sister. The king could not help but fall in love with you.'

Anne looked away. 'Those were different days, Cicely. I was married before him, did you know?'

'I . . . I had heard, Your Grace.'

'Richard and I were betrothed, but then the turn of political events saw me married to Henry VI's son, Edward of Lancaster, Prince of Wales. We were husband and wife for six months, or thereabouts, before he died at the Battle of Tewkesbury.'

'But now you have a much finer husband, Your Grace.'

'Yes, the king.'

'Not just the king. You have Richard Plantagenet, the man himself, and I know of no greater heart.'

'Cicely. I . . . carry guilt.'

Cicely gazed at her. 'Please do not tell me more,' she whispered. 'Please, for I could not bear to know. The king means everything to me, and . . . you mean everything to him. I cannot learn something I know would pierce him. Please, Your Grace, do not hand me that burden.'

Anne's thin hand gripped hers. 'Forgive me, Cicely, but I think I already have.'

'Not in words I cannot pretend to have misunderstood.'

Anne smiled. 'I see well why you are so high in his regard. You are not afraid to speak your mind to a king or queen.'

'Only *this* king and queen,' Cicely answered

'Richard always deserved better than me.'

Cicely looked away in tacit agreement. She was distraught for him. The gossip was right: Anne had always loved her first husband more than her second.

'I am sorry, Cicely, but I feel the burden too. I know I have failed him through our marriage. When we were first betrothed I thought I loved him so much, and I did. Truly. But then I was snatched away and given to Edward of Lancaster. I have tried to do right since Richard and I married, to love him as he should be loved, but we cannot always overcome our hearts. No woman can forget the first man she lay with, and that was Edward.' Anne smiled regretfully. 'And he was not worth it. Do you know that? He was not worth it, because he had no heart, but still I feel this way towards him. Still feel that if he had lived, I could have changed him. Is that not what all women think? We are all fools. I am perverse and selfish, for I have the love of a man who is all I know you believe him to be. This illness is my sentence. As was the loss of my son. I am a living wraith because I am a lie.'

Cicely's eyes filled with tears. Anne saw her child's death as *her* punishment? It was *Richard* who paid the real price. He was a king without an heir, with a wife who could not give him another and who had always loved someone else.

Anne watched her face. 'You think less of me now, do you not?'

'It would be naıve to say I do, because I have never been in such a position as you, and cannot begin to know how it feels. But I do not think love can be apportioned.'

Anne smiled. 'If it could, everything I am would be Richard's. I *do* love him, you see, I just cannot leave the past where it belongs. Fate is not dealing him a kind hand, but soon I will be gone and he will be persuaded to take another wife. I pray she gives him more than I have ever done. Cicely, no matter what you now think of me, I seek your promise that you will always be there for Richard. Your youth is no barrier, for it is your heart, mind and strength that can sustain him. He is closer to you than anyone, I know that, and you have earned that honour. My guilty heart will be eased if I know you will be there to support him when he most needs it.'

'I will always be there for him, Your Grace. Always.'

'That is what I hoped you would say.' Anne's face became a little wry. 'It is to be thanked that you do not feel as your sister does, for to be sure *you* could have had his heart and body long since.'

Cicely's cheeks flamed. 'Please do not say that! He is my uncle.'

'You and he have something, call it understanding, that is very out of the ordinary. Fate has made you his niece, but you would have been a far better wife for him than me. You would have warmed his bed. I was only ever warm with my first husband, and it has caused me pain ever since.' Anne gazed at her. 'But Richard is your uncle, and you only see him as such.'

'Of course!' Cicely was shocked.

Anne smiled. 'Of course,' she murmured, but then changed the subject. 'Please help me up for I must go to the bed.'

Cicely struggled to take in all the queen had said, but managed to attend her with the care and consideration she had always shown. 'Do . . . do you wish me to stay, Your Grace?' she asked when Anne was lying on the huge bed.

'No, you may go. But Cicely . . . ?'

'Your Grace?'

'Please try to understand me. I have never told anyone what I have told you today.'

'Nothing of this will ever pass my lips, Your Grace, and I do not think any the worse of you. It is not my place to judge something of which I know nothing.' *But I now feel even more for Richard, if that be humanly possible.*

Bess was nowhere to be found. Cicely searched the castle without success, and eventually found her quite by accident, standing on a chair to look out of the narrow aperture window of a small room that overlooked the castle bailey. She turned, and stepped guiltily down from the chair. 'You have found my secret place then? I come here often.'

Cicely stood on the chair, and saw the view below, where Richard, John and some gentlemen were viewing a pair of new horses. One of them was her cousin Jack, who had arrived from the north that very day.

Bess was defensive. 'I do no harm by coming here, and offend no one. Surely you do not pick fault with this as well?'

Cicely watched as Richard mounted one of the horses, a mettlesome chestnut that did not take kindly to its burden, monarch or not. Richard was not unseated, and seemed well able to control it. He gave no sign of his pain, and was as fit and accomplished a rider as any straight-backed man, probably fitter than most. Then she looked at John, and her eyes softened with love. *My own John.*

'I cannot undo my love,' Bess said quietly behind her. 'Could you undo yours?'

'John is free to be mine, Bess, but Richard belongs to Anne.'

Bess was silent for a while, and then looked at her again. 'Do you think you will marry John?'

'I pray so, but it might be that now that the little prince has gone, the king has a grander match in mind for his only son.'

'*You* are a grand match, Cissy. It would be a very popular marriage in the land.'

Cicely smiled. 'Shall I shock you, Bess? If I cannot marry John of Gloucester, I will lie with him anyway. I will be his lover, and will remain so for as long as he wants me.'

Bess gave a sad smile. 'What is so shocking about *that*? Cissy, I have been in that fleshly prison for what seems like an eternity.'

Cicely looked down into the courtyard again, at her cousin Jack in particular. He was handsome and roguish, with wild dark curls to his shoulders, brown flashing eyes, and a seductive smile — and charm that gained him access to numerous ladies' beds. Or so Cicely had been told. Looking at him, she could believe it.

The party mounted and prepared to ride out from the castle, Jack on a splendid white horse, called Héraut, that was the envy of most. It was probably more suited to the king himself than the nephew expected to be his heir. As the little party of horsemen moved slowly towards the gateway, in the shadows of the old walls, Richard and John were indistinguishable one from the other.

CHAPTER FIFTEEN

It was just before Christmas and Cicely stood in her room as close as possible to the fire. Biddy fussed around, arranging the folds of the gown that had been made up from the blush-rose satin, and which would be worn during the seasonal celebrations. At last the old nurse was satisfied and stood back to look at her charge. 'Lady Cicely, I declare you look lovely. Your father would indeed have been proud. There will be few to rival you.'

Eyes shining with anticipation, Cicely turned to look at her reflection and was well pleased with what she saw. The gown was all she could have wished, the soft cloth falling elegantly from a high waistline, the trimming of gold striking just the right note of contrast. Around her waist she wore a belt of mother-of-pearl from which hung a long golden chain, and at the end was an enamelled pendant of brilliant colours. Around her throat were twisted many strands of pearls, some hanging low past her waist and some tightly twisted against her skin. There too was John's ring, although still tucked out of sight. Her dark hair was brushed until it shone and on her head nestled a small cap hung with drop pearls.

She smiled at Biddy. 'What a fuss just to see if I will look well for the festivities. We could have employed our time to better use, I think.'

'Ah, but it was worth it just to see you. The king's son will be taken with you all over again.'

'Indeed he will,' Elizabeth's imperious voice declared from behind them. She stood there, for the first time at Richard's court wearing a gown of some other colour than black. She had not gone north with the court during the summer, but had remained in the south, near the riverside palace of Sheen, upstream of London, claiming piety and a need to retreat for a while. She was elegant in dark blue figured velvet, her hair tucked into a sky-blue headdress from which sprang a wired veil. She was an echo of the beautiful widow for whom Edward IV had formed such an intense infatuation. She dismissed Biddy, who had always been a little afraid of her, and then sat down to survey her daughter.

'Yes, indeed, Cicely, you look well. Is it all for John of Gloucester?' She smiled as Cicely's chin took on a stubborn set. 'I am not criticizing, far from it. In fact I will go so far as to tell you that when the time comes you will have my full consent to marriage with him. I will put no obstacle in your way.'

Cicely looked suspiciously at her mother and once again Elizabeth smiled.

'Jesu, girl, do not regard everything I say with such doubt. I may not have been with you when the court was at Nottingham but my eyes do not deceive me and I see how things have progressed between you. If you do not believe my intentions are good, then look at it this way. Richard Plantagenet dotes on his bastard son, and if John expresses a strong enough wish to marry you then I do not think Richard will deny him. Neither will he allow his son to live as a pauper. John is bound to be rich and influential. Ah, I see you begin to smile; you would rather believe in my mercenary instincts. I cannot blame you for that — I have not been a fond mother — but that is my nature. I cannot easily show affection.'

Cicely, trying to disrobe without help, found it impossible to reach the fastenings at the back of her bodice. Her mother went to assist. 'If only Bess's affairs were as simple and straightforward as yours. It is mostly on her account that I am here. She gives little sign of her feelings at the moment, although I heard rumours from Nottingham that she was making a pretty time of it drooping over him. Tell me, is she over him now? It is not merely an idle question, for I have good cause to ask.'

'I . . .' Cicely could not bring herself to answer.

'I will take that as confirmation that she is not over him. The Lord God only knows why.'

'You do know why, Mother.' Cicely looked at her.

Elizabeth paused, and then sighed. 'Oh, I suppose I do. Damn him for his appeal. Anyway, I ask because he has spoken to me concerning her possible marriage. And he is *not* proposing himself, I hasten to point out.'

Cicely stared. 'To whom?'

'The Irish Earl of Desmond.'

'The king wishes to send her into virtual exile?' Cicely's mind raced. Had Richard finally realized the truth?

'Hardly exile. Ireland is a stronghold of Yorkist sympathies, and it may be that in Richard's eyes the marriage has immense political importance in the securing of those sympathies.'

'Will you tell her?' Cicely wondered what on earth Bess's reaction would be.

Thoughtful, Dame Grey helped Cicely into a fresh peach velvet gown. 'Hmm, I do not think so. After all, Richard may still change his mind. He made no definite offer to me, he simply informed me he was considering it. Besides, if she thinks she is to marry and leave England she may reveal more than would be seemly. It is a possibility I wish to avoid at all costs. So, it is best left as it stands. If you breathe a word to her, you shall rue it!' With this echo of her old self, Elizabeth went to the window, clearing a patch of misting from the glass to look out. 'It snows again. I declare this is the coldest winter I have known, or perhaps it is merely that I feel the cold a little more than when I was younger. This last year has aged me, I fear. I once thought I would be glorious forever, but look at me now.'

The words made Cicely study her mother, for it was hard to think of her as getting old, but a closer glance revealed how much she had faded since the death of Edward IV.

Elizabeth turned her head. 'I have a message. The king commands you to go to him. Just hold your tongue about Bess.'

As Cicely reached the royal apartments, she found a familiar and beloved figure standing near a window. Well, two beloved figures, for one was John, the other Jack of Lincoln, who looked striking in kingfisher blue. John turned at the sound of her footsteps and he came to sweep her into his arms and plant a huge kiss upon her lips. 'It must be all of two hours since last I saw you, and it feels like a lifetime.'

'You flatter me, sir.'

'Never.'

She turned to smile at Jack. 'How good it is to see you again, cousin, *and* that wondrous amethyst ring I desire so much.'

He returned the smile and embraced her. 'It is good to see you too, sweetheart, but the ring remains mine, no matter how sweetly you flutter your pretty eyes at me.'

She hugged him tightly, for she really did like him. They had known each other from childhood and he had once saved her from drowning. His company was *always* welcome.

John reclaimed her. 'The lady is mine, Jack. Do not forget it.'

Jack spread his hands, and the light slanted through the coveted amethyst. 'I will be kind to you, John, and not steal her, which I am sure I could if I tried.' He winked at her.

John gave him a look. 'And how is your wife, sir?'

'I have no idea.' Jack grinned.

John cupped Cicely's face in his hands. 'We do not have long, for my father awaits you.'

'Why? What does he want?'

'You will soon know.' He kissed her again. 'I will wait out here.'

Puzzled, she went to the king's door, which the page opened before her.

Richard was standing in front of a freshly stoked fire, a sheaf of papers in his hand and many more lying on the floor around his feet. He was frowning at the topmost communication, stroking his chin thoughtfully, but he smiled as she approached. 'Be seated if you please, my lady, and my attention will be all yours presently.'

He was not alone, for Francis Lovell and Robert Percy were with him, as well as the king's elderly secretary, all helping with the volume of work that required his personal attention.

She sat down on a nearby chair, and watched her uncle as he dealt with the never-ending flow of documents requiring his attention. His grey eyes flicked quickly over the words, and he pushed his long hair back as it fell forward.

'Robert, I tell you we must be finished with this impudent Tudor before this next summer is out, for I cannot tolerate his presence in Brittany, causing unrest in England with his plotting. Or the French for *their* plotting.'

'By your leave, Your Grace, you should have beheaded his Medusa mother when you had the chance.'

'True.' Richard looked at Cicely.

Francis was seated at a desk by the window, working upon another sheaf of papers, a quill poised in readiness. He smiled at Cicely, and gave her one of his huge winks.

Richard still spoke of Henry Tudor. 'The wretch still declares his intention to marry my eldest niece, if you please! Well, he shall not have Cicely, and Bess will be married forthwith to Desmond and despatched across the Irish Sea.'

Cicely inhaled with swift dismay, and he heard. 'What is it, Cicely? Is there some reason why Bess should not be married?'

She swallowed nervously, searching frantically for an answer to his question. 'I fear Bess's heart may be given already.' Well, it was not untrue.

He continued to look at her, as if trying to divine her innermost thoughts. 'Already given? To whom?'

She was aware of his two friends exchanging glances. Even the secretary reacted.

Richard was puzzled. 'I have not seen her dallying with anyone at court. If you will tell me his name I will endeavour to please her. If he is available then she shall have him.'

'I . . . do not even know who he is, Uncle.'

He studied her. 'Hidden pages, Cicely?'

She lowered her eyes.

For a long moment he continued to look at her, and then cleared his throat. 'The fellow is married, I take it?'

'Yes.'

He drew a long breath. 'There is nothing I can do about *that*, unless he can by some miracle be *un*married. I have no appetite for annulments, they always smack of lies.' He handed his pile of documents to Robert. 'Well, Cicely, I shall have to know the situation soon, for I will have her beyond the Tudor's clammy clutches. She is the firstborn and should be married first.' He waved the others away. 'I wish to speak to the Lady Cicely alone.'

Francis bowed low to Richard and then to Cicely, gathered up the papers and went to the door. Robert Percy and the secretary followed on his heels, and she heard them greet John and Jack outside before the door closed behind them.

Silence fell upon the room and Cicely thought the crackling of the fire seemed to fill the air. Richard looked at her. 'Cicely, do you wish to marry my son?'

Her eyes widened. 'I . . . Yes.'

'Well, I knew as much already, but it is necessary to ask you formally. I made a great error in the case of Ralph Scrope.'

'This is formal?' She glanced at all the other papers and documents still scattered everywhere.

He smiled and spread his hands. 'For its sins, but I am not always at ease amidst grandeur.' Then he shifted a little. 'Are you quite sure? Beyond all doubt? Because you both matter to me.'

She looked at him. 'I love him, Uncle.'

'Well, he has requested my permission for you to be wed. I gave my consent, of course, but the match is fraught with the usual awkwardness of consanguinity. The Pope will grant dispensation, but it will take time. These things always do.' He came closer and touched his palm to her cheek. 'There is also the delicate matter of any children born of such a marriage, and their closeness to the throne. They will be the grandchildren of two kings. Do you see? You and John are illegitimate, but there will be a possible path open to your children. I have to consider it.'

'I do not think John and I would wish such a weight upon our children's shoulders. Whom we may never have, anyway,' she added.

'True, but somehow you both seem in rude enough health to provide me with an army of grandchildren.'

'I cannot imagine you as a grandfather.'

Again his smile. 'Now then, as I said, dispensation will take some time, and apart from that, I wish to have Henry Tudor over and done with before your marriage. I would have my realm at peace for such an occasion. I would also see Bess married first. Your sister Ann I wish to make handfast to Thomas Howard, grandson of my dear friend the Duke of Norfolk. She is eight or nine, and he is eleven, which is suitable enough, as such things go. This betrothal will also be kept in abeyance until Bess's future is decided. I have not been tardy in seeing to the husbands of my nieces, that you must admit! You will be thankful to know that I have yet to turn my industrious mind to your two youngest sisters.'

'How have you found time for all this?' She found she was looking at his lips. They were so sculpted yet quick, so ready to smile and . . . And what? What else was in her mind as she looked?

'Have I food between my teeth?' he enquired on a teasing note.

She flushed. 'No. No, of course not. Forgive me, I did not mean to . . .' She left unsaid what she had not meant.

'That is a relief. Cicely, I am glad about you and John. It warms my heart.'

He kissed her cheek and indicated that he had finished by drawing her to her feet. She smiled at him and went to the door, but he halted her. 'Cicely, are you sure you do not know the identity of the man Bess loves?'

She met his gaze squarely. 'Quite sure.'

'And here I was, convinced *you* would never fib to me,' he said dryly. 'Just tell me it is not one of my enemies.'

She returned, 'If it were, I would tell you. Bess may love unwisely, but there is no treachery in it. I swear.' But she knew he *should* be told. It mattered to his good name, and yet she could not betray her sister to him.

'I believe you, Cicely. Rightly or wrongly, I will always believe you.'

Guilt kept her where she was, and he came to her.

'What is it? Tell me.'

'I cannot tell you. You least of all. Please do not ask me.'

'Me least of all?' He searched her eyes, and she saw the beginning of enlightenment. 'Cicely?'

She put a shaking finger briefly to his lips. 'Please,' she whispered. 'Please do not ask me to betray her even more than I already have. What I suspect is in your mind now is the truth.'

He closed his eyes. 'Jesu.'

'I am sorry,' she whispered.

'Sweet God above, what a fool I have been. I should have known! Things become clear suddenly.'

'You should not be faced with such a thing.'

'You think me too fragile?' He smiled.

'It is just another thing to be a weight upon you.'

'And your silence has been because you think of me?'

'I will always think of you.'

He drew a long breath. 'Cicely, I will have to take steps to—'

'Do not punish her,' she said quickly. 'She cannot help her feelings, and if you turn your back . . .'

'I have to do *something,* Cicely. I can hardly continue to behave like the only idiot in the village. That is certainly how I must have appeared until now, I think.'

'It is talk. No more.'

'But not talk I would wish to continue. You do see that?'

She nodded. 'Yes, I know. Oh, I feel so guilty. I have broken her confidence, and now it is on your shoulders too. I am so sorry.'

'I should have had my wits about me, but it simply did not occur to me that . . .'

'A niece could desire her uncle?'

'Something of the sort.'

He was the King of England, but had an allure that breached boundaries. There was no side to him, nothing that could ever lead to mistrust. He eclipsed everyone around him. Had any other king ever been as natural and gracious? She did not know how long she had gazed at him, until he teased her again.

'Does my appearance meet with your approval, my lady?'

She coloured again. 'Yes.'

'And yours with mine.'

'About Bess . . .'

'I will not hurt her, Cicely, save by not being able to return her affection. I cannot view her in that light. She must understand that.'

'She does, but it is not always possible to fall out of love.'

His grey eyes were almost luminous. 'Oh, that is something I know only too well. Go now, because I think John is waiting.'

Cicely withdrew, feeling all that was disloyal to her sister, but it was done now and could not be undone. Then she saw John, and all else went from her mind as she ran to him. Jack had gone.

When Cicely next saw Bess, it was to learn that Richard had already sent for her.

'Cissy, I managed to turn the situation to my own advantage, but it cannot last too long, I fear. I admitted I was in love with someone already married, and said I accepted that the man in question would always be beyond my reach. I then asked Richard if he would stay his decision until I was over the heartbreak.' Bess blinked back tears. 'He said he would speak to me again when the New Year was well on its way. Jesu, if only he knew that it was *he* whom I longed for, *he* whom I loved so!'

Cicely could not meet her eyes, for he *did* know. 'He is our uncle,' she said.

'And do I not realize it. He was a little . . . changed, I thought. As if he did not feel entirely at ease with me. Do you think someone has told him, Cissy?'

'I . . . cannot say. Possibly.' Cicely felt dreadful.

'I do pray not.'

'Did he ask you the identity of your mysterious love?'

'No. Strangely. He simply said that when I was ready, he would proceed with the Desmond match.' Bess drew a long breath. 'I was so tempted to tell him the truth.'

'Maybe the earl will be to your liking, Bess.'

'No one can be to my liking. Only Richard.'

CHAPTER SIXTEEN

IT WAS CHRISTMAS and the tables in the dining hall groaned beneath their great load of festive delicacies. The banquet was lavish, the food sumptuous and the company brilliant as Richard's court celebrated the season. The spangled gathering made merry to the full. Everyone was there, except Bess. So many minstrels, jugglers, tumblers and fools performed that it was difficult to know which to watch or listen to first. The great hall rang with merriment, the noise was deafening and the spiced smell of the dishes still lay heavily upon the warm air. To Cicely, now so happy with John, the atmosphere was as sweet as nectar.

Richard had remained true to his decision on returning to London after his son's death. There had been no mourning, only a celebration of his lost child's life. He was bright, brilliant even, and gave no sign at all of what was in his mind. To many, especially Cicely, it was as touching as if he had enveloped himself in swathes of unrelieved black. Others saw it as callous disregard for the dead, especially those like Lady Stanley, who was always ready to defame him.

Cicely sat immediately below the royal dais, with her mother on one side and Robert Percy on the other. John stood behind his father and the queen. Cicely was wearing the blush gown, and it felt good. She was also wearing John's ring, no longer around her neck, but on her right hand — not her left — for all to see. Word had spread of Richard having agreed to her marriage to John, but somehow it was not yet out about Bess's proposed contract with the Earl of Desmond. This resulted, as always, in renewed whispers about why Bess had not yet been matched. Even the third of Edward IV's daughters had been found a future husband, but not Bess, the first. And now she was absent from the celebrations. Richard was subjected to continual glances. If he had looked towards the top of the steps, everyone would have believed he anticipated his eldest niece. But he did not look.

Robert's green eyes twinkled with laughter as he held a dish of cheesecakes before Cicely. 'You sit there without eating, my lady. Will you not partake? I vow they are the finest ever baked.'

'You are kind, sir, but I am too nervous to eat.'

'Nervous? Why so?' He discarded the cheesecakes and lifted a small dish of flowers of violet instead. 'Then these surely cannot offend.'

She took some of the sweet confection, and paused. 'I do not really know why I feel like this,' she confessed.

'Then you have no business feeling it at all,' he declared firmly.

She smiled and slipped the confection into her mouth, but as she savoured the honey taste, a great roar of approval was raised as the final great dish of the banquet, called a subtlety, was carried in upon a golden platter and placed before Richard and the queen. Such dishes were served at the end of every course of a banquet, but this one was the most splendid of all. The exquisite mixture of sugar and eggs was formed into the shape of the Virgin and Child, and was particularly beautiful.

Richard laughed aloud when he saw it, and lifted his goblet in a toast. The cheers that followed made known the court's delight. After that his attention was required to other small ceremonies, and John moved closer to engage the queen's attention.

Anne wore the cherry and gold gown, but seemed lost inside it. There was a trace of her beauty, but it was very faint, and she tried so hard to be strong but had often reached for Richard's hand. It was something Cicely found hard to watch, because he was being deceived. John was dressed in green, the green of Sherwood, and his father's badge was on his collar. He smiled at his stepmother, and was as kind and attentive as Richard himself would have been.

The king missed nothing. His hand went momentarily to John's arm, a gesture of appreciation even while he was diverted by so much else, and in that small moment, that fleeting acknowledgement from father to son, Cicely loved them both all the more. She had believed herself happy in her father's court, but the court of her uncle, Richard III, made her even happier.

Glancing around, she saw Jack, who raised his cup to her and winked. His almost black curls were as untrammelled as ever, and his dark brown eyes had that lazy warmth that could so easily seem to caress. She found herself blushing. Everything about roguish Jack de la Pole suggested he was a consummate lover. He was said to have left a trail of broken hearts behind him, and she could well believe it. Had she herself not wondered what it would be like to lie with him?

Many of Richard's friends and supporters were present tonight, and his true allies, but she knew Margaret, Lady Stanley, was not his only enemy. There was perfidy in the air, intercepted glances, pursed lips, bland faces that gave nothing away, except perhaps to the Devil. She could hardly bear to think of Richard being surrounded by false friends as well as implacable enemies. Why could they not see what a good king he was? How he was essential to England? Why did they not see him as she did? And if that were beyond them, why did *he* not deal with them as her father would have done? *Why?* She was unswerving in her support for Richard. Left to her, he would not long have such enemies.

She needed distraction from such dark thoughts, and what better distraction could there be than John? Richard's attention was all on Anne again, and so John returned to sit with Cicely, Sir Robert Percy making room for him. If John were legitimate, she thought, he would be a truly worthy heir to his father's throne. He still was, if such a thing were to ever be permitted. She smiled then, because if he were legitimate, *she* would not be allowed to marry him! There could not be an illegitimate Queen of England. It was another thought she did not wish to entertain, because for John to be king, Richard would have to be dead.

John turned to her suddenly. 'Why has not Bess come down?'

'I think she must be indisposed,' Cicely replied tactfully.

'Perhaps you should go to her. My father has asked where she is.'

'He has?' Cicely's heart sank.

'Yes, and knowing him, he is likely to ask again. He expects his brother's eldest children to be here tonight.'

What of Edward and Dickon? Cicely could not help the thought, for although Richard had permitted her mother to visit the princes at the Tower on one occasion, no one else had been so allowed. They were lodged in the Garden Tower which apparently suited them admirably as they could indulge in all manner of boyish activities in the bushes and gardens which surrounded it. Dickon was full of his apparent prowess at archery, and Richard's Constable of the Tower, Sir Robert Brackenbury, was well liked by them both. He took them occasionally to the Lion Tower and permitted them to watch the king's leopards and suchlike beasts that were kept there.

Now the boys were not seen at all, and Richard had told her, in the strictest confidence, that he had sent them elsewhere for fear of another attempt to abduct them, such as John Welles had attempted just before Buckingham's rebellion. Welles, although free, had now fled the country and was said to be in Brittany with his half-nephew, Henry Tudor.

A little whispering had begun about the princes' whereabouts. Or their dreadful fate. It was beginning to be suggested that their disappearance indicated a dark deed had been done at Richard's command, and their failure to be seen only fanned these nascent flames. Cicely had urged Richard to produce her brothers and put a stop to it, but he had not, preferring to keep them safe in obscurity. Maybe he was right, but somehow she did not think he was.

John sensed what she was thinking. 'Your brothers are safe, Cicely. My father would never harm them. You know that as well as me.'

Cicely managed a little smile. 'I know, for he has told me so, and I believe him. I always do. I wish they could be free and here now, though. Well, one of them. Dickon is all I could wish for, but Edward is . . . an odious little sack of self-importance.'

John was taken aback. 'Really? You have not said that before.'

'No, because I have always hoped he would change, but when Mother saw him at the Tower she said he was as irksome as ever. Apparently he behaves as if he is still the only person of importance in England. It is time for him to accept his new lot. I have had to.'

'How very disapproving you are,' John said sternly.

She smiled. 'And in the season of goodwill. Shame on me.'

He bent to kiss her cheek. 'You are perfect in my eyes, Cicely Plantagenet.'

'And you in mine,' she whispered, closing her eyes with the pleasure of his lips against her skin.

Something made him glance up at a gallery behind the royal dais, and she saw the three small, very sleepy faces of her youngest sisters peeping through the carved balustrade. They had been brought from Sheen to enjoy the Christmas festivities. He took her hand and they hurried up to speak to them. Little Bridget was almost asleep, but five-year-old Katherine squealed with delight and ran to them.

John caught her and swung her up high. 'Well now, my little lady, and how are you enjoying the celebrations?'

Katherine was excited. 'It is all so pretty. The ladies are so beautiful. One day I shall have a gown that is like a rainbow, and lots of jewels, and I will dance with all the princes.'

'Slow down, sweeting,' he laughed, 'for you must grow a little first. There is plenty of time yet! ' He put her down and turned to see young Ann — whom everyone called Annie — still peeping over into the hall. 'And what of you, Annie, do you try to seek your future lord in that crowd?'

The nine-year-old slate-blue eyes turned fully towards him and she smiled shyly. 'I have tried, but I cannot see Thomas Howard. Do you think he will be handsome? Maybe he is not here tonight. I hoped he would be. I want to be a duchess one day.' Pouting, she looked at the hall again. 'If I was old enough I would be down there dancing and not sitting in my room in a sulk like Bess.'

Cicely was concerned. 'A sulk?'

'She is dressed for the banquet but will not go down. She told me to go away. I think she has been crying.'

John looked quickly at Cicely, and with a nod she slipped away.

She found her sister alone by the fire, and the sight of her took Cicely's breath away. Bess was wearing the gown of cherry and silver brocade. At her throat shone a diamond necklet with a solitary black drop pearl, and her hair was held back by a small lace cap.

Caught unawares by her arrival, Bess struggled to compose herself. 'What brings you here, Cissy?'

'Annie told us that you were unwell. I have left John with our sisters. Why have you not come down, Bess?' Cicely sat in a chair opposite.

Bess smiled wryly. 'Can you not see for yourself? I did go as far as the gallery, but when I saw the queen, I could go no further. Cissy, the gowns are far too similar. I dare not present myself because it will look as if I seek to challenge Anne. Everyone talks of me as it is without it being any worse.'

'Bess, the king has noticed your absence.'

Bess closed her eyes. 'My absence, but not me.'

'Do not pick my words apart, Bess. He has noticed, and John believes he may ask again because he expects you to be there as well as me. You cannot stay away. Come, you will be with me, and with John, I am sure, for he knows nothing of it all and will gladly stand beside you.'

'You have not told him?'

'That my sister wants to bed his father? I think not. Whether or not he knows from elsewhere I do not know. He has never said anything, or indicated anything.'

Bess rose unwillingly. 'I will do as you advise, Cissy, but I think it is a mistake. Perhaps if I change the gown. . . ?'

'Richard chose it. He remembers so many things that it is quite possible he will remember that as well. Stay as you are, and outface them all.'

'I am not as brave as you. Maybe I once was, but no longer.'

'You are Father's favourite daughter, Bess. That is all you need, remember.'

John awaited them and was clearly taken aback by the gown. He looked enquiringly at Cissy, who answered, 'The king chose it.'

He did not say any more as he accompanied the sisters to the foot of the great staircase. There was a considerable stir, but to Cicely's relief Richard was engaged in conversation with Francis Lovell and Robert Percy. He did not even seem to notice the change in the atmosphere.

The revels faltered, but then continued, with the music, dancing and entertainments. Everyone watched Bess, but discreetly, as John conducted the sisters to where their mother was seated. Elizabeth's eyes flickered angrily over the gown but she inclined her head civilly enough. What else could she do?

Once Bess had taken her seat, her eyes lowered to the floor, her hands clasped in her lap, John led Cicely out to join the dancing. He spoke every time they twisted past each other. 'You did not mention the gown.'

'The king chose it,' she repeated.

'The devil he did.' John glanced towards his father.

'He did not know.'

'Oh, I am sure of that.' He glanced at her. 'I *have* heard the whispers about her feelings for him,' he said quietly.

Richard had perhaps not been as unconscious of events as perhaps seemed, for he glanced around at Bess, saw the gown, and then looked quickly at Anne. Although his face did not change, Cicely knew he had forgotten choosing Bess's brocade, and how dismayed he now was. He looked at Sir Francis and said something. Francis nodded and moved swiftly towards Bess, bowed, and clearly requested her to dance. Richard then turned to Anne, leaning closer to speak to her. She too looked at Bess, and then put her hand over his sleeve. Cicely saw her fingers tighten, as if in reassurance, and knew he had asked her forgiveness for his part in his niece's gown.

'Poor king,' she whispered, forgetting to dance, as Richard himself had done on that other occasion. She could have wept for him, and John led her swiftly from the floor.

'It is not *your* fault, sweeting,' he said gently, proffering a handkerchief.

'John, I feel everything so keenly where he is concerned. I cannot bear it when he tries hard to do the right thing, yet finds himself in a pit.'

'Of his own digging,' John added, smiling.

'His intentions were kind.'

'That is the problem. Time and time again we come back to his unwillingness to be firm and unflinching with those around him. Put him on a battlefield and he is the most formidable fighter and commander in Christendom.'

'You would have him wield his battleaxe here tonight?' she asked lightly, but remembered her earlier thoughts. *She* would wield that battleaxe.

'Yes, I would,' John replied. 'I saw you watching those gathered here. You sense it too. They play the friend, but will betray him. He will be sold, Cicely. Bought and sold.'

She stared at him. 'Please do not say that.'

He reached for her hand and pulled her near enough to put his arm around her waist. 'Forgive me, my sweet lady, but I suddenly feel . . . Oh, I do not know.' He fell silent.

Cicely did not know what to say. The empty shadows at the side of the great hall had suddenly crowded forward, and she was frightened. 'John?'

He saw the look in her eyes and caught her closer. 'I should not have said that.'

'Do . . . you really think it will happen?'

When he returned her look, and could not answer her glance flew to Richard. Please let nothing happen to him. Please.

John changed the subject. 'Your sister is a sight to behold. Whatever may have been said of her, no one could deny her loveliness.' He was watching Bess dance with Francis.

Richard watched Bess as well, but still without expression on his face. He toyed with his rings and lowered his glance to them. But then suddenly he looked up, straight at Cicely, and smiled at her across the crowded floor. He might almost have said her name and taken her hand. She returned the smile.

Anne did not look at Bess once, but then she saw Cicely with John, and beckoned them. They pushed their way to the dais, and Richard stood, almost with relief. 'John! You trod an excellent measure.'

'Better than you, Father?'

Richard smiled. 'That you will never do, you pup.' He turned to Cicely, and kissed her cheek. 'I have never liked blush-rose more than I do at this moment,' he said with feeling. Had he added, *'Anything but cherry,'* his meaning could not have been more obvious.

He looked at her. 'Please sit with the queen, Cicely, for I wish to talk to John.'

She inclined her head. 'Of course. It will please me, Uncle.' As she knelt by Anne, she heard her whisper, 'Jesu, of all the cloths in that room that day, he had to light upon the other cherry brocade.'

'He did not know, Your Grace.'

'Well, he does now, and is distressed, both because he thinks it has upset me, and — of all things — because he thinks *he* has caused your sister embarrassment!'

Cicely could only take her hand. 'It is not the king's fault, Your Grace. Please do not distress yourself.'

'Cicely, I intend to do what I can to take the sting from all this. When this measure is at an end, will you please bring your sister to me? And then I wish you to stay.'

'You are sure, Your Grace?' Cicely was concerned. 'You are not well, and—'

'Do as I request, Cicely.'

With great reluctance Cicely did as she was told, and as Bess accompanied her towards the dais again, she whispered, 'Not one word out of place, Bess, not one word. You are to be a dutiful niece.'

Bess smiled. 'You will not be able to pick fault, Cissy. I promise.'

As Bess sank into a deep curtsey, Anne was the very soul of gentleness. 'Bess, I wish you to join Cicely here with me, for what better time than Christmas to be reconciled?'

'I am honoured, Your Grace, and humbled by your kindness.'

'Bess, I will have you know that I think you look very lovely, the king has excellent taste.' Anne tried to sound strong, but could not. Her words trailed away into a whisper.

Bess could not speak, but kept her eyes fixed to the folds of Anne's gown. She was pale, her hands were clasped so tightly in her lap that her knuckles were white, and the queen could see how she shook.

'Have no fear, Bess. I mean you no unkindness for I know in truth that the gown is no fault of yours. It is no fault of anyone's, merely a stroke of awkward fate.' Anne paused, taking a shuddering breath and then glancing at Richard, who was deep in conversation with John and Francis. 'Bess, I know what is in your heart.'

Bess's breath caught, and her face went pale.

Cicely felt so guilty that she could only stare at the mingled folds of cherry brocade, one stitched with gold, the other with silver. Richard knew everything, and it was *her* fault that he did.

Anne looked at her. 'I know you love your uncle as you should not, and I know there is nothing you can do to stop. My poor Richard, he can draw hearts and keep them close ever after, without even having to try.'

Cicely looked away. But he does not have your heart, Anne, when he should have that one most of all.

Anne continued, 'I feel for you, Bess, because you can never know his love in the way you wish. I will not speak of this again, I only ask — *beg* — you never let him know. That is all I desire. His protection.'

Cicely felt so culpable she could almost have been sick.

Bess looked at the queen through tears. 'I will not fail you, Your Grace. I regret with all my heart that I have caused you such distress, and I am ashamed of what is within me. I will not tell him. How can I? I would rather take the crumbs at his feet than never see him again. Oh, there was a time when I wanted to tell him, but that madness has gone. My love has not, though.' Anne stretched a hand down, and Bess took it, still trying to fight back tears. 'I do not deserve your understanding, Your Grace.'

'Yes, you do, Bess, because we are two of a kind. Love is not always kind.'

Stifled anger stirred within Cicely, because she knew the queen was speaking of her first husband, not her second.

Bess pressed the queen's hand to her lips and then to her forehead. Her shoulders shook and she found it hard not to sob aloud.

A little later, Richard reignited the whispers by leading Bess out to dance. It was not anything to him other than a formal dance with his niece. A convention. Not to have done so would have caused more comment than to do it anyway. In due course he would dance with Cicely as well.

That was all it was. But the air seemed to stand still as the entire court watched the elegant shimmering Bess dance with her slender, beguiling uncle. Cicely watched, for her sister was ethereal, conducting herself perfectly, carefully avoiding Richard's eyes, and doing nothing whatsoever that should have warranted comment. But there was comment anyway; how could there not be?

As the dance came to an end, Richard conducted Bess from the floor again, returned her to her mother and then went back to sit with Anne, making it plain that his eldest niece was already forgotten. Bess did not gaze after him as once she would, but sat beside her mother. He had not even spoken to her, either during the dance or after. Before tonight he would have paused a while with her, maybe only for seconds, but nevertheless he would have done it. Now he was reserved.

If it had been an attempt to stem the flow of rumour and innuendo, it failed.

Cicely and John left the great hall in search of seclusion in the crowded palace. They chose a small chamber close to the apartment she shared with Bess. It was where her favourite tapestry had been hung on being brought from the abbey. There was no fireplace, nor even a brazier, and their breath was visible as John brought a torch from the passageway to light the candle on the table in the centre of the room.

Cicely gazed at the tapestry, its colours seeming to move in the undulating light that now filled the little room. Arthur, King of Camelot, riding his white horse down from the distant castle, followed by the Knights of the Round Table.

She smiled at John as he returned from putting the torch back in its place in the passageway. He stood behind her, his arms slipping around her waist. 'Cicely, there is something we have to talk of. I had not entirely believed all the rumours, but tonight I could tell that Bess really does love my father.'

Cicely lowered her eyes unhappily. 'But I love him too, John, and so do you.'

'The difference is that she is *in* love with him.'

'She did not do anything tonight,' Cicely reminded him.

'He did. He made his indifference to her very clear indeed. He may be fond of her as his brother's child, but it goes no further.' He turned her to face him. 'I would have liked it if you had told me, Cicely. Did you stay silent because you do not trust me? Did you think I would go straight to my father as I did about Ralph Scrope?'

'No! Oh, no.' Her fingers enclosed his. 'I did not want to put you in such a position. All this does harm to his good name, I know that, but she is my sister and no matter what she has done, I cannot stop loving her. I do all I can with her, truly.'

'You are often with the queen. Does she. . . ?'

'Know? Yes. And so does he,' she added unwillingly. Was she betraying Richard? No, not in this, for John was his son. And as loyal as Richard had always been himself.

John stared at her. '*He* knows?'

'Yes,' she whispered.

He continued to gaze at her. 'You told him?'

She described what had happened. 'I had to do it, John, because he knew there was something important I was not telling him. Lying to him is impossible for me, because he can always tell. Either way I was damned to be untrue to one of them, and in this he is more important than Bess.'

'Oh, dear God . . .' He removed his soft hat and put it on the table to run his hand through his hair. The candle flame shivered, the shadows danced, and his likeness to Richard became more pronounced. 'A pretty mess, is it not,' he said, as a statement, not a question.

'What I have confided should not have been confided, John. I beg you not to say anything.'

He gave her a reproachful look. 'You do not have to seek my word, Cicely.'

'I know. Oh, I feel so guilty about everything.'

'Do not. I know how close to my father you are, and that you would do anything for him. Well, perhaps not anything. At least I trust not.' John smiled.

She hardly noticed what he had said. 'He is always alone, John, and I did not want him to be alone in this as well.'

John looked at her. 'Alone? Are you sure of that?'

'What do you mean?'

'Oh, I do not know. Sometimes I feel . . .'

'What?' She looked at him curiously.

'I feel that there is someone else he thinks of. A woman.'

'If he has another love, he hides it well.' So well that Cicely did not believe it was a fact at all.

'I may be wrong.' John smiled. 'I am hardly so much a man of the world that I know everything about such things, least of all where my own father is concerned.' He pulled her closer. 'My poor Cicely, how tormented you are, having to listen to everyone's whines. Now then, enough of my father, your sister, and anyone else who would petition you for advice. We came here to be alone together, and time is being wasted. This Christmas is for us, for our happiness, and nothing shall mar it.'

CHAPTER SEVENTEEN

Cicely and Bess were in their mother's apartment, waiting for her to return from a visit to their little sisters at Sheen. Bess was at her embroidery, but Cicely stood at the window, looking out over the chill grey of the Thames. It was February 1485, and she had only just come from the queen's apartments. Anne was very unwell, and her physicians had sent all her ladies from the apartment, including Cicely, whom Anne wished to have close by most of all. Something was very wrong. The queen needed her.

As she looked at the river, a rich barge was being poled downstream towards the landing. 'Mother has returned,' she said, watching as the craft nudged the stone steps and was made fast. The sole passenger, well wrapped against the cold, was helped ashore and then assisted to walk into the palace. Winter did no favours to Dame Grey's health.

Bess glanced at her sister. 'You had best join me with your embroidery. We must look dutiful and industrious. She is not of even temper in the cold.'

When Elizabeth entered the warm room, she was so anxious to be close to the fire that she hardly noticed her daughters. Two of her ladies took her cloak away, and after she pulled her gloves from her frozen fingers, she held her hands to the log fire that crackled and flickered so welcomingly in the hearth.

'The winter is at its most inhospitable,' she declared, 'but at least Sheen is comfortable. However, you will be glad, nay happy, to know that your sisters are in sound health.' She looked at Bess. 'Or are you still so wrapped up in Richard that you no longer care about your siblings?'

It was a little unkind, and Bess blushed. She had been trying to tread the correct path where her improper love was concerned, and it hurt to be reminded of it. Richard's rather public rejection at Christmas had left her heartbroken because now she no longer had even the crumbs. He made certain he was never in an awkward situation with her, and if he spoke at all, it was merely to be civil as convention demanded. She had lost what little she had of him, but her love still burned brightly.

Elizabeth's attention returned to the fire. 'How long ago did you leave the queen, Cicely?'

'Two hours, I think. Since all the ladies were told to leave her apartments. I know she is more ill than before, but—'

'Yes, her condition has worsened considerably this last hour. I have just learned that for fear of contagion, her physicians have now *forbidden* Richard to go to her. The end is imminent, I fear.'

Cicely leapt to her feet. 'I must go to her!'

'No, Cicely. I was accosted by Sir Francis Lovell when I entered the palace. Richard has commanded that you are not to risk the contagion. It is his *command*.' Elizabeth was caustic. 'It would seem he knows you well enough to anticipate your reaction.'

'Do you mind?' Cicely prepared for a confrontation.

'What point would there be? You are his creature — you are *both* his creatures — and nothing I say will make any difference. But in this matter of Anne, *he* is the one who decides, and his decision is that you stay away. Is that clear?'

'Yes, Mother.'

Elizabeth turned to Bess. 'The queen's imminent demise must *not* encourage you, Bess. If he takes another queen, it will not be you. Bite upon the strap, girl, for one inappropriate squeak at this of *all* times, and I will strangle you. In person, not by the hand of an agent.'

Ten days passed, and Anne continued to linger near death. John stayed close to his father, and Cicely had seen little of either of them. Looking from the window again, she saw John arrive at the landing stage and ran to intercept him before he went to his father's apartments. Her feet flew as she ran through the palace to the head of the main staircase, but there she halted, for he was not alone in the hallway below: Sir Francis was there too.

The viscount was agitated, and gesticulated as he addressed John in an urgent whisper that did not reach Cicely. John listened intently, his expression disturbed as he stared at a carved shield boss high on the wall.

They began to approach the foot of the stairs, and Cicely shrank back into an alcove as their conversation became audible.

Francis's barely suppressed anger was more apparent at this close quarter. 'I tell you, John, if the king allows these latest rumours to continue, his character and reputation will be gravely sullied, perhaps irreparably. He obstinately refuses to believe the urgency of the situation. The Council's advice floats unheeded past him. Even William Catesby, his closest adviser, has been unable to move him. I have this past hour been pleading with Richard, but he merely looks at me as if I rant about the price of meat! I know he is distraught about the queen, and that this particular topic is the very last thing he wishes to think of, but he *must*! I beg you to speak to him, to make him see his folly.'

John's voice was quieter. 'I have your meaning, Sir Francis, and will do what I can, but if no one else can bring him to reason, it is unlikely I will.'

'If you fail, perhaps the Lady Cicely. . . ?'

John halted. 'No. That would be to ask too much of her.'

'But he listens to her, we all know that. She is dear to him and he trusts her.'

'To ask her would be to put her in an impossible position, surely you see that? I love her, Sir Francis, and cannot allow such a thing. My father would not wish it either. If he thought for a moment that she had been sent on such an errand, he would never forgive any of us, including me.'

Francis grunted and shuffled, knowing John was right. 'I concede the point, John, but there is not a moment to be lost. Go to the king now, do all you can, and maybe the worst of the situation can be averted.'

'Very well.'

Cicely heard Francis stride away, his sharp steps echoing as he descended the staircase. She peeped out of the alcove, and John sprang back in alarm. 'Jesu! You risk a great deal by creeping around like this.' He pulled her into his arms and kissed her on the lips. His mouth was still cold from the outside air. Then he drew back to look into her eyes. 'You have eavesdropped, I take it?'

'I had no choice. I was coming to meet you. What is it about, John?'

'There are fresh, more disgusting rumours about my father and your sister. It is now being spread around that he beds her already and fully intends to make her his queen when Anne is dead. It is also said that he is poisoning Anne, to help her into eternity.'

Cicely was horrified. 'But who would stoop to say such things?' Lady Stanley, she thought, answering her own question.

John leaned back against the wall. 'Sir Francis believes he knows where the rumour began, but he can do nothing for lack of proof and lack of belief on the part of my father. It appears that on the day he was finally forbidden to go to the queen, my father was closeted with the Lancastrian

Archbishop of York on some matter or other. During the course of their conversation something arose concerning my father's obligation to remarry, and the question of a suitable bride. I know not the exact content, but the gist was plain and it was too much for my father to bear on that of all days. He was angry and in his rage he cried, "What would you have me do, marry my niece? I think *her* lineage should suffice for the purpose!" He meant nothing more than a heavy sarcasm, of that you may be sure, but since that day these rumours have been growing and spreading. The coincidence is too great! The archbishop is the source. God's blood and bones, if I had that conniving prelate here I would slit his sanctimonious gizzard and throw the pickings to the rats!'

Cicely touched his arm, a little frightened by his violence and hatred. 'It may be that the rumour began elsewhere.'

John snorted. 'There is little doubt in my mind. The archbishop is known to be thick with the Stanleys, and is thus a friend to Henry Tudor.' John gave her a quick smile. 'The irony of it all is that my father will not listen, he chooses to ignore the furore as being less than the dust on the ground. Sweet God, I cannot credit his actions sometimes. No, his *inactions*. Now I must do as Sir Francis begs, but I do not think I will be listened to any more than anyone else. Not in this.'

'Should I try?' she offered, although it was not something she relished.

'What would you say? Can you imagine how to broach such a subject? You would have to tell him that he is accused of incest.'

She drew back. 'I know.' She had told Richard of Bess's love, but how could she possibly tell him he was now accused of returning it physically? How could anyone tell him *that*?

'He needs to be told, Cicely, but not by you. I will do it, although how he will receive it I do not know.' He took her hand and drew it to his cheek. 'He is the one who matters in this, not Bess, but her name will have to be drawn into any outcome. You do understand?'

She nodded, for there was no choice. It had all gone too far, and Richard had to do something to stop it.

He kissed her knuckles one by one, and then her lips. 'Oh, Cicely Plantagenet, if only you know how much I long to lie with you . . . My dreams would surely shock you.'

'No more than mine would shock you,' she whispered.

He stepped away. 'I would tarry here all day but cannot delay the unpleasant task I have undertaken. Every moment counts.'

Accompanied by Bess and Cicely, Dame Elizabeth Grey approached the carved door of the king's rooms. A page announced them and they were led before Richard.

He stood alone and when the page had gone, the three women waited. His hands were clasped behind his back and from where Cicely stood, she saw how they fidgeted. She noticed his right hand, with the shortened little finger and the ruby on the thumb. Then he gestured towards some chairs, his rings catching the firelight. 'Ladies, I pray you be seated for I have something of great import to say, something that it grieves me beyond measure to have to raise at all.' He met Cicely's eyes, and she knew he was forced to speak of the rumours concerning Bess.

He paused as they took their places, his face serious and more than a little embarrassed. 'Dame Grey, I must tell you that there have arisen certain contemptible rumours concerning my intentions towards Bess.' He shifted his weight from one foot to the other, and when he continued there was hesitance in his voice. 'It is being suggested that I mean to marry her as soon as I am able to so do. I will not embarrass you with what else is being said. There is, of course, no truth whatsoever in any of this.' He looked directly at Bess.

Her face drained of colour and she swayed a little in her chair, but Elizabeth steadied her, gripping her elbow tightly and warningly.

Richard took a deep breath. 'Dame Grey, I had hoped to be able to ignore this infamy but there seems to be no glimmer of abatement in the story and so my only course must be to make a public denial of it. Please believe me when I say that I have no wish to involve Bess, but there are some aspects of this tale that *must* be silenced. If I allow the rumours to continue unquestioned then it may be assumed that there is indeed some truth in the allegation. I do what I am forced to do by unquiet tongues. For her sake as well as my own. Do you understand?'

Elizabeth stood. 'Your Grace, provided my daughter's name is not maligned, I will accept whatever decision you make. I, no more than you, wish this calumny to persist. Richard Plantagenet, I would have you know how I despise the perpetrators of such a story, for I know well how it must pain you at this very sad time.' There was genuine compassion in the words, but then she took a few steps closer, and extended a hand for him to kiss. It was a proud gesture that completely spoiled her expression of sympathy.

If Richard disapproved of her hauteur he gave no intimation, but drew her fingers towards his lips. His hair clung momentarily to her velvet sleeve. Cicely watched it, strand by strand, and how it tried to stay as he released her mother's hand. She watched his hair. Him.

They took their leave then, Bess distressed and fit to faint as she hurried after her mother. Cicely hesitated before following, as so often she did, unable to leave him without speaking. He had moved to the fireplace, where he stood with his head bowed.

Her heart went out to him again, and she put her hand on his arm.

'Cicely?'

She gazed into his eyes. 'I am so sorry for all this, Uncle.'

'Why? Is it your fault?' he asked with a glimmer of his old humour.

'No, but neither is it yours.'

He put his hand to her cheek. 'Ah, Cicely, my joy and comfort.'

'If I could take some of your grief away, I would. I cannot bear to think of how you must be feeling.'

His hand fell away. 'You would not wish to know how I am feeling, Cicely. I pray it is something you will never experience.' He hesitated, and then kissed her cheek. 'Go now, before my sorrows are indeed transferred to you.'

CHAPTER EIGHTEEN

On an eerie day in March, the gentle soul of Anne Neville slipped quietly away into blessed oblivion. Even the sun had been eclipsed in the sight of Richard's grief. The whole land stared in wonder at the half-sun that threw such a haunting light upon the realm, a strange semi-darkness without even birdsong to pierce the silence before the bells boomed out yet again for the death of royalty.

Richard did not attend the funeral, for it was not done, but his grief was plain enough. If anyone had ever believed he did not love his queen, they surely could not now. On that sorrowful day, Cicely had needed to be alone, and with the coming of evening sought the solace of her favourite place in the walled gardens. The daffodils were there again, not quite in full bloom but close. They saddened her, because it began to seem that their coming signalled the loss of a member of her family — her father, Richard's son, and now his queen. It was too much and suddenly she could no longer bear the garden. Catching up her heavy black skirts — for this time Richard did order the court into mourning — she made her way back into the palace.

He withdrew as much as he could. He rarely smiled, and his face was now so weary that he tore at Cicely's heart. She thought of him constantly, and yearned to spend at least a little time with him, to try to lift his spirits, for she knew how he thought and felt. But he did not send for her at all, and she did not dare to go unannounced. Perhaps he now shunned his second niece as well. He immersed himself in his duties, attending very few court functions, and leaning more and more on his only remaining son. As a result, Cicely again saw little of John.

As spring moved into the rich green of summer, Richard travelled through his dormant realm, making preliminary preparations for the now inevitable invasion by Henry Tudor. He came once more to that rocky fortress of sad memories, Nottingham, his Castle of Care. There he waited. It was the promise of battle, of the hand-to-hand fight, that invigorated him, and lifted him from the morass of his sorrows.

On a warm June evening, barely two weeks after the arrival of the court at Nottingham, he sent word to his two eldest nieces that he wished to see them. Their mother and younger sisters had stayed behind at the palace of Sheen, on the banks of the Thames upstream of Westminster. Dame Grey no longer desired to travel, nor did she have a taste for court life. Life was easier at Sheen.

Richard awaited them in his apartment, alone and surrounded as always by letters, papers and communications of all sorts; the acrid smell of melted wax hung in the still air. His ruby ring lay upon the table before him and he looked up quickly at their entry. He was slender in a tight black doublet and hose, and seemed more delicate by the depth of mourning. 'Ladies?'

They sank into deep curtseys and when Cicely rose, she found his eyes upon her. 'It seems a long time since last we spoke, Cicely.'

'It is, Uncle.'

'The circumstances have not permitted it.' He looked at Bess, acknowledging her with a nod, but no more. He had maintained an air of aloofness towards her. He did not cut her, or refuse to speak, but he could no longer be comfortable with her.

'Ladies, I have decided to send you to more congenial surroundings that are also safer. I speak of the castle of Sheriff Hutton in the county of Yorkshire.'

Bess's face changed. 'But . . . when are we to go, Uncle?'

He took a deep breath, his mouth twisting thoughtfully. 'The sooner the better, I would have you in safety before Tudor invades. Your wardrobes and whatever else you will require are to be sent ahead within the hour. Simply keep behind what you will need in the meantime. I wish you to leave two days hence . . .' He picked up a quill from the table, and stroked the shaft nervously.

'Two days?' Bess stared at him as if he had announced she was to go to the moon itself.

'Yes. Your destination is to be kept secret, for there are those who would wish to intercept you, and perhaps do you harm. Or worse.' He glanced at her again, in a reminder of Henry Tudor's sworn intention to make her his wife. 'You will not be alone, for your cousins the Earls of Lincoln and Warwick are to go with you, as well as my son John. Your brothers will join you at Sheriff Hutton. Oh, yes, they are still very much alive, even though my enemies would have it believed that I have had them murdered. You will be in Jack of Lincoln's charge. I regard him as my heir, and should anything happen to me, I intend him to assume the throne. Nothing is formal, but that is my wish. Jack is also at the head of the Council of the North, and therefore well placed to have care of you.'

Cicely lowered her eyes. She had learned that Jack's roving eye had settled upon Bess. Perhaps he would be a welcome distraction from Richard. She looked at her uncle again. Could any man distract from him? She doubted it. Very much.

Richard's tiredness was evident as he continued, 'You cannot take your ladies with you, for this is to be a swift journey, unhampered by frills and fancies. A maid has been found who will attend to you both. Her name is . . .' He shuffled the papers before him, searching for the maid's identity. 'Her name is Mary Kymbe and she is the daughter of a Lincolnshire gentleman loyal to me, Thomas Kymbe of Friskney, which manor is actually of Jack's holding. So she is not lowborn and must not be regarded as such. Is that understood?'

They both nodded.

'Good. Now, you are to obey Lincoln in everything. I have placed you under his protection and he is responsible for you. Disobey him and I will learn of it. Your route north will be feigned. You will leave Nottingham accompanied by a detachment of mounted men-at-arms, bearing the banners and colours of the three lords in the cavalcade. Your route will take you south, into a particularly dense part of Sherwood, and once there you will part company from your escort. The men-at-arms will continue south, with as much noise and display as can be achieved, and they will be accompanying a party that only pretends to be you. In the meantime you will ride north along the bed of a stream in order to leave no tracks. You will not pass through any hamlets, nor make your presence known to anyone. You will have to take shelter, of course, but there are certain priories that I know beyond doubt will keep faith with me. God willing, you will reach Sheriff Hutton without detection. You will be safe, and Henry Tudor none the wiser. I mean at all costs to protect those who are close to me in blood. From there, if the need should arise, you will be able to flee to the coast and the safety of my sister Margaret, Dowager Duchess of Burgundy. The countryside around Sheriff Hutton is strong for me and there is little chance of treachery from the inhabitants. Should the day go against me, there will be at least seven scions of the House of York alive and safe across the sea.' He paused and glanced at them. 'Have you questions?'

Something gave way in Bess, and she so far forgot herself as to run to kneel at his feet and seize his hand so fiercely that the quill bent. 'Do not send me away. My place is with you. Please!'

Cicely was dismayed to realize that her sister was finally going to put the nature of her love into words. And to his face. It was not the time. There would *never* be a right time, because he had already made his feelings plain.

'My mind is made up, Bess,' he began, clearly embarrassed. 'You will go to Sheriff Hutton and that is the end of it. I *must* protect you. All of you.' His tired eyes encompassed Cicely.

But Bess was distraught and remembered only that she loved him. 'Make me safe from the Tudor by marrying me yourself! He can never have me then! I love you more than life itself, and willingly offer myself as your wife. *Your* wife, not Henry Tudor's Yorkist token!'

A silence fell upon the room, broken only by the sounds from the courtyard. Richard disengaged his hand. 'Bess, I cannot be to you that which you wish and deserve. I am not worthy of your love.'

'You are! No man deserves it more!'

He looked to Cicely, who hurried to draw Bess away. 'Come, sweeting,' she said gently. 'This does you no good.'

He remained calm, and tried to be gentle. 'You *must* accept it, Bess. I am your uncle, and it is only as an uncle that I see you. I cannot and will not contemplate anything else. Please do not persist, for it distresses me as much as it distresses you.'

His eyes were upon Cicely again. What expression could she read there? Something, she knew not what, but he again seemed to almost say her name. Just with his glance.

Bess was still distressed. 'No, please . . .'

'I am sending you to Sheriff Hutton, Bess. The discussion is at an end.' Any further argument was terminated.

Bess nodded through her tears. Her red-gold Plantagenet hair spilled down over the shoulders of her mourning gown, and as she left, her blue eyes were bright with the incredible force of her love.

Cicely began to follow, but he spoke. 'No, Cicely, for I would speak with you a while.'

She should have been torn, because she knew Bess needed her, but she had no heart to go from him. And so she closed the door and returned. To him. Close enough to touch him if she wished.

He smiled sadly. 'I prayed she would never say it. The whole court may know but while she kept it unsaid . . .'

'She cannot help herself, and today the thought of being sent away from you was simply too much.'

He met her eyes. 'And what of you, Cicely? Are *you* content to be sent away from me?'

'No. I would stay with you as well. You have no idea how much I wish it.' She gazed at him. Going away from him at such a time as this was . . . heartbreaking. She did not want to go, because even though she would be with John, she would *not* be with Richard.

'I appear to have two very loyal nieces, one for the wrong reason, the other for the right.'

'You seem surprised.' She continued to gaze at him, trapped by the force of her feelings. 'You must have some inkling of how you affect others. It is not only because you have power and are king, it is something within you.'

'I have my share of detractors as well,' he reminded her, smiling.

She knew he was not unaware of anything. Perhaps it was as Jane Shore had said, he simply did not use his fascination as her father would have done. His character was too different, but even knowing him as she did — as she thought she did — in this the pages were firmly closed. She supposed she had been green to think a man of his intelligence could be deceived about himself, but it made no difference to how she felt towards him.

She tried to smile. 'You are not so innocent, I think.'

Amusement curved his lips. 'Do you suspect me of feigning ignorance, Cicely?'

'Possibly.'

'I should not let you in so much.'

'You cannot entirely keep me out.'

He looked into her eyes. 'I know that too.'

'It makes no difference to me whether you know your power over others or not, only that you do not misuse it. Now you stand higher in my estimation.'

'Cicely—'

But she continued. 'I find you exhilarating to be with, and I am always so glad when you send for me. Or make me stay. You . . . are very dear to me. So dear.' Why had she said it twice? Why did she want him to know how profound she suddenly knew her feelings to be? Yes, her feelings ran far too deep.

There was a silence, during which she became ever more aware of him. It was as if the air crackled. Then he tracked a finger briefly down her cheek. 'You know so well how to warm my heart.'

Suddenly his touch influenced her in a very different way from any before. Everything about him bound her with fleshly desires. She loved him more each time they spoke. He was so much more than an uncle, so much more than . . . Her thoughts halted, for she was shocked by their unexpected path. A curtain was drawing back, allowing her to see within herself. Now, the glimmer of realization dawned so brightly through her that she could hardly breathe. Her love for him was no longer what it should be. Perhaps it never had been.

'Cicely?'

As he searched her eyes she wondered if he would see what had hitherto been unacknowledged.

When she did not answer, he severed the moment by going to the window. 'If it is the time for honesty, you should know how much of a pleasure and comfort you have been to me since you came to court. I have always felt able to converse with you, to seek your comment, and know that it will be worth seeking.' He paused and looked at her again. 'When we met again that first time I was taken with how earnest and direct you were . . . still are. It was so refreshing. Once you forgot to be frightened of me, that is.'

'I was childish.' Her newly opening eyes could not move from him.

'No, you were not childish. I have never found you *that.* You were simply afraid because your head had been filled with untruths about me. Cicely, if the world were to abound with such as you, it would be a very much better place, I think. I trust my son understands full well what a very fortunate fellow he is,' he continued. 'Have I already said that to you?'

She still could not look away from him, his thoughtful eyes, the lean curves of his mouth, his hair, his smile, his voice, his very weariness. . . . Everything. *Everything.* Now the comprehension almost blinded her. Sweet God, she loved him as Bess did! *She* loved him, and had done so from that same moment at the abbey. He had *always* meant everything, always drawn her in a way not even John had done. The knowledge was so dazzling that it seemed to blaze throughout her consciousness.

She had to say something. Anything. 'I — I am equally fortunate to have John . . . Your Grace.' Suddenly she could not address him as her uncle. Not now.

'Are we to be formal? Why?' He returned to her.

She trembled as she sought words. 'I cannot think of you as my uncle,' she answered unguardedly.

'Well, I *am* your uncle, I fear.' He paused, bowing his head for a moment. 'But if you cannot address me as that, *please* do not make me your king. I would rather be your friend.'

She did not want him to be uncle, king or friend. She wanted so much more. She wanted *him.*

Their eyes met, his unfathomable, hers still wide with her shattering new insight. She saw him in a blur of sudden tears. 'Please do not be kind to me, for I cannot bear it,' she whispered.

'Cicely?' He raised her chin. Always he would touch her, and always she would be glad of it. Such small gestures, so natural to him, so beloved to her. But now . . . now she did not have the sophistication to cope with it.

'You stop my heart, can you not see it?' she said at last, only too heedful that every moment she was with him like this, the greater the peril of following Bess into an awful admission.

'I would not do anything to hurt you, not for the world.' He hesitated, and then took a curl of her long dark russet hair as it fell past her shoulders. He spread it slowly between his fingers and thumb, an attention that was sensuous and bewitchingly enticing. His hair, her hair. So similar, so subtly stirring, rich and erotic.

Her tears stung. What had happened here today? How had it suddenly become so clear? How could she have failed to recognize how she felt about him? And yet . . . when he spoke to her as he now did, behaved as he now did, how could she have ever *not* known?

'Have I offended you?' he asked, taking his hand away.

'No.' She pressed her lips tightly together in an effort to control herself. 'I — I am afraid for you. When I leave here I will not know what happens. I will not know if you are safe.'

'What will happen is that I will trounce the Tudor upstart. I will be safe and then you will return.' He smiled again, but there was a shadow over him.

It was a shadow she could not bear to see. She was so acutely conscious of him that her whole body trembled. The room was filled with tension, overflowing with unspoken words and feelings that it was hard to draw breath. Finally she understood herself. She was guilty, exhilarated, confused and yielding, but above all joyful to see at last what had been there all along. 'I love you,' she whispered, a tear travelling slowly down her cheek.

He did not seem to hear, but brushed the tear aside. 'No weeping for me, please,' he said, hesitating but then permitting his thumb to stroke her.

Was it simply comfort? Or did it mean much more? She only knew that he was temptation itself, sin itself, and she had no defence. Nor did she seek any. Her fate was sealed, and there was no going back. She found her voice. 'There *must* be tears. Do you not see that I love you? I love you as Bess does, and I cannot stand the pain.'

'Oh, my sweet, sweet Cicely . . .' He whispered her name, and she saw more in his eyes in that moment than she had ever seen before.

'Do not hate me, please,' she begged, so overcome that she felt she drowned in the flood of self-knowledge that inundated everything. Common sense was denied her now, and she stepped right to him and slipped her arms around his neck and allowed her parted lips to move longingly over his cheek. She had become the very embodiment of love, a being of sheer desire, all restraint cast aside just for this one illicit moment of holding him, not as her uncle or king, but as the man she longed for. She hardly knew her lips dragged achingly towards his, with a carnal need of such passion and meaning that it laid waste everything she had ever believed of herself.

At any moment he would push her away, distraught that she, the niece he trusted, was as guilty as her sister.

CHAPTER NINETEEN

But Richard did not push her away. Cicely felt his momentary resistance, and heard the brief catch of his breath. Once again he was confronted by a niece's desire . . . but was this different? Would he be as repulsed as before, and thrust her away from him? Would he look upon her with disgust and disbelief?

Slowly, at first hesitantly — reluctantly, even — his arm slid around her waist and he drew her closer. His hand went to the nape of her neck and his fingers pushed richly into her warm hair. Her heart threatened to halt as he began to return her kiss. It was not the kiss of an uncle, for it burned her lips with its potency. He was no fond kinsman now, but a lover, ardent, aroused and unchecked.

He pulled her even closer, enveloping her in his arms and kissing her as if he would blend her body into his. She had never felt so much, or so completely. He tasted of mint, so cool, fresh and clean, and yet his lips were not cool, they were warm and pliable, cherishing and delighting her senses. She was weightless, adrift on pure emotion, loved and loving . . . until he drew back, brought to cold sanity by the degree to which he had given in. He removed her arms hastily and stepped away.

'No! For you are my niece, my niece!' Overcome, he ran his hand agitatedly through his hair. 'You should go, Cicely, and forget this has happened.'

Tears leapt to her eyes again. 'Forget? Never!'

'Please.'

'Being your niece does not stop me from loving you as I should not,' she whispered, so choked that her words were almost incomprehensible. 'I did not know. I did not know that the feelings within me were of this kind. Until now. Suddenly I see it all so clearly. If I embarrass you, disgust you, I cannot help it.'

He caught her hand and linked his fingers impulsively through hers. 'No, Cicely, you do not embarrass me, and you certainly do not disgust me. Do you think I could kiss you so if that were the case? You are not at fault. In your innocence, you did not know this for what it is, but I have known all along.'

She gazed at him through tears. What was he saying?

'I know what I do, Cicely. I am not an untested boy, and certainly not the innocent you may have thought me to be. Since my marriage I have never played with fire in my private life, because I have seen what it can do. So no matter how great the temptation, I have remained my own master. If that has made me the target of coarse curiosity, I could not care a jot. Your father gave in to temptation time and time again and eventually it ruined him. Forgive me, Cicely, but you know that the man he was in the end was not the man he had been in the beginning.'

'Yes, I know.'

'And now, *now,* I have permitted fire to enter my private life, and I am in danger of letting it consume us both. You do not deserve that. I am by far old enough to know better. You have every right to expect more of me.'

She could not grasp his meaning; her thoughts were spinning so out of control that she could only fix upon that one word, 'old'. 'You are but thirty-two, I am sixteen. I see nothing wrong in that.'

'In your seventeenth year?' He trapped her glance.

'Yes.'

'Cicely, have you not realized what I have just confessed to you?'

'I cannot think. I am in such . . . I do not know what I am in, save that it is more wonderful than I had ever dreamed. I love you, and that is all that matters to me.'

He searched her eyes. 'Oh, sweet Cicely, you say I stop your heart, but you have demolished mine.' He turned away. 'As for age, if that is what concerns you, you are old enough for it not to be any problem, but that does not matter because I am your uncle. Your uncle, Cicely. It is forbidden, and even if a thousand dispensations were to be granted, in my eyes it would still be wrong.'

'But not in mine.'

He smiled. 'No, not in yours, but there are rules, bars that should not be crossed, and this is one of them. I have not set those rules, but I do want to observe them. At this moment I am not doing so. Nor have I for some time. Since you, Cicely. Think back. Have I *ever* behaved towards you as just your uncle and king? Have I treated you as I have everyone else? The answer is no. I have often wanted to be with you, and have always made the opportunity.'

John's words echoed within her. *I feel that there is someone else he thinks of. A woman.* She stood there, her body and mind still in the grip of his kiss. 'You have done nothing wrong,' she said then. Nothing he had *ever* done to her had been wrong.

'Yes, Cicely, I have.'

'Then so have I,' she answered with raw honesty. 'I can hardly credit how blind I have been, but today, at last, I can see. Do you say that my love is the less for being so close to you in blood?'

'Please listen to what I am saying, for I think you do not understand. I feel too much for you, Cicely, and it is wrong. The fault is mine, not yours, because I have done precious little to prevent this, and I am the one who should know better. It was always within my power to stop myself. Now it is too late.'

He felt too much for her. He had said it, and meant it. The world seemed to move too slowly around her, and she was rooted, unable to do anything but gaze at the man she loved so very much. 'But you do not really want to stop yourself, any more than I do,' she breathed. 'I know it is wrong to feel as I do for you, but it is also too perfect to be wrong. With every second that passes now I am deeper in your heart, as you are in mine. It is what I want. What we both want. Do you not see this love for its beauty?'

'Yes, of course I see it, but you must accept the truth about me, Cicely. I am a hypocrite. Because of you, my love for Anne faltered in the end.' He paused. 'Not that she ever truly loved me. I know that. I have always known it.'

Her heart was igniting as she realized more and more that he felt for her as she felt for him. 'I do not know how *any* woman could not love you completely, utterly, without hesitation or doubt,' she said softly. 'What is there about you that *cannot* be loved? Nothing. Nothing at all.'

He smiled gently. 'Perhaps that is why I am so drawn to you, Cicely. I see in you what you see in me. I have always thought of you too often and too much. I have failed those who mean the most, especially you. And there is John. I behave as if pleased to permit him to marry you, when all the time I want you myself. I love you, Cicely, and not as your uncle.'

He loved her. He *loved* her. She could not speak. Could not breathe. All sound had deadened, except for his words. And they were so sweet to her that she could have wept.

'Cicely, my guilt and remorse is such that it weighs upon my heart. If I could turn time back upon itself and put a leash upon my weakness, I would, but now it is beyond my will to undo what I feel for you. It has never happened to me before, this feeling of intolerable need, this worship of your smile, of everything about you. So do not see me as a shining knight, beyond reproach, because every time I look at you, I make a mockery of my responsibilities.'

'No!'

Richard managed a regretful laugh. 'Our love is incestuous, Cicely. It is an ugly word, but true nevertheless. It is the self-same sin I stood up in public to deny so strenuously when it came to Bess. The self-same sin I have only just told *her* I could never countenance. Of course I could not countenance it with her, I do not *love* her. But I think of committing that sin with you, Cicely. I think of it often, and I long to do it. The gossip was so right, but it alighted upon the wrong niece. My honour is as distorted as my back.'

New tears sprang to her eyes. 'Please do not describe yourself like that. In my eyes you are peerless, and if you desire me, then I am the happiest of creatures. I love you as you are, as you always have been and always will be.'

'Oh, Cicely, will you *never* see me clearly?'

'I *always* see you clearly,' she cried, her voice breaking, 'and never more so than now. If you had another chance, and time really could be reversed, would you not have returned my kiss? Would you have rejected me?'

His eyes were expressive. 'I should say yes.'

She longed to go to him again, to steal another kiss from those lips, but something about him prevented it. She could only stand there, absorbing every beloved feature. 'I may be like Bess, but I am a thousand times luckier because I know what it is to be kissed by you. Not just a fond buss upon the cheek, or a polite bow over my hand, but a kiss upon my lips. The kiss of the man, not the uncle. The kiss of the lover.'

'Please, Cicely, for each word shames me more.'

'We have not lain together, we have done nothing wrong. A kiss is not a sin.'

'That kiss was, and you know it,' he countered. 'I feel so much for you that even now, when everything that has been unsaid is suddenly in the open, its hazards so manifest, I am in danger of letting my heart rule my head.'

She gazed at him, so tempting, so alone, so racked with guilt. The passion he inspired in her was almost insupportable. '*Please* do not turn me away from you now, for I could not bear it. I will go to Sheriff Hutton, I will do whatever you want of me, but please do not deny me your friendship. Do not be as cool with me as you are with Bess. I do not know how she can bear it, for I know it would surely deny me the will to live.'

Her words moved him. 'How can you still feel this for me? I have used you shabbily. I *know* how sad you are for me, how warm-hearted and gentle you are, how much you care for me, and today I made you stay with me. I knew it was wrong, that I was courting a danger that should never even exist, but still I did it. I could not prevent myself, because I did not want you to go with Bess, but to stay and feel for me what I feel for you. And you do, Cicely, you do. Now it has led to this. I have what I want — your love — but I cannot have you in the fullest sense of the word. If I could make you my queen, I would. Do you understand? That is how much I feel for you. I would honour you as no other, not even Anne, whom God knows, I loved at first. You rise above everything, Cicely, for you are my soul's mirror. With you beside me there is nothing I could not do. You make me feel . . . invincible. You comfort me so much that I cannot bear it when you are not with me.'

'You say such beautiful things,' she whispered.

'Maybe I do, but no uncle should feel that way. You are my brother's child, Cicely. Too close. Far too close.'

'And you blame yourself for what has happened tonight? I *made* you kiss me.'

He smiled. 'No, Cicely, I let you persuade me. There is a great difference. I surrendered without even a token pretence. For those brief moments I could hold you as I wanted to, kiss you as I wanted to. I knew what I did, that I made you love me even more. It was what I wanted so much. Your love. You.' He drew a long breath. 'I will always want you, but it is time to think of you, not me. It may be belated, but I *must* face my accountability. You need me to behave as I should, not as I wish.'

'As you *should*? No, that is not what I want! If you tell me to go now, and forget these past minutes, then I will, but without *ever* forgetting or discarding my love.' At last she went closer, to touch his sleeve with a hand that shook so much she could only stop it by gripping the rich cloth. '*Do* you want me to go?'

He was silent for a moment. 'Again, I should say yes.'

'But will you?' She made him look at her. 'Will you?'

'Cicely, I have just told you that I manipulated what has happened here tonight, that I contemplated your seduction and even began it. Do you not realize it?'

'I kissed you,' she repeated.

'No, Cicely. I enticed you. I played upon your feelings, and knew exactly what I was doing.' He held her eyes. 'I want there to be no misapprehension, for it is too important. If I do not say all this now, there will come a day when you finally do realize it, and then you may despise me.'

She hesitated. 'Why do you not see that there is nothing you can do that will change my love or regard? You can hurt me, yes. With one word, one cruel dismissal, you could destroy my heart so that it will never recover. But you cannot stop me loving you. Maybe it is now you who do not understand. Whatever it was that you instigated this evening, I am glad of it, because if you had not, we would not be standing here now, saying these things to each other. We would not know we loved each other.'

'Oh, I would still know I loved you,' he said a little wryly, 'but if I had left you alone, would you still feel as you do now, I wonder?'

'Maybe not tonight, but I was close to the realization. Just how many more times could I have been with you and not seen the truth? I have always known I loved you, I merely mistook the nature of that love. Even so, I knew it went too far, knew there was something too strong and different. You are an exceptional man, Richard Plantagenet, and if you thought of seducing me tonight, I wish you had, for by now I would have had all of you, and that would make me . . . Oh, I do not quite know, save that I would nurse my good fortune into eternity.' She ran a fingertip down his cheek, as he had earlier to her. 'I have been sleeping, but am now awake — to a love that has been waiting to be accepted.'

He was affected, and although he looked away, she was sure she saw tears in his eyes. 'It does not matter how we feel, Cicely, we still have to turn from this. It cannot be spoken of again, and we cannot let it be known in any way. To anyone. Certainly not to John.' His eyes became suddenly anxious. 'Not to John,' he said again.

'How can you imagine I would confide this? To do so would hurt him, but it would also hurt you, and that is something I could *never* do. I still love John. I will be all to him that he desires, but you alone will be in my deepest heart. Not even my confessor will know, for I value it too much to put it in danger.'

'Your confessor would not believe you anyway. He considers women to be incapable of telling the truth.' Richard observed with faint irony.

'All I am saying is that I will never fail you. Never.'

'I do not deserve you, Cicely,' he whispered. 'Believe me, it is best you go now. We should never be alone like this again.'

She could not go, not just yet. 'Please, I ask one thing of you.'

'Ask whatever you will.' His voice shook.

'One last kiss, to sustain me forever.'

'Cicely . . .'

'You cannot cast me away when my eyes are newly opened and my heart is newly bursting with this love. You cannot be so harsh.'

'I do not cast you away, Cicely, I protect you.'

'I do not want to be protected *from* you, I want to be *with* you, always, but I know I cannot. I know that if what has happened between us today were to be broadcast far and wide, it would destroy you. I love you too much for that, but I *will* have one small token, one unbroken kiss that I can always feel upon my lips, always be able to share with you again in my thoughts.'

'Oh, Cicely,' he breathed. 'You do not know how you splinter what is left of my heart.'

'Then kiss me. Let me understand, let me feel you close one last time. Must I go upon my knees to *implore* you?' Her voice was an almost silent whisper. '*Please.*' She moved closer, willing him to hold her again, kiss her again. He *must* grant her this small concession, this boon that would always mean everything.

She saw how he tried to resist, but his own feelings were too intense. He took her hand and drew her steadily towards him, holding her gaze as he did. 'We both know better than this, Cicely.'

'I do not care.'

She closed her eyes as his arms moved around her in that beloved way, only now it *was* intimate, and she wanted so very much more. If he was reluctant, he gave no sign. The kiss was sweet and true as his parted lips played with hers, teasing, arousing, yearning. He held her to him as if he would never let go, and she was vibrant with love, sinking weakly against him, so lost in desire and emotion that her existence centred only on him. His hair brushed her cheek, his livery collar was cold, his body lean and strong, his arousal tangible. It was a kiss that barely an hour before would have been unthinkable. She would not have believed anyone who foretold it. She knew it was wrong, forbidden, shocking and would be named by most to be unnatural, but she would not deny it. Ever.

He slid his hand to the nape of her neck again, twining his fingers in her hair as he had before. She closed her eyes and leaned her head back as his lips moved upon the pulse of her throat. She was so fortunate, so very fortunate. He, who was so enthralling and to whom she was so devoted, was in her arms, and she was as close to ecstasy as seemed possible.

Her hands roamed adoringly over his damaged back, and she kissed the rich cloth on the shoulder that was a little higher than the other. On this man the physical imperfection was astonishingly pleasing. He seemed so delicate, and yet was so strong, and his face . . . his face was so full of grace. She was kissing the lips she had looked at so often without understanding the wantonness of her feelings. Now she was with him as never before, and she did not want it to end.

If he had chosen to step further beyond the bounds in those moments, she would have stepped with him. There would be no hesitation, no second thought, no regret. She craved consummation, wanted to lie naked with him and give completely. She wanted him to fondle her breasts, to stroke her, love her, be inside her, *need* her as she needed him. Those feelings of suppressed emotion, of unnamed, undeniable desires, were now fully recognized for what they were: a need to love and be loved. She had known it of herself before today, but now, *now* it was tangible fact. At last she had a face to give to the lover she had only imagined before. This man was the reason she lived. No other would ever mean as much.

But this second kiss was to be as broken as the first, for they were interrupted by a knock upon the door. 'Your Grace?' Sir Robert Percy! They broke guiltily apart, and Richard ushered her behind a curtain and put his finger to his lips.

He paused to compose himself, and then called. 'Enter!'

'Your Grace, it seems the Lady Cicely has been missed.' Robert looked curiously at Richard's flushed face.

'And what has that to do with me?'

Robert shifted uncomfortably. 'Well, nothing, Your Grace.' He could hardly point out that the king had called his second niece back when the first had left.

Richard indicated the apartment at large. 'Do you see her, Robert? Perhaps I have her in a cupboard?'

'No, Your Grace, I only wondered . . . if she had mentioned where she was going.'

'I am not party to my niece's plans, Robert. I am sure she will soon reappear.' Richard waved his startled friend away, and the door closed quickly behind him.

Cicely emerged slowly from hiding. This was the only way it could ever be, for theirs was a love that was so secret and unacceptable that it must *never* be known to others. He spoke of protecting her, but she had to protect him too.

'I *must* go this time, must I not?' she said. 'I cannot try to delay the moment of parting?' she said quietly.

He caught her hand, linking his fingers warmly between hers. 'Wisdom demands it,' he said gently.

'Will you ever speak to me again? Send for me again?'

'Of course I will speak to you, Cicely. Jesu, I could not endure without at least that consolation, but whether I will send for you as I have in the past . . . perhaps that is not a very good idea. How long could we resist temptation? How long before we do lie together? It is as well that in two days you will go to Sheriff Hutton, and then, well, who knows what lies ahead?'

She knew he was thinking of the inevitable invasion, and her fingers tightened between his. 'Have faith in yourself, and you will triumph over Henry Tudor.'

'On my own? Cicely, I do not know who will be at my side and who will have deserted me. Oh, I have good friends and supporters, but there are others who would stab me in the back at their first opportunity. I will fight with whatever I have.'

'And you will not fail,' she whispered, pressing his palm fervently to her lips.

He closed his eyes. 'Please go, Cicely. Use the other door.' He indicated a door she had never noticed before. 'You are less likely to be seen that way. It was much used by your father for —' He stopped.

'For the same reason?'

Now he gave a reluctant smile. 'I fear so.'

'Let me stay a little longer. Just a little longer,' she pleaded, wishing she was not suddenly so weak.

'Please, Cicely, for we have no innocence now.'

'Nor have we sinned,' she said again.

'Not fully, but we want to.'

She nodded. 'Yes, we want to.'

This might be the very last moment she was ever alone with him, and she still found it impossible to simply go as he asked. Was that a sign of her foolish youth and inexperience? If it was, she needed to overcome it, but words and willpower had deserted her. The parting was such torment that all she could do was sink to her knees, wrap her arms tightly around his thighs and rest her cheek against him.

'I will always love you,' she whispered. 'If you could look into my heart, you would see all you could ever wish to. I belong to you.'

'And I to you, Cicely. And I to you.' He ran his fingertips over her hair. 'But now, as you love me, go before you unman me. I would not weep like a babe before you.' He bent to help her to her feet.

Choking back a sob, she wrenched herself away and ran to the other door, dragged back the bolt on the door and ran out of the royal apartments into a maze of small passages she had never known existed. She found a corner where no one would come, and there gave in to sobs that racked her body. No one saw her, no one could ever know what had happened and could never happen again. Her heart was rending for the love that could never be openly acknowledged, and yet was so essential to her.

Her heart also broke because she betrayed John. And because of her, Richard had too. She was still a maiden, but not in her heart, which belonged to Richard and only to him. Now she knew too well how Bess felt. And how Anne felt too. It was a terrible thing to love so much and yet not be able to have the object of that love.

And how could she ever face John after this? Or Bess? She was unfaithful to them both, and did not know if she could ever conceal it. But even though her conscience twisted within her, she did not want to undo a single moment of being with Richard.

'You *must* hide it, Cicely Plantagenet,' she whispered. 'Not for yourself, but for him.'

Slowly she regained her composure, and at last felt able to make her way back to the apartment she shared with Bess. She felt like Judas, because *she* was the niece who had Richard's love, and it was a beloved secret that could never be given a voice. Except to him.

CHAPTER TWENTY

It was a day later, the eve of their departure for Sheriff Hutton, when she next saw John, who had been entrusted with preparations for the journey and had to deal with them alongside his obligations to his father. She was on the castle parapet, watching the army encampments in the distance as Richard's forces gathered for whatever the coming days would bring. She could hardly bear to think of it, because he would be in such danger. He had ordered no more wearing of black, and so she was in fawn, a subtle colour that seemed suitable.

'Your thoughts, my love?'

She turned quickly, and John smiled at her. She returned the smile. It was much easier than she had feared, because she did still love him, just not in quite the same way she had previously believed.

He came close, glanced around to see who was near, and then pulled her to him for a moment, brushing his lips to hers. Then he released her and was discreet once more. 'One thing I look forward to at Sheriff Hutton is the chance to be with you more. It is the *only* thing to which I look forward, because as God is my witness, I want to be with my father.'

'He would have you safe, John.'

'I know.' He leaned on the parapet and looked out over the city. 'What were you so intent upon?'

'I was wishing Henry Tudor had never been born.'

'Ah. A worthy wish.'

She joined him, and they were shoulder to shoulder between the battlements. 'Will Richard be betrayed, John?'

He did not answer.

'I cannot bear to think of it.'

'Do you think *I* can? And he is sending me away. I am his son and should fight at his side, to the very last breath. Instead I will be lolling at Sheriff Hutton, doing nothing at all.'

'You will be staying alive, John, and that is all he wants of you.'

'It is not enough for me. It shames me.'

She straightened in surprise. 'Shames you? Oh, John, I had no idea that is how you felt.'

'I do not always say what I think,' he answered, straightening too.

'Does he know?'

'No. He has enough on his shoulders without my whining.'

He took a lock of her hair, parting the strands just as his father had done, and for a moment, only a moment, she was with Richard again.

John saw the nuance cross her face. 'What is it?'

'Sometimes you are so like him that . . .'

'Yes?'

'I do not know, it is simply . . . a great likeness.'

He looked at her. 'I do not think it displeases you.'

'What do you mean?' A pang of alarm struck through her.

'Simply that I know how high he rides in your esteem. Not in the same way as your sister's, God be thanked, but you *do* favour him.'

She forced herself to meet his gaze without giving anything away. 'How could I not? He has always been very kind, and I love him for it.'

'I am told he's desirable,' John said wryly.

'I did not say I found him desirable!' she said quickly.

'No, I know that.' His hand rested reassuringly on her arm. 'Please do not think I was suggesting anything, Cicely, for I was only going to say that he sleeps alone, as he has for some time now, the queen having been so frail. He could have any number of ladies of the court, but he takes no one. At least, I do not think he does, although I have already said I do suspect there is someone.' He smiled, but then pressed his lips together. 'There is a lot of pressure on him to find a new queen, but he has no stomach for it. He knows his advisers are at work. They seem to favour a Spanish princess who is known to desire a pious life, cloistered away in some religious house or other. Can you imagine such a sanctimonious slab of Iberian stone in my father's bed? I certainly cannot. He needs a woman's warmth and love, not her constant prayers.'

'Yes.'

'He could have any woman he chose — well, almost any — yet he does nothing about it. I do not understand him, but I certainly wish I knew his secret.'

'You have me, sir. Surely you do not long for more?' She teased, and hated herself for it.

'I do not have *enough* of you, that is the problem. That is another reason to wish Henry Tudor had never drawn breath.'

She smiled, and caught his hand to kiss it. 'I love you, John of Gloucester.' It was not a lie.

'And I love you, but already I must leave you. My father has a long list of tasks for me and I have yet to complete even half of them, but I saw you up here and was determined to spend some moments with you.' He began to move away, but then paused. 'I may not see you again before we leave tomorrow.'

'But then we will be together.'

'Yes.' He looked at her for a moment, seeming on the point of saying something, but then he hurried away.

She remained where she was, feeling so full of guilt that it almost made her feel sick. Guilt. Because she loved where she should not, and must be dishonest about it.

Her heart was heavy as she left the battlements, and descended through the castle, but then, without warning, she saw Richard. He was coming towards her, accompanied by Francis and Robert.

Richard's tread was as agitated as his voice was irritated. 'So help me, Francis, if you mention Spanish princesses to me one more time, I will put my hands around your throat!'

'But, Your Grace . . .'

'Enough!' Then Richard saw her, but continued to speak to Francis.

She sank into a curtsey, her skirts billowing. 'Uncle.'

'Cicely.' He came forward to raise her, his hand resting beneath her elbow as it had numerous times before, but now the physical contact meant so much more to them both.

Her entire body seemed to lurch within, from her heart and breasts, to those places between her legs where she longed for him most. Those muscles now clenched with the sheer joy and excitement of being close to him again. She gazed at him, the longing almost intolerable, but he alone knew how she felt, because she had sufficient control over herself not to give the truth of it to anyone else.

'I hope I find you well, Cicely?' he enquired.

She smiled. 'Yes, Uncle.'

'I will miss your sweet company when you go to Sheriff Hutton.'

'And I yours.'

They gazed at each other, and then he extended his hand for her to kiss, a signal that the meeting was at an end, but as she bent her lips to his skin, the emotion that gripped her was akin to torture because, unseen by the others, he squeezed her fingers.

She straightened again knowing her face was flushed, but it was not something she could help. Were her eyes too dark now? Did they tell tales upon her desire? Did they reveal to the entire world how much she loved this man whom unkind fate had made her uncle? Robert was looking at her. What was his expression? Had he realized something?

Richard inclined his head and walked on without looking back. But she did, she looked back until he and his companions had passed from her view. Even then she stood there, exulting because she could still feel the pressure of his hand and still bask in the warmth of his eyes.

The night before the departure for Sheriff Hutton was clear and starry. A shaft of moonlight slanted into the uncurtained bed where Cicely lay awake and Bess slept beside her.

She knew Richard was in the royal apartments, for there had been a meeting there late in the evening, but was he alone now? The warren of little passages that led up so secretly to his rooms was on her mind, for it offered another chance to go to him. He had told her that everything must end between them, but she knew he said it because he had to, not because he wanted to. And she had looked into his eyes again and seen his longing.

One thing alone kept her where she was, and that was the fear of his anger. If she went to him, would she test him too much? Would he lose patience, heed his conscience and send her away? She lay there, wanting so much, and daring so little. But then came the inconceivable possibility that she would ride from here in the morning and never see him again. What if he *was* to be bought and sold by those who professed to be his friends? What if he faced Henry Tudor and forfeited his life through treachery? What if that were to be the case, and she had lain *here* instead of going to him?

Such a thing, no matter how unthinkable, was so stark and cruel that she sat up, her dark hair tumbling over the shoulders of her ivory-coloured night robe. She could not stay here, not when she loved so very much. If he was angry with her, then so be it, but at least she would have been true to herself. And to him. She needed to give him her love, *all* of it, and for that she was willing to risk his displeasure.

She slipped from the bed without disturbing Bess, and flung her dark cloak around herself, because it would hide the paleness of her night robe. She did not want to be seen as she made her way through the castle. Starlight pierced every window she passed, and her bare feet made no sound. She did not encounter anyone.

It was only when she saw the door through which she had left his apartments before that it occurred to her it might be bolted on the inside. To leave it otherwise would place him in danger of murder. All was quiet beyond it, and there was no light shining beneath. Was he alone? What if there was someone with him after all? What if he was not even there, but had been called away upon some duty or other?

She faced the door, her hand upon the cold iron of the latch. Was she about to ruin everything they had? Should she knock? Should she turn away? With sudden resolve she lifted the latch, and to her surprise the door gave way before her. The room beyond was silver with moonlight, and she could see the table scattered with documents in need of his signature and seal.

She went inside, glancing all around for him, and at last saw him standing at the window, outlined against the moonlight as he looked at the army campfires and torches beyond the city. He wore a loose, floor-length robe — black brocade, she thought — and he did not glance around, so she did not know if he was aware of her or not. But then he spoke.

'One step more, Cicely, and our sin is as good as committed.'

He turned, his robe parting slightly. He wore nothing beneath. For a moment she saw all of him, his unequal shoulders, his irregular body, lean but not gaunt, pale, with dark hairs on his chest and loins. His loins . . . She had seen such things before, but this was different. This was *him,* and a quiver of new excitement stirred within her.

And so she took that one more step, and did it gladly. 'I have come to be with you, however you will have me, because in the morning I will go away from you and—' She broke off.

'And you may never see me again?' he finished for her.

'Do not say it,' she breathed.

He came closer and brushed against her as he stretched past to push the bolt across. She felt his warmth, and the scent of costmary on his robe and skin.

Her concern was his safety. 'It should always be locked, for your protection.'

'I do not wish to be protected from you, Cicely. That is the only reason it is open, because I hoped you would come. But it must be bolted now, because neither of us intends to do what is right.' He unfastened her cloak and tossed it aside, so that she stood in her night robe, pale and ethereal in the moonlight.

'But what we intend *is* right,' she breathed, 'because we love.'

'Oh, Cicely, I pray you will not come to regret this. I pray you do not awaken one morning and hate me because I am your uncle and should still, even now, send you from me.'

She looked into his eyes, those tired but memorable grey eyes that seemed to know everything about her. 'That will never happen,' she said.

'There could be . . . consequences.'

A child. Yes, she knew that. 'Whatever the consequences of lying with you, I will not change. You have not allowed me to enter this without knowing what I do, or without knowing how you feel. You have laid bare your own conscience, but it makes not one whit of difference. You can never turn me from you. I love you so much, want you so much, that nothing else matters. Nothing. So do not try to reason with me, for it cannot be done. If I do not make love with you tonight, it will be something I will regret for the rest of my existence. And so will you. You are *all* that matters in my life. My feelings for you are *that* complete. You are a treasured gift that is within my grasp, and I intend to reach for you. We both know this is right. We know what is happening to us and we know its importance.' She smiled gently. 'We are already one, Richard, and it only remains that we consummate an established fact. I do not wish to give myself to any other man. It must be you, because you are love itself.'

She undid the throat ribbons that gathered the voluminous folds of her night robe and allowed the garment to fall about her feet. It was so right to show herself to him. This was not to be a *surrender* of her chastity, it was to be a giving of it, freely, lovingly, and without any vestige of guilt or wrongdoing. She moved to him, sliding her arms around his neck as she had before. 'You do not seduce me or manipulate me now, for this is *my* doing,' she whispered, pressing her body to his and reaching up to kiss his mouth.

He returned her desire, and almost lifted her from her feet with the force of his embrace. His mouth demanded so much, gave so much. He had called her his mirror, and so she was, reflecting and revealing, hiding nothing. His hands moved longingly over her, sometimes to her back, sometimes into her hair, sometimes to her buttocks as he held her against his aroused loins. Wildly ravishing sensations erupted through her because it was him. Richard.

She slipped her hands beneath the black brocade of his robe and explored him too, his distorted back, his waist, his hips, and she was so consumed with love and desire that her inner muscles did not cease their urgent response. Ripples of enticing pleasure danced through her, and enticed still more as he caressed her.

'I love you, Cicely, so much that I . . .' He drew back gently, taking her face in his hands. 'That I have no words to describe my feelings at this moment.'

'Words are not needed,' she whispered.

'Cicely, you do know my honesty in this?'

'Of course. You do not hide pages from me now.'

He smiled. 'No, you see me as I am.'

'And you see my honesty too?'

His hand rested lovingly against her cheek. 'You have never been dishonest, Cicely.'

'Nor have you. Not really. You simply did not tell me what you felt. There is a difference.'

'My words turned upon me again?'

'Yes, because I will not have you blame yourself for everything. You had done nothing wrong when I realized what my love for you really was, you merely confronted me with it. I did not run then, nor do I now.'

He caught her hand to lead her into the bedchamber where he always slept alone. There she turned to him, and pushed his robe gently from his shoulders. As it fell away, she did not see his imperfection, only that he had no fault at all. No fault at all. She slipped on to the bed and laid her head back where she knew his had been, and then she held out her hand. 'Come to me,' she whispered.

He took her hand and joined her, leaning over so that his heavy hair fell forward. His eyes shone with love. 'Cicely, you are a maid. I do not wish to hurt you.'

'You will not, I know it, but should that be, I will welcome it.'

He lowered his lips to hers again, gathering her to him in a kiss that seared them both. He caressed her breasts, stroked her nipples, kissed them, ran his tongue over them, and sucked upon them until her delight was almost too much. His hand moved gently to her most feminine places, exploring that which had never been explored before. He was no untried boy, but a man who knew well how to give her all the pleasure she could seek.

She was adrift in the gratification he gave so tenderly, and when his kisses moved down to her thighs and then between them, she cried with happiness. Oh, the things she learned in those minutes, the things he taught her about her own body, things she had not imagined could be so. He took her to peaks of pleasure, and kept her there, showing her the secrets of her own flesh, as well as his own.

There were no boundaries. She covered him with kisses too, and ever more intimate caresses. She discovered that her instincts did not fail her, and she knew how to pleasure him too. There were things she did to him that made him arch with rich enjoyment, especially when she no longer resisted the temptation to explore his masculinity. Never had she believed she would go so far, or want to so very much. She adored his maleness, kissed it, tasted it, hid her face against it, until at last he could endure no more.

He pushed her gently on to her back, parted her thighs, and moved over her. There he paused, his hips lowered between her legs, their final joining yet to be accomplished. He smiled down at her flushed face and darkened eyes. 'Do you need to know again how I love you?'

'Do you need to know how much I worship you?' she whispered. Could she have wished for a more exquisite initiation than this? She gazed up at his face, the face of her king, her uncle and her lover, and was filled with every sweet emotion it was possible to imagine. 'Love me now,' she said softly.

Slowly, so slowly, he pushed forward. She felt his heat press against her, felt how he eased himself against her body's gentle resistance. Her senses were jubilant, liberated by his love and her own cravings. And *he* was the one with whom she shared it all. There was no echo now of this being a sin, no shadow to darken her happiness.

She gasped as her body accepted him and at last he was fully inside her. She moved against him, weeping as a torrent of joy undulated through her. Never could she have anticipated such a sweet torment.

He withdrew a little, and then returned, then he did it again, slow voluptuous strokes that imparted something akin to ecstasy. Even now he thought of her, taking his time, allowing her to do as she wished as well. There was no selfishness, only love. He was her first lover, and he would not spoil anything. It would be as wonderful an initiation as he could make it, because he wanted her to remember these moments as enchantment. But at last he could resist no more. His need became too imperative. But he carried her with him as he came.

She felt him pulsing inside her, and it was exquisite. Control abandoned her as a welter of unutterable gratification swept her away. Had she been able to melt into his flesh she would. The passion was almost brutal in its demands, and her fingernails dug into him as she willed it never to stop. But it had to stop. Not quickly, but fading away into gentle waves until she was so relaxed and drowsy that she could not do anything except hold him.

She felt his lips upon hers again, gentle, stirring and filled with tenderness. How could this be a sin? How could something so unutterably radiant be wrong? This man meant the entire world to her, and it did not matter that he was her uncle. It just did not matter.

He moved from her at last, and lay on his back beside her, as drained as she by the power of their lovemaking. She nestled close, her head upon his chest. His arm was around her, and he rested his cheek against her hair. 'Now we have tempted Providence,' he said softly.

'We defy it.'

He smiled and closed his eyes. 'I wish I could regret it.'

'Do not ever regret it! Ever.' She scrambled to sit up. 'I am so happy at this moment,' she whispered, tears springing to her eyes. 'You have made the sweetest love to me, and shown me more delight in one night than most women will know in a lifetime.'

'And so you cry?' He smiled. Oh, such a smile, for it made love to her again.

She tried to return it, but her lips shook.

'What is it?' he asked, reaching up to push a lock of her hair behind her ear.

'We should be able to love each other openly, not hide away like this.'

His smile deepened. 'Cicely, I do not think I would *ever* choose to do before the world what we have just done.'

She had to smile as well. 'You know what I mean.'

'Yes, but we cannot be open. For so many reasons. But I want you to know that I *do* wish you to be my queen. There is nothing in which I would exult more. With you I would be complete at last, and no queen would ever have been more cherished by her king.' He was silent for a long moment, and then added, 'I will not take any other wife.'

She was shocked. 'Not take a wife? But you must have an heir.'

'I have one. Jack de la Pole.'

'But he is not your son, not *your* blood, only the blood of your sister.'

'Cicely, do you really imagine I could take anyone else to my bed now? I have broken almost every rule I hold dear and defied my deepest conscience because I need *you*. No one else can ever be to me what you are now. I know what I do, and will not swerve from my decision. My loyalty is to you alone, and if that means keeping myself only to you, then so be it.'

'You cannot. You *must* have an heir of your own body. You know you must.'

He shook his head. 'No, Cicely. Some things are more important.'

'Then I wish we did not love, because I am now between you and your dynasty.'

'But we do love, sweetheart, and it can never be otherwise.'

Her tears would not go away. 'I am your curse.'

'My *curse*? Jesu, Cicely, you are the only thing that is good in my life!' He sat up to take her chin between his fingers and kiss her fiercely on the lips. 'Do you not see how I need you? How I cannot do without you? If I took another wife, I would betray her every night with you.'

She gazed at him through a mist of tears. 'I love you so much, Richard.' She put her lips to his, and closed her eyes, for the feeling was too much.

He drew her back down to the bed and gathered her into his warm embrace again. She slid her arms lovingly around his waist, and touched his back. His twisted back. 'Please tell me the pain does not get worse.'

'After all that had been said between us, would you have me lie to you *now*? It does get worse, but slowly. I can manage.'

'Would that I could take it away and make you straight again.'

He smiled. 'Oh, tonight you have, believe me.'

So great was her love that she would have allowed him to steal her soul. There was no question of it, no hesitation to mar the perfection of emotion he had aroused in her. She drew even closer to him, enjoying the beat of his heart, the leanness of his body, the scent of him. He was real. This was not another of her foolish dreams. She had lain with him, and he had made it sublime for her. The Bible said they sinned. But they did not.

'Cicely . . .'

She drew away, knowing by his voice that he did not wish to say what he was about to.

He took her hand. 'Sweetheart, we should think carefully of what we do, not only because I am your uncle, because even if I were not, I have still taken your innocence and there might be proof of it nine months hence. What then?'

'The lover in me would exult,' she said quietly.

He smiled a little. 'I would take care of you, you do know that? Maybe I cannot make you my wife, or — for your sake — acknowledge the child, but I will see you do not lack for anything.'

'The only thing I do not wish to lack is you. If you are in my life I do not care about anything else.'

But then he remembered John. 'Oh, dear God, John.' He got up from the bed and went to the window, an unprotected figure as the light of the moon fell over him. 'I speak of wanting you as my wife, when you are to be *his* wife. I have given him my *fatherly* permission, and now I have made a cuckold of him even before the event.'

'I cannot have you, Richard, but I know that you wish it were otherwise. I will not hurt John. I will marry him and be a good wife.'

'Will you then stay away from court? From me? Because you will have to if you are to be a good wife to my son and I a father to him. You and I will *never* be able to stay apart, and we both know it.' He pressed his lips together bitterly. 'How can I ever be a good father to him anyway after this?'

'You *are* a good father. What has happened here tonight is *my* fault. I came here because I could not allow us to part without having taken this one chance to be together as we need to be. Would you wish us not to have made love? This is not a battle stratagem, for which you must consider every possibility, it is love, which will not conform to military rules.'

'Cicely—'

'Please.' Fresh tears pricked her eyes.

His eyes were tender. 'You have me in your power, Cicely. I will do whatever you wish of me, you have only to ask.'

'Then come to me and hold me close again. Let the devil take the consequences.' She took his hand.

He smoothed her fingers with his thumb. 'Know always that I love you, Cicely.'

'Kiss me, for I will not waste another moment speaking of things that are in the lap of the gods. We only have tonight.'

Their eyes met for a moment, their thoughts upon the same thing. 'I *will* return after defeating the Tudor,' he said.

'I know.'

The words were hollow, and they both knew it. There was no guarantee of anything, especially when there were possible traitors near him.

She would not cry again, she thought, and smiled again. 'Make love to me, Richard, for I can never have enough of you.'

CHAPTER TWENTY-ONE

THE NEXT MORNING, as storm clouds scudded low over the land, a small group of swift horses and palfreys was gathered in the courtyard. Nearby waited a small detachment of men-at-arms, no more than twelve in all, their livery and leopards' head banners asserting their allegiance to be to Jack de la Pole.

There were no other colours, nothing that would identify John of Gloucester or Cicely's ten-year-old cousin, Edward, Earl of Warwick, attainted son of the dead Duke of Clarence. The story had been put about that Cicely and Bess were to go to Sheen, to be with their mother, and that their little cousin Warwick would be with them.

Jack, usually so carefree, was grim-faced and angry, snapping at a groom who had trouble controlling his famous white horse, which had to be seen at least for the first portion of the journey. Going to Sheriff Hutton was as little to Jack's liking as to John's, for they did not relish the safety of the north when Richard was under threat. Jack was fiercely courageous, acutely perceptive and infinitely thoughtful, and he longed to do battle with Henry Tudor, as he had been heard to protest loudly to the king.

'Uncle, I cannot skulk like a fox in a hole while you defend your realm! I should be at your side, and so should your son!'

Richard's response had been to the point. 'Well, skulk you shall, my lord of Lincoln, because England would not benefit from the forfeit of *both* our lives. You are also no stranger to Sheriff Hutton, because the Council of the North is centred there and *you* are its principal member. And I want you safe for the future. Do you understand?'

'But—'

'Sweet Jesu, why will no one simply do as I command? I know you are all loyal, but as God is my witness you make it hard for me! I have endured enough from John, who all but tugs my hem to change my mind. And Francis, who almost weeps because I wish him to go to the south of the country to guard it for me. And now you. Jack, you will *all* do as I say, and like it!'

There the matter had ended, and Jack bowed to his uncle's authority, but with as bad a grace as John had before him.

Cicely waited quietly with Bess, who had managed to remain composed and dignified since finally confessing everything to the man who wanted to hear it least. Cicely's heart was heavy, because after today she too would be far away from Richard, without any hope at all of seeing him, happening upon him, or even hearing him in another room. She would not be able to watch him toy with his rings while someone read a document to him, or close his eyes as he listened to sweet music. Or kneel, head bowed, at Mass. She . . . would not see him at *all*.

She had not been alone with him since last night, but the kisses they had shared still warmed her. She had those hours with him that no one could ever take away. Her body still treasured him, still needed him. She would never again be the same. Never again sweet, innocent Cicely, because she had been exposed to the full force of a powerful love that would be with her for all time. Richard Plantagenet, King of England, that matchless man, was her lover. She tried to think only of his victory against Henry Tudor, and the time when he would send for them all again. It was the only comfort she could have.

There was a bustle of activity from a nearby doorway and Richard appeared, accompanied by Robert Percy and John Howard, Duke of Norfolk. Behind them came Norfolk's son, the Earl of Surrey. The old duke was pleading with the king, and as they approached the waiting company Richard's answer carried clearly.

'Very well, I will give no further argument, my lord, you may do as you wish. The cannon at the Tower are at your disposal. I will send word to Brackenbury this very day.'

'Richard, I will put them to good use, maybe even blast the Tudor's miserable Welsh head from his scrawny neck!' The duke roared with laughter at his own words, slapping his great hand on Richard's shoulder with the rough camaraderie of a long and trusting friendship.

Richard smiled and then inclined his head to both men before coming over to the waiting group to say his farewells.

Cicely watched him, loving him so much that she knew the coming few minutes would be perhaps the most difficult of her life. To go from him when she had so recently truly found him.

He did not meet her eyes as he smiled at them all. 'I bid you Godspeed for a safe journey and will await word of your timely arrival in Sheriff Hutton. I trust you know what you must do, Jack?'

The Earl of Lincoln knelt before the king and pressed his hand to his forehead. 'I do, Your Grace. As few as possible shall know of our journey or its destination, but they had better take care of Héraut!'

'You have my word. Your horse will not come to harm, and will be returned to you in due course.'

Jack looked earnestly into Richard's face again, determined to try one last time to make him change his mind. 'Sire, will you not reconsider? Let me ride by your side against the enemy!'

'Jack, as you are my dear sister's son I will ignore your continual requests, but my mind stays firm. If the tide should turn against me, I shall at least have the knowledge that York may continue through you . . . through all of you.'

Jack stood dejectedly and bowed low to the uncle he idolized. There was only ten years between them, but the difference was great. Richard was collected and hard to read, his nephew wore valour and brilliance on his sleeve.

John went next to kneel at his father's feet, bringing the boy Warwick with him. 'Father, my heart is heavy at this leave-taking.'

'My dearest son, my love for you knows no bounds and I would be proud indeed to have you ride into battle at my side, but this is not to be. You must be as safe as Jack here, and for the same reasons.'

With a heavy heart John went to where his horse waited. Jack remained where he was, and Cicely thought that even now he deliberated whether to press the king yet again.

Richard stepped to his brother Clarence's son and put his hand on the boy's shoulder. 'As I loved my brother George, your father, so I love you too. May God watch over you.' He raised the boy, who immediately went to stand with Jack, whom he followed like a puppy.

Richard looked at last at his nieces, who came forward together to kneel side by side. 'I trust I will have your prayers, ladies?'

Cicely could not answer, the moment was too affecting, and seemed so very final. He had not changed his mind about anything. She would have to go away from him, and it felt as if he cut her in half.

Bess looked at him. 'You will always have my prayers,' she said in a shaking voice. 'And you will always have my love.'

'I know, Bess.'

'I cannot tell you how much I hope for your victory in the coming weeks. I will call upon God's protection for you.'

'Thank you, Bess.' He stretched his hand down, but she pulled swiftly away and rose without his permission. She looked one last time into his eyes and then hurried away to the waiting palfreys, where the new maid, Mary Kymbe, waited, cloaked against the wind, her soft brown hair aflutter.

Now only Cicely was left, kneeling before Richard, wanting to embrace him as she had before, to kiss his lips and feel his love for her. But she knelt there, giving nothing away when she longed to give her whole self.

'Cicely?' Her name was a caress on his lips.

She raised her eyes, and drank the love in his gaze. 'Be safe,' she whispered. 'Be safe for me, for I cannot bear to go from you.'

He bent so that only she would hear. 'I do not want you to go, Cicely, for I want more than anything to keep you here with me. I want to fall asleep at night in your arms, and wake up in them in the morning. I want to make love to you, only to you, sure in the solace that your love is only for me. How can I say more of what is in my heart? You shine in my darkness, and I want to reach for you. Whatever happens, always remember what I have said to you today, for it is an expression of the great truth of my life. There are many *un*truths, but truths as well, and *this* truth surpasses them all. You and I are not supposed to be like this, but we are, and nothing can change it. Take my love with you, and always keep it close, for it can never belong to another.'

She wept unashamedly, so moved she could not rise when he indicated. He put his hand out. 'Come, let me help you.'

His fingers were strong and firm, and she clung to them as she found her tongue at last. 'May a fond niece hug her favourite uncle farewell? As she would once have done?' she whispered.

She saw there were tears in his eyes. 'Yes, Cicely, she can.'

She flung her arms around his neck and held him tightly, burying her face in his dark hair, against his neck. 'Every night when I go to sleep, I will think of you,' she whispered. 'I will make love with you and adore you, and I will be with you when you ride against Henry Tudor.'

He held her close but knew that to let the moment hang would draw unwelcome attention, and so he released her.

'I am a fortunate uncle to be held in such regard,' he said lightly, intending to be heard. She felt Robert Percy's eyes upon her again, and this time sensed his dawning understanding. But he looked away again, and she knew he would never speak of it.

Richard turned to Jack. 'Take good care of her for me.'

'I will.' But Jack's glance moved to Cicely and then back to Richard, and she knew he too had observed.

She was hardly aware of walking to her palfrey, or of the party riding towards the barbican. She looked back, oh, how she looked back, for that last glimpse, that final moment before she could not see him anymore.

Take my love with you, and always keep it close, for it can never belong to another. . . .

From the black shadows of the gatehouse the small cavalcade destined for the north emerged into the dull daylight, where the wind blew across the hillside and a group of travel-stained horsemen gave way for them to cross the drawbridge. With a huge effort, Cicely drew herself up, determined to show pride and dignity, for she recognized the thin, shrewd face of Margaret's husband, Lord Stanley, the banners above his head bright with the silver buck's head of his cognizance. He swore allegiance to Richard, but the veil over his shifty eyes was to hide his treachery; she could sense it as surely as if 'Iscariot' had been branded into his forehead. She sat decorously on her mount, her back straight, looking straight ahead. She would *not* acknowledge him, not the man who was Henry Tudor's stepfather!

Bess instinctively did the same, and the sisters rode past Stanley together, heads held high, their Yorkist pride and disdain there for all to see.

But the unexpected encounter with Lord Stanley was an unfortunate stroke, because Richard's small party knew its departure had already been noted by someone who was most likely in the wrong quarter, and the chances of being followed had now increased tenfold.

Only when they were riding south through the narrow streets of Nottingham did Bess speak of the king. 'You have no idea how I envy you, Cicely. His affection for you is so freely given. You can hold him and allow your fondness be known to one and all, whereas I . . .' She gave a mocking laugh. 'I ruined what little I had, and can never be close to him again.'

Cicely stared at her palfrey's ears, so culpable that she did not dare to look at her sister. She could hear his voice again. *Take my love with you, and always keep it close, for it can never belong to another.* The tears flowed. Her shoulders shook and great sobs were dragged into the open air. She could not stem them, and Bess could not soothe her. Poor Mary Kymbe, so new to her place, did not know what to do, except sit on her pony and stretch out a nervous hand which she immediately withdrew again, as if she had presumed upon her position.

John turned his horse back. 'Cicely? What ails you?'

'We have left him,' she wept. 'He needs us all but we have left him.'

'It is *his* command, sweeting, not our wish.' John put his gauntleted hand on her arm.

They were passing beneath the city gate, where the shadows deepened, and he was his father's son again. She gazed at him through a blur of hot tears. She was untrue to him because of his father, and she could not bear it. 'I do not deserve your love, John.' She fumbled with her glove, meaning to return the ring.

He was dismayed. 'No! Never say that! What is wrong, Cicely? Please tell me.'

'I cannot.'

He did not understand. 'If you will not tell me, I cannot hope to offer you comfort. But I still worship you, no matter what. Keep the ring. Spurn me if you must, but keep the ring.'

She swayed in the saddle, trying to hold on to what remained of her fortitude. She heard John's anxious calls, and Bess's, but the last voice she heard was Richard's. *Take my love with you, and always keep it close, for it can never belong to another. . . .*

It was Jack who took her up on Héraut, although she hardly knew it. She was adrift in the grief of leaving Richard, and could only hide her face against her cousin's broad shoulder. His arm was around her waist, strong and steady, and although he did not speak, she was glad of him. It could not be John, not now, when guilt was all she had.

John led her palfrey and was clearly upset by her, to him, strange behaviour. He could not know how she had failed him, but nothing would have made her behave differently towards Richard. The love was simply too powerful. So much had happened to her, so much had changed . . . and was more exquisite, yet more filled with torment than she would ever have believed.

They rode south as planned, the men-at-arms following, Jack's leopards' head banners on display, making certain that no one they passed would be in any doubt what party they were. Into the forest they went, following a little-used track that wound between the wet, whispering trees. Suddenly another group of riders appeared ahead, waiting by a small bridge over a stream. They were clad as Richard's party, and all but one mounted on similar horses. The one stood with a dark bay mount that would not draw particular attention, and he and Jack exchanged steeds.

Jack lifted her down from his horse. 'Can you ride on your own now, sweetheart?' he asked kindly, adjusting her hood as the wind threatened to blow it back from her face.

'Yes, I think so.'

'Be sure, sweetheart, for we need to be swift, not held up.'

'I can manage.'

He kissed her cheek and then lifted her lightly on to her palfrey. They watched as their replacements continued south with the men-at-arms, Jack's white horse giving the party the appearance of complete authenticity, then the party for Sheriff Hutton rode down the side of the bridge into the stream, the bed of which they followed as it swept around to the west and then, out of sight from the road, to the north.

Anyone who now rode along the road from Nottingham could not know the party from the castle had even checked its speed.

After riding about two hundred yards, to a point where the stream wound behind a screen of young sycamores, Jack reined in and nodded at John. 'Be careful, for one slip will be our undoing, but I *must* know.'

John dismounted and waded back the way they had come.

Jack manoeuvred his horse close to Cicely and then leaned to speak only to her. 'We are all distressed, Cicely, but I think your distress cuts into your soul.'

Her lips parted and she could not meet his eyes.

For a moment his arm was around her shoulder. A gesture of comfort, a sympathy she had neither expected nor sought and she knew he had realized the truth as she parted from Richard.

John reached a clump of willows within sight of the bridge, and hid behind it to see if anyone had followed. Almost immediately he heard a single horse coming from the direction of Nottingham. When it came into view, the rider was hooded and impossible to identify. The horse did not pause but rode on over the bridge in the wake of the cavalcade, and by the way the rider leaned over in the saddle now and then to look at the ground, he was making sure he followed a trail.

John waded back to the others, and nodded at Jack. 'Whoever he was, he took the bait and went on south.'

Jack grinned. 'Stanley's arse-creeper, no doubt. Let us be on our way, and mind now, no one is to leave the stream, is that understood? We follow it for some time now.'

They continued, but three hours later the racing clouds at last gave up the rest of their rain. It poured down, slanting in the wind and banishing even the vestiges of the English summer. The dripping trees of Sherwood Forest crowded above their heads, rustling in the sodden wind, blotting out the failing daylight. The rain fell ever heavier, coming down in such torrents that it was not long before the stream's flow increased. They came to a swirling bend, where the water span around and the bed deepened without warning.

Cicely's palfrey blundered into it first, and plunged down, head tossing, eyes rolling as it floundered for some footing. Cicely clung to the saddle. She was such an indifferent horsewoman that doing anything to help her mount was beyond her. John urged his horse in beside her, and spray flew as he struggled to seize the palfrey's bridle.

'Be still, now, Cicely!' he cried. 'For the love of God stop swaying around!'

'I cannot help it!'

'Yes, you can. Look at me. At *me,* not the water!'

She did as she was told but was frightened as the palfrey continued to toss its head, trying to find purchase on the stream bed.

John held her gaze. 'Now, just sit there like that and let me take over. At me, Cicely. That is better.' He smiled, and then turned his own horse, and managed to coax the frightened palfrey to shallower water. Only then did he reach for Cicely's hand. 'You are safe now, sweeting.'

The endearment was like a warm cloak that wrapped comfortingly around her in a way she did not merit, and she clung to his hand.

He smiled again. 'I will look after you, Cicely.'

She gazed at him as the rain sluiced down his concerned face. His fair hair clung to his cheeks and dripped down his back, and he was so anxious about her. It was a moment that forced her to face herself. She loved his father as much as it was possible to love any man, but she loved John as well. He was Richard's flesh and blood. She prevented the thought from continuing, because maybe that was the truth of it. Did she love John for himself, or because of his father? Was she so selfish and without true kindness that she was capable of such deceit? She did not know, except that for whatever reason, John of Gloucester was precious to her and she hoped he would never know how she had failed him. But she would always belong to Richard Plantagenet. Always. 'Forgive me, John, I have not treated you well.'

He smiled. 'You are upset, I know that. I can wait until you are yourself again.'

She *had* to do right by him, and be as she had before. She smiled and squeezed his hand.

He turned to Jack. 'We have to find shelter. It is impossible to continue in this deluge.'

'We are not far from Newstead. St Mary's Priory is among those on the list of places true to the king. This stream passes the walls.'

'Then we must go there.'

As Jack hesitated about a final decision, Bess looked at him angrily. 'Cousin, I care not *where* we go, merely that we find shelter before we all die of the ague.'

His knowing eyes surveyed her. 'My lady, such an ague would be worth the catching if you would be my nurse.'

Her face flushed red and she raised her chin haughtily. 'My lord of Lincoln, your wife would no doubt be glad to perform that service. Or maybe it is so long since you were in *her* bed that she no longer even recalls what you look like!' She flicked her reins and rode slowly on down the stream towards the haven at Newstead.

Jack grinned broadly at John. 'Oh, such spirit. I would gladly be the first to tame her.'

Cicely was cross. 'How like a man, Jack de la Pole. Why do you *all* have to speak of taming a woman as if she were a horse? Can you not coax her into your questionable bed by other means? Maybe force is your only talent in that respect?'

John winced, but Jack only laughed. 'Good God, John, your lady is even more spirited than her sister! Lady Cicely, if you ever tire of this paltry fellow, I will gladly coax you. You have no idea how sweet and persuasive I can be when I try.'

'I think I probably do.'

He smiled at her, and again there was a nuance, a suggestion that he understood — or guessed — at least something.

She remembered he had been close by during those final moments of parting from Richard. It had all had been too expressive. And that had been her fault, not Richard's.

The prior of St Mary's took them in willingly. His name was Thomas Gunthorp, and he was anxious to show all possible hospitality to his illustrious guests. Cicely and Bess were led to two small cell-like rooms, all too reminiscent of their sanctuary at Westminster, but Cicely could not have cared less as Mary Kymbe, having already waited upon Bess, came to attend her as well. She was of an age with Cicely, and had a heart-shaped face, brown eyes and rich brown hair. She and Cicely already liked each other, but Bess was not able to unbend sufficiently to chatter with a maid.

Cicely was glad to be out of her wet clothes and warmly wrapped in a large blanket, but hardly had Mary commenced brushing her hair than Jack appeared in the doorway.

Mary tried to shoo him away but Cicely prevented her. 'Mary Kymbe, I think I am sufficiently covered by this blanket for my lord of Lincoln to only see my toes.'

The maid disapproved, but as she hurried past Jack, he suddenly caught her arm. 'Your name is Kymbe?'

'Yes, my lord.'

'Of Lincolnshire?'

Mary nodded. 'Friskney, my lord. My father is Thomas Kymbe.'

'He entertained me at dinner a year or so ago. You were not there. I would have remembered.'

'I have not been back to Friskney in three years, my lord. Is something wrong?'

'No, of course not.' Jack smiled, and then let her go.

When Mary had gone, Cicely looked at him. 'You leave my maid alone, Jack de la Pole.'

'I will be a saint, I swear.'

She searched his face. 'What was that about?'

'Mere pleasantry.'

'Oh no, there is more to it. Tell me.'

He closed the door. 'Until just now I had not realized her name was Kymbe. Cicely, your brothers may be at Sheriff Hutton now, but they *were* at Friskney.'

She stared at him.

'It is my manor,' Jack reminded her, 'and it is close to the sea. Your maid clearly does not know. I merely wished to be certain.'

'How long have they been there?'

'Since John Welles, who has neighbouring Lincolnshire manors, was fool enough to try to abduct them from the Tower. Welles fled to Brittany to Tudor, but could be anywhere now. Wherever, he is not likely to visit Friskney if Thomas Kymbe is Richard's man. Your brothers have been perfectly safe there. Dickon has been in good spirits, but Edward is sickly. Not too sickly to make the journey to Sheriff Hutton. Now you know as much as me.'

'And you really can trust Mary's father?'

'He served with Richard at Tewkesbury and has not swerved from him since. I gather that his son, your maid's brother, Tom Kymbe the younger, is not so steady to York, but he has been estranged from his father for some time and has been with relatives on the Isle of Wight — do not ask me why. I am not a fount of all wisdom concerning the Kymbes of Friskney. Remember now, your maid clearly knows nothing. She has not been back to Friskney and her father keeps his secret close, so do not enlighten her unwittingly. It may be that she is close to her brother, who appears to have close connections with John Welles and is therefore most likely a Lancastrian.' Jack smiled. 'Enough of that. We should speak of Richard, I think.'

'There is nothing to say,' she said quickly.

'But there is.'

'No.'

He came closer. 'Jesu, Cicely, do you really imagine I could have been standing where I was in that courtyard and *not* see how you and the king love each other? I felt your pain so keenly that I shared your tears.'

'It was merely a fond leave-taking.'

'Do I look like a gull, Cicely? I make no judgement upon you, nor do I feel compelled to rush to the nearest confessor with my horror. And God knows, I could find enough of them here.'

'But do you feel compelled to tell John?' She met his eyes.

'No.'

'Do you promise?'

He smiled. 'Do I need to? Then you have my promise. The secret belongs to you and the king, and I would no more betray it than I would desert him on the battlefield. I know what I saw today, Cicely, and it moved me more than you can imagine. He has long needed someone like you. Needed you in particular, I imagine. I am glad for you both, even if it must be a secret.' He came closer. 'I only wanted you to know that I saw no sin, and that if you ever need to talk, I will be close by.'

She managed a smile. 'Thank you, Jack.'

He hugged her tightly, kissed her cheek and left her alone.

Moments later Mary returned to resume the brushing of her mistress's hair. Cicely closed her eyes and saw Richard again, wearing the black brocade robe, his body pale and slender. *One step more, Cicely, and our sin is as good as committed. . . .* His voice filled her head, his lips kissed her still, and it was too much. Fresh tears began to fall.

Mary saw. 'My lady?'

'It's nothing, Mary. Just my foolishness.'

'I see no foolishness, my lady. I see only great sadness.' The maid put a soft hand on her shoulder. It was brief, a daring to touch, but it was heartfelt.

Later, when Mary had gone, Cicely lay down on the hard board that was the bed. She listened to the steady patter of the rain outside the narrow window, and the drips that struck the ivy leaves against the wall. The priory was in a clearing, with the forest banished some fifty yards in all directions, but the wind so soughed through the trees that it sounded like the sea. The sharp smell of wet moss soothed her, and she closed her eyes, to drift away into Richard's waiting embrace. She knew that whatever he was doing now, he would be thinking of her. *Take my love with you, and always keep it close, for it can never belong to another. . . .* His love was with her now, and the knowledge was so good.

How long she slept she did not know but it was dark when she awoke suddenly. It had almost stopped raining but the clouds still rushed across the sky, breaking now and then to allow swift shafts of moonlight to slip across the room. Someone was in the room! But it was only Mary, standing by the narrow window, looking out intently.

'What is it, Mary, can you not take your rest?'

Mary turned, startled, and bobbed a curtsey. 'My lady! I thought you slept.'

'A miracle on this horrid plank.' Cicely smiled. 'What is so interesting outside?'

'I am not really sure. The window looks to the edge of the forest to the south, and a moment ago there was moonlight. I thought I saw something move, but the bushes were heaving in the wind so it seemed but a trick of the eye. And yet . . .' The maid looked out again.

'What do you think it was?' Cicely asked, slipped from the bed to join her.

'A horseman, but if so he is well hidden in the bushes and wears a hooded cloak that hides his face.'

Could it be the man who had followed them out of Nottingham? Cicely searched the edge of the trees. Were they discovered? The moon emerged again, and sure enough, there was a rider among the bushes, his cloak billowing in the wind, his muffled face turned towards the buildings. As they watched he turned his horse away and rode slowly into the forest, leaving behind only the empty bushes, where torn leaves scattered like emerald rain. Then clouds covered the moon again.

Cicely was disturbed. Who was he? Not a friend, for a friend would have come to the abbey. Who then? She caught up her skirts and ran to find the others.

They left the priory before dawn, slipping out quietly and riding once more along the bed of the stream. Behind them no hint was given of their departure, of them ever having been there. Whether the lone horseman had been friend or enemy, he would have to find them again.

CHAPTER TWENTY-TWO

THE BEAUTIFUL OLD city of York was crowded, its bustle and noise scarcely less than London itself. It was evening as they rode under the southern gate and into Richard's beloved city of the north. Cicely looked up at the towering minster which hung above the narrow cobbled streets and was visible from every corner. To her delight their arrival in the city did not attract much attention, for they rode without banners or signs to reveal their identity. The clatter of their horses against the smooth stones was barely audible as they rode past the clutter of market stalls and pens of animals. Street traders of all sorts shouted their wares, jostling with each other for customers.

Soon the riders passed into the shadow of the minster itself. The hot, dusty sunshine was suddenly eclipsed by the mighty church, which cast a blessed coolness. Cicely looked up at the carved walls and arched doorways, and finally at the three towers reaching up to the very heavens above. Richard's city was dear to his heart, and Cicely could understand it. He had prayed here, listened to the music, was its patron. She could almost feel him. York would always support Richard III, its beloved Duke of Gloucester.

Beside her, Bess rode without looking to left or right. She had said very little since leaving Nottingham, and

Cicely no longer felt able to speak to her in confidence. It was impossible now that Richard stood between them, even though Bess did not know he was there. Cicely's sister was enveloped in her own unhappiness, and it would not have occurred to her that she was not alone in the misery of having left him at Nottingham.

At last they rode out of the city, beneath the ancient north gateway, and Cicely was relieved because they were now embarking on the final stage of their long journey to Sheriff Hutton, some ten miles ahead. Soon the dusty road led downhill through the Forest of Galtres towards a small village on the bank of a wide, deep, fast-flowing stream that was spanned by a narrow stone bridge that had no parapet. Next to the bridge was a sprawling tavern with a creaking sign depicting Richard's white boar badge. Some hundred yards or so beyond the bridge the dense forest continued.

It was as the little party descended towards the bridge that Cicely had a very disagreeable feeling of being watched. There had been nothing since the horseman at the priory, but now she was sure secret eyes were upon them again. She was about to mention it to Bess when Mary urged her pony alongside. 'My lady, do you recall the horseman at the priory?'

'Yes, of course. Why do you ask?'

'I pray you, look just beyond the tavern, to the horse beneath the ash tree.'

Cicely put her hand up to shade her eyes from the dazzle of the sun, and saw the ash tree. Her brow creased, for at first there seemed nothing to see, but then came a flicker of movement as a horse lashed its tail at flies. There was a man standing with it, although he kept in the shade. He might have been anyone but instinct told her it was the same man. He had to be tracking them, and knew their only route north was across this bridge.

She shivered in the warm evening air, and moved her palfrey between John and Jack, who was steering his mount around a pair of mangy hounds that snapped and snarled at each other in the middle of the street. He cursed as his steed reared but then smiled at Cicely.

'You find me in poor shape, I fear, Cousin,' he said.

As his horse became quieter, Cicely looked from him to John. 'We are no longer alone.'

'Have you seen someone?' John asked quickly, the concern in his grey eyes a reflection of his father.

'Yes. Down there, beneath the ash tree.'

Jack scowled. 'Damned maggot,' he breathed.

John glanced around. 'Do you think he is alone?'

'How in God's own holy carcass should *I* know?' Jack snapped.

John pulled a face. 'What a dear fellow you are today.'

Jack was a little contrite. 'Forgive me. I awoke this morning filled with resentment that you and I are here on this dairymaid errand.'

Cicely flushed. 'Thank you, Coz.'

He drew an irritable breath. 'Very well, I apologize to you as well, but none of this will help our difficulty. The king has charged me to get us all safely to Sheriff Hutton without Henry Tudor knowing, but it seems the Welshman's grubs are aware of us and seem to have been since we left Nottingham! That blood-sucking turd Stanley is behind this. Securing Richard's heirs, especially Bess and Cicely, is the Tudor's principal purpose, and so I imagine that by now there are many more than just one horseman. They will be waiting in the forest, where our capture is less likely to be witnessed.'

John was looking at the bridge as he answered Jack. 'Jesu, why do you always see the dark side of things? Have some optimism. Look, we have to use the bridge, the stream is too hazardous. The bridge is dangerous as well, of course.'

'And you say *I* am the pessimist?' Jack growled.

'I have a plan, Jack, so hear me out. The road forks some fifty yards beyond the bridge, to the right leading to Sheriff Hutton, to the left further to the north-west, but they *both* enter the forest, which gives excellent cover. If we could get across and take the road that leads *away* from Sheriff Hutton, we could follow it for a mile or so at a good speed and then cut across through the trees to rejoin the road we want. It has to be possible, if we simply complete the triangle.'

Jack remained irascible. 'Oh yes, it will be so easy even a babe could accomplish it.'

'My father has other castles and numerous manors here in Yorkshire, we could be travelling to any one of them. Whoever follows us will not know which. Sheriff Hutton is no more likely than any other. With God's help, we will evade pursuit and soon be safely within its walls. There is a garrison there, and Stanley will need a large force if he is to have any hope of taking it. Yes, our whereabouts might be discovered, but capturing us will not be possible. If you have a better plan, Jack, by all means let us share it.'

'You can be an impudent pup when you choose,' Jack muttered. 'I do not have another plan, if you must know, but I do see a flaw in your reckonings. What do you imagine the unwelcome tail will do while the dog makes a run for it? He will be immediately behind our flea-bitten arse all the time.'

'If you will but look behind us, I see something that will delay any follower quite considerably.'

They turned and saw a woodcutter's fully laden cart, drawn by two oxen, lumbering carefully down the slope behind them.

John continued, 'When it is on the bridge there will be no room for anything else, and I believe the oxen will take some time to negotiate such a narrow way. I suggest we pause at the tavern, as if to rest, and that as soon as the cart is within yards of the bridge, we mount and make a dash. We could go over just in front of it, and our follower will have to wait. He would have to be a very brave rider and his horse particularly strong and fresh to try the water. It would mean we gain several minutes' grace.'

Jack's troubled eyes brightened. 'You are right. Damn your boots, you have your father's military guile after all! Come, we will ride on, but slowly, and on reaching the tavern we will halt, but the ladies will not dismount. Do you hear? Nor you, my lord Warwick,' he said to the little boy, who said so little and obeyed the Earl of Lincoln without question. 'John and I cannot be lifting you all on to your horses *and* hope to get to the bridge before the cur's tail wakes up enough to wag.'

They continued downhill with the woodcutter's cart rumbling behind them, the oxen straining to hold the weight back. John watched the man by the ash tree draw his horse back into the shadow of a hut as they approached. 'Jack, he *has* to be in Stanley pay, yes?'

'I hope so,' Jack replied, 'because if we can send him off on the wrong road, I think he would rather tell Stanley he followed us to some fictitious destination rather than admit he had lost us! I know I would. Stanley sets my bowels griping. Let him believe we have gone anywhere but Sheriff Hutton. God knows, Richard holds such great tracts of this land, Stanley's men could comb back and forth and still not be sure if they had missed us. Let them go around in circles, because while they are here in the north, they cannot act against Richard.'

The man kept well out of sight as they reined in at the tavern. John and Jack dismounted, and they gathered as if at ease and simply resting; the ladies and little Warwick remained mounted, but relaxed. The cart rolled slowly onward, the yards between it and the bridge closing so slowly that Cicely held her breath. What if they did not all get to the bridge before it?

The moment came at last, John slapped Bess's horse and that of Warwick, while John did the same for Cicely and Mary. Then the two men climbed swiftly into their saddles and urged their mounts in the wake of the others. Bess and Cicely crossed the bridge and continued riding, with Mary and the little earl right behind. Jack was hard upon their heels, but John only just made the gap before the ox was upon the bridge and the cart blocked all pursuit.

He glanced back. The watching rider had been caught off guard and had only just remounted. He had no chance of crossing the bridge. His hood fell back. It was Ralph Scrope!

The fleeing party reached the fork in the road and bore to the left. Soon the Forest of Galtres closed upon them, shutting out the dying day and cooling the air with ever lengthening shadows. There was a scent of evergreens as they galloped further and further from the bridge. Surely their pursuer would have crossed by now?

Jack called out. 'To the right! Now!'

They turned, leaving the road and riding almost silently on a carpet of pine needles. Only the jingle of harness told of their presence, and shrill birdsong drowned even that. They reached a dip in the land, and Jack drew them all into the shelter of a thicket. They listened, and after a moment heard the faint clatter of hooves along the road they had left. On the hoof beats went, and soon disappeared into the distance to the north-west.

John grinned at Jack. 'Not a bad plan after all, eh, Cousin?'

Jack sniffed. 'I suppose so, but we are not there yet. Come on, because if I do not reach Sheriff Hutton soon, I vow I will lie down and die!'

'Well, do not succumb just yet, for I know who our follower is. Ralph Scrope.'

Cicely's lips parted. Ralph's hatred for her, and for Richard, who had taken her side and prevented the match, had become so poisonous that he had turned upon the House of York.

John glanced at her. 'For what it is worth, I have always suspected that deep within he was of a Lancastrian persuasion. It was so vague a suspicion that I did not really take notice. Now I wish I had.'

Jack breathed out heavily. 'Scrope would be lying in an unmarked grave if I had anything to do with it.'

John glanced at Cicely. 'And I am sure you would help to dig it, mm?'

'Oh yes.'

They found the other road without trouble, and followed it out of the forest over open moorland that was shaded to purple in the twilight. The dark forest clustered all around in the valleys and clefts, and lapwings tumbled high overhead in the last of the light. Eventually the village and castle appeared ahead. Dust flew again as they rode through a street that was sunk between its cottages, worn away by the frequent traffic to and from the great fortress. At the castle gateway both Jack and John were recognized and the small party was allowed entry. So, at last, the weary travellers passed over the drawbridge and into the bailey. They were safe.

John dismounted swiftly and came to assist Cicely. She slipped down from her palfrey and he held her close. 'Journey's end, sweetheart,' he said, kissing her forehead.

'Hold me tighter, John,' she begged 'Hold me tighter.'

His arms enclosed her more, and when she raised her mouth, he kissed it. His lips were hot from the frantic ride, and she could feel his heart thundering. She now knew what she should not, the difference between the kiss of a boy and a man. John was young and ardent, as she herself had been, but he was not Richard. She made herself kiss him as she would once have done, eagerly and without hesitation, but he drew back to look deep into her eyes.

'You do still wish to marry me?'

'Of course. What makes you ask?' She had to know if she had already given herself away.

'You seem . . . changed. Maybe you have cooled towards me?'

'No! No, of course not. I love you, John.' She was so anxious to reassure him that she knew her reaction seemed all it should be.

'You were going to return my ring,' he reminded her.

'I was so upset about everything — leaving Nottingham, the danger the king is in, the upset with Bess . . .' *Oh, how despicable you are, Cicely Plantagenet.*

He smiled. 'It has not been easy.'

'No.'

'But I will make it better now, I swear it.'

She held him again, defying herself to cry for the wrong reason.

Suddenly he caught her firmly and swung her up from her feet and twirled her around. 'I love you, my lady, and I do not care who knows it!'

She laughed, for there was exhilaration in the moment, but then he stopped twirling her. 'I have an ulterior motive, of course,' he said, lowering her to the ground again.

'Oh?'

'Yes. I want to make love to you.'

'Fie on you, sir.'

He grinned. 'Is it not said that honesty is always the best course?'

She lowered her eyes. 'It cannot *always* be the best course, John.'

CHAPTER TWENTY-THREE

CICELY AND JOHN were alone together in a small anteroom at Sheriff Hutton. The life of the castle went on all around: the training of the men-at-arms, the sound of horses and hounds, shouted orders, everything that was always associated with a great fortress.

They had been at the castle for a week now, and the princes had yet to be brought from Friskney. There had been no word from Richard and Jack's mood was still as angry as it had been on leaving Nottingham. He would *never* take kindly to inactivity, but especially now. There was no sign of any enemy. It seemed they had definitely fooled Ralph Scrope, who might, as Jack had said, have told his shifty Lord Stanley anything at all but the truth — that he had lost his quarry somewhere in the Forest of Galtres.

John was seated in a chair in their sun-filled room, and Cicely was on his lap, her black skirts tumbling to the floor, her arms around his neck. Their heads rested together. It was a quiet moment they both wanted and were content to share it in silence. But then, as had happened two years ago in Westminster Abbey, a conversation was overhead. It was one that kept them as still and quiet as it was possible to be, because Jack was pleading with Bess for her favours.

'Sweet lady, will you not be a little kind to me?'

'My lord of Lincoln, you have a wife who will be kind to you, that should suffice!' Bess was stiff and cold, clearly resenting being lured into the adjoining room on whatever pretext he had invented.

Jack was impatient. 'My wife is far away and cannot relieve my misery of mind and body.'

'Then send for her.'

Cicely and John had to press their hands to their mouths as they pictured the scene.

'Oh, come now, Bess, do you not find my hapless existence appealing?' Jack was at his most pleasing and attractive, which was quite considerable. There was a pause, and then the sound of a sharp slap.

'You presume, my lord of Lincoln!'

'God's blood, woman, are you made of granite? A kiss is not an assault upon your virtue! '

'It is from my viewpoint. Do *not* trespass further! Your person is not of the slightest interest because I love the king — he is my only joy in this world, and will always be.'

'Then you are doomed to a lonely life, my lady. *You* will never have Richard.'

Cicely could not look at John.

Jack laughed. 'I *will* have you, Bess of York, on that you may count. Oh, I would take your sister first, but unfortunately her heart is already engaged.'

Steps were heard and then the outer door closed.

John leaned his head back and smiled. 'Jack was ever the faithful, loving husband, eh? I doubt he was true to his wife on their wedding night. I did not know *you* would be his first choice.'

'Nor did I. He will never win Bess over. No one will take her mind off your father. No one. He is impossible to forget or replace.'

'Good God, Cicely, not even my father can be that much of a paragon. I no longer think I envy him, but have become downright jealous.'

She managed a laugh. 'Well, you have no need to fear because I am just another of his nieces and therefore prohibited.'

That night Cicely's sleep was disturbed by the dull, groaning sound of the drawbridge being lowered, and then a company of horses clattered over the drawbridge into the confines of the castle. She heard a voice she recognized.

'Tell the Earl of Lincoln that Sir Francis Lovell is come from the king with my lords Edward and Richard of York!'

Cicely gasped and peered out. She saw Francis's silver wolf banners floating in the moonlight.

The following morning, her brother Edward proved to still be disagreeable. He was rude, condescending and superior, even when addressing Jack. The first hint of his hauteur came when they all awaited him at breakfast in the great hall. The minutes dragged but still he did not attend, even though Jack had sent peremptory word that his presence was required without further ado.

Dickon was very different, and seemed set to grow up in the very image of his father, Edward IV. He was strongly built with the blue eyes and pale coppery hair of the Plantagenets, and his manners and disposition left little if anything to be desired. Like the young Earl of Warwick, he had swiftly formed a devotion to Jack, and imitated his every gesture and action. Jack of Lincoln was everything such boys would worship.

Francis, who sat beside Cicely, smiled at her. 'Your beauty grows with each passing month, Lady Cicely. Who would have imagined that the little, dark-haired, freckled girl I once knew could become so lovely?'

'Why, thank you, sir, but please do not mention the freckles. They only come in summer, and I hate them.'

'They are charming.'

She changed the subject. 'Have you seen the king? I would know how he is.'

He met her eyes. 'As well as might be expected without you,' he answered softly. 'But I left Nottingham only two days after you.'

'So you know my secret too?'

'Robert Percy and I are in his confidence. He knew we had realized the truth at your leave-taking.'

She looked away. 'I pray nightly for him. No, I pray more often than that.'

'He would be glad to know it, I am sure.'

She smiled. 'I wish a thousand plagues on Henry Tudor, and upon every deceitful Yorkist and treacherous Lancastrian. If the earth were to open up and swallow them all I would gladly brandish the shovel that buries them.'

Francis pretended to be startled. 'And you look so gentle and amiable.'

'I would strike down anyone who betrayed him, or who even *thought* of betraying him.'

'Perhaps the white boar is not a fierce enough emblem for him. Mayhap your kerchief would serve better.'

'I would give him a thousand kerchiefs if I thought that was so.'

At that moment there was a stir, and all eyes moved to the far end of the hall. There stood her brother Edward. He was tall and angular, his thin face hollow-eyed and almost chinless. His dull hair hung limply to his shoulders and he gazed down on them now, his complexion sallow in the morning light. He looked quite dreadful, and yet had clearly not been mistreated. He was simply very unwell.

Edward descended the steps, an insolent expression upon his face, and they all observed in awful silence. He walked serenely past the benches of onlookers, nodding his head briefly to his brother and sisters and halting at last next to Jack who, naturally, sat at the head of the table.

Cicely's fascination was tempered with horror. His voice proved as shaky as his appearance. 'You dare to break bread without me, my lord of Lincoln?'

Jack's nostrils flared at such insolence. 'Dare?' he repeated in a dangerously controlled tone.

'Aye, my lord, I had thought the King of England would sit at the head of a table and not one of his subjects.'

Jack folded his napkin and began to dip his fingers in the finger bowl proffered by a page. 'Sir, in case you are not aware of it, the King of England is not present, only his heir.'

'If you speak of my uncle, the usurping Duke of Gloucester, then of course he is not present. I speak of the true King of England, my father's trueborn son. Myself.'

Jack surveyed him. 'Oh, I am tempted to fling you over my knee and thrash you for the tyke you are.' He dried his hands on a napkin and then rose until he towered over the boy. 'I do not dispute that you are your father's son, but your *uncle* is the rightful, anointed King of England. If this is to be a sample of your manners then I think your Woodville tutors were grossly at fault. In this hall there are seven members of the House of York, and of the seven *I* am the head! I am legitimate and have the blood and rank. Next follows my lord John of Gloucester, son of the present King of England, *then* you may take your true place in this hall! But you may be sure that if you continue in this vein, I will consider the Earl of Warwick to outrank you, attainder or not. Do I make myself understood?'

'You lie, my lord, you are merely the son of my aunt and the Duke of Suffolk, no more, no less. My father's marriage was true and *I* am the rightful monarch.' Edward was clearly a little frightened of Jack but to his credit stood his ground like a lanky young cockerel, but then his fear made him cough. It was a hard, dry cough that brought echoes of the late queen.

Jack exchanged a glance with Francis, for it was clear that the one-time Edward V was very ill indeed. Jack lowered his head for a moment, and when he addressed Edward again it was in a kinder tone. 'My lord Edward, I forgive you your breach of manners. If you will sit with us now I will say no more.'

Edward's chin, such as it was, was raised pugnaciously. 'I will not sit unless it is in my rightful place.' And with that he turned and stalked away again.

A nerve twitched at Jack's temple.

Francis looked at him. 'I fear, Jack, that your patience is going to be sorely tried.'

Jack found a little humour. 'And let us be honest, Francis, I do not possess an abundance of it in the first place.'

'That, unfortunately, is true.'

'Are you sure I cannot persuade you to stay? I know you like hawking, and I am determined to risk detection today by flying my favourite white hobby, which is kept in the mews here.'

'You feel able to take such a chance?' Francis was surprised. 'That damned hobby is as conspicuous as your horse. If it is seen overhead it will be known from whose wrist it flies.'

'I believe our presence here is unknown, and I intend to go to the north, an area where I doubt there will be anyone watching.'

John looked at him. 'Then you go without me. I do not intend to invite an arrow because *you* wish to look splendid.'

Jack was not pleased. 'Oh, very well. We will go hawking, but without my hobby. Will that do?'

'Yes. A little disguise and caution, and it will be a welcome diversion.'

Francis folded his napkin and dipped his fingers into the little bowl of water provided. 'I wish you well of your sport, but fear I cannot take you up on the invitation, tempting as it is. I must leave for the south coast, having been diverted to Friskney. Placing me there is not likely to make the slightest difference, because I do not believe Tudor will arrive there. He will land somewhere else. Wales, in my opinion. However, Richard has to take all precautions. I wish you all farewell. May our next meeting be under triumphant circumstances.' He bowed to them all, and then hastened away.

Jack caught Dickon's eyes. 'Please reassure me that you are everything your brother is not.'

'I am, my lord.'

'Thank God for that small mercy.' But Jack still held his eyes. 'Are you for King Richard?'

'Yes.'

'Without hesitation?'

'Yes, for I have known nothing but kindness from him. If I were older, I would ride with him against Henry Tudor.'

Jack smiled. 'That is what I like to hear. You are a good fellow, Richard of York.' He raised his cup of mead and drank it all in one.

The following day, when Francis was well on his way south again, and they were all closeted in the solar, a messenger arrived from Richard. It was Sir Robert Percy and, incredibly, he came alone, without even a few mounted men-at-arms for protection. It was strange that he should undertake the role of messenger when Richard had many trained riders and horses at his disposal.

Robert was closeted with Jack for a while, and then both men joined the others in the solar. They were all — Cicely excepted — to go hawking a little later, as Jack had planned, but Robert had declined to join them, stating he had other tasks to attend to before riding back to the king. Cicely was not going hawking for the simple reason that she did not like it. She preferred to stay behind and read, for she had discovered some of Richard's books, and because he had read them, she wished to as well. She longed to question Robert, to learn of Richard, but as yet there had been no opportunity. At least, not one that was sufficiently private.

Jack, it seemed, had already enquired after the king, for it was not long before he mentioned Richard. 'I find my uncle an enigma. He can be provoked into punishing those who warrant it, but the prodding has to be almost savage to bring him to that point.'

Robert nodded. 'I do not think he will ever change. Mercy is generally part of him.' He glanced at Cicely. It was a strange glance, seeming at once casual and yet deliberate.

She did not notice, for she was reading. A younger Richard had signed his name inside the book. *Ricardus Gloucestre. Loyaulte me lie.* He had also written a poem, although whether it was his work or simply something he liked, she could not tell.

To be without you is to fade a little within
To not hear your voice is to lose the sweetness of music
To forfeit your smile is to be plunged into darkness
To never feel your touch is to lose all sense of being
To know you have gone forever is to steal away all joy.

She ran a finger over the long-dried ink. If he had composed it, which, knowing his skill with words, he well might have done, who might it have concerned? Someone he had lost some time ago. John's mother? Possibly, for it was surely a love poem.

The words brought a lump to her throat and tears to her eyes. She put the book hastily aside and rose to go to the window, there to compose herself before facing her sister and cousins again. She longed to simply ride back to Nottingham to be with him again, to confront the odium, simply to be in his arms. She gazed towards the dark blue-green of the forest shimmering in the haze of summer. Larks fluttered and warbled against the sky, and the call of a curlew echoed across the wooded hillside to the south. The air was warm, and insects droned sleepily against the warm stone. It was all so peaceful and serene, and it was all Richard's England.

Leaving the others, Robert came to her side and lowered his voice. 'I have a message for you, my lady.'

'A message?' She searched his earnest eyes. 'From . . . ?'

He nodded. 'Oh, do not fear that your confidence will ever be betrayed, for I am a man of honour.'

'I had already guessed that you knew,' she answered. 'And I am aware that Francis does as well.'

'I trust your love is truly given, my lady, because it will surely destroy Richard if it is not.'

'Never was love more truly given, Sir Robert. I would die before I failed him.'

He smiled. 'Then I am charged to take you to him.'

'To *Nottingham*?' she gasped, but then for some reason her glance fell upon the letter Jack had received. It was so fresh, so uncreased, and the seal was as bright and crisp as if it had only just been pressed with Richard's ring. 'He is not in Nottingham, is he?'

'No, my lady, although no one but you and I know it. It is believed he is indisposed and confined to his apartments. In fact he and I left Nottingham at dusk yesterday, and we have used fast relay horses to come here. Eighty miles is a long way for horses that have not been so trained.'

'Just the two of you?'

'Yes.'

'But he is the king! How could he put himself in such danger? He has so many enemies.'

'He would rather face any number of hazards to be with you than stay where he is without you, even though it can only be for a few hours.'

'Oh, Richard.' Tears shimmered on her lashes. 'Where is he now?'

'But half an hour away to the south. There is an old hunting tower.'

'I believe I know it . . . I have seen it above the trees.' He was so near? How had she been so unaware? How had she not *sensed* his closeness?

'Never did any man need his lady more.'

'He is well?' she asked quickly, alarm springing.

'As well as could be expected. He is not ill, but he is under a great strain. It would be better for him if you were still in Nottingham, but that cannot be. And besides, there are . . . obstacles for you both.'

'I am aware of that, Sir Robert. No one could be more aware.' She had to take a deep breath to compose herself. 'When may I see him?'

'Are you still to stay behind when everyone else goes hawking?'

'Yes.' Jack must have told him.

'Do you know which way they go?'

'North.'

'You are sure?'

She nodded. 'Yes, perfectly sure. I think it probable they will stay overnight at one of the manors. I do not know which one. Jack is determined it is to be quite an outing, even without his white hobby. I wonder he does not wear white as well,' she added.

'So *virginal* a colour for Jack of Lincoln?' Robert raised an eyebrow. 'However, if everyone is to be away from Sheriff Hutton today, and if they know you do not like hawking, perhaps you and I could ride together? I am sure I will be regarded as a harmless escort.'

She smiled. 'You are a gentleman, Sir Robert. The king would not send you to me if you were not.'

'I am first and foremost his friend, Lady Cicely.'

'And for that, I hold you in great respect.' She smiled sadly. 'If only I were not his niece . . .'

'My lady, fate has dealt him so many blows that I wonder he does not break beneath it all. He is but human, and his life is filled with sorrow. Except for you, Lady Cicely, because you have warmed his heart again, and for that alone I am your most willing servant. No one deserves happiness more than he. He is the most loyal and supportive friend any man could have.'

She looked at him. 'He *is* well? You would not deceive me?'

'He is well, my lady, as you will soon see for yourself. The long ride caused him pain, but he was bathing when I left. Warm water eases the discomfort, although it does not banish it, of course.'

'I . . . I cannot believe he is near.'

In the room behind them John laughed at something Jack said, and she lowered her eyes guiltily. She was making arrangements to go to Richard while John was in the same room. It shamed her, and yet she could only place his father first.

Robert saw. 'It is not easy for you, I think.'

'In the end, there is no choice. It will always be Richard. It can never be anyone else.'

She turned towards the room again and felt Jack's eyes upon her. His fingers rapped quietly upon the king's letter and he smiled. He knew.

CHAPTER TWENTY-FOUR

THE HUNTING TOWER stood on a hillside, its parapets above the trees. When it was built there were not any trees, and those who stood on its roof would watch stag hunting across the valley below and the hills beyond. A brook trickled down the slope against its eastern walls, and everything was very quiet. There were no horses, no sounds. A curl of smoke rose from the chimney of one of the low outbuildings that clustered against the tower's uphill wall, for there was a keeper and his wife who took care of everything no matter if there was hunting or not.

It was the middle of the afternoon and the air was very warm and still as Robert and Cicely rode up towards the tower. Harnesses jingled, and their mounts trod easily on the soft mossy track that wound among the trees.

Cicely's heart was pounding with such hope and anticipation that it seemed set to burst. She too had bathed, and then chose a gown of honeysuckle gold silk that she hoped would brighten Richard's heart. Her hair was free about her shoulders, without even a small cap to control it, and her skin was sweet with rose water.

When they were almost there, she glanced at Robert. 'Please tell me I will not suddenly awaken and find myself back at Sheriff Hutton.'

'It is real, my lady. He awaits you. This is no jest or deception. He has come all this way, risking much just for a little while with you.'

They reined in close to the brook, and he dismounted to help her down. Then he nodded at the doorway, which was reached up a flight of stone steps against the tower wall. The door stood open. 'Go to him, Lady Cicely. You will be alone together, for the tower keeper and his wife are loyal and I will busy myself elsewhere.'

Cicely hesitated in an agony of breathless excitement. In a few moments now she would be with him again. With Richard. She caught up her skirts and mounted the steps. Her gown rustled, her hair moved in the light breeze and her heart thundered in her breast. She took a step inside, where the air was noticeably colder. Little warmth penetrated the thick stone walls. There were more steps, leading steeply up to the floor above. She climbed slowly now, her eyes upon the shadows ahead. At the top she found light from a single narrow window. It revealed a wooden-floored chamber with a beamed ceiling, a huge stone fireplace where the hearth was black with soot and ash, and shadowy furniture, chairs, a settle, a table . . . upon which she saw his hat and gauntlets.

'Richard?'

'One step more, sweet Cicely, and our sin is as good as committed,' his voice said softly, and he emerged from the shadow beyond the fireplace.

There was not much light, but sufficient for her to see he was pale, marked by sleepless nights and the pressure of rumour, speculation, treachery and preparation for a foe who might not even come. He was not dressed as a king, but as a traveller, in leather doublet and hose beneath a simple sleeveless coat unadorned with fur or embroidery. He might have been any man, except that he had that touch of royalty, that demeanour and sophistication that marked him as highborn. His eyes were more tired, and his face drawn. That face, those lips, all so incredibly dear to her. 'Oh, my love,' she whispered, taking that one deliberate step again.

Then she ran to him and he held her tightly, his face buried in her hair as he breathed the scent of her. He could not have crushed her closer, drained her more of love than he did now. It was as if he could be renewed through her, could find again his strength and purpose, his will. He did not speak, did not caress or kiss her; he simply embraced her as life itself to him.

Her tears flowed as she moved her cheek against his hair. She wanted to sacrifice her own self if it would return him to his. He was so precious, so needed, so susceptible that her heart turned over with the incredible love she had for him. Now it was *her* fingers that sank into the warm hair at the nape of his neck, her fingers that coiled and stretched, twisted and twined, imparting the sweetness of her emotion, the completeness of her desire. His clothes, poor or not, still smelled of costmary, and it was a scent that pricked her nostrils, aroused sensations and worked its rich way through her body and limbs.

She kissed his hair. 'I cannot believe you are here, that I can touch you again. I have missed you so much.'

At last he drew away. 'I could not stay away. I need you, Cicely.'

'You have my love, *all* of it, forever. No man can ever mean to me what you do.' She took his face in her hands and moved her lips tenderly against his, savouring the caress as if it were the very first. Then she looked into his eyes. 'You must be strong,' she whispered. 'Be strong for me, because I cannot live without you. Do not let your enemies win even before you face Tudor. He is a petty lordling, not worth the ground you tread upon.'

He smiled. 'You are my courage, my sweet Cicely.'

'No, *you* are your courage. Never think that if I am not at your side you will falter. I *am* with you, every moment of every day. Richard, you are my lover and my king. I could not hold you in more regard if you were also a god. Can you not see why I love you? Why I would give my life for you? You are the anointed King of England, you have God and right on your side, and the people support you, but I see so much more. I love you for the man you are. I will always love you for that.'

'You lift me, Cicely. Always you lift me.'

She smiled. 'And you excite me. Do you know how difficult it is to stand here and not make love to you? I have *never* loved before as I do now, and I never will again. There is nothing that could ever be finer, greater, more inspiring or rewarding than what is between you and me. Tell me you know it too.'

'You know I do.' He put his hand to her cheek. 'It has been intolerable without you.'

'When must you go?'

'In the morning. Neither Robert nor I can contemplate riding back today, it is just too much. I certainly cannot. We will leave at dawn, and reach Nottingham at nightfall.' He smiled. 'I will return to my apartments by a certain secret doorway. And sleep.'

'Then we must make the most of now.' She covered his face with foolish, loving kisses. 'Give yourself to me again, Richard, for I need your physical love as you need mine. Oh, I believe I could kiss you forever.'

'And if I could let you, Cicely, believe me I would.'

She smiled. He had brought her to life, and she could not imagine that life without him. 'There was never such a king as you, Richard Plantagenet.'

'That may or may not be a compliment.'

'It is when I say it.'

'Ah, then I am comforted.' It already seemed his face had lightened. The terrible heaviness that had weighed upon him in those first seconds had been banished, simply because he was with her.

He took her hand and conducted her up to the room above. It was very much the same as the one they had left, except that it boasted a large posted bed that had clearly at one time graced the lord's quarters at the castle.

She wondered if he had ever been here like this before. Maybe she somehow imparted the silent query, for he knew. 'No, my lady, I have not.'

She gazed at him. 'I really cannot exist without you,' she said again.

He came to unlace her gown, and she shivered in the cool air as the honeysuckle brocade slipped to the rush-matted floor. Then he turned her to face him. 'You *can* exist without me, Cicely.'

She shook her head. 'No, for I would not wish to draw breath if you were not here.' She remembered the poem, and recited it. 'Did you write it?' she asked then.

'Yes. It was when I realized that Anne loved her first husband more than she did me. I had forgotten it.'

'It is very beautiful.'

He smiled. 'Such agony did not last long. A year later I would not have written it at all.'

'Will you mind if I remember it?'

'No, sweetheart, for I *would* write those words for you. It is yours, sweetheart. As am I.'

'You are beautiful to me, Richard. No man can come close to you.' She began to undress him, slowly, tantalizingly, kissing every portion of him, worshipping and caressing him. She stroked him, ran her gentle fingertips over his back, his shoulders, his chest, his waist, his loins. She knelt before him, holding him close, hiding her face against him, kissing him more. All of him. There was no part of him that was not precious to her. Nor was there any thought now of their close blood, of rules or sin, only that they were together again.

He bent to her, taking her hand and raising her to her feet. 'Sweet Jesu, Cicely, would you have me part with what is yours before we even get to the bed?'

'I would have you now, then again, and then again.'

'After riding as I have today, I do not know how capable I am,' he said, smiling.

'You do not have to do anything. You have taught me well what to do.'

His eyes were amused. 'I am that good a teacher?'

'Oh yes, I think we can safely say you are.'

He remembered using the same phrase that night at the abbey. 'Is there anything I have ever said that you do not recall?'

'Not a word.' She took his hand and led him to the bed. 'Come, for we waste time and that is something we do not have.'

She lay down, and drew him with her. The joy of pressing their bodies together was infinite. His arms were around her, his lips were upon hers. She would taste him, smell him, and see him so clearly. He was hers, all hers, and she was so happy that she wept as he made love to her. He was passionate, tender, vulnerable, and so in need of her that she could not have cared more for him than she did there in the hunting tower.

She stretched her body up to him with pleasure as he moved within her, and she gazed up at his face as the final moments exploded from him. His eyes were closed, his dark chestnut hair tangled, his lips parted. What it was to see such a man at such a moment! His beauty almost fractured her heart, and when he sank into her arms again, she gathered him close. Dear God, how she loved him. It was an ache that engulfed her, and wrenched her heart from her body. Could she let him go again? Could she let him ride away, back to whatever fate awaited him? 'No,' she whispered to herself. 'No, I will not part with you again.'

He raised his head. 'We have to part,' he said gently.

'Take me back with you.'

'No.'

'Please, I beg you. Take me with you.'

'No, sweetheart.' He leaned up to push her hair from her damp forehead. 'You have to stay here, and never speak of our meeting today. We knew how it would have to be.' He kissed her on the lips, a long, sweet, gentle kiss that seemed to spread into her veins.

'That does not ease my heart now,' she whispered.

'Nor does it ease mine, but at least I have held you again. It was too much to be there without you. I have been longing for a sight of you, a word with you, a touch. Oh, I have *so* ached to touch you . . .'

'And I you.' She pulled him into her arms again, and they lay there, wrapped in an intimacy neither of them wished to bring to an end. Just for this while they could forget and simply be themselves, lovers, sharing only one soul.

'Cicely, if we were back now in the abbey, could you ever have envisaged we would be like this now?'

She closed her eyes as she moved her cheek against his hair. 'I knew I had left childhood far behind. I was so affected by you, so drawn and caressed by your smiles and kind attention, that I knew I would never be the same again. You meant nothing wrong in what you did, you were simply being your own self, but I had never known such feelings before. I know now what you had aroused in me, but I did not know it then.' She leaned up on an elbow to look down at him. 'I also know that I will not leave you until morning.'

'Cicely—'

'No. In this I will *not* obey you, Your Grace. You may be the King of England, Richard Plantagenet, but *I* rule here. Tonight we can go to sleep together and wake up together. Just this once.'

'And how do you intend to explain your absence from Sheriff Hutton?'

'Jack will know where I am and who I am with. He realized at Nottingham, and he is nothing if not accustomed to the intricacies of clandestine trysts.' She put her hand to his cheek. 'I *must* sleep at your side tonight, do you not understand that? I want to wrap my arms around you, rest my head against you, hear your gentle breathing. There must be one occasion when we see the morning light together, warm and close. When might there be another opportunity like this? Please, Richard, do not deny me.'

He smiled a little. 'Staying here overnight is intended to recoup my strength, not vanquish it completely.'

'It need only be sleep. It's the being with you that matters. I need to be close to you like that. And you need to be with me. You cannot come here like this and not spend every moment with me.'

He drew her closer. 'Once again I should send you away.'

'But you will not.'

'No, I will not.'

'Let me love you. I vow you will not need to move a muscle.'

He laughed, a real laugh that transformed him. 'Not even one? Then it may be a pointless exercise, my love!'

She laughed too. 'Well, maybe just one. The most important one. This one . . .' She slipped her hand down over his lean abdomen and into the dark hairs around his loins. Then she began to stroke him. 'There, you see? It works very well.'

'That is because it knows what I am thinking.'

They fell asleep in an embrace, but not before they had made love several times more. She did not want to sleep, just to hold him while *he* did. But his warmth lulled her, as did the mere fact that he was with her like this. The morning would come all too soon, but she would be here when it did, with him in her arms.

Sleep still enveloped them, and dawn had yet to come when Robert came to the tower. He carried a lighted lantern and stood at the bottom of the steps to call up. 'It is time, Your Grace.' He left the lantern on the steps, so that its light shone up to where they lay.

Richard stirred, and then remembered. His arms went around her and he kissed her again. Her eyes opened slowly and she smiled at him, but then the smile faded. 'You have to go?'

'No, sweetheart, you do. Robert will take you safely back to the castle.'

'No.'

'You must go this time, Cicely. I have already risked too much to be here. I need to be at Nottingham when word arrives that Henry Tudor has set foot in my realm, not lying in paradise with you.'

'This is paradise?'

'Yes, because you are here.' He kissed her again, adoring her with his lips in such a way that she knew it signified parting. She wanted to hold him back as he slipped from the bed, but he moved beyond her outstretched fingers.

She got up and stood behind him, her arms around his chest, her body pressed to his damaged spine. 'You will not be able to come here again, will you?'

His hands enclosed hers. 'Not until it is over.'

Please God, keep him safe for me. 'Has anyone ever loved as we do?' she whispered.

'I would wish *everyone* to be able to love like this,' he answered, leaning his head back so that his hair mixed with hers. Then he drew away and bent to hold her gown for her step into it. He paused after he had drawn it up around her. 'We will be together again, I vow, but I do not know when.'

She had to close her eyes because the tears were near again and she did not want to make it even harder for him.

He laced the gown. 'See how adept I am?' He smiled.

'I envy all the women who had ever lain with you.'

'You do not need to,' he answered. 'Not one of them could put you in the shade. Now, let us see how nimble-fingered *you* are.'

'I have not dressed many kings,' she said.

'I trust you will only dress one, my lady.'

'There is no question of it, because there is only one king I would wish to assist with even his gloves.' She helped him, but as he was about to fasten the front of his doublet, she halted. 'One moment, my lord . . .' She moved close and put her lips to his chest, moving them adoringly over his warmth. Then she opened her purse and took out a small kerchief she had placed there earlier. It was the first thing she had ever embroidered — in a design of sweet cicely flowers and leaves — and it meant a great deal to her. She pushed it gently inside the doublet, against his heart, and then completed the fastening herself. 'Carry it with you, my love, for it will remind you of me.'

'Jesu, Cicely, do you think I need reminding?'

Their lips joined again, and then she pulled back slightly. 'I will go now, but parting from you is still so hard that—'

He put a finger to her lips. 'No more words, Cicely, for we do not need them. We know what is in our hearts.'

'Sometimes words say more than they seem to. The last time we parted, you said such beautiful things to me, and one keeps returning. Now *I* say it. *Take my love with you, and always keep it close, for it can never belong to another.*'

He pressed her palm to his lips, and then led her down the stairs again. He picked up the lantern and went to a table, upon which she saw the few things he had needed to write to Jack. There was another letter there, folded, sealed, and he gave it to her. 'Put it in your purse. Do not read it now, but when you are private.'

'Richard . . .'

'In your purse,' he said again.

She did as he bade, but her hands shook so much that he had to help her. His fingers were firm and steady. 'I have not said how the colour of your gown pleases me. It is a colour to gladden the heart,' he said.

'That is why I wore it.'

'I know.' He smiled. 'Now, Robert will see you safely back to Sheriff Hutton.'

She gazed at him, absorbing every detail, every small thing that made him what he was to her. 'I love you so very much,' she whispered.

'And I you.'

She hesitated a moment more, finding this parting so much more difficult than the one before, and that had been anguish enough. There was something else now, something she could not identify but which touched her with a cold finger. He was alone and in peril, and he affected her so much. Where he went, she wanted to be as well, but she could not. Not now. She had to let him go away from her to a fate that might be his salvation and vindication, or might equally be his death.

'Please, Cicely,' he said softly. 'Go.'

Choking back her tears, she turned and went from him. She felt as if her heart tried to leap out of her breast to return to him to whom it belonged. It was all she could do not to return to him. Not to even look back. The pre-dawn light was blessedly anonymous, hiding her distress as she went to where Robert waited with the horses.

He was kind. 'You will see him again, Lady Cicely.'

'Will I?'

'Do not even think that you will not,' he said quickly, almost superstitiously.

She struggled for composure. 'I cannot bear to leave him, I simply cannot bear it.' She turned on impulse to go back but he prevented her.

'No, my lady. Let him be. Do you think he finds this moment any easier than you? I must take you back to Sheriff Hutton, and then he and I must make all haste back to Nottingham.'

'Look after him for me, Sir Robert.'

He nodded. 'You may rely upon it, Lady Cicely.'

The others had returned the previous evening, but at this early hour she saw no one. Except Jack, whom she encountered on the steps that led up to the private apartments.

He halted before her, the light of a wall torch in his eyes and through his amethyst. 'How now, sweet Cicely? Creeping home at dawn?'

'Yes.'

'How is he?'

'Who?'

He folded his arms. 'The king.'

'Well.'

'And lusty, by the air about you.' He smiled and stepped aside for her to pass. 'He is a fortunate man, Cicely Plantagenet, and the only one whose place in your heart I could not take.'

'Do you ever stop flirting, Jack?'

'I cannot help it. I was put on earth to pleasure the fair sex.' He grinned.

'The dazzling gift God presented to womankind?'

'Could I be anything less?'

'No doubt your wife is in full agreement.'

'I doubt it very much.'

She hid away to read the letter from Richard, and when she broke his seal, the words he wrote were so moving and tender that she was overwhelmed. Tears coursed down her cheeks as she read.

'My dearest, most beloved lady, I send this because I have to put down in writing the feelings I have for you. You are all around me, every moment of every day, and there is not an hour when I do not think of you as many times as that hour has minutes. Being parted from you is to be likened to purgatory, and I am but half a man because you are not with me. I am a king, yet lack that one jewel that will make me complete. I know that I am in your heart, and for this I cannot measure the honour I feel. Your sweet, forthright nature, your voice, your touch, your constant support, all of these make a slave of me. If our love is crossed by fate, I no longer care. It is an eternal love that will carry me to whatever lies ahead. No spirit could ever be more true than mine is to you. Be safe, my beloved. My heart and soul are forever in your keeping. Richard.'

She could hardly bear it, and raised the letter to her lips. He had touched it, written it, folded it with his own hand, and it made her feel close to him again. She wept unashamedly, because Richard Plantagenet was as eloquent with the written word as he was with the spoken. When he wanted to convey his love, he did it so incomparably that it was as if he held her in his arms.

CHAPTER TWENTY-FIVE

It was August, and Cicely sat with Bess on the grassy slope beneath the castle walls. Mary sat nearby, stroking a tabby cat that had begun to follow her around. The maid's eyes were fixed upon the gatehouse, from whence a wine cart would soon emerge.

Cicely could not help teasing the maid about her new sweetheart. 'Has Will disappeared, Mistress Kymbe?'

Mary blushed. 'Please, my lady.'

Bess looked around from the daisy chain she was making. 'Who *is* this Will? Is there some secret to which I am not party?'

Cicely smiled. 'Mary has a lover.'

'Oh, my lady, he is not my lover!' Mary exclaimed indignantly.

'Then it is surely not for want of him trying.'

Bess was interested now. 'Come, tell me all about him.'

Mary blushed even more. 'He is the son of the innkeeper at the White Boar.'

Bess was surprised. 'The one who brings the wine? Mary, he is built like York minster itself, has bright red hair and legs like tree trunks.'

Mary hid her flushed face.

Cicely smiled again. 'He entered the castle an hour ago and is still there. Mary threatens to fall down the bank in her eagerness to see him again.'

'Oh, my lady, it is not fair of you to mock me so.'

But at that moment they heard the deep rumble that announced the wine cart's passage beneath the gatehouse. The old grey horse moved more easily with only empty barrels to haul, and the muscular young man with the reins was whistling jauntily. His gaze moved to Mary, who met it without pretending to play the silly girl.

Cicely looked at her. 'Mary, Bess and I will not mind if you wish to speak to him.'

Eyes bright, the maid pushed the annoyed cat aside and scrambled to her feet to run lightly across the grass towards the slowly moving cart. A pleased smile spread across Will's cheerful face as he saw her, and he drew the horse to a halt.

Bess gazed at them wistfully. 'Oh, how envious I am, Cicely.'

'Surely *you* do not have a fancy for Will?' Cicely kept a straight face, for the thought of cool, elegant Bess with such a fellow was almost too comical.

'I will ignore that,' Bess murmured, finishing the daisy chain by making it into a little crown which she placed on her head. 'There, now I am at last a queen.'

A single horse galloped along the road from York, and Cicely shaded her eyes, a finger of alarm travelling up her spine as he moved towards them along the hollowed village street, casting a cloud of dust in his wake.

Bess stood. 'He wears Richard's colours. Oh, please, do not let it be bad news.' She pressed her hands to her mouth.

Cicely got up as well, her heart beginning to pound with trepidation.

The horseman passed the wine cart without checking, and rode full pelt into the castle court. Then the sisters heard Jack being called.

Bess's hand crept to take Cicely's. 'I will not believe it is bad news, I will *not* believe it.'

They stood there, undecided whether to go inside as well, but then they heard more hooves, and the rider emerged on a fresh horse, this time swinging away from the road, around the south-east tower and into the waiting arms of the forest.

Cicely's hand tightened around Bess's. 'Why does he go in that direction?'

'We are about to find out, for Jack and John are coming to us.'

Jack waved a letter as he approached, and the sisters saw the king's seal. 'Well, ladies,' Jack said, 'the moment of truth is almost upon us for Henry Tudor has landed.'

A pang of such force passed through Cicely that she thought she would be sick. It was upon them all at last, and Richard would soon face this latest challenge to his crown.

Jack read from the letter. 'Tudor reached Shrewsbury two days ago, the seventeenth, having passed unhindered through Wales. Unhindered and in part aided! '

'There are more potential enemies among English lords than the Welsh,' John replied.'

'Richard is mustering his men but still instructs us to remain here.' Jack all but crumpled the letter. 'If you and I were at his side, we would strengthen his arm and his resolve. Is that not so, John?'

'Yes,' was the simple answer.

'However, we must continue to play at nursemaids, for which fact I am so filled with resentment that, with your exception, John, I could happily strangle everyone.'

Bess was icy. 'If we do not strangle you first, Cousin, for you are as rude and disagreeable as it is possible to be.'

He grinned. 'Ah, you are coming around to me at last, Bess. Soon you will be begging to be admitted to my bed.'

She looked away.

'Oh, cruel heart,' he declared, grinning. Then he looked at John and Cicely again. 'There is some good news come out of this, for Richard has at last moved to secure the Stanleys' allegiance in some manner. Lord Stanley, it seems, requested leave to depart for his estates, which means he was slipping away from the king's side. Richard granted him permission, but only provided Stanley's son and heir, Lord Strange, remained in royal custody! A hostage, by God! That will serve to make Stanley think twice before unfurling his banners for his wife's puking son. Jesu, what I would not give for a chance to strike at the Tudor weasel.' He kicked at a clump of harebells, destroying them beyond recovery, and then he turned to Bess again. 'My lady, the king speaks also of you and your sister. He is most emphatic that you shall be prepared to leave the country with the utmost haste if need be. He does not wish you to fall victim to Henry Tudor.'

'Victim? I thought I was marked to be his consort.' Bess was bitter.

'Levity sits ill upon your lips, especially when it is at the king's expense. Or are you no longer in love with him?'

Bess flushed. 'You go too far, my lord of Lincoln.'

John was angered. 'For Jesu's sake, Jack, you do not only speak of Bess's uncle, you speak of *my* father!'

Cicely lowered her eyes to the daisy-strewn grass. *And you speak of my love. He is mine. Only mine.*

Jack repented. 'I crave your pardon, John, but Bess, you must be sensible on this. Because for you to be forced into Henry Tudor's bed is, in Richard's eyes, to make you a victim! Or you, Cicely.' He met her gaze, and she heard his silent addendum. *'Especially you.'*

Bess sighed. 'I cannot have the man I really love and so I wish I had agreed to the marriage with Desmond, for I would have been away in Ireland, out of reach.'

Cicely kept her eyes fixed upon the daisies around her feet. *She* had the man her sister loved, and now there were consequences. Her monthly bleeding was late. She was never late. Never. And she felt different. So different. She had become an observer, trapped in a hazy world that existed alongside this one. It was a wonderful secret, known only to her and to Mary, and she did not fear the day when she had to reveal her condition. She would never say whose child it was, though. Jack would know. Jack seemed to be aware of everything, but she would not *tell* anyone before Richard himself. May God care for him and bring him victory.

Bess's fresh statement about the king made Jack's handsome face grow cold. 'The fact is that you are *not* married to Desmond, nor are you destined to warm your uncle's nights. So, for you the alternative falls between flight or Henry Tudor's ardent embrace! Richard has commanded that you flee, and I trust you intend to obey him. He remains the king, no matter how you may lust after his body.' His glance flew to Cicely, and then away again.

Bess flushed. 'Cicely and I will do whatever the king wishes.'

A silence fell upon them and Cicely remembered the messenger. 'Jack, where does the king's rider go now?'

'He has Richard's commands for the Earl of Northumberland who lies at present at his manor of Wressle. There not having been any sign of him as yet, the king has to jostle him to raise his forces immediately and ride south to join the royal army, together with the men of York who would fight for their duke. Richard should not have to make such a request. Damn Northumberland. I think he bears a grudge because he still resents my having been appointed to the Council of the North. Harry Percy considers himself to be the commander hereabouts. I believe he is one of those who will hold back when Richard needs him most.'

Cicely was concerned. 'But Sir Robert Percy could not be stronger for Richard.'

'Robert is but distantly related to the earl, and has known Richard since childhood. Northumberland, however, is for Northumberland, and is a spineless knight, not worthy of carrying Hotspur's name, but Richard has need of his forces. More is the pity, because men of Percy's calibre are worthless. Bah, he is no fitting topic of conversation, I am more concerned with Henry Tudor. The battle will be bloody when Richard meets with him. You must pray your Lancastrian suitor is defeated, Bess.'

With a start, Bess remembered the foolish crown of daisies she still wore, and hastily removed it.

A vigilant lookout called down to Jack. 'My lord, many riders pass close to the castle from the south-east.'

Lincoln looked up quickly. 'Do you make out their colours?'

'Aye, my lord, they bear the crescent moon of Northumberland.'

With an oath, Lincoln turned towards John. 'What makes Percy ride *north* at a time such as this? His way lies *south*! What manner of cousin and supporter is he? I detect a stench! Come, John, we will ride out to intercept him. Keep your eyes and ears alert for anything, no matter how small, that may indicate his ultimate intentions. A few prudent questions should prove illuminating.'

Leaving Cicely and Bess, the two young men hurried back into the castle, emerging only minutes later with two standard bearers and a small detachment of mounted men-at-arms. John would later describe to Cicely exactly what happened.

Jack had grinned at him as they rode towards Northumberland and his leisurely retinue. 'It will be worth this effort just to see Percy's face when he realizes who we are. He would not come this close to Sheriff Hutton if he was aware of our presence. Nor would be he trotting along at such a lazy pace.'

Harness jingling, the small cavalcade cantered out to where the earl had halted on seeing them. As they drew near, they saw the expression of uneasy suspicion on his fat face. He was thirty-six, but looked older, and there was a set to his mouth that told of a cruel nature.

At last the party from the castle halted as well, and Jack and John manoeuvred alongside the earl's horse.

'Greetings, my lord,' Jack said, inclining his head.

'Cousin Lincoln, I greet you. I had no idea you were here. My lord John.' Percy's jowls bulged over his collar as he inclined his head.

Lincoln looked levelly at the shifting eyes that would not fully meet his own. 'My lord of Northumberland, I saw you passing and came to pay my . . . respects. It surprises me to see you riding north at this time. Did you not encounter the king's messenger barely minutes ago?'

'Ah yes, indeed, but I must first prepare. At the moment I have only half my promised strength. There is plague in York and I will need another route for fear of the contagion. I go now to my manor at Topcliffe with urgent matters to discharge.' Percy did not entirely conceal his dislike for Jack.

Jack shared the hostility. He knew there was plague in York, but also that if Percy really wished to travel south to Richard, he could. He grinned without humour. 'I will write to the king of your eagerness to attend him with your forces, but now, if your, er, business is of such great import, my lord, I will delay you no longer, and bid you farewell.' With a salute of his hand he turned his mount, and he and John retraced their steps to the castle, their standard bearers and riders following.

On the grassy slope, Cicely and Bess saw the earl shade his eyes to scan the castle battlements. He could see nothing unusual, no great force, no encampments, nothing. But he also glanced around at the forest, and signalled two riders to comb the glades. If there was a force true to Richard in the vicinity of Sheriff Hutton, he would find it.

Bess turned and walked back into the castle just as Jack and John returned from their confrontation with Northumberland. Jack reined in and turned in the saddle to watch the earl's company move on. 'How many like him are there, John? How many who hate York, wish to restore Woodvilles or Lancastrians, or look to Henry Tudor because they hate it that Richard is proving to be a loved and just king. They all come together now, all against the one man whose claim to the throne by far outranks any other. The question must be, are there enough of them to succeed?'

John swallowed. 'I pray not, Jack.'

'I will act upon Richard's wishes, and get everyone across the sea, now, without further delay. But when I have done this, I mean to join the king. Will you be at my side?'

'But, my father's wishes—'

'I know what Richard *wishes,* John, but I feel I *must* be with him. I can impose upon the three boys to leave now, although whether the two ladies will obey, I really do not know.'

'Bess said she will go, but I doubt she will leave England while my father is . . .'

'Alive?'

John nodded. 'Nor will I, for I do not think my father intended us to go unless the battle went against him. Jack, you are his heir and must be safe at all costs, so I think you are right to go now, and take the boys with you. But whether you are right to then go to my father instead of accompanying them to Burgundy is another matter. I am not in line to the throne, merely Richard's by-blow. If Cicely or Bess will not leave, I will stay here too.'

'Damn it all, John, it is Richard's express order that Bess and Cicely do not fall prey to the Tudor. They *must* leave as well.' Jack ran his hand agitatedly through his hair. 'Jesu, we speak as if Richard is already defeated, and yet . . .'

'Yet?'

'I have a feeling of foreboding. There *will* be too many Percys, John.'

Best course or not, when it came to the final moment, Bess would not leave, and because Cicely felt she must stay with her sister, John remained as well. Jack would have to set off in charge of only the three boys. His mounted men were waiting to depart as he came to his remaining cousins to say farewell.

He looked at Bess. 'Why do you fail Richard? Mm? Simply to be in the same land as him?'

'To breathe the same air? Yes, Jack, I do.'

'Then I trust you mean to take poison if things do not go as we pray?'

She did not answer the comment. 'Take care, Jack, God be with you.'

He turned to John. 'I need your promise, John. If you receive any word at all that the day has gone against us — against *him* — you must get you and the ladies gone from here immediately. Immediately, do you hear? I should be forcing you now, but will not force Bess, who is well old enough now to know the gravity of what she does.'

The words could not have been more indicative of Jack's bitterness, which extended to Cicely and John for permitting Bess to have her selfish way. He looked at Cicely in particular. 'You cannot fall into Tudor's hands, sweetheart.' He took her hand and kissed it soundly, before leaning close to whisper, 'I believe you have another secret, my lady.'

Her lips parted and she gasped. 'I do not understand, my lord.'

'I think you do. Be safe and well, Cicely Plantagenet. I pray that when it comes to names, you remember mine. But Jacqueline will do as well, I suppose.' He smiled and spoke very softly. 'Your eyes give you away, sweetheart. I can see your child in them.'

She caught his hand. 'You be safe too, Jack. I will miss you.'

'But not enough, dear lady, not enough.'

He kissed her on the lips, and then hurried away, out into the courtyard where the cavalcade awaited. Moments later Richard's heir and three young nephews rode out of Sheriff Hutton and turned east for the coast. And the safety of Burgundy.

Cicely gazed after them. She knew how Richard would feel if he were to learn what had happened, and what he would say. She, more than anyone, knew his feelings.

CHAPTER TWENTY-SIX

It was the twenty-sixth day of August 1485, and there had been no further word from Richard. Everything seemed so peaceful, as if nothing could possibly be happening — have happened — that would decide the fate of the throne.

Jack had sent word from the coast that their ship would sail on the next tide, and that was all those at Sheriff Hutton had heard. Whether he had accompanied the boys on the voyage, or merely sent them safely on their way, was not revealed. It could be that he was now with Richard, a fact that John found increasingly hard to bear. *He* should be with his father as well, no matter what Richard's instructions had entailed.

Yet, no matter how great his frustration, John obeyed his father and his conscience. In that, he was truly Richard's son. The king's instructions had been to flee only if they received word of defeat, and while John agreed with Jack's decision to leave before then, it was still not what Richard actually instructed. And so he did all he could within the bounds of his father's wishes. Last-minute flight was fully prepared for. Saddled horses were always kept in readiness in the stables, and a small armed escort would respond in an instant were an order to be given. They could leave within minutes, but no word came. Time hung in a way it had never done before.

Today, the twenty-sixth, John could not pace around inside a moment more, but went out riding. He stayed within sight of the castle, always able to see if anyone came or went, but his attention was not on the castle when someone *did* arrive.

Bess had not left her apartment that day, but Cicely was as restless as John. She walked in the castle courtyard, where the wind blew through her hair and excited the rooks around the towers. She had just reached the rail by the steps to the main castle apartments when suddenly there came the sound of hurrying footsteps, and Mary came out to her.

'My lady, Will is coming!'

'Will? But why the alarm? Surely he comes to see you?'

'I do not think so, my lady, because he rides at speed. I feel there is . . .' Mary did not finish, but her unspoken words were there anyway. She thought there was urgent news.

Cicely's hand crept to her throat. Make it good news. Please let it be so. But why would *Will* be the one to bring it?

Will urged his grey horse into the courtyard, shouting for the Earl of Lincoln, but he found only Cicely and Mary. His face was pale and his eyes filled with dismay as he slid down from the foam-flecked horse's bare back. 'Where is the earl, my lady?'

'He is not here.' A feeling of utter dread was beginning to seep through Cicely. *Richard*. . .'Please tell me what you have come for,' she managed to say.

Will went to his knee before her, tears pouring down his cheeks. 'My lady, King Richard is dead and Henry Tudor ascends the throne of England! May God rest our dear duke's soul.' Will crossed himself.

The very air seemed to be sucked from her. She was in a vacuum, with no feeling, no sound. Richard? No, he could not be dead. Not her dear love, the father of her unborn child, the most cherished lord of her heart.

'Lady Cicely?'

Will's voice echoed from afar, but as he addressed her again, she knew the air was returning, and with it came the agony of what she had to face. No, she could not confront it. This was not happening. All was really as it always had been. Richard was on the throne and would soon come to her again.

'Forgive me, my lady,' Will continued, 'but I came as soon as word began to spread. You still have time.'

'Time?' She could not think. She saw Richard everywhere, felt his touch, heard his voice. No, please, no, for he was the only reason she lived and breathed.

Mary came to steady her, and after a moment Cicely managed to look at Will again. 'What more do you know? Anything?'

'My lady, at this very moment a party of Henry Tudor's men are at the White Boar. They come to seek King Richard's heirs, but especially the Lady Elizabeth, your sister. They know you are here, and the Lord John, and also have word that the Earl of Lincoln and the Earl of Warwick are here as well. They are wild with victory.'

'Do they know of my brothers?'

'No, my lady.'

'When did the king die?' she whispered.

'On the twenty-second day of this month, my lady, at a place called Bosworth, somewhere south of Leicester.'

'There is no doubt? The battle was not a defeat from which he escaped?'

'No, my lady. Henry Tudor has sent a party with all haste to secure your persons. They hope to take you completely unawares. I know this to be true for I overheard their two leaders, Sir Robert Willoughby and Sir John Welles, talking at the tavern. They did not know I was nearby or that I managed to steal away to warn you. I do not know how long it will be before they are here. They may even be close behind.'

Sir John Welles? The same John Welles who had tried to abduct her brothers from the Tower? He had been knighted?

Will spoke urgently. 'You *must* leave, my lady! They cannot find you.'

'Do you know anything of how he died?' Cicely tried to maintain her composure, but her voice trembled and some of the words did not sound as they should. Her head was spinning and she could hear the blood pounding in her ears. Richard was dead. The man she loved and treasured above all other treasures was dead.

Will's voice was filled with anguish. 'Our Duke of Gloucester, our King Richard, was slain in the battle, cut down in the very heart of the fight, as were the Duke of Norfolk and many others. He almost reached Henry Tudor before he was slain. They say he cried treason, for he knew he had been betrayed.'

She closed her eyes. 'Oh, my beloved,' she whispered, gripping the rail by the steps.

'The Stanleys deserted him and threw in their forces with the Tudor. The Earl of Northumberland was there, but withheld himself from the battle altogether, so they say, and if that is discovered to be true then I do not give his life much value if he returns to the north. He will surely meet a violent death one dark night.'

'So my dearest Richard *was* bought and sold.' The words were uttered almost silently. That such a shining man should die because of false friends was almost too great an agony for her to bear. If ever there had been a good king, a just and fair one, a king who thought of the people, it was Richard. Henry Tudor was not worthy to even speak his name, let alone usurp his throne.

Will was confounded by her inaction. 'My lady, you cannot delay.'

'The Lady Elizabeth and I are alone here. Lord John has gone out riding, but promised to always have the castle in view.' She turned to Mary. 'Go, tell someone to ride to him without delay. Tell them that for pity's sake they must find him and warn him to escape.'

'My lady.' The maid bobbed a curtsey and then ran towards the sergeant's door.

Will was deeply cut by the tragedy of Bosworth Field, as would be all true Yorkshiremen. 'They have commanded my father to take down the sign of the White Boar. They say he must rename the tavern, for they will not have King Richard's badge shown anywhere.'

Cicely felt faint, and supported herself by gripping the rail even more tightly. Her other hand went to her belly, where Richard's child was lying snug and warm.

Will looked helplessly at her. 'You and your lady sister *must* go. *Now.* There is no time to wait for Lord John of Gloucester to return. You cannot become Henry Tudor's prisoners, my lady. Please. If you feel anything for our dear lost king, you will not permit his murderer to gain the very reward he seeks. Henry Tudor will not be long on his blood-ied throne if he does not have one or other of you as his wife.'

Cicely's orders were already obeyed, and a horseman clattered out as fast as his mount could carry him to find John. But he did not know where to seek John, only that he said he would always be within sight of the castle.

She struggled to make herself think clearly, her fingers slipping inside her purse to touch Richard's letter. 'Will, return to your father, for I do not doubt he needs you.'

'My lady—'

'Go.'

He obeyed, and urged his lathered horse outside again, cutting immediately towards the trees in order to avoid encountering the Lancastrians. Or were they Tudors? All he knew was that they were the enemy.

Cicely suddenly thought of something both Jack and John had overlooked, something very important. The fact of her brothers having been here seemed not to be known, and so all trace of them had to be removed. She turned to Mary. 'See to it that there is no evidence of my brothers. Burn or bury whatever you find. The same applies to anything left by the Earls of Warwick and Lincoln, and my lord John. If it is possible to convey the impression that my sister and I have been alone here, I will do it. Arouse as many servants as you can. Do not fail me in this. And . . . tell my sister.' She hardly dared to imagine what effect such news would have upon Bess.

Mary ran off just as the sergeant presented himself, and Cicely turned her attention to him. 'King Richard lost the day,' she said, her voice choking because saying the words was so harrowing.

The sergeant was stricken. 'No, my lady. . . !'

'It is true. He . . . is dead, and we must do what we can to defy those who slaughtered him. Henry Tudor's men are soon to arrive here. Display Richard's banners from the turrets and battlements. I want *his* colours and standards to confront his murderers. Do you hear? This is the true king's fortress.'

'My lady.'

'But there is not to be armed resistance, do you hear? I do not want any more of Richard's loyal men to lose their lives. I will permit his enemies to enter peacefully.'

He hesitated. 'But, my lady—'

'You have your order, sir, or do you wish to challenge my authority?'

'No, my lady.'

'See that our mounts are still in readiness. If the Lord John should return in the coming minutes, there may yet be a chance of escape, in which case, you and your men are at liberty to do the same. Richard would not wish any more to die in his cause. He would wish us all to live to fight another day. So, whatever happens in the coming minutes, Henry Tudor's men are to be allowed to take the castle.'

'My lady.'

All she could see was Richard's bloodied body, carved and stabbed on Bosworth Field. His body, his dear body. Her sweet Richard. She closed her eyes for a moment, trying to keep control of herself.

The sergeant was shaken to the core, but he managed to bow to her. 'You are truly the king's niece, my lady.'

'I am so much more than that,' she whispered. 'So very much more.'

He did not understand, but hastened away to carry out her orders.

Cicely remained where she was, leaning against the rail, and then holding her arms around herself to protect the child that would keep Richard with her forever. His colours flapped from the towers and against the curtain wall. Would she ever see them again after today? Would the white boar ever be displayed in all its brave pride?

To be without you is to fade a little within
To not hear your voice is to lose the sweetness of music
To forfeit your smile is to be plunged into darkness
To never feel your touch is to lose all sense of being
To know you have gone forever is to steal away all joy.

He had given the poem to her. To her. And oh, how poignant the words now. He was the one who had gone, and yes, all joy had been stolen away. She forced the tears back, determined *not* to weep before his enemies. She had her pride. And Richard's. But it was so very hard to bear the pain, to know she would never see him again, kiss him again, be loved by him again.

Minutes passed, but then the breeze brought the sound of horses. Was it John? No, it was the rhythmic drumming of many horses. She and Bess were about to be captured by Henry Tudor. She drew herself up proudly, and clasped her hands in front of her to confront the oncoming sounds.

Somehow, from the depths of her heart, she found the courage to face whatever peril was about to enter Sheriff Hutton. The hooves were upon the drawbridge, echoing beneath the gatehouse, and then clattering in the courtyard, as Henry Tudor's armed men entered Richard's undefended stronghold. The red dragon of Cadwallader and red rose of Lancaster streamed above them, as did the prancing black lion of Welles and the ships' rudders of Willoughby. But far overhead Richard's banners fluttered the more proudly. She glanced up at them again and drew strength. His enemies would not learn *anything* from her. Anything. And she would delay them here for as long as she could, the better to allow John's escape. Please, let him have already taken flight.

The first face she saw amid the enemy horsemen in the castle was Ralph Scrope's, a sly, vengeful, *smirking* presence. To think that in her fourteen-year-old naivety she had once favoured his basilisk smiles. Now she abhorred him more than he could realize.

The two leaders, both several years older than Richard, she guessed, dismounted slowly, glancing warily at the battlements for any sign of a trap. They had gained entry so easily that it surely had to be trickery. The younger of the two approached her, bowing low, his lips set and unsmiling. He was grim-faced and inclined to stoutness, with an unfashionable beard sorely in need of washing as she noticed that flecks of food were caught in it. He had small brown eyes and full lips that he smacked every now and then, as if anticipating a long overdue meal. Or the sweetness of more punishment for the Yorkist nobility.

He swaggered in front of her, his arms akimbo. 'By your bearing and the colour of your hair, I imagine you must be Lady Cicely Plantagenet?'

'Who are you to so imagine?' she demanded in a clear voice.

'Sir Robert Willoughby, your servant.'

Servant he definitely was not, she thought, for arrogance almost dripped from him. She managed to nod with a calm she did not feel. Richard was dead, and she wished she had died with him. How could she live now? Except . . . Her hand crept to her belly, and stayed there. She carried him within her, and for *that* she would survive Armageddon itself.

Willoughby had not finished. 'I am charged by Henry, by the grace of God, King of England, to bring you and every one of your family here present to London.'

'I am alone, Sir Robert. As you see.' She spread her hands.

'We will see about that,' he replied.

Sir John Welles — who else could he be? — stepped forward then, and she noticed that after a second of hesitation, Willoughby gave way to him. Welles was younger than she had expected, tall and lean, with very deep blue eyes and thin lips. He was as unfashionably bearded as Willoughby, but took greater pride in his appearance. The bow he executed was far from unfashionable, and she knew that he was as much a courtier as soldier.

'Sir John Welles, my lady,' he said, bowing.

'So, you are *sir* now? Surely you were not elevated by your nephew for *failing* to abduct my brothers from the Tower?'

He smiled. 'I do not have a stick, yet appear to have poked a viper. Lady Cicely, I have to believe that you already know of Bosworth Field?' His voice was clipped and business-like and yet had none of Willoughby's unpleasantness.

'I do.' Margaret's half-brother did not resemble her in any way. Clearly he did not take after their shared mother, but after his attainted Lancastrian father, Lionel, Baron Welles.

'I am here to represent to you the kind greetings of King Henry VII.' He held out a sealed document.

She did not even glance at it. Touch something that bore the seal of any other king than Richard? She would perish first. There *was* no Henry VII, only Richard III.

Welles stepped further forward, caught her hand and placed the document in it. Then he folded her fingers tightly around it. 'It *must* be accepted, my lady.'

She stood there, holding Henry Tudor's missive. 'There is no King Henry, Sir John. Only Richard.'

'Who is now exceedingly dead,' he pointed out, not unreasonably.

'Not to me. He is the only true King of England, crowned so in the sight of God. Do not speak to me of your treacherous Henry, who has little claim to the throne, save a small drop of illegitimate royal blood and a mass of traitors to support him. King Richard was foully betrayed at Bosworth, by men without any of his greatness. I pray you all burn for your part in the sacrilege of killing the anointed king.'

Willoughby took an angry step forward, but Welles prevented him. 'Lady Cicely, I am endeavouring to be reasonable.'

She looked through him and did not respond. If only he knew that her brothers had been hidden away at Friskney, right next to his own lands in Lincolnshire.

Willoughby had not done with her. 'There is something unnatural about your veneration of crook-backed Richard, my lady.'

'Better to have a crooked back than a crooked spirit. And how can I be unnatural to love him? He was my uncle and he honoured my siblings and me as his nieces and nephews. My father's marriage *was* false, my mother admitted it. What would *you* do in Richard's place, Sir Robert? Allow your brother's by-blow to inherit everything? Would you deny your own son's patrimony, and at the same time condemn the land to strife? Or is that too uncomfortable a question? You would rather speak ill of Richard than admit he was entitled — *obliged* — to act as he did. My siblings and I are all illegitimate, yet in order to marry my sister, your shabby new king is prepared to stand before God and claim my parents' marriage was true after all. Oh, no doubt he will overturn Richard's rights in order to do so, but he will still bear false witness to the Almighty. Henry Tudor may be king by right of conquest and usurpation, but he will not perch upon his rickety throne for long unless he unites York and Lancaster. I pray God is so outraged that He sends a bolt of lightning to sever Tudor's head from his noxious body. *That* would be true justice.'

She thought Willoughby would lunge for her, but again Welles restrained him, this time with more difficulty. His piercing blue eyes rested upon her. 'How valiant you are, my lady, but it is all in vain. I have been charged to present you with King Henry's greetings, and I have so done. Sir Robert is charged with bringing your persons safely to London. By that I mean the Earls of Lincoln and—'

'The Earl of Lincoln was not at King Richard's side?'

'No, my lady, and you know it.'

'I believed he was,' she answered frankly. Her mind began to race. Then where was Jack? What had happened? Had he sailed with the boys after all? How she hoped so.

'So, you claim the Earl of Lincoln is not here?'

'I *know* he is not here. If he was not captured at Bosworth, then he must have escaped. I truly believed he was there.'

Willoughby spoke. 'I have to bring the persons of the Earls of Lincoln and Warwick, the Lady Elizabeth of York, you and John of Gloucester to the king in London.'

'Well, you have found me, sir, and that will have to do.' They definitely did not know about her brothers! She could scarce keep the triumph from her eyes, and she had never been more regal than in that moment. 'I recognize no King Henry,' she said again. 'I am the Lady Cicely Plantagenet, King Richard's vehement supporter and ally, his proud, loyal and loving niece, daughter of King Edward IV, and representative of the House of York. I will *never* submit to Henry Tudor. *I* am not the traitor here, you are. All of you. I am outraged that you dare to raise your eyes from your shame.' Her hand crept to shield her belly, and Welles saw.

There was a sullen stir and Willoughby could stand no more of her defiance, but as he stepped towards her, Welles again prevented him. More forcefully this time.

'For the love of God, Willoughby, can you not see her distress? Remember you may be addressing the king's senior sister-in-law, possibly even his queen, so do not be a fool.' Welles turned to her again. 'My lady, I can understand your loyalty, and respect it, but in these new times it is a dangerous thing.'

'Loyalty cannot be changed, not if it was true in the first place.'

'Enough of all this dilly-dallying, my lady. Please tell Sir Robert Willoughby where he may find — if not Lincoln — then Warwick, and Richard's bastard son, John of Gloucester? And, of course, your sister, the Lady Elizabeth of York.'

‘I am alone here, Sir John,’ she said again, although she knew that a cursory search would soon lead them to Bess.

‘I hardly think that to be so, my lady. Of late your name has been linked with Richard’s bastard, so he at least will be here.’ Welles noticed again how she defended her belly.

A new voice broke into the courtyard from the direction of the gatehouse. ‘You would have words with me, sirs? Or is it your unmanly Lancastrian practice to terrorize defenceless women?’

Cicely could have wept with dismay as all eyes turned towards the gatehouse from whence the words came. It was John, astride a dappled horse in the shadows, hair darkened by the gloom, his jewelled clothing flashing. Henry Tudor’s men fell back in fear, seeing Richard Plantagenet’s vengeful ghost risen from the blood-soaked earth of Bosworth.

Ralph Scrope was so terrified that he eased his horse away until it almost crushed his leg against the wall. John saw him, and smiled contemptuously. ‘So here you are, Scrope, with the other human excrement. Ready to be scraped from my boot.’

Willoughby’s face had waxed pale with such fear that he backed away, caught his spur on a step and fell rather ignominiously. He was obliged to scramble up again, but he knew his fear had been observed. Welles stood motionless, and Cicely realized he was not of a sufficiently superstitious nature to be taken in. He saw Richard’s son, not Richard himself.

John moved his heel and rode further into the courtyard, where Henry Tudor’s unnerved men parted before him. His silvery hair told immediately of his true identity. He was proud and upright, the son of whom Richard had always been proud, and as he looked at Cicely, smiling his love, she struggled to keep control of herself. Her heart reached out to him across the hostile air. Why had he not fled for his life? Why had he come right into the lion’s den?

Willoughby snapped his fingers at the men nearby, and in a moment John’s horse was held, and he himself hauled from the saddle. His hands were bound and he was dragged away.

She looked desperately to Welles. 'You cannot harm him! Please, I beg of you! Does your Henry not wish him to be taken to London? Does he not want us *all* to be taken there?' She was reminding him again of Henry Tudor's need for a Yorkist bride.

Welles looked at Willoughby. 'You heard what the Lady Cicely points out. You had better stay within the strict terms of your remit. I do not need to remind you that I am close to the king.'

Just then they all heard a terrible wailing shriek from inside the castle. Mary had told Bess of Richard's death.

Welles looked at Cicely. 'The Lady Elizabeth, I imagine? For fame has it that she alone would grieve so for Richard Plantagenet.'

'How unwise you are to speak of such things, sir,' she answered, 'for she may be about to become the new queen.'

He was amused by the turning of his own words upon him. 'You are right, of course, my lady. I should listen to my own advice.'

'King Richard did not intend to marry my sister, my lord. I can state that without hesitation, because I have always been sufficiently in his confidence to know. I tell no lie. My sister is as pure a maid now as she was before going to Richard's court. He always behaved impeccably towards her, as an uncle should, and if you believe otherwise, or repeat otherwise, you will deserve eternal damnation.'

'Eternal damnation, eh? Well, I would not wish to risk that,' he replied, and she again sensed that she amused him. And that he admired her courage.

Sir Robert signalled to some of his men, who dismounted and accompanied him into the castle to find and detain Bess, but Welles called after him, obliging him to halt on the steps. 'Find the Lady Elizabeth by all means, Willoughby, but if you do one thing that offends her or causes her distress, I *will* see that the king hears of it.'

Willoughby's tongue passed over his lips and as he proceeded into the castle, Cicely knew he loathed Sir John Welles. At that moment her glance fell once more upon Ralph Scrope. Still he smirked, still he gloated. Still she despised him.

'Sir, may I request one thing of you?' she asked Welles.

Surprised, he inclined his head. 'I am at your disposal.'

'Please send Ralph Scrope from Richard's castle.'

He was caught unawares. 'Indeed? But are you not handfast? I have seen the contract.'

She stiffened. 'Certainly not!' Again she saw Richard, leaning against the abbey wall. *Do not worry, Cicely, for you have heard the last of such a match. I will not coerce you into Scrope's bed.* Nor had he, for Richard was nothing if not a man of his word. But clearly he had not destroyed the document. She knew he would not have signed it, or appended his seal.

Welles spoke again. 'The contract is evidence of a binding agreement between you and Ralph Scrope It was drawn up at King Richard's instigation and states that your father wished it, and that you and Ralph were compliant.'

'Does it bear my uncle's signature and seal?' she asked quickly

'It does, but I have to admit I am not entirely convinced by the signature. Richard was a very educated man, with an excellent hand, whereas this more resembles the trail of a spider through ink.' Welles turned to Ralph. 'I will have your version of this.'

'The Lady Cicely and I are handfast, my lord,' Ralph declared in a boasting tone. 'The late King Edward IV took my part and spoke to his brother on his deathbed. King Richard had the document drawn up, signed it and affixed his seal. It is as binding as marriage itself.'

'Liar!' Cicely cried. 'You worm, you insect! Richard was in the north when my father died and could not have heard *anything* said on the deathbed. I was *never* handfast to you, and my uncle would *never* have proceeded after he knew I did not want such a match. The only man to whom I am handfast is the Lord John of Gloucester, and the fact curdles your spiteful bile with jealousy. You are beneath contempt.'

Welles looked at her again, clearly weighing the one version against the other.

She collected her tumbling thoughts. 'Think on, Sir John Welles, if you take Ralph Scrope's part in this, you could be elevating him to the position of Henry Tudor's brother-in-law, with all the influence and power that entails. And remember also, sir, that your nephew may yet marry me himself. He will not be pleased if you interfere in his plans by supporting Ralph Scrope in this sham. Incidentally, Ralph was in Richard's household until recently. He only went over to your cause to be avenged on me. A mongrel that can turn its tail once will do it again, this time over Henry Tudor's kingly new shoes.'

'That is calumny!' Ralph cried.

'It is the truth,' she replied levelly.

Welles' mind was suddenly made up. He jerked his thumb at Ralph. 'Return to York, if you please, and stay there until you receive word either from me or Sir Robert. I do not believe this marriage document to be genuine, and will submit it to King Henry's justice.'

Ralph went pale, his nostrils flared, and he kicked his heels to fling his horse out of the castle of Sheriff Hutton.

Cicely watched him go. To whom could he now offer his traitorous self? Who was left?

CHAPTER TWENTY-SEVEN

Later, when darkness had fallen, Cicely, Bess and John were permitted to be alone together for the first time. John had been released from his bonds, but like Cicely and Bess was obliged to stay in the rooms allotted to him, without access to the rest of the castle. Now they were brought together in the solar and told they had a few minutes of privacy before Welles and Willoughby came to speak with them.

Cicely ran into John's arms and held him tightly. 'I thought Sir Robert would kill you. I was so afraid . . .'

He returned the embrace, and she could feel his shoulders shaking. She had lost Richard the man, the lover, but John had lost the father he admired above all other men. She knew now that she loved John of Gloucester for himself, not only because he was Richard's son. Father *and* son were in her heart, and if she could no longer reach out to Richard, she could to John. At least, she could until it was no longer possible to hide her condition. She could not weep, but seemed to have entered another room within herself, a private room, without windows, cool and quiet. She could be alone there with Richard, hear him again, touch him again, make love to him again. There was no world outside, just them. And the room. Hers was a silent grief, but John could weep, and did so unashamedly. She drew him close, whispering gentle words, offering comfort, when all the time she was seared by her own desolation. She just could not show it, not yet, when she still had to confront Richard's enemies. Nor could she look to anyone else for understanding.

Her love for Richard was a great secret, and now he was lost to her. Forever. She had only her own counsel, and must think what Richard would have wished her to do. She closed her eyes. Her heart was in a thousand fragments, and could never be repaired, but at least she could console John.

Bess was also calm. Too calm. She might not have been Bess at all, but an identical stranger. She was measured, a mistress of ice. The high-backed chair upon which she sat was probably the most uncomfortable in the entire castle, but she gave no sign of anything. Her hands were clasped in her lap, she gazed straight before her, and there were no tears in her eyes.

John struggled to be himself again. 'Forgive me, Cicely, but it is such a shock and bereavement to me. And to you, I know, but—'

'I understand, John. Truly I do.'

He smiled at her through his tears, and pushed a lock of her hair back behind her ear. She caught his hand to stop him, for it was too evocative and poignant an echo of his father. 'I was so proud of you today, Cicely,' he said. 'I did not see the Tudor banners, I knew nothing until I was actually beneath the gatehouse. Even then I could have made my escape — well, attempted it, at least — but when I saw you facing them all like the daughter of York you are, I could not have left you.'

'I had your father's banners raised in defiance, did you not notice them?'

He gave a choked laugh. 'I did, Cicely, and I thought it signified his victory. Oh, dear God, for those minutes I was exultant. I thought it was all over and the future stretched gloriously ahead. England would prosper under my father's rule, we would be married and be happy together. I was an idiot in paradise.'

She was stricken, for it had not occurred to her that what was defiance to Henry Tudor's men might be construed as good news by John. 'Oh, John, I did not think. I lured you here when that was the very last thing I wished to do. Bess and I have so much to answer for. If we had not refused to leave, you would have escaped.' She could not have met Richard's eyes were he to walk in now. . . .

At that very moment the solar door was flung open, but it was Sir John Welles and the unlovable Sir Robert Willoughby. Both men had changed clothes and were clearly refreshed, but by the set of the latter's lips it had not improved his temper. Welles was now clean shaven, and Cicely saw that he was not ill-looking, but neither was he handsome. He had bearing and presence, was adroit, missed little and was probably able to deal with most difficulties that came his way. He had certainly been better chosen by Henry Tudor than his companion, because Willoughby did nothing at all to enhance the usurper's reputation.

The two men placed themselves across a table from the three representatives of the House of York. Bess looked at them without expression. Cicely and John had pulled hastily apart, but not before their embrace had been noted. Sir Robert's small eyes were hard and his voice even harder. 'Small wonder Scrope's presence was so unwelcome.'

John reached for the dagger that was no longer on his belt because it had been confiscated. His fingers closed over nothing. 'May the devil claim you soon, Willoughby!' he breathed.

'Ah, the young mongrel thinks he has teeth?'

Welles was in no mood. 'Enough,' he snapped, and then nodded at Cicely. 'Please be seated, my lady.'

She wanted to defy him, but his conduct had been all that was correct, and so she obeyed.

He turned to Bess. 'My lady, we ask for information as to the possible present whereabouts of John de la Pole, Earl of Lincoln and Edward Plantagenet, Earl of Warwick.' He stood in the circle of light thrown by the candles on a table.

Bess did not even look at him. 'I have nothing to say to you, sir, only to my new lord, Henry Tudor.'

Welles turned to John. 'Have *you* anything to tell me?'

'I do not know where my cousins of Lincoln and Warwick are,' John replied.

'Lady Cicely?' Welles' dark blue eyes moved to her again.

'I have already said I do not know, my lord.'

'How astonishing, for to be sure you were *all* here together. Oh, do not deny it, my lady, because whether or not you despise Ralph Scrope, he *did* confirm that he followed you here. Well, perhaps not here, exactly, but certainly to this side of York. I cannot imagine Richard would have sent you three here and the others elsewhere.'

'I was not in the true king's complete confidence,' she said defiantly, and untruthfully, because no one had been more in Richard's confidence. She wanted to do as Bess requested, behave as Bess did, but could not. Her feelings for Richard transcended everything, and to deny them was impossible. She would defend his name with all her might.

'I shall overlook that remark, my lady.'

'Do with it as you wish, my lord, because if you expect me to betray anyone or anything to you . . .'

'I do not *expect* anything, my lady. I am not that much of a dupe. You have made your feelings towards Richard very clear, and while I think you misguided, I cannot in all honesty blame you. He had great charm when he chose to use it, but he *is* believed to have had your brothers murdered in the Tower.'

John stiffened, but she caught his arm, her fingers urgent. 'No, John, do not rise to such feeble bait.' Her eyes implored him not to mention that her brothers had been here at Sheriff Hutton, and to her relief he relaxed again.

Bess said nothing, did nothing.

Cicely regarded Welles again. 'My uncle the king would never have committed such a terrible crime, my lord. And you certainly believed they lived in August 1483. Or did you just scramble into the Tower for the thrill of it? Perhaps you hoped to do away with them for your paltry Henry and then blame Richard?'

'I clearly have that stick somewhere about my person. Perhaps it will further satisfy your venomous loathing to know that I was involved in the Buckingham rising and that I was one of Henry's captains at Bosworth.'

'So, you succeeded in only one of the three,' she answered.

'Your fangs are effective,' he observed. 'I am sorry if I have turned into Beelzebub before your eyes.'

'You stink of brimstone, sir.'

At that he laughed. 'Then I will have to take another bath.'

'You will still stink.'

'You have a noble heart, Lady Cicely. I wonder if Richard ever knew what a ferocious kitten he had for a niece.'

She could not help a small smile. 'Oh yes, sir, he did. He knew it full well.'

'So where are your brothers now?'

'Still in their apartments in the Tower, I imagine.'

'How admirably cool you are, Lady Cicely, but given your unusual and illogical support for Richard Plantagenet, I cannot believe you. If he removed them, then I would hazard you know where to. Why do you guard him so well? Rightly or wrongly — you would have me think he was justified in having you and your siblings declared illegitimate. You, who were once destined for the King of Scotland's heir, must now settle for someone far lower in rank. John of Gloucester, it seems. Do you insist that you are handfast to him?'

John replied. 'The match had my father's consent, if that is what you mean. But it had yet to be formalized.'

'So you are *not* handfast in the strict meaning of the word?'

John fell silent.

Sir Robert gave a grunt. 'Unless you have anticipated your vows.'

Welles frowned at him and then looked at Cicely again. 'I am charged to act for my nephew, my lady, and I will not be defied on it because *you* are so strong for dead Richard. This is not a musical diversion with ribbons and fashionable trifles, it is a matter of the utmost political importance, so do not think to toy with me.'

John faced him. 'Choose your words with more care, sir, for it is my father of whom you speak, and to my lady that you are so unbecoming.'

Welles inclined his head. 'As you wish, I apologize for any offence I may have given.'

But Cicely rose to her feet anyway. 'Ribbons and fashionable trifles? My lord, do you *truly* believe that such things are in my mind at this time? You have murdered King Richard, and I hate you for it.'

His lips twitched. 'I did not kill him in person, my lady.'

'But you were there. That is enough.'

'For what it is worth, Lady Cicely, I have nothing but admiration for the way he died. Never did any man show more courage. Whatever else I may have thought of him, he was brave and resolute. He was alone, and fought so brilliantly that he almost reached my nephew. There would have been a very different outcome if his horse had not been cut from under him and his helmet dislodged. But for those last few yards, he would have won the battle. Too many betrayed him, and the fact is that he did *not* carry the day.'

'And now you raise a nonentity to his throne.' She trembled inside.

Welles paused, his lips pursed. 'Lady Cicely, Richard Plantagenet is dead and buried, and—'

'Buried? Where?'

'When I left I think it was to be imminently at the Grey Friars in Leicester. His naked body was first to be put on display, to prove he was indeed dead.'

John turned away, unable to bear it.

Now Cicely shook visibly. 'Your soulless, pinch-stomached nephew did not even show *honour* to the body of the anointed King of England, but stripped him and left him to be ogled at?'

Welles nodded. 'I fear so.'

'I trust you are proud of your half-sister's foul offspring, sir.'

'No, my lady, in this I am not, but I am not the new king. I would not have treated Richard in such a way, but at the same time you have to understand that it was necessary that his face be seen, to *prove* his death.'

John closed. 'Jesu, they abused him. . . .'

Cicely closed her eyes weakly, unable to bear the pain of it. His face. His beautiful face.

'My lady?' Welles came quickly around the table and ushered her gently back into the chair. 'I am sorry if this is too much, but you *must* understand my position.'

She strove to reclaim her outward air of control. 'Did you ever meet Richard, my lord?'

'Yes.'

'Then you must understand my grief, understand why we *all* grieve for him. He had a fine heart; there was none finer.'

'I envy him such devotion.'

'A courtier's response, sir, glib and insincere,' she retorted.

Willoughby had had enough of such delays. He was a man to beat the truth from anyone, even a woman. 'For pity's sake, Welles, have done with this nonsense. She has lied about Lincoln and Warwick, and would lie again if she thought she was protecting Richard Plantagenet's cause!'

Cicely's eyes flew at him. 'You are a disgrace to your already disgraced Henry Tudor, but even you admit Richard has a cause. The throne was his by *right*, not by knavish scheming! His blood and his claim to the throne could not be matched when he lived, and cannot be matched now! I detest you, *all* of you!' There were tears in her eyes and she would not have held her tongue even had Willoughby held a blade to her throat.

He uttered a terrible oath and stepped towards her with his hand raised, but John leapt at him, striking his chin so violently that for the second time since arriving at Sheriff Hutton, Sir Robert Willoughby was jolted from his feet. With a cry of rage, he scrambled up again and lunged at John.

Welles pulled them apart as if they were fighting dogs. 'Willoughby, stand back, I say! Stand back! *And* you, sir!' He shoved his boot against first Willoughby's knee and then John's. 'If you cannot conduct yourselves in a civilized manner, I will have you both removed and placed in a convenient dungeon. *There* you can fight to the death for all I care.' He held Willoughby's gaze. 'Oh yes, sir, for I think that in the eyes of the king I far outrank you.'

Sir Robert's face was stained red with anger and fear, but when he managed at last to speak it was to John, whom his words provoked to further passion. 'I retract nothing, Sir Bastard. Your father was a tyrant, a felon who usurped the throne of his own nephew and deserved to die!'

Suddenly Bess rose slowly from her chair, and the room fell silent. 'I will not have this misconduct in my presence, my lords. As it seems I am to be Queen of England, I believe King Henry would wish my family to be treated with due respect.'

Welles bowed. 'My lady, I disassociate myself from Sir Robert's insults. My reason for being here is to extend King Henry's greetings and love.'

'Love?' Bess's eyes flickered. 'It is a little soon for that, do you not think? His greetings I can gladly accept, but that is all.'

'Nevertheless, he is eager for your first meeting and begs you to ride south at your earliest convenience. He will send a magnificent company of ladies and gentlemen to accompany you on your journey in a fashion as befits his future wife and her family.'

Bess looked at him. 'I will ride south to meet the king, and my sister and cousin will ride with me. There is no one else here at Sheriff Hutton in whom you need be the slightest interested, and we do not know the whereabouts of either my cousin Lincoln or my cousin Warwick. They were briefly here but have long since departed. We believed my cousin Lincoln was at Bosworth. Now, I think this interview is at an end, for I intend, with my sister and cousin, to go to the chapel to pray for the soul of my uncle, King Richard.'

'By your leave, my lady, before you go I wish to say something.'

'Say it.'

'A thorough search of the castle has been instigated, without your permission, and for that I seek forgiveness. I hope you understand the delicacy of my position. Although York and Lancaster will soon be united by marriage, at the moment there are many of Yorkist persuasion who are not friendly to the new king. Until we find Lincoln, we know not if he is to be trusted to swear allegiance to my nephew. The same goes for the Earl of Warwick, although he is, of course, a child. I *have* to search the castle because it may be that they both hide here unknown to you, of course.'

Cicely was forced into an unwilling admiration. This man had a smooth tongue and was well able to avoid offence.

Bess nodded. 'You speak well, sir. Search as you please — you will not find anyone.' She swept out in a rustle of bronze brocade, followed by Cicely and John. They spoke not a word, because there were guards at every corner, every doorway, every window.

The chapel lay across the courtyard by the gatehouse, and was deserted in the flood of moonlight that now softened everything. Candles burned on the altar, and the golden cross upon it shone richly. The spangled window behind the altar was pierced by the moon, shedding crimson, azure, green and gold upon the glittering richness of the holy vessels. Bess went to prostrate herself on the altar steps, but when Cicely went to her, she shook her head. 'Leave me, Cissy, for I would pray alone.'

Cicely turned to John, who leaned against a pillar in that way so reminiscent of his father. He held out a hand, and as she slipped her fingers in his, he pulled her close and gave her a kiss that was at once passionate, anguished, loving and filled with sorrow. She would have needed to be fashioned from ice to resist, and so returned it with all the avidity of which she was capable at such a time. She wanted to help him, to give him all she could. Was it atonement? Maybe. Maybe.

He kissed her face, her eyes, her throat, savouring each caress, but her eyes were closed in shame, because it was Richard who held her. Richard, who had been so noble and yet was dead, his body desecrated, his resting place unworthy of his royal station. Unworthy of the great love in which he was held by so many.

At last John drew away. 'Dear God, I need us to be together tonight.'

'Then we will be.'

He looked at her. 'Cicely, we cannot. Not under Willoughby's nose. Nor Welles' for that matter.'

'Willoughby is a cruel man, but Welles is not, I think.'

'If he and Margaret Beaufort share a mother, count upon it, he will be cruel, and do you really imagine he would be lenient if he found Richard Plantagenet's son and niece together? Can you imagine how such a union might result? Any child would be dangerously close to the throne.'

Richard's words of warning echoed inside her, the more so because they had already come true, and the child she carried was even closer to the throne than any she could have with John of Gloucester. Her baby was the child of Richard III and the grandchild of Edward IV. Illegitimate or not, a child of such blood would attract Yorkist sympathies. Especially a boy. She was afraid, for herself and her baby, and there was no one in whom she could confide. No one at all, except perhaps . . . She wished she could talk to Jack. Dashing Jack, who teased and flirted, but whom she knew to be a good friend. Yes, she could talk to him. But not John, whom she had let down so grievously.

Bess got up from the steps and came to them. 'It chills my soul to think I must speak with courtesy to Richard's murderer, but I will do it. I do not forget that Henry Tudor has gained support only because of his promise to marry me. I am important to him, and until he has me in his bed, he has to treat me — us — well.'

Cicely could not understand her sister's abject surrender to fate. 'Bess, I look at you now and see a craven submission that is unworthy of your blood. You are a Plantagenet, and should have the pride of your lineage!'

'What would you have me do, Cissy? Refuse to marry Henry?'

'*I* would.'

'That is the difference between us, Cicely. You have the sort of passion I do not. Oh, I still have the wrong passion for Richard, but that is different. You are more fiery in nature. Entirely. I admire your strength and honesty, for I have neither quality myself.'

Turning on her heel she left the chapel.

Later, at the witching hour itself, as owls screeched across the moor and in the depths of Galtres Forest, from whence night travellers could be guided by the distant lamp on the steeple of All Saints in York, Cicely slipped silently from her bed and drew on her robe. By the light of the solitary candle she could see Mary deeply asleep on her pallet against the wall, and the maid did not stir as her mistress crept from the room.

There were guards everywhere, but they were not alert, either dozing at their posts or talking among themselves, so that she was able to reach John's room without being observed. His guards were asleep and snoring, which would not have pleased Willoughby and Sir John Welles if they learned of it. She tiptoed past them, and managed to turn the ring handle without making a sound. Then she went into the moonlit rooms beyond.

John's apartment was in darkness, without even a candle, and she saw a page asleep on a board beneath the window. Her feet were silent upon the rushes, and then she held aside the heavy green velvet curtain that separated this outer room from the bedchamber beyond.

He knelt naked beside the bed in the shaft of light from the window, his face buried in his hands as he prayed for his father. His shoulders shook and his fair hair curled against his pale shoulders.

'John?' She said his name very softly, but he did not hear. She went closer. 'John?'

He leapt to his feet with a start, but then relaxed as he saw who it was. 'Jesu, Cicely, I thought—' He gave a slight laugh. 'I thought my time had come.'

She gazed at him, so strong and virile, so much the heir Richard had needed. 'You are very handsome, my lord,' she said softly, smiling.

'I did not think you would really come here tonight.'

'I said I would.'

'But with so many guards . . .'

'They are not as mindful of their duty as your father's would have been. And I do not think Welles and Willoughby imagine we might creep around to each other's rooms.' She smiled again and went closer to him. 'I could not stay away tonight when you need me so much. We need each other, I think, for we have lost someone we both prized above any other.' She removed her robe and then untied the nightgown beneath. As it fell away, she stood naked before him in the moonlight.

He came to her, and they embraced, flesh to flesh for the first time. Memories and sensations moved through her, of that other body, that other man. Her arms tightened around John, and she stood on tiptoe to kiss him.

He did not taste of mint, there was salt on his lips, and his need rose strongly against her. He drew her to the bed and they lay down, kissing, caressing and whispering together. She so wanted him to be sure of her, to know she was his. Until she could no longer hide her guilty secret, and what she would say to him then she really did not know. But the time had not yet come. She was unable to fail him physically with Richard now, but Richard would always be in the deepest recesses of her heart.

John's lovemaking was not as assured and skilled as his father's, but hot and brimming with youth and passion. He thrust into her with a force that only just stopped short of causing her pain, but he was still exciting, still beloved. When he reached the peak of emotion, he did not think of her as Richard would have done. He was so impetuous, so tortured with loss to do anything except surrender to the force of his need. Afterwards, he knew he had not treated her as he should, and he rolled away and lay ashamedly with his back towards her.

'Forgive me, Cicely, forgive me such selfishness. I . . . could not help myself.'

'I know that.' She leaned over him and kissed his shoulder. 'I do not think tonight is a time for restraint, do you?'

He turned back to her. 'You always know what to say, Cicely. You make things better simply by being here.'

'I know — it is because I am far too ancient for my years,' she teased.

He smiled. 'I am callow, I know that.'

'No, you are not. This is a terrible strain for us all, and we all cope in our own ways. I know that one day soon you will make love to me as sweetly as I could wish.'

He kissed her lips. 'Do not pretend all is well, Cicely, because we do not know what Henry Tudor has in store.'

'Maybe he is a man of his word?' she ventured.

He snorted. 'Swine will fly around York Minster before that is proved true!'

'Do not speak of the future. We are here now, and I wish to lie with you again.'

'Already? I do not know that I—'

'You are a Plantagenet.'

He smiled. 'So I am,' he whispered, and pulled her close again.

But she still held Richard, and always would.

The cold grey of dawn stained the sky, all too soon, all too quickly. John slept at last as she left, passing guards that still slumbered on. She had almost reached the safety of her room when a tall figure suddenly barred her way. It was Welles, and she knew by his eyes that he was aware where she had been.

'My guards are not as alert as they should be, I think,' he said.

She did not answer, but looked at him with such pride and hauteur that he smiled. 'You are indeed a ferocious kitten, Lady Cicely, and an impudent one. It does not please me that you have lain with John of Gloucester while you are in my charge, but I rather think it is a little late anyway to attempt safeguarding your chastity.'

She flushed. 'That was not well said, sir.'

'No, my lady, but I fancy it was accurate. You carry John of Gloucester's child, do you not?'

Her breath caught. 'Certainly not!'

He smiled again. 'I am man of the world enough to interpret the signs, my lady. I saw how you protected your belly when I arrived. You *do* carry his child, unless you have given yourself to others as well?'

She raised her hand to strike him, but he caught her wrist. 'Please, Lady Cicely, female temper has no place in this. I know where your loyalty lies, and that you hold me in contempt, and also my nephew.'

'I hold all Lancastrians in contempt.'

'For good measure? As you wish, but in spite of that I am not your enemy in this. You are with child, and if my nephew should discover it . . . well, a Yorkist child so close to both Richard III *and* Edward IV is not something to ease his spirit, if you understand my meaning.'

'I am not with child,' she insisted.

'Deny it if you will, but soon it will be evident enough. You will not be permitted to marry John of Gloucester, you must know that.'

'What would you have me do? Throw myself from the highest tower and thus spare your nephew any awkwardness? Well, I will *not*.'

'You present me with a very testing problem, my lady.'

'Then be tested, sir.'

'God spare me Plantagenet princesses with more pride than sense,' he murmured, but then looked at her again. 'I do not know how to help you, for you and I will never be on the same side, I fear, and how anyway can I protect you from your own folly? I will do what I can, as best I can, but ultimately, you have to face the consequences alone.'

'I know that, sir.' She made herself look at him. 'But I must beg something important of you. Important to me, but no one else.'

'I trust it is something I can do without putting my head on the next block?'

She held his eyes. 'I wish you to say nothing to anyone about what you know of me. Apart from my maid, you are the only one who knows.' *And Jack.*

'The only one? Surely your sister at least must know?'

She shook her head. 'No. Nor does John of Gloucester,' she added.

The implication of this did not pass over his head. 'So he is *not* the father?'

She held her tongue.

'If I keep your secret, Lady Cicely, will I be guilty of treason?'

The question startled her. 'Treason? I . . . cannot think so.'

'I have already pointed out the importance of your child to any Yorkist cause. The identity of its father is therefore of the utmost significance. My nephew has no option but to have you and your siblings declared legitimate again, and—'

'Legitimate or not, I am with child outside marriage. It is a wedding band that will make the difference, and there will not be one.'

'Who is he, my lady? Why has he not done right by you?'

She smiled. 'He would have done all he could, sir, but he did not know, and I ask you to honour my request.'

'He *did* not know? He is dead?'

She bit her lip. 'Yes.'

He gazed intently at her. 'My thoughts begin to take an uneasy path, my lady. Perchance the whispers concerned the wrong niece?'

She wanted to admit it, she wanted to shout out that she carried Richard's baby, but she did not really know this man. He seemed so open and, yes, trustworthy, but he might well be Margaret Beaufort's half-brother in far too many ways. 'You should not stoop to listening to court gossip,' she said.

'It is only gossip if it is not true.' He continued to look at her.

'Do you really imagine Richard Plantagenet would bed his own niece?' she enquired.

'My lady, if I am honest, I believe *you* could tempt the Archangel Gabriel.'

'You flatter me. Now, regarding my request. I will keep faith with you, sir, do not fear otherwise. No one knows that you are aware of anything, and it will stay that way. Oh, my lack of purity will be obvious soon enough, as you say, but by then I will no longer be any concern of yours. I cannot be a personal worry to you anyway, for I was already with child when you arrived, so your nephew cannot possibly suspect *you*. I need time to find the courage to admit to being with child. . . if I am *ever* to find sufficient such courage. But I will *never* name my baby's father publicly.'

A faint smile played on his thin lips. 'The man who marries you will need fortitude, I think.'

'Perhaps you would care to take me on?'

He laughed. 'I would have harmony in my bed, my lady, not a repeat of Bosworth Field, with me as Richard.'

'Oh, there is no chance at all of you taking his place, Sir John. If your miserable Henry ever inspires even a morsel of the devotion that was given so gladly to Richard Plantagenet by his many close friends, he will perceive a glimpse of sweet fortune. Richard was a good man, and would have been a great king. He was loved, and he earned it. There was nothing mean and paltry about him, he was just at all times, lenient when he should have destroyed his enemies, but strong for England. A true prince among men, and I will grieve for him for the rest of my life.'

He was silent for a long moment. 'I would be honoured if you were to speak even a quarter as well of me. Which will never happen, I know.' A glimmer of humour lit his eyes again, but then he returned to seriousness. 'I think I should also envy Richard Plantagenet for another reason. I am not taken in, Lady Cicely. The facts are written plain enough to me. But only to me. You have my pledge that my lips are sealed, but I pray you never make me the greatest fool in the land.'

It was an odd moment that pricked her heart and made it bleed. Unstoppable emotion caught within her at last. Richard seemed to stand in the shadows, waiting for her to go to him. She could feel his presence as if he touched her again. Those touches, so quick, so honest and tender. So heartbreakingly moving now.

The words of his poem rang around in her head, over and over, like a round song. She leaned back weakly against the wall, sobs rising in her throat as tears welled down her cheeks. Her knees gave beneath her, and she sank to the floor, helpless with misery.

'Sweet Jesu,' Welles muttered, unsure what on earth to do. 'My lady?'

'I have l-lost him,' she tried to whisper. 'I h-have lost h-him.'

'You have two to be strong for,' he said awkwardly, putting his hand on her hair.

'I have n-nothing to be strong for.' She seemed to crumple even more. Her head was spinning, her memories were filled with sweet, echoing pain, and her heart was trying to stop beating. She knew nothing, cared even less. Richard was dead. He was dead, and she had been left behind.

Welles bent to lift her strongly in his arms, and she clung to him, her arms tight around his neck, her face buried against his clothes. He could feel how her body was racked with distress and shock. He held her close, stroking her hair rather clumsily and trying to find suitable words of comfort, but feeling unable to do so, not when he had been on the wrong side at Bosworth. She was beyond hearing anyway, he thought.

All he could think was to hurry her to her maid. Comforting stricken women was not something to which he was greatly accustomed, nor did he wish it to be. So he carried her back to her room, and laid her gently on the bed before shaking Mary awake.

The maid sat up with a start and scrambled to her feet on seeing Cicely. 'My lady is ill?' she cried.

'No, she is simply overcome. The news of her uncle's defeat is too painful for her, I think.' Welles straightened and looked at her in the candlelight. 'Are you not Tom Kymbe's sister?'

'Why, yes, Sir John. I know he is your man.'

Welles smiled gently. 'Not a good thing in the eyes of your Yorkist father, I think. Mary, there is perhaps something you do not know. Your father was at Bosworth, and paid the price of his loyalty to Richard.'

Shocked, Mary stared at him. 'My father is dead?'

'You were close to him?'

'No, my brother Tom and I did not get on with him at all, but he was still our father.'

'Tom will take over at Friskney now. Not a Yorkist at all, mm?' Sir John looked kindly at her. 'I am so sorry for having to tell you such news, and for now telling you to attend your lady, for she is overcome with sorrow for her uncle. I think you know her condition.'

'Yes, Sir John.'

He studied her again. 'You are in her confidence?'

Mary paused. 'I am only her maid, Sir John. She tells me nothing.'

'Hmm. Very well. Care for her now, and if she attempts to leave this room again, you had better prevent her, otherwise you will incur my wrath.'

Mary's eyes widened. 'Yes, Sir John.'

'By whom is she with child?' he asked suddenly, hoping to catch her off guard, but Mary was not easily tricked.

'She is with child, Sir John. That is all I know.'

Clearly it was not John of Gloucester, so who else *might* it have been? He had to know, because he truly did not want it to have been Richard. 'Was it that libertine Jack of Lincoln?'

Mary gazed at him. 'I do not know, sir,' she said again. 'I have not seen her with anyone. She was — is — very discreet.'

'And is able to slip from her room at night without you seeing *anything*?' he responded disbelievingly.

'If she has left in such a way, Sir John, tonight is the first time.'

'So it happened at Nottingham?'

'I only became her maid when she and the Lady Elizabeth left Nottingham, Sir John.'

He drew a long breath, knowing there was nothing more to be elicited from Mary Kymbe. He looked down at Cicely, who still wept so pitifully that she was oblivious to the world around her. For a moment he considered putting a comforting hand on her shoulders, but then drew back. Not appropriate, he thought, and turned on his heel and went out, now certain Richard had fathered her child.

It was a dangerous secret, but he had promised her his silence, and she would have it.

CHAPTER TWENTY-EIGHT

IT WAS EARLY September when Elizabeth of York's procession rode out of Sheriff Hutton Castle and down the gorge-like village street, where the people lined the way in silence. They mourned Richard and had no time for Henry Tudor, and it was silently made very plain indeed to the cavalcade that Henry Tudor had provided for his bride.

Cicely could hardly take her eyes away from her sister's splendour. Bess rode at the head of the procession, and on either side of her rode Sir Robert Willoughby and Sir John Welles. Bess wore a gown of mulberry silk — murrey, for York — that had pendulous sleeves lined with blue cloth-of-gold. Upon her red-gold hair there was a blue headdress embroidered with silver and murrey. Her hair was still loose beneath it, but the headdress denoted that she would soon no longer be a maid. She glittered with jewels for there was many a dazzling necklace twisted around her throat and draping down her bosom, and her fingers were clustered with precious rings. She was a daughter of York, with a white rose pinned to her breast. Another such rose was fixed to Cicely's wrist.

The ladies sent from London by the new king had spent many hours shaving her forehead and plucking her eyebrows into the tortuous arches that were considered so desirable. The result was a fashionable beauty that well deserved the hand of the King of England, although perhaps not such a mean king as Henry Tudor, who surely did not warrant any prize so rare and lovely. But Bess's face did not match the richness of her garb, for it was pale and taut, her eyes fixed unseeingly upon the horizon. She had wept many times more for Richard, but always in private, and never for her captors to discover. She smiled only occasionally, and laughed not at all.

Cicely was grandly attired as well, in a dusky blue brocade gown, the skirt of which floated as her palfrey trotted. She had refused to have her forehead shaved and eyebrows plucked, even though the ladies implored her. Richard would not have wished it. He loved her as she was, and she loved him in the same way. Thus her face was still as God had made it as she rode just behind her sister.

John was in the middle of the cavalcade, seated on his dapple horse, his hands bound before him. His head was bare, his Plantagenet blood evident in his looks and bearing, and everyone he passed knew who he was. He was cheered from the outset, first by the villagers of Sheriff Hutton, and then by everyone he passed thereafter, much to Willoughby's impotent fury. And so Richard's by-blow was led like a felon. Nothing would do for Sir Robert but that John of Gloucester was seen as a prisoner for the ride south, and no amount of sweet reason by Sir John Welles had moved him. Sir Robert was convinced that the new king would wish that what had been done to Richard at Bosworth would soon be done to his bastard son.

'Remember, Willoughby, my nephew may wish to receive John of Gloucester as graciously as he does the princesses,' Welles warned, but Willoughby would have had John of Gloucester hooded as well, perhaps even slung over his horse as his father had been, but in this Welles prevailed.

'Do that, and I will complain to the king that you have conducted yourself with egregious discourtesy towards the Houses of York *and* Plantagenet. He will not be amused, you may count upon it, not when he himself is to take a Plantagenet bride and claims Plantagenet descent.'

The cavalcade rode over the moor and down into the forest again, passing near the hunting tower. It could not be seen from the road, but Cicely knew it was there, and relived those final moments with Richard. She was so glad he had come from Nottingham for those few hours, so glad he had needed her so much that he took such a risk. But how she wished he had flouted everything by letting her return to Nottingham with him. There would have been more hours then, more lying together in the dark hours of night, lost in the love they felt for each other. And with her there to support him in everything, he would surely not have lost the battle. She would have sustained him, carried him to victory, and exulted in his just triumph.

Out of the forest they emerged, and over the narrow bridge by the White Boar, except that it was no longer the White Boar, but had been renamed the Blue Boar, its sign hurriedly repainted in order not to provoke memories of Richard. Will watched them pass, and gave Mary a sad smile, for they knew they would not see each other again.

As they rode beneath the gateway of Richard's city, where the minster thrust against the sky, there were more crowds, sullen and hostile to the representatives of Henry Tudor. But those crowds were wild with cheers for the House of York. They knew John, if only by his looks, and he was lauded. His mount, lacking his sure touch, was nervous in the enclosed, over-hanging streets, and its hooves slipped many a time upon the smooth cobbles.

A man — a merchant by his clothes — emerged from the crowds and held the bridle. 'God bless you, my lord. Keep faith with your father, good King Richard!' There was jubilance as the man kissed the ropes that bound John's wrists. The horse danced still more, but John smiled at the man. The cheering rose to a roar as York made known where its loyalty lay, until Willoughby's men were ordered to set about anyone showing disrespect for Henry Tudor.

Willoughby was frightened, even though he had armed men enough to put down any riot that might have ensued. Welles gave no sign of any discomfort at all, although he was not pleased when Cicely turned her palfrey and rode back to John, who smiled at her, but there was a devastating sadness about him. It was there in his eyes, those eyes that brought Richard to life again. 'Do not fret for me, sweetheart.'

'Lady Cicely, you should be at the head of the procession,' said another voice, and she looked around to see Welles had ridden back. He leaned to grab her palfrey's bridle and looked angrily at her. 'Show a little sense, my lady. I cannot watch you every moment, nor do I expect to. If I can tell tales on Willoughby to my nephew, then so can Willoughby tell tales of *your* conduct. Do you understand? Your only use to Henry is to be his wife should anything befall your sister. Other than that, he can marry you off to a lowly squire if he feels so inclined. Your place is with the Lady Elizabeth, and that is where I intend to see you!'

'You cannot order me, sir.'

'I think you will find that I can, my lady. I have charge of you, and I am damned if I will let you flout my wishes. Willoughby will report everything, you do understand that, do you not? If you persist in showing your support for York and contempt for Tudor and Lancaster, you will soon go too far.'

John looked imploringly at her. 'He is right, Cicely. There is nothing you can do for me. My fate is uncertain, but you can protect yourself. Behave as Bess does.'

She was close to tears. 'My place is with you, John,' she whispered, her voice almost drowned by the noise of the crowd.

She heard Welles' tut of annoyance as he turned her palfrey and forced it to go with him. 'Do not try me too far, my lady,' he said. 'And do not rely upon my always being able to control Willoughby!'

York soon fell behind them, but every village town they passed through was loud with support for the House of York.

The people of England did not want their new king, they wanted Richard.

The long journey to London took many days, but finally came the early morning when the towers and steeples appeared on the horizon. The last time Cicely had seen them was when the court had gone north to join Richard at Nottingham. It was a beautiful memory now. Such a beautiful memory.

Bess was as elegant and lovely as she had been at the outset, but Cicely found it more difficult. She often felt sick, especially in the morning, and it was difficult to hide the fact. There came the distant sound of a fanfare, and Cicely saw the glint of sunlight upon metal as Henry Tudor came out to greet his future bride. Bess heard, and looked briefly at her sister. There was a moment of communion, a moment of regret and weakness that might easily have been the undoing of them both, but then Bess was herself again, her back straight, her head held high as she rode to meet the new king.

Closer and closer they drew, but the haze of morning sunshine made it impossible for Cicely to make out Henry Tudor. All she knew was that she would soon confront the man whose craven, perfidious, execrable lords had slaughtered Richard.

Welles' horse appeared beside her. 'Remember now, my lady, you are to take great care. My nephew is not me.'

'I know, and thank you for your gallantry, Sir John.' She looked anxiously at him. 'Did you take the book as I asked?'

'The one in which Richard wrote the poem? Yes, I have it. It is safely in my baggage.'

'Please take care of it for me.'

'You know I will. I will see that you have it as soon as the moment is sensible. But not just yet, I fancy.' He nodded at the ring on her right hand. 'I am given to understand that it is John of Gloucester's keepsake?'

'Yes.'

'Then put it in your purse. There must not be anything that will raise my nephew's suspicion that you do not support his marriage to your sister.'

Without a word she removed the ring, and pushed it into the purse at her waist, next to Richard's letter, which she caressed for a moment with her fingertips. How many times had she read it? A thousand or more? Was it possible to wear ink away simply by reading its words? If so, Richard's writing would by now have vanished forever.

Bess commanded Cicely to ride beside her, but just a few feet back, and so they were together as they at last saw Henry Tudor. His appearance came as something of a shock, for he was younger than they expected, only twenty-nine, and his face was thin and pale, devoid of Richard's warmth and attractiveness. He was taller too, with hair that was reddish-brown in colour, without the burnish of gold of his bride's family, and it fell in waves to the shoulders of his costly doublet. His clever, deep-set eyes were hooded and of a slate-grey hue, almost like the winter sea, and upon his head gleamed the circlet of gold that had last graced the brow of Richard Plantagenet. His rich purple doublet was embroidered with gold and scarlet dragons. His face bore no expression whatsoever, except for the guile in his eyes, which were strangely uneven, one not entirely in time with the other.

Bess halted to await his final approach, her face calm and still, giving nothing away, but Cicely knew that inside she was afraid. He reined in a few feet away from his Yorkist bride, and they gazed at each other. Cicely watched his face as he took in every detail of Bess's appearance and she saw his admiration, not of the woman, only her beauty.

He dismounted and walked to Bess, taking her cold hand and pressing it to his lips. 'Madam, I greet you.' His voice was quiet, a mixture of accents — English and French, with perhaps the faintest trace of Welsh. 'Do not be afraid of me, my lady, for I welcome you with great warmth and happiness.'

He smiled, but it was reserved, Cicely thought. He was not a man of charm as Richard had been, and he lacked Richard's effortless presence, but perhaps he meant what he said to Bess.

Bess summoned a smile. 'My lord, I have long awaited this meeting.'

He kissed her hand again and then approached Cicely. 'Lady Cicely? I had no idea my bride had so lovely a sister.' He bowed over her hand, bringing with him a faint scent of cloves, and a strand of his red hair clung to her wrist. As Richard's had done. She wanted to brush this man's hair away, brush *him* away, but she sat there and returned his smile as best she could.

'You are flattering me, Your Grace,' she said.

He watched her face. 'Flattering? I do not have that art, my lady. I leave that to the likes of your practised uncle, Richard. It seems *he* would utter whatever silken words were necessary to get what he wanted.'

At that moment she saw he wore Richard's ruby ring. *He* wore Richard's ring! Outrage welled through her, but she felt Welles' warning gaze upon her, and bit back the bitter words that rose so hotly to her lips. It required a great effort. A very great effort.

Henry knew her difficulty. 'You will have to do better than that, my lady,' he said softly, but still with a smile. 'My attention is upon you, and I overlook very little.'

She knew more of him in that second than he could have imagined. He was clever, observant and dangerous. He knew what her feelings were towards Richard. Not that she loved her uncle as she should not, but still that she loved him very much. 'I do what I can, Your Grace, but it is not easy to denigrate an uncle who always treated me well. If our positions were reversed, would you be able to accept bad things being said of *your* uncle?' Had she gone too far already? Maybe, but she could not endure it when Richard's memory was insulted.

Henry paused, and then rubbed an eye as if he would rather go to sleep than speak to her, but his answer was civil enough. 'I have two uncles, Lady Cicely, of whom Sir John Welles is one. I do not think even you would wish to insult him.'

'I respect Sir John, Your Grace. He has been courteous and considerate, and has my high regard.'

'*High* regard?' Henry glanced slowly around at Welles, and then back at her. 'I believe you do not hold me in similar regard, because I had Richard's carcass displayed in Leicester.'

Who could have reported *that* to him? Not Sir John, she was sure. It had to be Willoughby, who no doubt also wrote to Henry that his half-uncle had criticized him for what had been done to Richard's body.

Henry linked his hands and tapped his forefingers slowly to his lips before speaking again. 'It would seem that you engage me in conversation as much as you did Richard. I must be wary of you, I think.' He smiled.

It was not a sincere smile, or light-hearted, but a subtle warning. She managed a bland smile in return. 'My uncle liked to talk to me, Your Grace, but I think you probably do not.'

'That remains to be seen.' He looked at her for a long moment, as if undecided, and she was very conscious of the depth in his eyes. She was both menaced by him and disturbingly fascinated, and she could feel his interest in her. What had he heard? Why did he spend more time with her than with Bess, whose annoyance was perceptible?

Then Henry nodded and moved on through the procession, which parted for him to pass, and he halted before John. It was clear he saw the resemblance to Richard, but it was of the ropes that he spoke. 'I gave no order for anyone to be bound. Am I served by idiots?' He took out his own dagger to cut John's bonds. 'Your father was a brave and brilliant soldier, sir. He almost had me, and no doubt you wish he had succeeded.' He did not wait for a reply, but returned to Bess and Cicely.

'Ladies, the past must be put behind us now, and we must look only to the future. Lady Elizabeth, our marriage will bring everyone together in peace, which is my fervent wish.'

'And it is mine, Your Grace,' Bess replied, inclining her head.

Cicely did not move. Henry's eyes swung to her, again with that undecided expression, and from the corner of her eyes she saw Sir John Welles shift on his horse.

'Come, ladies,' Henry said then. 'We will ride to Lambeth where the royal barges await. Sir John, my uncle, yours will be the honour of riding with the Lady Cicely. It is fitting, I think. A member of my family to ride alongside a member of my bride's family.'

And so they went back to London, where the cheers for York were ill disguised. As the barges slid downstream, passing through billowing flocks of swans, Cicely glanced back at a following vessel, in which she knew John to be, but she could not see him.

Welles was at her side. 'I think you have impressed my nephew, my lady.'

'He frightens me.'

'That is probably a good thing. You may think him cold and without charm, but he has a way of worming the truth from even the most reluctant lips. Stay afraid, and always temper your attitude towards him.'

'Is that sound advice, sir?'

'It is well meant advice. The coming weeks are going to test you as never before, and you will need to stay on the right side of Henry VII. Unfortunately, it is far easier to be on his wrong side.'

'Poor uncle, to have such a view of the nephew he helped to the throne,' she responded.

He smiled. 'And poor niece to have put herself in jeopardy for the sake of a few stolen hours of love with her uncle.'

She flushed. 'But at least it was — *is* — love.'

So she admitted it, he thought. 'Somehow I do not doubt it, Lady Cicely, for you do not strike me as a lady who would do it for anything less than love. Just take care, I beg of you. I will still do all I can to protect you, but you *must* help yourself. Do not bristle like a bantam every time a derogatory word is uttered about Richard. Your love for him is far too clear, and believe me, would indeed provoke my nephew. Please assure me you understand what I am saying.'

'I do, sir.'

They passed Westminster Palace to the sound of trumpets and more cheers. Cicely saw the walled garden, and the apples on the trees. There were more and more vessels now, crowding the water, with waving people and rising jubilance. But for whom did they cheer? Henry? Or Bess? Cicely smiled. For it was Bess. And it was for her, Cicely. And for John of Gloucester. Perhaps for him most of all.

At London Bridge the mayor and aldermen in their gorgeous robes waited to greet the royal party, and as the barge nudged the landing, she was glad of Sir John Welles' sturdy hand. He helped her up the steps to where mounts awaited. Henry helped Bess on to a white palfrey that was caparisoned in silver, with a silver saddle. A mount suited to a future queen. The new king was attentive and courteous, but Cicely could not tell if he was also truly well disposed. But then, could not the same thing be said of Bess?

Sir John helped Cicely to mount, and paused for a moment, his hand over hers. 'Are you well enough for this, my lady?'

'I have to be, Sir John.'

He took her hand suddenly, and drew it to his lips. 'Be safe.'

'I will try, sir.'

He released her and went to his own waiting horse, and a minute later the royal procession set off through the ancient streets of London.

But as Cicely rode behind Henry Tudor, it was another king she saw, another king more dear to her than her own life. *Richard, by the grace of God, King of England and France and Lord of Ireland.* 'May his beloved soul rest in peace,' she whispered, blinking back tears.

And again Sir John Welles' hand steadied her.

AUTHOR'S NOTE

ALTHOUGH WRITTEN AROUND known historical events and people, this book is fiction, not fact. Please do not think I have a sound basis for writing of a deep love between Richard III and his second niece, Cicely. Their intimacy is entirely of my doing, although it is not impossible. Nor do I have a sound basis for creating a love affair between Cicely and Richard's illegitimate son, John of Gloucester. That Richard's queen was in love with her first husband can never be proved.

There is some suggestion that Cicely's elder sister, Elizabeth of York, did love her uncle romantically, and apparently wrote a letter, now lost, in which she confessed as much and expressed a wish to marry him. Whether Richard returned this affection is very doubtful indeed, and I do not believe he did. He publicly denied any intentions towards her.

I do believe that Richard was honest and above all ethical in everything he did. He was shown proof that Edward IV's marriage to Elizabeth Woodville was bigamous, and therefore *honestly* believed that all Edward's children by her were illegitimate, with no right to the throne. This was important. With the middle Yorkist Plantagenet brother, George, Duke of Clarence, having been executed and attainted, his children were thus barred from the throne. That only left Richard, who had no option but to accept the crown. It was his by right, he had a son who was legitimate and could succeed him, and so he had to follow his destiny. Not to have done so would have meant knowingly placing a baseborn twelve-year-old boy on the throne, with the attendant dangers of a minority rule. Why do that, when his own claim to the crown was entirely right and legitimate? He did not want to be king; he had been happy watching over his vast lands in the north of England, where the people loved him, but king he had to be.

Apart from keeping Richard in the public eye for centuries, Shakespeare did him a terrible injustice. Richard is surely one of our best-known kings, even though he was on the throne for a mere two years. He was only thirty-two when he died, but Shakespeare portrays him as much older, in events in which he had no involvement, and others when he was only two years old. Too many people accept Shakespeare's version of Richard as fact — but then the Bard flourished when Tudor propaganda was superbly crafted and Tudor power to be greatly feared. One simply did not speak up for Richard when there was a Tudor on the throne. And, as we all know, history is written by the victors.

I do not believe Richard killed his nephews, the 'Princes in the Tower', but I do believe he had them removed elsewhere, for their safety, and also because he did not wish them to be a rallying point for those who opposed his reign. Nor did he want them to be in danger from those who would see an end to the House of York as a whole, not only himself. Richard was not a child murderer; everything known of him makes such a thought almost preposterous.

There were others with motives for being rid of the boys, including Margaret Beaufort, Lady Stanley, Henry Tudor's mother. She was ruthless, ambitious and conscienceless enough by any century's reckoning. Henry himself was obliged to make the boys legitimate again in order to marry Cicely's elder sister and unite the opposing factions of York and Lancaster. He had promised this to gain support. If he entered such a marriage on such terms, and the boys proved to be still alive, he made their claim to the throne infinitely better than his own. He was too shrewd for that, and if he'd found them I think he would have disposed of them on the quiet.

But even so, I do not think this happened. Henry had the Tower searched from top to bottom after Bosworth, and certainly he feared the boys' return throughout his reign, because he had no idea where Richard had hidden them or what had happened to them. If Henry thought Richard had them killed, he was wrong, and would better have looked much closer to home for the guilty party. His fanatically religious and sanctimonious mother would have stopped at nothing to see him securely on the throne. Henry was to have to deal with at least two 'pretenders', one — Perkin Warbeck — who presented him with a very great threat indeed. We will probably never know the boys' true fate, and so we form our own opinions. Mine is that Richard was innocent, but then I am, unashamedly and unreservedly, his supporter. Does that make me blinkered? I don't think so. Too many facts speak for themselves where he is concerned. In my opinion, it is his detractors who wear the blinkers.

Henry Tudor invaded and won Bosworth by right of conquest, not his own Lancastrian bloodline, which descended from the illegitimate Beauforts, who had been specifically barred from the throne by Henry IV. There is also a question mark over the legitimacy of Henry's father, Edmund Tudor, which if true, would have weakened Henry's claim even more. Through treachery and amazing good fortune, he was able to overcome the anointed King of England and usurp the throne. Richard was betrayed, but died with astonishing courage that even his enemies admired.

There are other characters in this story who need to be mentioned. I have blackened poor Ralph Scrope's name unfairly, for it seems he probably *was* married to Cicely in some brief way or another. I have conjured the part-genuine/part-forged marriage contract. Henry VII was to have this 'marriage' annulled. Ralph succeeded his elder brother to the title of Baron Scrope of Upsall, dying in 1515.

Sir Robert Willoughby is also my victim. He may well have been as I have portrayed him, or he could have been a true knight. If he was the latter, I apologize to him too. All I know is that he was definitely the man Henry sent to Sheriff Hutton to secure Bess and those with her.

The Kymbes of Friskney are an actual family from the time, very well known in Lincolnshire, but Mary Kymbe is my invention. Her brother Tom Kymbe is fact. I have no basis for making their father a Yorkist sympathizer who sheltered the royal boys under his roof. Friskney *was* Jack de la Pole's manor, or so some delving suggests.

To return to Richard. The discovery of his resting place at Leicester has once again focused attention on a man who has been unfairly treated for half a millennium, and I wish to praise and applaud all those who worked so hard to find him. At last, a proper burial, fit for this fascinating king, with as much dignity and honour as every other monarch of England.

My Richard has the physical features that have been revealed by his skeleton. His character is how I personally interpret him. He was a man ahead of his time, taking care to look after his people, not merely the interests of the nobles, as had always been the case before. His reign was short, with only one Parliament, but he introduced the bail system, decreed that the law of the land should be in the language of the land, standardised weights and measures and banished the awful injustice of benevolences, which allowed the rich to purchase high positions. He believed — and made law — that husbands should always respect their wives and treat them well, and not once did he really punish the women who conspired against him. Nor, unfortunately, did he deal harshly enough with the nobles who proved to be dangerously untrustworthy. His fault was ever leniency, and trust.

He was a man of honour and expected others to be the same. Ultimately, this creed cost him his life.

What might he have achieved had he lived?

Sandra Heath Wilson
Gloucester
May 2014

ALSO BY SANDRA HEATH WILSON

THE CICELY PLANTAGENET SERIES
Book 1: CICELY'S KING RICHARD
Book 2: CICELY'S SECOND KING *
Book 3: CICELY'S LORD LINCOLN *
Book 4: CICELY'S SOVEREIGN SECRET *
* Coming soon!

Don't miss the latest Sandra Heath Wilson release, join our mailing list:

www.joffebooks.com

FREE KINDLE BOOKS

Do you love mysteries, historical fiction and romance? Join 1,000s of readers enjoying great books through our mailing list. You'll get new releases and great deals every week from one of the UK's leading independent publishers. Join today, and you'll get your first bargain book this month!

www.joffebooks.com

Follow us on Facebook, Twitter and Instagram @joffebooks

Thank you for reading this book. If you enjoyed it please leave feedback on Amazon or Goodreads, and if there is anything we missed or you have a question about, then please get in touch. The author and publishing team appreciate your feedback and time reading this book.

We're very grateful to eagle-eyed readers who take the time to contact us. Please send any errors you find to corrections@joffebooks.com

Printed in Great Britain
by Amazon

80596227R00192

Book 4 TAINTED

A botched attempt to extort money has tragic consequences.
An embarrassing DNA match to an unsolved rape and murder twenty years before means DI Colin Strong has to use his best diplomatic tactics.
Simultaneously, journalist Bob Souter is tasked with writing about that same case to re-focus public attention.
Will the newspaper's actions help or hinder the police?
Meanwhile, Strong's team has two separate murder enquiries to run.
With their friendship under duress, will Souter and Strong be able to work together?

Available through Amazon:

Getbook.at/Tainted-DavidEvans

Printed in Great Britain
by Amazon

51979189R00178